CW01511933

Copyright © 2019, 2021 by Geoff Bunn

All rights reserved. This book or any portion thereof may not be reproduced or used in any manner whatsoever without the express written permission of the publisher except for the use of brief quotations in a book review or scholarly journal.

First Printing: 2019, This Version 2021

ISBN 978-1791338176

Geoff Bunn
www.geoffbunn.com

"A beautiful, evocative story of young love...".

"One of the saddest stories I've ever read. My heart is shattered... Loved it".

"Wonderful". The TIMES

"I absolutely loved this book. It is beautifully written, moving, with characters you will fall in love with. It will make you laugh... and it will also make your heart ache".

blond(e) BOY

red LIPSTICK

GEOFF BUNN

1

If I'd never met her, where would I be now? I'd asked myself that question so often. But of course it was impossible to answer. So many times a day we make choices that could lead us to entirely different lives. We turn left instead of right, walk rather than take the car, we say yes instead of no. And each time, we shape our futures almost without a care.

I had moved to Ireland at the start of the millennium. I lived there still. Alone now, in a large stone house on the west coast, with a wide and impressive view across Mulranny Bay towards Croagh Patrick – Ireland's 'holy' mountain. That great dark rock was often moody and sombre, but as a solid and reassuring presence I also felt it watched over me the way a stern grandparent might watch over a child playing before an open fire.

I still didn't quite know how, coming from a tough sink estate, I'd ended up with a mountain on my doorstep. Many years earlier I had left school with just one low grade pass in woodwork and – with nothing else on offer – I had gone to work in a car factory in the English Midlands. The beginning and end of a career for tens of thousands of men before me. But I'd escaped. And despite the foul air, grime and sheer boredom of that place, I'd learned a lot there, both good and bad, and some of it had certainly helped me to find my own way in life.

Years had passed since then and today, somehow, I was self-employed and financially very secure. Working from home or wherever I was with my computer, I had major clients in Germany and Scandinavia who were continually offering me work. I could pick and choose which jobs I took. So it wasn't a lack of success or empty hours that were making me unhappy – and yet, unhappy, I knew I was.

I leaned back in my chair, sighed and stopped typing up my thoughts.

Kate, my daughter, would have laughed to see me sitting in my hotel room on my first night away from home, trying to make sense of myself.

Laughed? Either that or told me off. Most probably both. A few days earlier, she had arrived unexpectedly at the house in Ireland, to find me searching frantically for something, almost in a state of panic. "What have you lost, Dad?" she'd asked, standing among the chaos of the living room.

"A photograph", I had replied, hauling cushions off the sofa and checking underneath, with Kate following along and replacing them as I moved on to the next chair. And then the bookshelves. And then to rifling through the drawers again.

"What photograph?" Kate picked up a few paperback books that I'd just pulled off a shelf and stacked them neatly back in their place.

My reply was not much more than a grunt.

"Shall I make us both a cup of coffee?" Kate suggested.

"Yeah, please", I said. I sat down heavily, temporarily giving up my search and slumping into an armchair as she went off into the kitchen.

I peered through the window as a sudden shaft of sunlight illuminated the dark water of the bay, the Irish sky offering a panoramic mixture of ragged grey clouds and mustard coloured light. It was beautiful here. Often stimulatingly so. But today it just struck me as melancholic.

It was more than just *a* photo. It was *our only photo*.

I had begun searching for it because I'd given myself some time off the previous evening, rather than begin work on some hugely complicated scaffolding diagram for an important engineering project in Stockholm. It was late and the job was going to be exacting. Long and intense. But there were probably only three or four people in Europe who could handle it. So my deadlines could be flexible, up to a point. There was no pressure. Not yet.

Setting the project to one side, I had switched off two of my three monitors and listened to some music on YouTube, letting my thoughts wander as I did so. Then I had watched a film. A biopic, set in the 1980s. As soon as it began I knew I ought not to have watched it. It would be painful. Yet I just couldn't switch it off.

I'd felt the inevitable sadness welling up as I watched, but tried to ignore it. Paused the film, got up, poured a glass of whiskey. Told myself not to care, not to be so soft, all that kind of thing. But it was no good. There were too many reasons, too many connections, between the images in that film and events in my own life. So I gave up. I let myself feel sad and sat back in front of the rest of the movie, with the wild dark night outside, filled with black and whispering rain, doing little to alleviate my mood.

The film had ended, and then I had gone in search of the photograph. And I hadn't been able to find it. When had I last seen it? I couldn't remember. But I knew I would have put it somewhere safe. It was very precious to me. In the end I had gone to bed much too late and feeling pretty sorry for myself.

And it was the next day that Kate had arrived.

Because life can be strange like that.

Singing to herself tunelessly as she always had, she showed up out of the blue, planning to spend some time with me and to visit some of her former school friends who still lived nearby.

"So tell me about this photo, then", she said, putting a mug of coffee down in front of me.

I stared at my coffee for a moment. Searched for a reply. "It's the only one I have of someone", I began. "Someone very special. It was taken in a photo booth. You know, those things where you get four pictures for 50p or whatever..."

Kate began to make a face implying that these days they cost a lot more than 50p, but I cut her short with a quick shake of my head.

"No, I know. I know. I'm sure they cost a lot more now. Anyway, we were out together one day having a great time, and we went into one of those booths with the last of our money. And of course we picked the wrong option and ended up with a strip of four identical pictures. Later we cut them up so that we each had two, and promised to always keep them. And I've always kept mine. Always. Only now I can't find it. Them."

Up until then, Kate had been standing, but now she sat down on the sofa facing me. "Is that the girl you and Mom split up because of? I remember there being a big row about a photo."

I laughed, a small laugh, and shook my head. "No. Not really, darling. There were lots of things. Mainly she couldn't settle out here. It was too isolated for her after the big city."

Kate nodded, but said nothing.

That bloody film. It had brought so many things back to the surface. Not just the whole break up with Lisa – my ex, and Kate's mother – but it had also reminded me that I had made a big mistake back then. I'd left a part of me behind.

As if I had needed reminding. For very many reasons it had always haunted me, affecting the whole of my life.

"Well...", I continued, looking into Kate's piercing blue eyes.

9

"Yes. A bit. Yes. That did play a role too, I suppose. The girl in that photo. "

Kate already knew some of it, what had happened and what hadn't. We'd talked it over before. She had been 16 when Lisa and I had split up. We had tried to keep her out of it as much as possible, but of course she had picked up on much more than we realised. And after the separation she had spent two more years here with me before moving to her mother's place and going to university.

All the same, I guess I deliberately understated the role 'that photo' had played in our breaking up. In part that was because I didn't want Kate to feel antagonistic towards the girl. In part because it just wasn't *her* fault. One day, when things were already fraught between Lisa and I over – of all things – a small but unpaid phone bill, she had come across the photograph by chance and turned on me. "Who's this?"

She had held it out to me.

I had shrugged. "It was years ago."

Lisa had then said something else, something wholly inoffensive but – feeling guilty, I guess – I had nevertheless taken offence, and I had suddenly blurted it all out.

From there the 'phone bill' row had escalated. I remembered it well. I had gone over the whole thing countless times.

So yes, as I had just told Kate, and had told her before, although there were many other deep-rooted problems in our relationship, it was nevertheless true that the photo – which I couldn't now find – was at the heart of the argument that finally drove her mother and I apart.

"What was she like?" Kate asked suddenly. "I mean, what did she look like?"

By way of answer, I showed her a bit of the film.

"She was very much like that." I said. "Sure. Unsure. Mature, yet so young. And alone too." I paused the film on one image.

Kate tilted her head to one side. "And was *she* that pretty?"

I smiled. "Yes".

I stopped the film.

"And I've always known that I should have done more than I did for her." I said at last, speaking as much to myself as to Kate. "We reached each other. I understood her strengths and weaknesses. I had seen where and how she was vulnerable. But in the end I failed her. And me too."

I wanted another whiskey, but because Kate was there I didn't have one.

We talked a little longer.

And eventually I reached the point – which I had done before – of saying that I ought to go to the UK and revisit some of my old haunts. To try and free myself up a bit more, maybe, for the life I was now living.

"Look, Dad", Kate said at last. "You haven't been back to Birmingham for the best part of 20 years now, as far as I know. You should go. Stop saying you might and actually do it. Go. Take your laptop. You can work from any cafe. I can stay here for a week or two and look after the place. You never know, it might help you stop feeling so sad about it or whatever. I'll even try and find your photo for you – assuming it's still here somewhere."

I hesitated.

"Just do it!" she'd insisted.

And so, only a few days later I was on a plane to the UK, to make a train for Birmingham and a very comfortable hotel.

And it was sitting there, that first evening, a little tired from travel, unable to think of work, that I had tried to get some of my thoughts down in writing.

How was it all so long ago?

*

We first met in 1981, on a cool day in mid-August.

I had just turned 18. I was good looking, with dark eyes and thick dark hair. At the time I was seeing a girl, but we were going nowhere. I knew that was largely down to me. I had a public face, a persona, which girls found very attractive. Outgoing, talkative, with an almost arrogant charm. That was how I appeared. I dated any girl, every girl, as and when I chose. But in private, once we were alone together, I was much less sure of myself. Quieter. More reserved. Shy really. And that, I knew – but couldn't easily change – was less attractive. We were teenagers, and life was supposed to be fun.

Back then, I was still living in Birmingham, my home city. But on that day, a day I would never forget, I was in London, on a dreary work-related visit to the south east, travelling on a local train slowly making its way back into the city centre. Then at some anonymous suburban station, voices caught my attention and I looked up from my book to see a group of punks or something on the platform. They were just talking, laughing. Fooling around a little. Doing nothing in particular.

I watched them for a few seconds, focusing mainly on a slender girl with strikingly blonde hair and a short pink mohair jumper. She did a little dance and seemed to be making all the others laugh. For some reason I found it impossible to even look at her without smiling.

Then I went back to my reading: *'There are moments in life that are given to us. Moments where we can make a choice. There is much more to the world than we realise, and those moments should be treated with special care when they do arrive. They are often crossroads or junctions. A clear choice between action and inaction. Sometimes mundane. Sometimes – and often, and we do not see it – one of them will be very precious. A chance to change a whole life. To act or not to act. If only we make the right decision, we might be able to change a whole story.'*

Suddenly, just as the train was about to leave, someone jumped on board, opening the door right next to me and then dropping into the seat directly opposite. That felt a little odd. It was one of those open carriages with lots of woodwork and as many doors as there were windows. Strong smells of dust and warm moquette. But the train was almost empty too, so there was no need for them to sit so close. And as we moved off, I half looked up.

It was that same girl.

Other than the pink jumper, she was mostly wearing black. She had also scattered a half dozen glossy magazines on the seat next to her.

Then, once again, I returned to my book.

What happened next? A misunderstanding. That was all.

The train slowed down for the next station and I felt a strange sensation. I didn't look up, because I could tell what it was.

And I was embarrassed by it. I even felt myself blushing. It was the girl opposite. She appeared to be periodically rubbing her shoe against mine, against my boot.

The train stopped. And then she did it again. Very lightly, but – to me at least it was quite definite – she pressed her shoe against mine. I tried to ignore it. Sure, it wasn't much, but it wasn't the kind of thing most strangers did on a train.

Then it happened once more.

Still I didn't look up. At least, not fully. But I did glance over the top of my book, past the words I was no longer able to read or think about, and notice that she was wearing a longish, black, tight fitting skirt and leather high heels.

I guess because it was daytime and August, albeit a cool day, those clothes surprised me. And maybe that was why I looked at her legs for longer than I ought to have done, as she later assured me I had. In any case, from her, I went back to staring at the pages of my book, turning them slowly to make it look as if I was reading. Not sure what to think. I hoped that staying quiet would make her stop.

The train moved off. And then it happened again.

I didn't know what to do now. Should I say something? I'd never had anyone sit opposite me and do that before, and it felt strange.

Why would she keep doing that?

As we approached the more urban parts of London, I glanced out of the window, first to my side and then across her to the other window, as people do, by way of an excuse so I could look at her without being too obvious. Not obvious? Well, that's what we tell ourselves.

Oh. Fuck.

I don't know why, but I hadn't expected her to be so attractive. There was not only the startling bleached blonde hair, which I'd always loved, but above night-club-red lipstick, she had high, fine cheekbones which gave her an almost sculpted appearance, and narrow almond-shaped eyes, outlined heavily with eyeliner, the lashes darkened to black with mascara.

There was a coldness in that face too, yet at the same time, a vibrancy, a liveliness that bordered on the insolent. I could see all that immediately.

But there was also something else there that I couldn't place. Not then. Nor could I study her for too long, because those almond eyes flashed a sudden glance at me and a bright smile passed across her face. I couldn't tell what colour those narrowed eyes were, but I could see that they sparkled, that they shone.

I turned back to my book. The train stopped again. And we were stuck at another nondescript station for quite a long while.

I knew the girl was now watching me now. I could feel her gaze on me.

Then she lit a cigarette, took a few drags on it and seemed to blow the smoke straight at me. "Ooo, sorry, is that bothering you?", she said immediately. The accent was a little strange, but where from exactly? I couldn't place it at first. It was also, somehow, not an ordinary girl's voice.

"Nah", I said, making myself smile at her. "It's fine. Really. I smoke myself sometimes."

"Mmm", she said quietly. "I thought it might be bothering you. Sorry."

I didn't reply. And she picked up one of her magazines and, very quietly, began humming to herself as she flicked through it. Maybe even singing a little. Then she tossed the magazine back down onto her seat.

"People can be rude like that, though, can't they? With smoke." She spoke quickly. The voice was nervous and I found myself watching her mouth, and those very red lips. "Sorry", she said again. With a shy but wide smile. "I am. I'm sorry."

That was it! There, in that final apology.

That was when I realised.

Those few extra words. They had given it away. The something about her. The something about her face. About her body language. About her movement. Everything. We made proper eye contact for the first time and I froze as we did so.

The girl opposite me wasn't a girl. *She was a boy!*

That was what I'd finally picked up from that last 'sorry'.

She was a boy.

Maybe my age. Maybe a little younger. It was hard to be sure.

I saw all that and I guess it shocked me. It must have done, because I wanted to speak but couldn't open my mouth and get any words out.

But there must have been an expression of some kind on my face. Because by way of response she smiled at me again. She knew that I knew she was a boy. But it was a gentle smile, with no hostility in it. Her face may have been finely chiselled and almost perfect, but there was something very gentle in there too. Definitely. And yet... and yet... also something quite deliberately provocative.

"You're not from round here, are you?", she asked. He asked.

"Erm... no", I replied, the words coming out by themselves. "No, I'm not. I'm from Birmingham."

"Mmm...", he said, smiling another quick smile at me and fanning a cloud of blue smoke out the window with a lively flourish of one hand. "I could tell. I could. Your accent." He pinched a small piece of tobacco from his upper lip. Then the train finally started up again. "I am. I'm more or less from round here. Well. I am. And I'm not. Not really."

I didn't know what to do. What to say. Nor what to feel. And, at first, I told myself that it was just out of politeness that I kept the conversation going, "Oh, whereabouts are you from, then?"

He waved the cigarette a little. Another flourish of the hand. "Here. I live in London." He glanced out of the window. Then back at me. Straight into my eyes. "No. Guildford originally. So I'm not really from around here either. But I do live in London now."

I looked again at his face.

Bleached blonde hair, challenging red lipstick, boy or not, I could hardly take my eyes off him. He was stunning.

"So what are you doing down here then?", he asked, again speaking quite quickly and partially covering his mouth with his hand as he did so. He was very forward. But also, at a deeper level, it struck me that he was shy. I could tell. I could see it. He was very much both things. And, instinctively, I felt drawn to that shared characteristic.

I told him what I was doing, keeping it as brief as I could. Said that I had been down for the day for work. The job was boring, I said, and not worth talking about. Then I stopped, because I realised that the whole time I spoke I was being watched very carefully by unflinching eyes.

"What about you?" I finally asked, trying to shake off his gaze.

He blew smoke straight at me and widened those eyes a little. Smiled. And then just shrugged. "Actually some of my friends live in a big house. Out in the suburbs, the posh bit. And we've been there all week partying. Partying on and off, and now I suppose I'm going back home. It's a shame really, I wouldn't have minded spending another day or so out there. It was fun."

I nodded. "I'm jealous. It sounds ideal. Was it out in the country? I love the countryside. But I never get out to it."

He shook his head a little.

The train stopped once more. And a half dozen biggish lads got on and sat right behind us. They made no impression at all on me, but he, the girl opposite, glanced up at them and winced. Then, leaning forward and lowering his voice, almost conspiratorially he asked, "So what are you doing now? Where are you going? Somewhere lovely?"

The truth was I was going back into the centre of London to catch the first train back home, but I lied about that. Lied because I knew now, already, that I wanted to keep this going, keep this boy talking. This girl. Boy. Girl. "Oh, well, before I go back to

Birmingham I guess I'll go and have a drink somewhere. Do something."

I didn't really understand myself at that moment. I knew I wanted to say more. To talk. Yet this was a boy dressed as a girl, and I also knew that I was totally straight. So why did I want to talk to him? Why? I had to be honest with myself. I wanted to talk to him because I was breath taken. He had simply crashed into my space. He looked like a girl but chatted me up like a boy. And I was impressed. Almost dumbstruck.

Once more those eyes fixed me. A hesitation.

The tip of his tongue briefly touched his top lip. "Isn't life strange?", he said at last. "Actually we're all going to be in Birmingham this very weekend. Do you know the Aussie Bar? Yes, you must do."

I smiled. He asked and answered his own questions. I liked that.

I replied, saying I knew the Aussie Bar.

The truth was that I'd heard of it but had never been there. Actually I wasn't really focusing too much by this point as the voice, his voice... I suddenly realised that I found it attractive. It was a little bit husky, as if he had spent a weekend smoking, or at least dancing in a smoky club somewhere. It was also quite effeminate, for want of a better description.

But there was something else in there too, something that

fascinated me. Another accent I couldn't definitely place. Not at first. And I wanted to ask him about it.

"I'm sorry", he said, in that soft, light voice. "Do you want a cigarette?"

"No thanks. No. I'm fine."

He lit another cigarette and sat back in his seat. I looked at him a little more closely as he did so. In addition to a short pink mohair jumper, those heels and uncomfortably tight looking skirt, he was even wearing black fishnets. In many ways it seemed like an outfit from the 1950s. Even I could see that much. I wondered if he was a so-called 'New Romantic'. They were making the news a lot. Maybe those others on the platform hadn't been punks.

Then I saw that he was watching me again.

I smiled. And he smiled back.

"My turn to say sorry", I said, "as you've already said it to me about five times. But I think your accent's a bit strange too. Where is that from? It isn't an ordinary southern accent, I can tell. There's another sound in there. It's almost like a foreign accent." I had met and dated a Swedish exchange student on holiday the year before, and a Finnish girl the year before that.

"Oh my god!", he laughed, sitting up sharply. "Thank you. How did you hear that? That's quite sweet. That's really very perceptive."

"Sweden?"

"Yes and no. I'm not, I'm not English. Well, I am. And I'm not. My father was English, but my mother is French. And I was actually born in France. We moved over here when I was little. Then we lived for a while on the south coast before moving up to Guildford. How could you hear that?"

I laughed.

"Oh, I..." I opened my mouth to carry on, then paused. Why was I saying all this to a boy I didn't know? A stranger on a train? But I said what I'd been thinking anyway. "There's supposed to be a million-year-old man living inside each of us. Well, I think I'm him. I seem to know and feel everything sometimes. Just... I don't know, everything. So that's it, I guess. I'm a million years old."

Those dark narrow eyes lingered on me again.

He drew on his cigarette and held the smoke in for a moment.

"Really?" And then he pouted to exhale a big cloud of blue smoke. "Well you don't seem a day over fifty thousand." He smiled.

I laughed.

"Thank you." I said.

Yes, to answer my own question, I liked him, I liked him a lot.

That was why I was talking to him.

He looked at me. Still intense. Almost a scowl. And once again I felt under examination. But, somehow, from somewhere, I think I understood why he did it, and it felt OK. It even felt right. Maybe he needed to suss a person out. Of course he did, being dressed like that. And perhaps he did so just by scrutinising their face.

"What are you reading?" he asked me at last. Nodding at my book, which was now on the seat beside me.

"Oh that", I said. "It's philosophy, I guess. Religion. A bit of both. Eastern." I paused. "If we could live our lives like that, I think we'd all be a lot happier."

I was reading a lot in those days, too. Serious stuff like Jung, Rousseau, even Nietzsche. Sometimes novels by authors like Gide, Balzac or Camus. That was a big part of the inner me. The real me. I had begun doing so as an escape from the boredom of the factory, where I felt so trapped. In fact, to kill those seemingly interminable hours, it was read books or read newspapers. In practice I did both. Oil stained copies of The Sun and the Daily Mirror, cover to cover. Leather-bound copies of the Timaeus and Critias of Plato, cover to cover. I could relate to either. And I liked that.

"Read me a bit, then", he said.

'Bloody hell.' That was my thought. But instead I shook my head. "No, no. It's a bit heavy going, really."

"Go on", he said. "Please. Just a bit."

Thirty minutes ago, maybe a little more, I had never met this boy, this girl, boy. Girl. Now I was reading him philosophy? What had he said a few minutes ago? 'Isn't life strange?'

I picked the book back up, opened it where I had folded one corner of the page to bookmark it, and read: '*Past and future are the same. Neither is here now. Only the present is here now. Time is shaped so that we can alter the past, and therefore the future, to heal ourselves or even to heal others. What we did not live, we may yet live, but first, in the present we must give shape to it*'.

I shut the book.

Was I boring him? I wasn't sure.

"Like I said, it's pretty intense", I said. "Sorry."

He nodded.

And for a moment neither of us spoke.

"So... anything that we missed, or anything we did that we didn't like, we can change it?" he asked suddenly. "Tell a different story? And if we change it, then that will change who we are today for the better? And maybe change our future for the better too?"

"Yeah. Exactly that." Inside it surprised me that he had followed the passage so clearly and summed it up so concisely. I didn't think I could have done that.

"Hmm. So how does that work, then?"

I wasn't really sure, but I had a stab at it anyway. "I guess the point is that reality isn't what we think it is. It's very different. It has so much more potential. It's just that, as humans, we don't really get it. There are dimensions and all sorts of possibilities..." I tailed off. "Maybe we just have to have faith."

He watched me very carefully as I spoke, almost as if he was looking for truth or lies in my gestures and facial expressions. "I like that", he said at last. "I like the idea that our past is actually as open as our future."

"Me too", I agreed.

What was I saying? What was I doing? This was a boy dressed as a girl. Were we flirting with each other? I was straight. What was I doing? I looked at him, and as I did so he returned the favour, deeply, almost piercingly. I didn't flinch away, having already learned not to.

"What about you?" I said, trying to change my focus and nodding at the fashion magazines by his side. "You read a lot too?"

He laughed. "Oh those. Yes. And no. I read a bit. And I cut out some of the pictures and put them on my wall."

"You bought all those just for a few pictures?" I was surprised. One of them was Vogue. Big glossy magazines like that would have cost quite a bit.

He shook his head. "Oh, I didn't buy them". A quick gesture with his hand implied that he must have stolen them.

I smiled. There were at least half a dozen magazines. He'd taken quite a risk.

"You know what?", he said finally. Out of the window there were all kinds of railway lines meeting up as we neared central London. "I've made a decision. I'm going back to my friend's house right now. Why should I go back home today? It can wait. It can all wait. What's a few more days?" He paused. And took a last long draw on the cigarette, still fixing me with those eyes. "Birmingham", he said, changing the subject. "We're going to go to a wine bar there. On Saturday. The Hostaria. It's a very 'in' place. The Hysteria. Why don't you come? If you aren't doing anything else, I mean."

"OK", I said, trying to look back at him as hard as I felt he was looking at me. "But where's that?"

"Sorry", he said again. We seemed to both be saying that a lot. "Actually it's right by the Aussie Bar. Come on, come. You'll enjoy it. I promise. Why not?" He laughed. It was a small laugh. Quick. Almost a giggle.

Saturday was only two days away. On Saturday nights I usually went to a club in the city centre with some friends. But I had been a bit bored with that for a while. So, yeah, I could do that another time. I was going to go to that wine bar. I wanted to do that instead.

"OK", I said. "I might. I will. It sounds good. The Aussie Bar. The wine bar by it. Saturday night. What time?"

The train was coming into a station and he was clearly going to get off. He blew out a long breath. "Oh anytime. Any. Time. I shall be there... all night. Until we leave."

He stood up. Not tall. Not short. But very slim, his trim figure enhanced by the tight fitting skirt. "Are you getting off here too?", he asked.

"Oh... er... no", I said. "No. I don't think so. A few more stops yet, I think."

We both paused. I don't know why, but I instinctively opened the door for him. He exited the carriage in much the same way I imagine a film star from the Golden Age of Hollywood might have done. Then he turned back to me, and smiled. A huge broad smile. "I'll see you there, then."

It wasn't a question.

I smiled back. And he was gone. I tried to read my book again. But I couldn't. My mind was already elsewhere. I couldn't really believe what had just happened.

*

Suddenly my phone beeped with a text from Kate. "Dad, Hope you OK. Stop sitting in ur hotel feeling sorry. Get out and go see things! Have found your photo. He is beautiful. Love Kate xo".

I rang her back immediately, got no reply and sent her a text instead. "Wow. Brilliant, well done. Thank you. So much. Guard it with your life. Going out right now. Love Dad."

Kate's news, that she'd found my photo, cheered me up. It was only two small identical black and white images, but they were the only ones I had. Today, with cameras in phones, every step, every moment of a life is logged and posted on social media. One long-running photo-saga. But in the 1980s, we had none of that. And most of our memories were locked up inside our heads, with no permanent visual record ever existing.

Despite my promise to my daughter that I was 'going out right now', I turned back to my laptop. Not to write. Not to put down any more memories but to catch up on my work. First, several business emails. And then I had to work on a detailed drawing for the parts needed for some unusual scaffolding to be used on a new hotel in Stockholm.

An hour or so later, looking up from my screen, I realised that outside it was now dark. I had already showered, eaten, watched some nonsense on the TV and now I really did owe it to myself – and Kate – to get out and explore a few sights.

It wasn't easy to motivate myself to do that, as my hotel room offered the kind of comfort I could never have dreamed of years ago when I had once drunk in the bar downstairs, as a prelude to going on somewhere else with my mates. But, somehow, after one last bout of wrestling with the scaffolding diagram, I managed to shake off my lethargy and go out into the Birmingham night.

To begin with, I knew that what I needed, wanted, simply had to do was make a visit the Hostaria wine bar. Where, in so many ways, this story had really begun. But first, I would walk across the city centre to get a feel for my home town.

My hotel was situated adjacent to the central cathedral, churchyard and graveyard where, all those years ago, the punks used to hang out on a Saturday afternoon and where, sometimes, there would be fights. Benches and iron railings. Trees. Rows of bus stops. It all looked and felt exactly as it always had done during my youth. And despite the typical background noises of the city, all around me I could hear starlings, arguing and chattering in their distinctive manner as they settled down for the night in treetops and on buildings. I'd always associated that sound with this particular churchyard.

My first impression was that nothing really had changed. It still felt like home. Time hadn't even passed. The sky was dark, of course, and so bright lights were everywhere. A city centre shines. Attracts. Especially at night. I soon realised how wrong first impressions could be.

People who didn't know the city thought it was grim. Concrete. Built for cars, not humans. But it was also a good city, with a big heart and when I was young, the centre of Birmingham had been small. We all knew the names of every club and pub 'up town', as we called the city centre. It was intimate. Much more so than other cities. But now there were lots of bars. Lots. Many more than we had known or needed. And I had the clear impression that the names of the bars were now changed almost every weekend. Each finding it increasingly difficult to have a unique voice. I wondered where people found an anchor in such rapid change.

There was something else, too. The further I walked, the more I realised that town was packed, with crowds roaming pavements in ways they never used to do at night. I tried to avoid some of that by cutting through some dark alleyways and the hardly used side streets of my childhood. But even these were now filled with people, drinking outside, crowds smoking sugary electronic cigarettes ignoring one another and talking to friends on phones, and a lingering smell of hair gel.

Wasn't any part of the city centre still dark and quiet? It seemed to me that the answer was no. And that was very different from the old city that I had known.

Further on, the old Bull Ring shopping centre had gone from the centre of town, but 'The Ramp' was still there. I smiled. 'The Ramp'. New Street. Where so many people would arrange to meet, at the foot of 'The Ramp', or on it or at the top of it. A long sloping walkway, ugly concrete with a plain black iron railing. A McDonalds. Some other fast food shops.

It had been many years since I last sat in a McDonalds, and I wasn't about to go into one now. But as I walked past it, I vividly recalled how this was the very first one I'd ever seen or ever used.

When? It had been 1979. I remembered the date so clearly because I had taken a girl there, from my school. A girl who used to backcomb her blonde hair and make it stay upright with far too much hairspray. The date hadn't worked. We hadn't really got on. But I remembered her name very clearly – it was Lisa.

The same Lisa I would later live with and have a daughter by.

As I recalled that first, failed date, I hesitated outside the shop. Then I laughed out loud to myself. I had ordered a horrible sugary apple pie, the watery contents of which burned the roof of my mouth. I had spat it out. Lisa had not been impressed. Did they still sell those ghastly things? Surely not.

From McDonalds and the Ramp I went along New Street itself to where the Golden Eagle pub had once stood.

A wonderful old pub and a great venue for live music. I had seen bands like Birmingham's own 'G.B.H.' there and stood in awe watching Mark E Smith's 'The Fall'. But now? Just a small and largely inaccessible car park.

I might have lingered a bit longer in New Street and even gone for a drink somewhere, but it had been a long day travelling, and, in any case, the closer I got to the Hostaria Wine Bar, the more excited I felt at the prospect of seeing it once more.

As I walked along I visualised it; the wine bar was out past New Street Station, beyond any of the main shops, through dark and windswept underpasses, with very little to brighten the area up except for the headlights of passing cars. The relative isolation of the area had allowed it to develop a Bohemian character all of its own. Which was probably part of the reason it been so appealing to those who felt themselves to be outside of 'normal' society...

Sadly, for me anyway, very little of all that now seemed to remain either.

What used to be such an offbeat part of the city was now a bright and vibrant Chinatown. Large red brick restaurants, new hotels, crowds and traffic. The Aussie Bar, the old public house, was still there, albeit now blacked out. But I had hardly ever used it. It had always been merely a sort of bookmark for me to find the Hostaria, or to tell people where it was.

But the Hostaria? No. It was gone. Not only the wine bar itself, but the whole brick building and courtyard had been demolished and replaced with a characterless modern structure, largely unlet despite being perhaps 10 years old, that did very little for me or for the city. Some might call it progress. But elsewhere old industrial buildings were being preserved and brought back to life. An industrial city needed its industrial heritage. The Hostaria could have been renovated, renewed. Instead it was gone as if it had never existed.

2

That Friday. 1981. Back at work in Birmingham. Then that Saturday. I was uneasy the whole time. Would I really go in the evening? To the Hostaria, a wine bar I had never been to, on my own, to meet a boy who dressed like a girl. Would I really do that? A wine bar on my own was easy enough. It was the last bit that was unsettling. I wasn't meeting a girl. I was expecting to meet a boy, and that made me uneasy. Was I really going to do that? I was straight. Or so I thought. At least, I wasn't gay. Or was I? Actually I didn't know. How do you know? I was good looking. I'd had great-looking girlfriends. But never a boyfriend. I'd never wanted one either. So yes, I was straight.

But I also knew that I didn't care. I just didn't. My parents were easy going and brought me up the same way. It may not have been the same for others, but for me if I found someone attractive, I found them attractive. Did it matter what was between their legs? It wasn't about that. And I had felt that way ever since I could remember. More of that million year old man inside me, perhaps.

All the same, I had never before even seen a boy that I fancied. Nor had I ever looked. And I had definitely never had a sort of date with a boy. Not that this was a date. We were just going to meet up and... Actually I didn't know what we were going to do. Would we get on? We had got on fine on the train. Though, the way he'd appeared to flirt with me... With those shoes. That was strange. Why did he do that? I didn't know that, either. Later, I would understand.

All I knew for sure was that if someone had asked me right then, I guess I would have said that I was pretty *unsure* of any boy, especially this one. But maybe I was even more unsure about myself. Yes. That was it. I was confused. By all of it.

So.

Would I go?

Saturday night came around. And at about 7 pm or so I went upstairs to get ready. I hadn't ever answered the question "Would I go?" But nor had I stopped expecting to do so.

Getting changed, listening to different bits of music, nothing felt right. I didn't know what to listen to. I didn't know what to wear. In the end I wore those same old battered suede boots that I had worn on the train. I tied up my longish hair. Put on tight, pale blue jeans and a white t-shirt. I knew I was more than just good-looking, even dressed plainly like that and, in any case, there was no point wearing anything else. Anything else next to him would have just been a waste of effort.

So that was it.

I planned to go. And I was ready.

Then a bus. First a long wait, creating more tension. Then a protracted journey, seeming to stop every few hundred metres.

On that bus, I sat reading an old hardback copy of a dusty book; Pascal's 'Provincial Letters', and more than once I glazed over, couldn't see the words and asked myself what the fuck I was doing on that bus to town that night. I didn't know where the wine bar was. I didn't even know for sure where the Aussie Bar was.

At one point on that long slow journey, I looked out of the window at the dark, industrial Saltley Viaduct. Old houses stood empty all around it. Waiting to be demolished. Old factories too. Remnants of a world order that seemed to be neat and tidy; a world where men had been men and women had done as they were told. Of course it hadn't really been like that. But it somehow shouted at me "Look how *we* were. What are *you* doing? Where do you think *you're* going?"

Finally the city centre. Town. I went into one of the first pubs I came to and had a pint. I told myself I didn't need a drink and that I was only in there to ask someone for directions. And, after a second drink, I did ask someone.

It turned out that I was going to Digbeth, more or less. A gloomy area on the edge of the city.

The Aussie Bar was hard to miss, apparently.

And the wine bar? It was just a few doors further up from the Aussie.

That walk over, through town, in a cool dusk, felt awfully long and I felt ever more nervous the closer I got. No, I felt much more than nervous. Again. The same thing. This wasn't a date with a girl. This was a date with a boy. Or a meeting anyway, if not exactly a date. Was it a date? What the fuck was I doing? I had never looked at any boy twice before. Was I being teased or laughed at by life?

I even asked myself some half-arsed questions, such as did I hold doors open for him? I swore at myself for asking them. Nevertheless all sorts of similarly dumb and naive questions still came into my mind. I realised I had no idea what I was doing. I stopped. Should I just go home? Go to an ordinary pub and maybe chat up a girl? I didn't know what to do. I was out of my depth.

Yet despite all that, something was making me do it.

There was a pull. And I couldn't resist it.

And I remembered those words from the train. "Isn't life strange?"

And I wanted to do it too, I wanted to.

Then, suddenly, there it was.

A wine bar called the Hostaria.

The sky overhead was just beginning to darken as I went in.

Inside there was a long corridor. Brickwork walls painted white. That was the first thing. A corridor with glass panels overhead made to look like the courtyard of some Spanish tavern. I liked it, and it worked. The place did seem to be indoors and outdoors at the same time. And it did resemble a Spanish or Italian cafe. Something like that. The kind of place that might have been in a spaghetti western.

At the far end of the corridor I could see a large crowd of people. Darkness. Orange lights. And there was music. Chatter. A bar. That was obviously the main room. But to my immediate left, as I began to walk along the corridor, there was something darker. Spaces underneath a lower ceiling. People seated and standing. They were alcoves. Alcoves with tables. Clouds of smoke. Sounds of laughter. Drinking.

What should I do? Go and look in there? No. That was out of the question. So I kept walking straight along the corridor. Towards the main bar.

There were only a few tables and chairs in the corridor. And maybe a dozen or so people standing. They had just come in, perhaps, and were saying hello to friends. Everyone else was 'inside' and that had the effect of making any entrance all the more conspicuous. And as I walked along I felt exactly that; conspicuous.

Bastard. I said to myself. What am I doing?

In my own places, I was often pushy, talkative, confident. But here? I wouldn't have agreed to come if I'd known it was laid out like this. I'd need to search the dark spaces with a torch like a fucking cinema usherette to find my blonde boy in here. And I obviously wasn't going to do that, or anything like it. All the more so as he probably wouldn't even be there.

Could I change my mind and leave? Turn around and walk back down that long corridor? No. That was no good. I could feel people starting to look at me already. I couldn't do that. So I walked on. It was too late to turn back. I would buy a drink. Stand at the bar, drink it. Then go. That would be fine. I'd be alright.

And that was exactly what I did.

As I was being served, I glanced at the faces around me. There was some bleached hair, but no one shone in the way my boy had done. In fact no boys seemed to be wearing girl's clothes. There were one or two odd outfits, but if the boy from the train used this place, he was a one-off. This was not about cross-dressing. Nothing like that. New Romantics? Yes. But that was just a fashion. Or so I thought.

I stood there for maybe 20 minutes or so. Carefully, but without moving from the bar, to which I felt safely anchored, I also tried to look into the darkness of the alcoves, but they were too crowded and, in any case, they disappeared off into the distance. I couldn't see all of them.

I can't do this, I told myself finally. And I finished my wine and left.

That long walk back down the corridor.

Feeling flat. Hugely disappointed.

I was within two metres of the exit when, from the last of the alcoves, now to my right, I heard a voice I thought was somehow familiar. And I hesitated. Taking the chance to light a cigarette and look up, just a little, at the shadowy figures in the dark.

"Hey!" That voice. I did know it. "Hello!"

I peered into the crowd.

And there, emerging from a haze of orange light, haze of blue smoke and appearing in a haze of blondeness, was the boy from the train.

Very heavily made-up with eye shadow, eye liner, and mascara all exaggerating his naturally striking almond-shaped eyes. Blusher emphasising his already fine cheekbones, a cream foundation that made him look even more feminine and a bold red lipstick that drew the eye to his pouting lips. He looked gorgeous. Every bit a girl.

"Hello!" he said again, squeezing past a few people to get to me, and then, once free of them, half dancing up closer to me and stumbling a little as one heel slipped on the tiled floor. "Hello!"

He adjusted his shoe and stood up straight and looked at me. I was surprised to find his eyes almost level with mine. "Are you leaving? You're not leaving?"

"Noo", I lied, "I was just... I was..."

"Had I missed you? Were you leaving? Deserting me?"

I nodded. "Yeah. I didn't think you were here."

"Oh no", he said. "You nearly left. If I hadn't seen you at the last moment."

There it was again. Life was strange. Wasn't that what we had said on the train? It kept happening. The night had only been saved at the very last moment. But it had been saved. And that was what really mattered.

"I did keep watching out for you", the boy continued, speaking quickly. "But we must have missed each other."

He laughed. That same small, delicate and fast laugh that I had heard on the train. Almost shy. Almost nervous. A little giggle.

He held a cigarette for me to light and I lit it for him. He took a long draw on it, then slowly blew out a huge cloud of smoke. "I knew you'd come, though." He smiled, a sexy smile. "I just knew it!"

I laughed.

Feeling rather unsure and nervous, yet wanting to say something positive. Because I did feel positive. Very. I had been so looking forward to meeting this boy again ever since that train journey. "Er... I had to come", I said. And then added "I had to. I wanted to see what you'd... Anyway, the other day, it was so strange. Good. Good strange. We can't ignore life when it offers... And you made me laugh, anyway. You did. Thank you. I'd had a terrible day. Really boring and you lit it up".

He smiled. Then offered a hand.

Just like that.

And to my surprise I took it.

"Come on, come and buy me a drink. Buy me a drink for making you smile and getting you out of your usual routine on a Saturday night." And with that, he led me back along the corridor to the main room. Past some faces who were – I'm sure – very green with envy.

"Stop", I said.

And we stopped.

If my blonde boy was a bit of a show-off, so was I in my own way. I could see that, ahead of us, the main room was packed. But here, at the end of the corridor, everyone could see us clearly and I wanted those envious looks to last a little longer. "I don't even know your name."

Those heavily mascaraed eyes blinked back at me. "What's yours?"

I told him.

"Mine is Alley", he said. "As in alley cat."

I laughed. "As in alley cat?"

"Yes!" He nodded, then meowed and scratched the air in a feline fashion. "Well, no. It's short for Alexander." He paused. "Or Alexandria. Take your pick. It was how I spelled it at school anyway and it kind of stuck." And with that he gave me a huge smile and then tugged on my hand and we were off, squeezing between people as we entered the main room.

We stood at the bar and didn't talk. The music was loud. It was stuff I didn't know. But I liked it all the same. It worked. The whole place worked and I was already hooked. Suddenly a cigarette, his, was put to my mouth. But it wasn't the same cigarette I had just lit for him, it was a joint. He had been passed it by one of the door staff. I took it. Smoked it. "What can I get you?" I said.

"Anything white. By the bottle. Then come down to where we all are", he said.

And with that he whirled around on the spot and disappeared towards the alcoves again.

I stood there for a moment, took another draw on the joint and wondered if I had died. How had life suddenly and so miraculously taken this strange turn? Had I really just walked into a wine bar holding hands with a gorgeous blonde boy, dressed as a girl and wearing red lipstick? Inside I fizzed with excitement, and it probably showed on the outside too.

I think if someone had asked me, right there and right then, where the hell I was, I wouldn't really have been able to answer them. I wouldn't have been able to say how old I was. Or who I was. One meeting on a train and then all this? I should catch the train more often. That was the only clear thought I had right then.

Then, suddenly a line of music cut into my thought:

I will be king, and you, you will be queen...

I knew the track. It was David Bowie. Heroes.

The line stopped me. Froze me.

This *really was* something else. It was. Queen. *Queen.* All the connotations of that word. What the fuck was I doing there? I was straight. Since Thursday, when we met, I had been sleepwalking. What was I doing here?

At that moment I think I might have walked out. But right then, cutting into those shocked thoughts, I realised that the man behind the bar was asking me what I wanted to drink. Maybe my natural politeness got the better of me, I don't know, but I forgot my panicked thoughts and asked for a bottle of white wine. I had no idea what. They suggested something Italian and I bought a bottle of white wine in a tall, oddly shaped bottle.

"Two glasses, please", I said. And they passed me a second glass.

By now the place was really quite crowded. All sorts of faces and styles. I didn't look too hard but I saw that there were other men in make-up. That was fine. I was fine with that. Though none of these others looked like a girl. Unlike Alley. Who did. And there were lots of women too. So it wasn't just a gay club. That was fine too. And hair styles of all kinds. I liked that. On the one hand it all made me feel very plain and out of place. Yet, somehow, in plain jeans and a white t-shirt, I also felt I stood out a little. One of the few not trying to be other than I was.

I squeezed past various groups of people and then walked down towards the alcoves. I could see Alley's blond hair and I was sure I could hear his voice above the others. Was that because I already recognised his voice and was drawn to it? Or was it because he was a bit loud and showy? Both. I decided it was both.

Seated and standing, Alley and his friends were all in and around two alcoves. Dark wood. Dark tables. Benches. White plaster walls. And fake windows with orange lamps inside them. As I got closer, I had to stop as someone squeezed past me with a handful of glasses. I looked up. One of the boys standing by Alley's alcove seemed to be almost two metres tall, with his hair tied up vertically and bound up with ribbons. It was pretty impressive.

Another was dressed entirely in yellow. A yellow suit. And thick yellow make-up. A third, a woman, was all in leather and wearing a heavy German peaked cap from the war. She appeared to be trying clothes on another woman who was, in effect, topless.

I laughed. I couldn't help myself. Not because I was laughing at them, but because I had been reading a book about Hieronymus Bosch a week or so before, and the whole scene vaguely reminded me of one of his pieces. And perhaps that was it, perhaps I had died in a train crash last Thursday and now I was up in heaven or down in hell. All of this couldn't be real, could it?

Alley, though, was on another level to the others. She shone. She was beautiful. More than beautiful. And as I thought that, I realised that I now thought of him as *her*. Quite suddenly. Why had I done that? I didn't know, but it made me smile to myself.

Just then she looked up, and smiled hugely back at me. She nudged someone sitting next to her to move over, patted the bench beside her and I squeezed in and sat down. I held out a glass for her. She took it, and I poured her a glassful of wine.

I looked around – well, sort of half looked around – and realised that not everyone in the company was quite so Boschlike. There were boys in bizarre clothes, yes, but some others were in relatively normal suits and plain thick cotton shirts. And one man, who must have been nearly 60, was even wearing a threadbare tweed jacket. I figured he was the father of one of them. And I guess that made me feel a little easier. For a while I had actually felt conspicuous because I was wearing jeans and a t-shirt!

I turned to look at Alley, but she was talking to someone else. Then she sat back holding one of her wrists and rocked slowly from side to side, as if she was waiting for something.

And then, suddenly, the something arrived. A cigar packet flew through the air from somewhere and landed right beside her. She glanced up, waved at a face I hadn't seen and then turned to me. She opened the packet and inside were two ridiculously long and fat, but tidily rolled, joints. She offered one of them to me. I took it. She put the other in her mouth and lit it, and then she lit mine for me.

For the next hour or so I watched, learned and laughed.

There was quite a bit of a cattiness between Alley and some of the others, and a lot of that made us both laugh too. I noticed just how sharp she could be at times. Almost too much with some people. But I already felt that she didn't mean to hurt, it wasn't that, not at all. She was just on a different level.

Then I offered to get some more wine. And she clapped her hands and said "Yes, yes please", like a child asking for an ice cream. I liked that about her. Her every gesture seemed designed to be attractive, and I wondered if she practiced any of them in front of a mirror somewhere.

Going away from the alcove felt cold, though. I didn't like it. Sure, the whole place *was* full of strange-looking folk, but there was something, somehow, not right about most of them. I could see that now. Yes, they wore make-up, but they didn't seem to have the same body language as those in the alcoves, who all seemed at ease and to know one another. As I stood at the bar I looked around more. It struck me that the whole thing wasn't about clothes or make-up. It wasn't just about that. There was no harm in doing any of that, but the people in the alcoves... they weren't doing this for the weekend. It wasn't just a fashion for them. Unlike the rest of the crowd, this was how they *really* were. That was the difference I saw. What about me? Did I fit? No. I wasn't any of them. Neither in fashion nor yet like the ones who lived like this all the time. To be a weekender would have been too shallow for me. Too inauthentic. But to be like it all the time? I didn't have that need. Or that desire. Or those balls.

I seemed to be at the bar forever. And I wanted Alley to come up. To hold my hand again. To talk to me. In front of all these people. All these part timers. But she didn't come. And eventually I was served and then squeezed my way back to the now even more crowded alcoves.

As I got there, Alley, wearing the German military cap, was posing for her photo. I stood and watched, getting the distinct idea that she had no idea who the photographer was. After a few more poses, she removed the cap and skimmed it back to its owner. Looking up, she saw me and made room for me at the table once more. She could make others move out of her way if she wanted them to. There was a hierarchy of the Bosch-set, and she was clearly right at the top.

49

I sat down and filled her glass for her. My own too. Another joint was passed to me. I gave it straight to her. She took it without flinching. She spoke to me. I replied. And my reply made her almost choke with laughter.

As the night wore on, and the alcove we were sitting in got even more cramped, I found myself getting ever more pressed up against Alley. Against her legs and the black silky material of her skirt. Her arms too, which were mostly bare. I kind of stepped aside from myself for a moment and asked myself how that felt. Fine. That was how it felt.

Alley was also wearing a sparkling bracelet on her left wrist, and it kept catching on wine bottles or other things every time she leaned across the table to make a point or tell someone off or whatever. Reaching for a bottle, it finally caught someone's glass and brought it crashing down, spilling wine all over the table top. From then on, she just kept hold of her wine glass and tilted it towards me in a dramatic sort of way whenever it needed refilling. Others laughed at that. I adored her all the more for doing it.

At one point she turned towards me as I turned towards her and our faces were only ten or twelve centimetres apart. She looked slightly upwards to meet my eyes and I felt things then that I had no place to feel. I said something to take my mind off those feelings. I can't remember what. And by way of reply she put her hand across her mouth and leaned closer towards me. And whispered. Then someone shouted something at her. She taunted them back in return. Then turned to look at me again. Narrowing her already heavily mascaraed eyes.

"Really?", I said. She sniffed and I laughed.

"It's the inside that counts", she said finally.

"I know", I agreed. "Being good inside is what really matters."

What else did we talk about that night? I don't remember. We mostly laughed. That's the image I have of it. Fun. And, by the time everyone started to leave, we were enthusiastically talking to each other about art and how to draw.

"Are you an artist then?", she asked me. I wasn't. Not back then. But I had read everything I could about movements like Cubism and Impressionism and I loved Turner and painters like Gainsborough and Brueghel. And I could talk about art or listen to people talk about art for hours on end.

And then suddenly it was time to go. Sad moment. Who ever wants such a great night to end? We ought to be able to bank such hours and return to them when we need them.

They were all going on to a club, or so I thought, and I wasn't. But as we got up and she reached for her coat, I put my hand on her arm and stopped her. "Alley", I said. There was something I just had to clear up for myself, "You know... on that train... the other day", I began.

She looked at me a little from under her eyelids.

I liked her. A lot. And we got on. Very well. But something was worrying me. "That was kind of... very, I don't know... odd. What you did."

"What?" her voice was a little bit hoarse, and all the sexier for it.

"You sitting right opposite me. When that train was empty."

"Mmm. Life can be like that. Strange. I told you. And we never know where things might lead. We have to go with them or give up loving and living!"

I didn't say anything.

"Oh no", she said suddenly, eyes finally widening. "No. I see what you mean. No. Oh my god, no. We were all standing on the platform, you know, just talking. Gossiping really. And then someone said 'your train Alley'. It was going and I just ran and jumped on. First door I came to. And I found myself sitting down right opposite you."

She smiled.

By now we were outside and she was ready to leave with the others. What she had said made sense. And I liked the answer too. But I still didn't say anything. Even if she had sat right opposite me by chance, hadn't she then deliberately rubbed her shoe against mine to get my attention? I felt uncomfortable with that.

But was that what she had done? Now I wasn't at all sure. But I still felt uneasy about it.

"Yeah." I just had to say. "You were still pretty forward, though."

"Excuse me?" she said again. "I was so not. It was you who kept staring at me!"

"I didn't."

"You did too. Every few minutes, actually. You kept pretending to look out the window but really you were looking at my legs."

"Oh, I never! You kept rubbing your foot against mine!" I protested.

She opened her mouth as if to say something but out came just a short "Ohh! I so did not!"

"You did!"

She reached down and put a finger in between her heel and the back of her shoe. "These shoes", she said. "This one. It pinches." She stood up a bit straighter and twisted her foot around a little. And moved it a bit. A few inches. Wriggled it around. "See. I keep having to do that. Wiggle it about. They'll soften up."

I sighed.

I had been wrong.

And she had been right all along.

It was just that life was strange.

What I thought had happened on that train hadn't happened. Yet, somehow, that very misunderstanding had brought us together.

"Oh", she said, mock horror in her voice. "You mean you thought... Oh all that. You thought I was hitting on you?"

"Yes."

She laughed. "I thought you were hitting on me!"

"No!" I said. "I wouldn't do that. Not like that."

"Oh my god. No. Nor would I."

By now we were both laughing. "Why did you invite me here, then?" I said.

"Hmmm. Well", she said, slowly, weighing the words, "actually it's not at all the kind of thing I normally do. I'll tell you about that sometime. But if some sexy-looking book-reading boy is going to try and chat me up, but can't find a way of asking me for a date, well, sometimes you have to push things along a little."

I looked up at the sky. Then back at her face and smiled. And we both laughed again. What the fuck was I doing here? I had no idea. The same question as before. Only now it didn't seem to matter. Life was running things, not us.

Suddenly a voice said "Come on, everyone". It was the woman in leather with the German military cap. And in a flurry of movement, all sorts of shapes and clothes and faces and make-up were moving and getting into taxis.

Alley was about to go, too. I tried to both feel and appear unmoved. Yet I knew that if she did go, we would never see each other again. And at the very last moment, I'm sure she knew it too. I'm sure she did. "Come on", she said. "It's a party. Not a nightclub."

"Am I coming, then?" I asked.

"Yes", she said. "Of course. Why not? Come on!" And she smiled that big quick smile again.

The party was in Handsworth which, back then, was still unknown to me. A dangerous kind of place with a reputation. Full of big redbrick houses, drugs and parties. Or so we'd been told. To some of the people I knew, the area was all about crime. And they were happy to blame 'the blacks' for that. I had heard that too. Far too often.

The taxi sped through streets lined by Asian shops that were still open. On my own estate, steel shutters had closed off all such places some hours earlier. The contrast made me smile. So much for the bad reputation.

Eventually we stopped next to what looked like a park; trees, tall and dark, their tops blowing in a freshening wind. It was a street that must once have been for the very wealthy. And maybe, in some of the houses, it still was.

As we arrived we all fell out of the taxi. Reminiscent of that scene in the Marx Brothers film where everyone tumbles out of a suddenly opened cabin door. Laughing, with more bottles of wine being produced from somewhere, we staggered up the drive – Alley losing one of her heels for a minute – to a front door larger than some houses I had known.

Inside, the house was truly vast. Though by now, to be honest, it was all a bit of a blur to me. There was so much to see and take in. The hall was oak panelled. A wide wooden staircase had a landing half-way up with a settee flanked by huge blue and white Chinese vases. Windows were leaded. Curtains were long, heavy and hung from chunky brass poles.

There were already lots of people at the party, too. Some singly, some in small groups, some in larger ones. Quite a few were standing but quite a few more were seated on the floor. For a minute or so I stood beside Alley, in the hallway, and studied the faces and shapes around me. Some of them were similar to those from the wine bar but, yes, there were fewer of them and those that were here were somehow older and maybe more settled. Wealthier, even. That may have been it. They were wealthier. And in addition to the wine bar types, there were very many 'straight' looking people in jeans or casual clothes.

Then I realised that I had a wine bottle, but no corkscrew. So I went off to look for one, with Alley and the rest disappearing behind me into rooms and spaces and who knew what.

I found a corkscrew in a huge and cavernous kitchen, opened the bottle and then put it down and lost it. Someone took it and I was without a drink again. So I took someone else's beer. I don't recall exactly what I did next but there was music, so I danced for a while in a spacious, darkened living room. I danced with a very tall girl. And I remember wondering if it was a girl. And that made me laugh. It wasn't the kind of question I'd ever asked myself before at a party.

Time went by. I had no idea how long. I wandered from one room to another and found myself talking for a while to someone who was looking for a singer for a band he had formed. He asked me if I could sing. Told me that I had the right look. I said I had no idea if I could sing. He told me I looked the part again, and apparently he had a studio in the cellar of his parent's house with all kinds of keyboards and instruments. He was only about 20, and I remember thinking as he droned on that my parents had taken years to afford even a basic record player. When I realised he was also trying to hit on me, I lost myself in the dark of the party.

Even though all kinds of windows and doors were open, the house was already thick with the smell of smoke from cigarettes and joints. It was almost too much. But when I sat down and found myself offered a joint obviously made of home-grown cannabis – the smell gave that away – I smoked some of it anyway.

Then the man in need of a singer found me again and sat next to me and told me some awful long-winded joke while he finished the joint off. Some music that I knew came on and I got up. I wanted to dance. With a girl.

"Hello", said a voice I now knew and already loved. It was Alley. But as I moved towards her to take hold of her and dance, another girl pushed in between us and I found myself dancing with the wrong girl instead. She put her arms around me and within a few moments I had lost sight of Alley. She wasn't dancing. And I wondered why not.

I danced for a while, but my heart wasn't in it. And when, for the third time, a very pretty but incredibly squeaky-voiced girl sat down next to me and started to come on to me, I had to get out of there and find Alley again.

That, too, was an odd moment. One of very many. Walking away from a good looking girl and searching for a boy instead. I laughed at that. I would never have done that before. But then, in this case, the boy was so much better looking.

Eventually I found Alley.

She was at the foot of the staircase but more or less pinned into a corner by a man, possibly twice her age, who appeared to be lecturing her.

I caught her eye and, over his shoulder, as he put an ashtray down, she mouthed a quiet 'Help' to me.

"Got to go", she said abruptly, ducking past him and grabbing me. "Get me out of here", she laughed.

"Me too!" I said. "I'm being followed!"

"Oh my god, let's hide somewhere!" she said.

I realised then that Alley was clutching my hand, almost dragging me along.

"Come on", she said, still that laughter. Still the smiles. Still making all the running.

And run we did.

We ran up that huge flight of stairs. A crazy, breathless run. But who cared? We were young. We laughed and clutched at our sides as we reached the top and half collapsed on the landing.

At the top of the stairs there was another flight of stairs. I looked at her and she looked at me. "No", she said. Around us, in all directions, were doors leading to unknown rooms. "This is far enough. One of these will do. Quick!"

I hesitated and looked at some of the people sitting on the landing, smoking yet more joints. I glanced down at the hall, the big front door, and saw it open and more of the crowd from the Hostaria pouring in. Then we saw Alley's 'man' coming up the stairs. The 'lecturer'. Alley yelped and we ducked into the first room we found, before he had a chance to see her.

Going into that room felt as though we had entered the wardrobe in the book with the Lion and the Witch. There was a calmness in there. A magic even. And I think we both felt it.

No one used the room very often. That was clear. It was dark too. No lamps, no bulbs. It had a slightly dusty feel. Like no one else had been in there for days, or even weeks. And it was cool. I liked it. It felt safe.

For a moment we both stood. "Mmm lookit that", said Alley. There *was* a wardrobe. Just like the one in the book.

"There might be another world in there", I said. "Let's look inside!"

We did. But all that was inside were a few heavy winter coats.

Then Alley almost danced over to the huge window. She opened it. Waved out and shouted to some people in the front garden. They shouted back. Then she closed the window. And pulled the curtains shut. They seemed to shimmer with dust as she did so. And they were thin too. I hadn't expected that. They should have been of a thick material, velvet maybe, but no, they were thin.

"Candles", she said. "We need some candles." But there were none. And soon, thanks to the thin curtains, the room was just about light enough, our eyes adjusting quickly.

Alley sat down in a big old armchair and kicked off her high heels, pulling out and lighting yet another huge joint at the same time. And I sat on a bed that was big enough for ten people to sleep in and still not touch each other.

Once more, for a moment, we were silent. Not uncomfortably so. Quite the opposite.

Eventually, I got off the bed and sat down on the floor next to her, glancing at her discarded high heels, which seemed to fascinate me. Then she offered me the joint, and suddenly got up and ran out of the room without even putting those shoes back on.

A few minutes passed. Then a few more. And I began to feel awkward. Had she gone? Would she return? Of course she would, her shoes were still here. But how long would she be gone for? And what was she doing? I felt as if life was teasing me. Trying to change my mood for the worse. And as more time slipped by, it began to win. Was this all some sort of game? What was I doing here?

Then, finally, the door opened and she came back in, shouting over her shoulder to someone on the landing, and laughing, carrying a bottle of wine and two huge orange candles.

A difficult few moments had passed.

We lit the candles and she sat down in the huge armchair again. The bottle was already open and we drank some of the wine. And then we re-lit and finished smoking the joint, which I had allowed to go out.

The candlelight revealed a few more things in the room. In one corner a strange, maybe African, sculpture, made of wood with horns of some kind and a few spikes. Neither of us wanted to take a closer look at that.

In another corner, there were some old clothes that looked like children's school blazers. And lastly, by one wall, there was a pile of magazines.

I went over to the magazines and picked a few of them up. I had expected them to be old and dusty. But they were all quite new.

"What are they?" Alley asked. Seeming quite small, tucked up inside that armchair.

"Oh, you know", I said, flicking through a few of them. "Celebrity news. Gossip. Stuff like that." I picked up a particularly thick magazine. "And horoscopes."

"Ooh!" her face lit up. "Let me see! Let me see!"

I took the magazine to her, and sat back down on the floor beside her once more.

She turned a few pages. "Oh no. Oh my god. 'Who is your perfect love match?' Oh, we must read that."

I took a sip of the wine and had another quick glance at the strange wooden statue in the corner to make sure that it hadn't moved or somehow come to life.

"Here we are", said Alley. "Here we are. You're Aries, you told me earlier your birthday was in mid-April. Mmm. So Aries. Aries man. Let's see." She took another draw on the joint, which was now very near its end, and handed the last of it to me. She blew out some smoke and continued. "Sometimes reckless. Oh. And very, very passionate. But, it says, always a gentleman when he needs to be."

I nodded. "Yeah, that sounds about right." Then I took a draw on the joint.

"Wait. I haven't finished." She peered at the text and – I was sure – definitely edited it verbally as she read it out. "An Aries man would make a Scorpio woman feel wanted and protected."

She paused and looked at me. "I'm Scorpio", she added. "Oh. They are ideal lovers, love making will be both exciting and fun. There will be doubts and mistrust in the beginning, but if they can get past that he will be incredibly loyal to her and loving and she will be able to trust him completely." She looked up at me. Smiled. Then read a bit more. "Oh, but I am to lightly touch his arm, or smile sweetly and do little things like that in order to encourage him to make his move because actually, although he's quite wonderful, he's not sure of himself. Not really."

She put the magazine down. And I passed her the wine. "Mmm. So I suppose rubbing my shoe against his on a train is another way of encouraging him to make his move."

We both laughed.

"Wait, though", I said. "Let me read it too." I picked up the magazine. What else did it say? What had she not read out?

Alley sipped the wine and took the very last of the joint from me. But it was already dead.

"Here we are", I began. "Both will demand a lot of love in any relationship." I hesitated. It said 'and sex too', but I didn't want to read that bit out. Alley raised her eyebrow in a singularly sexy way and then nodded. I continued reading. "His masculinity and his nerve is what does it for her. She admires his cheek and his strength of character. While for him, her magnetism and loyalty are what is important." I paused. "What does it say about that, magnetism? Oh, here it is. She is charismatic and glamorous and could seduce any man on Earth."

"Ha!" She blew out some smoke.

"But she can be very suspicious too!" I added.

Alley screwed up her nose. "Yes, and it says he's possessive. So that's evens."

I nodded.

"Well, of course he would be possessive about a woman like that. She's gorgeous."

'Wait', I thought. Don't say any more.

And so I put the magazine down.

In that room, in that candlelight, we then sat and talked, on and off, and smoked our last few ordinary cigarettes and drank for an hour or so.

Just the two of us.

I think we spoke about art again and she talked once more about drawing. I thought it sounded like an ideal form of expression for her. She seemed very keen on it and I wished that we had a pen or pencil and some paper with us so that she could sketch something for me to see but – naturally enough – we didn't have either.

Then, and probably inspired by the statue in the corner of the room and the huge dark wardrobe, we began talking about magic, and I told her ghost stories that I'd heard when I was young. I told her about a strange black dog that had watched over me as a child. And about a golden procession that used to pass over my bed when I was small. And Alley sat and listened to it all. Like a child being told bedtime stories.

When I'd finished, she smiled at me. "People normally bore me about their Ferrari or how much champagne they can drink." She paused. "I prefer listening to your ghost stories. Thank you."

Then we fell quiet. Said nothing.

A few minutes passed. Again it wasn't uncomfortable, though. And I felt glad that we could just be quiet together if we wanted or needed to be.

Suddenly Alley's voice cut into my thoughts. "I want...", she said, quietly, "I mean, can we talk?" Her voice was almost a whisper in the dark.

For a moment I honestly thought she was going to tell me that she was 'actually a boy' – as if I hadn't already noticed. But of course it wasn't that. It was something much more delicate. Deeper. And it began to change everything that we were or could ever be.

"I don't...", she began, hesitantly, "I don't really have relationships".

I didn't reply. Not yet. This was a time to listen, not speak.

"Oh, no", she said. "I haven't got that quite right. What I mean is that I have to know someone. To trust them. I mean really trust them before, before I can..."

The party, if it was still going on, which it must have been, seemed to belong to a distant and detached world, not intruding on us at all.

"No." She stopped herself once again. "Even that isn't right. It isn't that straightforward. I wish it was. But it's much more than simple trust..." But no more words came.

I picked up the wine bottle and took a sip from it. There wasn't much left.

"I'm not so different", I said at last, thinking about it as I spoke. "I like to keep people at arm's length really. Almost as if I'm scared to let someone in."

She watched me closely. One of those examining stares. Making sure that I was telling every bit of the truth. Reading my body language. Following and trusting her instincts.

"With me, but even more with you", I continued, digging into myself as I spoke, having never thought about it before, "it's like a shield almost. Protective. Yours is very beautiful and it attracts, but it also cuts you off. It is real. Again, like me. But it's just the outside. And so far no one has been allowed past that shield. But there is another you, inside... I'm sorry", I said, stopping myself. "I don't know."

Sunken ever more into the armchair she shook her head very slightly. "Go on", she said. "Please."

"Well... the inside...", I began. But stopped again.

She looked at me. Not exactly wide-eyed because her eyes were never that. But in spirit they were. "Yes", she said. "The inside..."

"That's less easy to say", I said, not sure if I was interrupting her or not. "Inside. The inner you? The inner me too, I guess. I think it's more that the inner, the inside, it enjoys the games played out here. But... but somehow it's also in there and looking out onto the world and sort of waiting."

This time it was her turn not to reply.

"It's waiting for someone to reach in. For you. For me too."

For a moment she was silent. I felt sure I was right. I felt it so keenly because I was, in no small part, describing myself and how I felt.

Then, and slowly, she said the most poignant of all things and it made my eyes sting a little as I heard her words. "If only someone could give to me. Really just give. I would give them the whole world. And more besides."

She paused. I felt that she did so because if she hadn't she would have begun to cry. And I wondered how and why she had opened up like this to me.

"I really would. I know I would. I'd be the best. The best lover and the best partner ever", she said at last. "So I just don't feel that I can let anyone in. Not unless they're the right someone." She was now on the edge of tears.

"Hey", I said. "It's OK. I know. I know."

She looked at me. Those dark eyes. Narrowed more than ever. "How?" was the only word she was able to say, her voice almost breaking. "How do you know?"

I shook my head a little. "I'm just like you", I said. "Really. I am. You don't know how much I'm like you. And right now, here, in this house, I don't know anybody. And you? All those faces downstairs that you recognise, and you don't know anybody either. Not really."

She gave me a quick and rather sad smile. "That's so true", she whispered.

There was something so dangerous and circular about where we both were. As I spoke I saw it, knew I would do something about it – but I don't think she saw it at all. At least, not clearly. Without letting people in, how could the inside develop? Where would it gain the strength it needed for when someone did reach in? Life isn't about waiting to share yourself. If you do that, one day someone will crash in and it'll be almost impossible to cope. The floodgates will open and they will fill the space with themselves and you won't have any defences. And then when it ends – because it always ends one way or another – you'll have believed every word they told you, the good and the lies. And you won't know the difference.

"There's no such thing as the right person. There's more than one of them", I said at last. "But they're hard to find. Because we don't know what they look like. And when one comes along, we have to let them in. Then they might take us over. But when it's finished, and they go, we have to move on. Because... there are more of them out there. There are. They may be next door. They may live a hundred miles away in another city, or across the sea in another country. But they are out there. Let them in. Love. Then when the time comes, move on. Move on or become stuck forever in just one storyline. Their prisoner, almost."

I looked at her. Sitting there in that candlelight. And she seemed very precious to me. We were both only young. Teenagers. But I felt so protective of her at that moment. And I wanted to just hold her.

But I didn't.

I didn't do that.

Instead, with that almost overwhelming feeling of wanting to protect her, and wanting to respect her own words – 'I need to trust someone first' – I went back to the big old wardrobe and took out a few of the thick winter coats. "Here", I said. "Let's just wrap ourselves up in these. Forget the whole world for a while."

And for a while that was what we did.

Under a few big coats she curled up in the chair. And I lay on the floor. Just beside her.

Probably no more than half an hour passed before someone crashed into the room. It woke me up. They saw us. Said sorry and left.

Half asleep, already cold and uncomfortable, I expected to find myself at home and alone in my bed. I expected to find that none of it had happened. It had to be a dream. I had not met a beautiful boy on a train. We were not, already, somehow, friends. It was not real. It had happened too fast. I had dreamed it all.

But no.

None of those things were the case.

I was still in that strange, magical room. I was still in this huge, extraordinary house. I could see shadows of trees through thin orange curtains. On the floor were two wine bottles. The room smelt of dust and smoke. There was a saucer filled with cigarette ash. It was all real. Wonderfully so.

There too, right beside me, was a huge armchair. And a few coats lay next to it on the floor. And in front of the coats there were two shiny black high-heeled shoes. And right there, in the quiet and dark of that room – which, the crashing door aside, still seemed strangely and wholly removed from the house and party that must have been going on around us – right there was a boy, in a chair, and asleep.

But she was no longer covered by any of the coats. They had all slipped onto the floor.

I sat up. I looked at my sleeping friend. This boy. This young man. This young woman. Or girl. Whatever the fuck would I call her? Labels didn't matter, but I wondered all the same. Her eyes were even more like slits when she slept. The thick black mascara exaggerated it too. And that blonde hair. I wanted to touch it. Stroke it a little. But I did nothing. She was fast asleep and I wanted her to trust me. I wanted that because I wanted to trust her too. We were not so dissimilar. I had been right about that.

Then I sighed.

I don't know why. Maybe because I knew that somewhere out there in the world was the woman for me. My woman. The right woman. And that was good. And fine. I was more than happy about that. But for now? Who was I? What did I want? I looked at Alley again. Had I ever seen such an exquisite face so close up? No. No I hadn't. Not close up. Not at any sort of distance either. She had a woman's skin too. Her arms. They were those of a girl more than a boy.

Fucking hell.

I felt all that in a heartbeat. Then I more or less pinched myself. Whatever this was, in my head, in my thoughts, whatever it was supposed to be, it would be. I would let it be. I knew that and I made sure I promised myself the same thing. There was no pressure. If I was to find my woman one day, that would come. But right now, right here, although we were just friends, I felt that this boy was all that mattered. And how.

I looked around the room. One of the doors to the huge wardrobe was open. I expected to see a dwarf or unicorn coming into the room from Narnia. Here, beside me, asleep was the White Witch. Surely this was her? That witch.

I lay back down on the floor. Tried to sleep again. Stared at the ceiling. Then I sat up. What was I doing? I couldn't leave her asleep like that without any covers. She would be cold. It must have only been about 3 am. She needed to sleep and so did I.

But what could I do?

At length I decided that there was only one thing I could do. And that was to treat her as I would have wanted to be treated and stop being so afraid of making a mistake.

"Alley", I said quietly, gently shaking one of her knees. "Come on. Get up. Get on the bed and let me cover you over properly."

She woke up.

I smiled. How could such narrow and heavy eyes even see?

But she, by contrast, instinctively felt the need to defend herself. "No", she said. "I told you, I don't."

I shook my head. "I know. It's OK. Neither do I. I promise. I just want to put you on the bed and cover you over with a blanket. It's a massive bed. Come on." Then I added a lie to try and reassure her a little. "You're not my type anyway." I said.

She didn't move.

"Come on." And to my amazement I actually took her hand. "I promise."

Sleepily, she got up. She padded over to the bed. And lay on it.

"I am", she said. Then again, looking straight at me, almost defiant. "I am!"

I wasn't sure what she meant by that. And so I just dragged a big heavy counterpane over her and, within moments, she appeared to be asleep once more. Then I picked up the coats and covered myself with them, as I lay down on the bed too. Not too close. I had given her my word.

Anyway, I was full of enough doubts of my own.

All the same, in that half-light, I turned and looked across at my friend's face. Who was she? In truth? Who was she? She would let no one in. Why? I didn't know. Yet she laughed so much, too. She was fun. Sharp too. Yet I also knew she was probably the most gentle person I had ever met. She really did have an unworldly beauty, both inside and out.

Lying there, from the rest of the house I could hear all sorts of noise. As if the party had finally come back to life. There were people talking and doors slamming. Music downstairs. But in this room, it was calm enough. So I lay and I listened to her breathe.

She breathed like everyone breathed. What was that stuff from Shakespeare? If you prick us, do we not bleed?

No. No. I was wrong. She didn't breathe like everyone breathed. She breathed with a different rhythm. I told myself that it was because she was that witch. And that thought made me smile.

I was drifting off to sleep too. Suddenly a voice cut into my thoughts. "Are you asleep?"

Had I fallen asleep? Was I dreaming? I didn't recognise the voice.

"Hey?" It was a strange sexy voice that sort of purred. Half asleep. Of course. It was Alley's voice. I gulped. My mouth was really dry. I hadn't realised that before.

"Are you still there?"

"Yes", I almost whispered.

She shivered. "I'm cold."

And it was cold. It was mid-August but cold. All the same, at first I said nothing. What was I supposed to do? I just lay still. I remembered our words from earlier and I knew she had meant them, too. As had I. And I wanted to be strong for her. For both of us.

For a moment there was silence.

"I'm cold", she said again, almost sulkily. There was something childlike in her behaviour at times, and I liked that too.

"I don't think there are any more covers", I said at last.

Facing me across that great wide mattress I could see her red lips. The blonde hair. But the contours of her face were all shadows and lines in the flickering of the one candle that was still alight.

"I'm cold!"

Fucking hell. I looked at that face. At that moment she appeared a lot younger than me. For the first time since we had met. "What do you want me to do?" I asked her, quietly.

She shivered again. Whether for real, or to make me do something, I don't know. Either way, I slid across that great wide bed towards her and put my arm out towards her so that she could lay her head on my chest.

She smiled and moved across to me and did just that.

For me, and I'm sure for her too, it felt a magical and gentle moment.

There was also something else. A relief. Some stress gone. Because everything, so far, really, had been down to her. She had made all the running. Often quite literally. She had held my hand on a few occasions, not the other way around. She had led it all. And all the time I had felt that I was out of my depth. But now, suddenly, I realised that much of what she had done – between the two of us, I mean – had been bravado. A show. And so far she had gone out on a limb. She wasn't sure either. Not that sure. Not of me. Not of herself. And I had only now, finally, offered any real sign of feeling the same sort of things for her.

3

Some hour of the morning arrived. Alley woke first. During the night she had moved her head off my chest, but she was still lying beside me and so as she woke and moved, I woke too. And then with heads on pillows, and a small but clear gap between us, we both lay for a while and let our minds catch up with our bodies.

"Shall we get up and see if the world is still out there?" she finally asked.

We did. I hauled myself over to the big chair and almost fell into it. I was still dressed. Except for my boots. I looked at her. She was dressed too. Except for those high heels. And, somehow, at some point in the night, the fishnets had gone too and now she was searching for them. I wondered how and when she'd taken them off. She soon found them and I only half looked away as she wriggled into the black nylon, glimpsing long, slim and pale legs. I thought they were very sexy. And that thought surprised me.

Then she turned, ruffled her blonde hair and smiled at me. That soft voice again. "Where are my shoes? Have you seen them?"

They were still beside the chair. I bent forward and picked one of them up, and held it out to her. There was something about that black leather that summed this all up. The shoes were, I assumed, originals from the 1950s and they had an authenticity that mattered. And that was it. She had that too. She wasn't in any way a fake. Inside that long skirt there wasn't a woman. But inside that body? Yes, I think there was.

She took the shoe and bent for the other one. Fit. Supple. Quite beautiful.

And once more I felt surprised at myself for thinking of her like that. She was a boy, after all.

She put the other shoe on. And then she began to come back to life.

She skipped to those thin orange curtains and drew them apart, almost pulling them down as she did so. And the sun shone weakly into the room. She opened the window. Shouted. At who? Maybe at no one. Just at the day itself.

"Come on!" she said, heading for the bedroom door. I pushed my feet into my boots, and we were away again.

I don't recall all the details. We ran downstairs. We seemed to run a lot. We said – or, rather, she said – various things to various people. Some of them looked like middle-aged college teachers. Pleasant looking men in suits or jackets or casual clothes. One of them offered her a cigarette and she took it. Some of the other faces were much more bizarre. Probably from the wine bar. But I no longer recognised any of them.

And we continued at a fast pace into the kitchen.

It really was a very large but also very modern and well fitted kitchen. It took us a while to find the fridge, which was hidden in a cupboard – something neither of us had ever seen before – but we eventually managed to unearth what we needed and make coffee. And we took it out through a heavy wooden door into a huge back garden.

We didn't stop. We kept walking. She kept walking, and I followed. Down the full length of the long garden to the very end, where there was an old pale blue shed, a bench, some large plant pots and a swing.

We sat on that bench. And we drank our coffee there.

"Have you been here before?" I asked.

"No", she said. "But I always like to go as far as possible."

At that I raised an eyebrow and we both laughed.

"Isn't life strange?" she said. Those words again.

I nodded.

After finishing our coffee, we wandered around the garden for ten minutes or so. And then a dog barked. A big one, too, or so it sounded to us. It might not have been in the same garden, but it made Alley nervous, so we quickly returned to the house, just in case.

Once back there, a man called to Alley and they talked together for a few moments. I stood a few metres away, trying to take the whole thing in. The whole experience. At one point the man glanced over at me and smiled. A nice smile. A genuine smile.

"That's John F", said Alley as she came back over to me a few minutes later. "He's a Brummie like you, but he's also half Italian." It struck me then that she was slowly introducing all the 'in crowd' to me. One by one. And, to my surprise that felt sweet. Sweet? It wasn't a word I normally thought of. I wasn't used to thinking that something was 'sweet'. But she was being sweet to me.

After that we wandered around indoors for a while before sitting on a sofa that nearly swallowed us both up. Another hour or so passed in that big house on that Sunday morning with people coming and going and saying forgettable things. Some she knew. Some neither of us knew. And so we sat. Talking or listening. But never touching.

Slowly, some people seemed to disappear. And, oddly, some new faces seemed to arrive.

Lazily, we extricated ourselves from the big sofa and soon found ourselves sitting down on the old bench by the shed again. I don't think either of us knew what we were going to do next. Both only 18 years old. We didn't know what the time was or when we were going to leave. We weren't even sure where we were. Little or no money, long since out of cigarettes. No one had a joint left.

I picked up some twigs and snapped them into smaller pieces. There I was. Sitting in a garden on a cool summer afternoon with the prettiest boy in the world. A boy wearing make-up and red lipstick.

A boy I had spent the previous evening sleeping next to. But not with.

A boy I thought I had connected to. But who had said nothing about it since.

And those were the thoughts that were beginning to occupy my mind.

Suddenly, the day came to an end. In a rush. Someone I didn't recognise told Alley that there was a car going back to London. And she wanted to go. "We're going." She jumped up from the bench.

"Where?" I asked.

"Back to London," She replied. "There's even a car!"

It was all over? She was going to just leave like that? Would we meet again? How? When?

"No", she said. "No. It's fine. You're coming too." She must have seen those thoughts flash across my face.

But I didn't want to go to London. Not then. Not like that.

Anyway, I couldn't. And I guess my expression must have told her that too. She stopped smiling. Stopped for almost the first time since we had met.

"You don't have to come if you don't want to", she said.

I think, now, looking back, that she actually felt rejected and a little hurt at that moment. Except for those few quiet shared hours the night before, she had shown her public face ever since I had met her. And a big part of that public face was to keep going. Keep partying. Go where events took you. We had spent most of the last 24 hours doing just that and now, suddenly, things were moving down to London, and for her it was natural that I should come too. All that, at least, was the public face. The outer one. That shield. Quite real. But not the whole story.

"No", I said. "It's not that. Not at all. I'd love to come. I would. But I can't. I've got work tomorrow." And that was true.

By way of response she looked at me in such a way that I just felt like an idiot. What the fuck did some job matter compared to living now? Living for the moment. And with her, life was just that. It was living. Real living.

But she didn't press it. Instead, she did something that I adored her for. Something that would change our lives and bring us closer together at the very moment I had felt I was losing her.

She sat down in front of me, squatting, which wasn't easy to do in a tight skirt, and took my hands. "Look. Look at me." And I did.

She looked into my face, straight into my eyes. "Life is much more than we realise. You know that. You told me that on the train remember? Life is strange. It really is. I don't meet people on trains and invite them out. I never do that. And then find myself spending a night talking to them and trusting them. No. Never. I just don't do that. Never. That is so not me. Really." She paused.

I nodded. "I know", I said. "I can see it all too. I don't do those things either. We're the same."

"Yet", she continued. "We've done all that. Both of us. That meeting, it was more than an accident. Life has made things happen just when we needed them to. And that isn't something either of us should walk away from, is it?"

A car horn sounded.

I shook my head.

She straightened up. "I have to go."

I smiled. In truth I felt very sad and it must have showed. But I also knew that she was right. This was something we couldn't just walk away from. But for now? We seemed to have no choice. "I'll miss you", I said.

She smiled and looked straight into my eyes.

"If I ever need you, will you come?"

I nodded. "Always."

She took a step away.

"I'll always come for you." I added. "Whenever you need me. Even when you don't expect it. In the future. Whenever. I promise."

With that her face lit up. She turned. Walked away a little. Stopped. Turned back to me and gave me a sexy Monroe-esque wink. Something else she had perfected. Then she skipped quickly off along the garden, into the house. And a few moments later I heard a car pulling away from the front drive. And she was gone.

Life suddenly felt very flat and colourless.

And how the fuck were we ever going to meet? I didn't know where she lived in London. I didn't even know her real name. I had no idea if we would ever see each other again. Yet it felt as if it was meant to be. And I hung onto that feeling.

Going home, as I crossed the big city and stood around at bus stops, at first I felt pretty happy. It was summer, albeit cool. And every face seemed to smile.

I also felt light headed. It had been a strange few days. Mysterious.

A girl I thought had flirted with me on a train, hadn't flirted with me on a train. Instead, she thought I was flirting with her. And that 'girl' was a boy. Then she'd invited me out because she thought I was too shy to ask her, and she liked the look of me because I was good-looking and reading a book. And then, last night, we'd met up on what I supposed was a date, we'd gone out, mixed with the most curious of people and had a really good time. Laughing, talking. And in the end? During that party, those few close hours together, we seemed to have made some kind of connection. And then that gentle but sudden goodbye.

No wonder I felt light headed!

I knew we would meet again, too. I felt sure of that. Worried. Uncertain how it would happen. But sure of it all the same.

But what about me? Where was I in all this? What had I felt during this last day or so?

I looked into myself and I was surprised by what I saw... No. No, I wasn't surprised. I expected to be surprised, but I wasn't.

I liked Alley. Much more than that, I already felt close to her. She, he, she, whatever, had gotten through to me with ease. Where most boys saw only an arrogance and often wanted to challenge it, and where most girls saw the same thing and usually wanted to date it, Alley had conquered it already simply by being even more like me than I was! Of course her exterior blew mine away. Yet we both had that outer face – and a much gentler, more

85

sensitive inner one. And as he cut through my outer, so I cut through his. We had a lot in common, despite some very obvious differences.

I was also sure, reasonably sure, that I didn't care that Alley was a boy. Not really. It made no difference to me if someone was a boy or a girl. Male or female. If I found someone attractive, I found them attractive. And I did find her attractive. Very. And that was a good feeling, too. A wonderful feeling.

But, although I felt all that about myself, I realised that things weren't so clear cut for others. Worse. Back in my 'normal' life, I felt there was absolutely nobody I could tell about those strange few days or the fascinating girl who was actually a boy.

My parents, for instance, didn't have anything against gays... That word stuck briefly. Was Alley a gay then? I didn't know. Was I? As far as I knew most of my friends didn't have anything against gays either. But the truth, the real truth, of how people would react, that can't be known until people are confronted with it.

In any case, even if my friends and parents were fine, others, elsewhere, surely would have issues with Alley. Homophobia was rife. And with or without me in her world a time would come, if it hadn't already, that Alley would be on the receiving end. And when I thought back to those words last night, that made me feel very sad. "If only someone could give to me. I would give them the whole world back and more besides." Those were very touching words. And when she'd said them, I knew that she longed to love and be loved more than anyone could have imagined. But most people wouldn't see that. They'd just see the lipstick, the hair or the clothes and react accordingly.

Nor was the big rough edged council estate where I lived the kind of place to talk to anyone about it. I couldn't sit in my local pub and say "You should see this gorgeous boy I've just met... he's such a nice girl". I would have been glassed. At the very least.

And that, too, made me uneasy.

Made me sad.

Both.

Because I saw that, for me, in a way I was almost playing. Just an outsider. I could go back to that estate and say nothing. Give nothing away. And no one would be any the wiser. But that wasn't the case for Alley. Or for people like her. For her, for them, it was all very real. She was a boy inside those clothes, but a girl inside that body.

And as I walked along I wondered again what hard times she must have had at school or from other pupils.

I wondered, too, if anyone had ever hit her for being who she was. I wondered very many things as I made my way home. And I knew that I would never really know or be able to understand what it was like for her.

Alley had given me a brief glimpse of a world where many people could have a very hard time of things. And that made me even sadder. I wanted to hold her and hit out at all of them.

Suddenly the summer faces seemed harsh to me. Their smiles all gone.

*

A full day in the city centre. Breakfast in the hotel, then out and look around a bit more. In my 20s, after taking voluntary redundancy from the factory and before I went to university, I had spent much of my time in the cafe, situated in the City Art Gallery. It was a place to pose. An intellectual sort of pose. By then we all had books, not just me. We talked about art. We smoked cigars. We played chess. It was a very ascetic, Bohemian lifestyle for a few years.

We played chess. That's right. I'd forgotten that. An old Polish man, who had moved to the UK during or just after the war, used to bring a chessboard. I can still see him in my mind. A slight figure, round glasses, tweed suit, a little goatee beard. He could beat any of us at chess. All of us. I'm sure I gave him a few good games, yet he still won every time.

On occasions, some of us sat and sketched in the gallery too. I drew the same Polish man a few times, and from one of those sketches I painted him on a small canvas once back in my own run-down bedsit. I think I may even have sold that canvas. And I probably used the money to buy basics like food. Unemployed, students... it was fun but it wasn't at all easy in terms of money.

So I just had to visit the art gallery again.

It hadn't altered, not really. There was a sedate calm to the gallery. A timeless quality. It had always had it.

There, still, was the painting by Claude Lorraine, which most people seemed to walk past but which totally captivated me. The marble horse's head was there too, into which we often put our cigar butts so that it looked as if the horse was smoking a cheroot. The hugely impressive bronze statue of Buddha was still in a prominent position too. In the mid-1980s, with only enough money to share a cup of coffee, the statue was alleged to be worth £1,000,000 and we often wondered if we could smuggle it out of the museum. And remembering our plots, I laughed as I walked past it. It was fucking vast.

Outside the gallery, however, things were very different, it had changed quite a lot. More pedestrianisation. Which was good. And a new library, the old one demolished. To many people the old one had been an eyesore. But I used to love that grey concrete lump. It was instantly recognisable and architecturally, for its time, quite unusual. Sadly, and evidently, the planning department of the city council hadn't shared my opinion of it. I vividly remembered the hours I had spent in there reading about all kinds of things while I was clocked into, and ostensibly present at, work. Those days now seemed a very long time ago.

Other things in the city had changed too. And although, in some ways, it felt like home, I knew that it no longer was.

I then had to spend most of the afternoon and early evening working on my laptop in the hotel, altering and making other last minute changes to some detailed technical drawings and the texts that went with them. By the time it was dark I still hadn't eaten. So I grabbed a quick bite to eat downstairs in the hotel and then raced out to meet a face from the past. Someone I had long since wanted to meet again.

Tall, red-haired and willowy, Megan had been a good friend back in the 1980s. We had first met at one of Birmingham's specialist clothes shops, Eva and Lyn's, a little place in a side street which sold period clothes from the 1950s and modern designer wear made by the two women who owned the premises. They were hugely in fashion, and all the 'New Romantics' wore their clothes.

At the time Megan was a fashion student and she worked as an assistant in the shop on odd days. Part-time. I wanted good quality shirts, linen and white or cream, and I couldn't find anything like that in the ordinary stores. So Megan and I came to an arrangement. She would set aside shirts like that, and every now and then I would call in, try them on, and buy one or two.

A little later on when I was very much into period suits, she helped me complete the image. Once she set aside an Italian suit for me, which was about the most stylish thing I had ever seen for a man to wear, but it was just a little too small for me.

Later still, maybe around 1985, after a few abortive attempts, she finally had her own stall in Birmingham's famous Rag Market, one of the country's most important centres for avant garde or period clothes outside of London. She was doing very well, but something happened that left her with a huge cash shortfall. Having received my first student grant and, by then, being accustomed to getting by with next to nothing, I loaned her the money she needed to keep going. Some months later she took me out to dinner – at the time, the most expensive dinner I had ever eaten – and from then on we had been very good friends. Though never more than that.

Somehow, we had lost touch during the 1990s and beyond. And it was only recently, via Facebook, that we had come into contact again. And meeting her, after all these years, was a big part of the reason why I had finally been persuaded by my daughter to revisit my home city. Megan had given me the name of the place, in the city centre, where we were to meet, with rough directions as to where it was. I got there a little earlier than our planned time, and rather than wait outside, I went in and ordered a coffee.

When I had lived in Birmingham, like so many other buildings in this part of the city centre, the place had been a bank, or head office for an insurance company. Something like that. A grand building with columns and a long, wide, marble staircase. Now? As with the others, it was an American style bar. And while the facades of each building remained mostly intact, the downstairs of each had been opened up with big new plate glass windows.

I didn't like the style. But it was the way things were moving.

Studying the plasterwork high up on the ceiling, I had only been sitting at the bar for a few minutes when a pale hand tapped me on the shoulder and I turned to find Megan standing there. Same red hair. Same huge smile. I stood. We hugged. We said hello. A little unsure. And then we hugged again.

"You're drinking coffee?" she asked, a little disappointedly.

"No", I said, pushing it to one side. "No. And it isn't very good anyway. Let's have something better!" I ordered a bottle of French red wine. And we sat at a table in one of the big windows, mainly in order to be furthest away from the vast TV screens that now seemed to flicker in every bar and bistro in the UK.

"My god", she said, mouth open. "You look good. You've not changed."

I said, "Thank you", with a laugh, then pretended to smooth out some of the wrinkles around my eyes.

"Oh no", said Megan, "no, really. You do. You look good compared to most of us".

"Don't you have a mirror in your house?" I replied. "You don't look a day older."

And so it went on for a while. We talked about names and faces and even some places that we remembered, and those that we still knew, as we caught up on the old days and current times.

"So, what are you doing now?", I finally asked her. "Still designing?"

She nodded. "Yes, I am. But I live out in Solihull now... Don't laugh!" Solihull was a bit of a joke to those of us who were born and raised in Birmingham. A place for the wannabe rich, with the really wealthy mostly having moved out some time ago. "I have a shop too. Not far from Earlswood. But I only rent the space. I mainly sell direct from home..."

"The internet?"

"Yes. You too?"

"Yeah. Though not designing clothes, of course!"

And so we talked for a while about where we were with our lives, and how we had got there. We talked about some of the differences between the UK and other countries, both good and bad, and after a while I went back to the bar and bought us a second bottle of wine.

As I returned from the bar, I realised that the whole place, the whole 'experience', had a Hollywood theme. I never paid very much attention to modern decor and, anyway, talking to Megan had completely held my attention. But as I sat back down, I also noticed that one of the big screens – the only screen we could see from where we sat – was showing short clips of famous film stars from back in the day. A few minutes of Gerry Lee Lewis doing some sort of gag. Then a clip of Frank Sinatra on holiday in what looked like the Cote d'Azur.

For a moment, we both sat and watched the screen. After a short clip of Elvis Presley looking incredibly young and handsome, there was one of Marilyn Monroe. She was walking down the steps of an aeroplane, waving to the crowd.

"You know something", said Megan as I poured each of us another glass of wine. "I had a strange idea about you once."

I looked up at her and put the bottle down on the table. "Oh, what was that?"

"Well", she began, picking up her glass but not taking a drink. "Back when I was working in the shop, you know, before I got my own stall in the Rag Market, all the gossip came through there. And one afternoon, I was sitting have a cup of coffee with Eva and she told me a little story..."

I laughed. "Yeah. I remember what it was like in there. If you wanted to know what was happening or who was dating who, that was the place to go."

Megan smiled, a small and slightly mischievous smile.

"Well, anyway", she continued. "Eva told me that she had seen 'that boy you keep those shirts for' walking around the Rag Market, one afternoon, hand in hand with a certain very stunning blonde."

Immediately I felt myself going a little red.

Megan put her glass down, and looked straight at me. "You kept it very quiet."

My mouth opened. But no words came out.

"It's fine", she laughed. "I didn't know. I didn't. Not for certain. But I can tell by your reaction. I know now. Wow. You had a thing with Alley, didn't you?"

I had never told anyone. Even Lisa, my ex, had only found out by accident. And I had always assumed that no one else knew. No one. And now I didn't know what to say.

"I didn't know what to think at first, when she told me", said Megan. She reached into her bag and brought out a packet of cigarettes. Sighed. Looked up at the high ceiling and threw the packet back into her bag. Smoking was for outdoors only. "I didn't really believe her. But Eva was quite certain it was you. Oh, I never told anyone. Not that it mattered. But I knew you when you were going out with that model, later on, and when you were seeing that Italian girl, the painter. Remember? You were such a ladies' man. The girls all fancied you and so I thought no, she must have been wrong. Oh, but yes, I'd always wondered."

I still didn't know what to say. But I could tell from the inside that I was red enough to have given it away totally. So I just nodded and raised my eyebrows by way of acknowledgement. I had known Megan for years, but hadn't the faintest idea she had suspected that Alley and I had been lovers.

I picked up my glass and took a sip of wine. What struck me, then, really struck me, as it had so often throughout my life, was how strange things were. How almost pre-arranged life could sometimes be. I had come here to meet an old friend and look around at my past. But was that all? No. No it wasn't. Why was I back here visiting my home town? I hadn't planned to tell anyone about Alley and yet, equally, I somehow half expected to do so on this trip, needed to do so, and now the opportunity had just presented itself. It was all so strange. Set up. As if each part was meant to be.

"I'm sorry", Megan cut into my thoughts. "I shouldn't have said. I shouldn't have said anything."

I shook my head.

"No. No. It's fine." I glanced out of the big plate glass window. Up towards the dark sky overhead. I shrugged and turned back to her. "Yeah, it's true. It is. We did go out for a while, Alley and me. And I've never told anyone..."

"No, you don't have to explain", said Megan, cutting in straight away. "I mean, it's OK. I just wondered. You know me, I had to know."

I shook my head again. "No. I want to. I want to tell you". I hesitated and took a sip of my wine. "I wish I'd been able to tell someone at the time. All those years ago. I needed to."

Megan wrinkled her nose. "You've never told anyone? Not even back then?"

"No. Like I said. Who could I tell back then?"

Megan shook her head sadly. "Oh, you poor thing. Why didn't you tell me? You could have told me."

I knew immediately that was true. It had been a long time since we'd last met, but I had always been able to trust Megan. I knew that. And to have been able to tell someone, someone who even knew Alley, albeit distantly. If only I had done that back then... No. I stopped my thoughts. No, this wasn't a time for regrets. I could do it now. Tell her now. The past could be changed. Alley and I had once read that in a book together.

I finished my drink and poured another, then pushed it aside. I didn't feel the need for that now.

"Back then", I began. "Well, it was like you said. I went out with the best-looking girls. A six foot two blonde Irish model. I'm not boasting. That's just how it was. In a way, I imagine, it must be like that if you're famous. If I went into a bar, often a girl would come over and chat *me* up. Not the other way around."

Megan wasn't at all fazed by my confession. "Oh, I know. I knew all that. I saw it myself when we went out together a few times."

"And then, suddenly, there was Alley. And I couldn't tell anyone about her. Not then. Not really. I hated that. I mean, on the one hand, as for boys, she was just a complete one-off. I'm not sure that I ever looked at a male, before or since."

I paused, hesitant, unsure what I was trying to say.

Megan came to my rescue. "It was so much different then though, wasn't it? In the 1970s, a gay man was John Inman or Larry Grayson. I loved them but it was all camp. And, really, when you look back, it was the early 1980s that helped change that..."

"I'm not gay", I interrupted her. "I'm not. For me a person is attractive, or they're not. And mostly they're not. Sex, gender I should say, just doesn't come into it."

She shook her head. "No, no. I know that. I just meant that those times, the early 80s, and then with AIDS and everything, it all changed from what we'd grown up with. Gay became accepted. Mostly. Much more so than before, anyway. And much less of a caricature of itself. But it was people like Alley, really, who helped shape that better way of thinking."

I nodded.

"Yeah. That is true. I know it is. And that's what I've always thought, too." I hesitated. "Alley and some of the others, they helped change people's outlook. But they were in London. That's always been a very different world. On my estate, I'm not sure I'd want to grow up gay even today. Not there. It's a hard place. And back then, before attitudes had changed? Well... that's part of the reason I couldn't tell anyone."

For a moment we sat in silence. I looked up at the screen and watched Humphrey Bogart in Casablanca, with Claude Rains. Then I turned back to Megan.

"Maybe I should have just toughed it out, like Bogey would have done."

She laughed. "Well I could definitely have got you the rain coat."

I hadn't said a great deal. All around me people were still drinking or talking, some, as ever, tapping at their phones. The world hadn't changed. But inside, I knew, after all those years, I finally had some release.

"So you've really never told anyone?" Megan asked at last.

I screwed up my nose. "Not really. But Lisa..."

"Your wife?"

"No, we never married. And in any case, she's my ex now. We separated a few years back."

"Oh yeah", Megan nodded. "Of course. Sorry. I saw that on Facebook."

"Well, anyway Lisa". I stopped myself and laughed, I'm not sure why. Maybe because the whole thing seemed daft, or maybe it was a sort of release of nervous tension. "Well, she did find out. In fact we had a huge row over Alley, and that's one of the things that split us up. Lisa and I had known each other at school. Dated. Got nowhere. Then we met up again at the end of the 80s. She, really, was the woman of my life. I still adore her even now".

I paused and took a drink. There was a small particle of cork in my glass. I tutted and took it out, but drank the wine anyway. "I suppose, no, I mean I know... Lisa and Alley were the loves of my life. They were both very different, obviously, but those were the two people I... Well. I don't know. But it makes me feel fucking sad to think I'll never have that again with anyone else."

Megan shook her head, just a little, "Oh, you never know. Life is strange."

I laughed. That phrase again. "Life is strange. How often have I heard that. But yes, I suppose that's true. I do miss them. I really do. But I should just be grateful to have known them both."

After that we carried on talking for a while longer, and Megan told me about her current partner. A Scottish man who, like her, had very strong pro-independence views.

Then we left.

And, walking arm in arm, we strolled through the city centre for a while, chatting and peering in shop windows. Then it was time to say goodbye. Her partner was picking her up and I waited with her until her lift arrived. As the car pulled up, we hugged. She turned and opened the car door.

"Hey", she said, just before getting into the car. "Thank you. I'd often wondered. Thank you for telling me about it."

I smiled.

Megan smiled too. "And let's not leave it so long next time!"

As I walked back to the hotel, it struck me once again how strange life could be. That Megan had known all that time. And that the flickering image of Marilyn Monroe descending the steps of an unknown flight had, just by chance, flashed before our eyes and so triggered the whole discussion. Just by chance? No. The older I got, the more I doubted that. There was much more to the world than we realised.

As I reached the door of the hotel it also struck me that, in many respects, I was still asking some of the same questions about myself, and even about Alley, that had been asked and answered so many years earlier. And, in some ways, I still didn't know the answers.

We get older. We don't necessarily get wiser.

The following morning I checked out of the hotel, already booked for the next couple of nights into a different hotel in one of Birmingham's suburbs – a place that would be, for me, rather special.

I walked across the city centre, heading for the bus route that I knew so well. The service that would take me back to the housing estate where I had grown up, in the east of the city. How many times had I caught that bus as a child, a boy and even a young man? It would be strange to travel on it again. A little sad. But I was also looking forward to it.

As I crossed the city I realised just how many of the old sights and places had now gone.

I used to love the Gaumont cinema, as a child, but I think that had already been replaced when I was living in Birmingham. But the pub a few doors away that we used, all those years ago, where had that gone? It was still there, in a way. Although now it was boarded up, painted a grubby black and looking pretty sorry for itself. Such a shame. It had always been a busy place. Lots of brass, dark polished woodwork and bright lights. All gone now.

As I walked along, I realised that even the layout of some of the roads had changed, often quite substantially. Gone were the underpasses too, or subways as we used to call them. That, really, I supposed, was for the best. They had been dark and sometimes dangerous. A mugger's haven. Though, for me? I missed them. They were part of my city's signature.

Gone, too, were the big department stores. Some of them, anyway. The one where I used to visit Father Christmas as a youngster. I wondered whether that had gone recently or if it had been lost years ago. I didn't have the answer.

That was part of the problem. There was so much change that it was hard now to remember which things had gone and when. In fact there was too much change. That was my overwhelming impression. Was I feeling that because I was getting old? Or was I right, that it would be better to let a city change more gradually?

Change everything you are. And everything you were. Lyrics from somewhere came into my head. They seemed appropriate.

Finally, from outside the Law Courts, I caught my bus. The bus that would take me back to the estate where I once lived. But first, it would go past my old factory at Drews Lane. 'British Leyland' as it had been at that time.

Strangely, the first real changes that Alley made to my life were at the factory. I remembered that and it made me smile.

Up until the weekend of that party I had gone to work, even though I hated it. I planned to stick around and finish my engineering apprenticeship and then leave and go to college and maybe university. But I had gone to work all the same, more or less dutifully.

That attitude began to change immediately after I'd met Alley.

Maybe because of the sheer size of the factory I worked in, it was pretty easy to be there and not be there at the same time. I mean, someone could clock you in on one of those ghastly clock punch machines, and you could still be at home in bed. Sure, it could go wrong if one or the other of you weren't careful. But there were ways around it. And if you had a good friend, someone you could rely on, maybe take turns, you could be there without actually being there.

And so, from then on, that was what I began to do. I'd get up on time. Leave the house as if going to work and then stay on the bus – this very route, the one I was on now – straight past the factory gate and into the city centre. Once there, sometimes I'd spend a few hours in the art gallery. And a few more hours in the central library. I studied art and, for some obscure reason, I even studied Swedish. Then I'd sit in the cafe in the art gallery. On other days I'd catch a local train and go to places like Sutton Park or Earlswood Lakes, where I'd spend hours and hours walking or sitting, my head more or less empty. Just waiting for the clock to slowly move around so that I could go back home – pretending that I had been at work the whole day.

My god, that factory. The things that happened there. The stories I could tell. The work force usually got the blame. But it was run so badly, from the top downwards.

Again I smiled to myself as I remembered the coal man. For several years after the whole place had switched to oil fired heating, his job remained unchanged. Every month he'd order the

104

coal. Every month the coal would arrive. Then he'd then bag it all up in individual sacks and sell it – very cheaply, to be fair to him – to the other men who worked in the factory. Nobody further up the management structure ever thought to query his role, or the fact that Leyland was still paying for a few tons of coal every month.

Strikes. That was the word associated with the place. 'Always on strike.' But that was another media myth. Nine times out of ten, when the workforce was idle, it was due to a strike elsewhere leading to a stop in production. There were never sufficient materials in store to keep working for more than a day or so if one of the suppliers went down.

What a place. I'd had some good friends back there at British Leyland, though. It hadn't all been dull or shambolic. We'd had some good times too. And, as the bus finally approached my old factory, the one person who did spring to mind was Andy. Andy the skinhead.

Andy had grown up on an estate rougher than my own. And he had survived by becoming a skinhead. Not just any skinhead, but one of the toughest of the bunch. He'd had skinhead magazines. He had a few tattoos relevant to skinheads. He drank protein drinks several times a day, stopping work once an hour to pump some weights. All that and much more. Yet one morning – I never forgot it – he came into work and the first thing he said was, "Fuck me, did you see Top of the Pops last night? That band. Was that a man or a woman?"

I hadn't seen it, so I didn't know what he was talking about. But I picked up the name from the replies some others made and overheard their comments too. Which weren't nice. Things like 'Fucking queer', 'Should be locked up', and so on.

And then I heard Andy's distinctive voice. "Fuck off", he said, quite loudly, and almost challengingly. "If he's a lad and he wants to dress up like that, then so fucking what?"

I had laughed and the others had shut up. Looking back on it now, I should have said something. I should have said 'Well put, Andy' or something. Yet I didn't. And I regretted that.

Finally, the bus reached the point where my factory had been. A place where thousands of men and women had worked and very many more had earned their living by servicing the industry. I knew it had all changed. I knew that those days were long-gone. All the same, as the bus pulled up at the stop I jumped off, expecting to see the original huge red brick factory, or a large modern replacement.

But there was nothing. Just rubble. Acres of it.

When I first met Alley, I'd been so desperate to get away from this place that if I'd turned up for work one day and found it demolished, I'd have been delighted. But now? It was just another lost connection with my past, my youth and even with her.

4

August 1981 was dragging. I wanted to see Alley again. To break away for a day, or even an hour, from the suffocating world of work and ordinary lives, and see her. She was taking me over. And I felt it throughout my entire being. Was glad of it.

But I had no idea how to find her. So the very next weekend, full of anticipation, and carried along by the things we had done, I went to the Hostaria wine bar again with the vague hope that she would be there. Friday night, and then the same on Saturday night. Of course Alley wasn't there on either occasion, and while the wine bar itself was busy, those shadowy alcoves were virtually empty.

What else had I expected? Alley and some of the others were from London, or at least they lived there now. And they probably only rarely came up to the Second City. But on the other hand, what else could I do? Even so, as I left each night, I felt miserable and all I could think was, "Will I ever see her again?"

As a result of those disappointments, the next week at work was quite different. Harder. Painful. It was like dying a slow death. I wondered if I should just go down to London. But she might as well have been on the moon. It wasn't the 100 miles distance; we would be just two faces in a sea of millions. I didn't know the place at all. Did she live near Hampstead or in Bromley? Did people still hang around in Carnaby Street? I knew that had been very big back in the 1960s. I had no idea. She could have been anywhere.

Most evenings I just sat in my bedroom, playing music. It felt so hopeless. "Where are you? Where the fucking hell are you?" I asked out loud. I heard no reply. On another night, I went for a long walk and shouted the same thing to the stars. Still no reply.

Eventually the next weekend came around. Friday. I was so worn out by then, so stretched, nerves shattered or shattering. But it was the same story. Friday night at the Hostaria and no one was there. Not really. Certainly no half-crazy blonde with a huge smile and dark mascaraed eyes. Utterly desolate, I propped up the bar for a few hours. Would I ever see her again? I put down my unfinished bottle of wine and left.

Saturday. My fourth lonely visit. Two weeks gone now. It was nearly September. And still virtually no one was in the alcoves. I sat at the bar with my head in my hands. One of the door staff came over to me and asked me if I was OK. I said that I was, but he could see that I wasn't. He even offered me a joint, which I gladly took. I decided I would smoke it and then leave.

And then someone said "Hello".

It was the Italian Brummie, John F. He had a girl with him who was very pretty but he had left her sitting alone at a table near the bar while he talked to me.

"You were at that party a few weeks ago, weren't you?" he asked.

"Yeah", I said. "In Handsworth." Trying to smile but feeling desolate.

We talked. Just a few words. This and that. And then he said he had to take his girlfriend some more wine.

There are moments in life that are given to us.

Moments where we can make a choice.

There is much more to the world than we realise, and those moments should be treated with special care when they do arrive.

They are often crossroads or junctions. A clear choice between action and inaction. They can be many or few. Sometimes mundane. Sometimes – and often and we don't see it – one of them will be very precious. A chance to change a whole life. Or two lives. A chance to create another heaven or another hell.

We simply have to make the right decision. To act. Or not to act. We might change a whole story.

I had reached just such a moment. And I had a decision to make. One that would have lived with me forever. I was going to put my glass down and leave. Give up. Walk away.

But I didn't do that. There was no crossroads.

Not this time.

Instead, John F came back to the bar before I'd had the chance to move.

Life is strange.

With his suit jacket in his hand, he came over to me, fumbling in the inside pocket of the jacket, "I've got something for you", he said, slowly unfolding a crumpled piece of paper. "I had a phone call. From that dizzy blonde. I seem to be some kind of central telephone exchange for the whole of Birmingham. Either nobody else has a phone or they never answer it. I'm not sure which."

He passed me the note. And I'm sure I was visibly shaking as I took it.

"She asked me to find you."

I looked at him. Open mouthed.

"I know. In a city of three million. But, well, here you are. I found you."

I laughed. More from nerves than anything else.

"Apparently there's been some kind of trouble", he added. "Some sort of upset. And she wants you to go down this weekend and see her." It was already Saturday night when he told me this and I must have gone pale, because John F looked concerned. "I'm sorry", he said. "She phoned me on Thursday. Twice. I did look for you yesterday, but you weren't here."

He must have come in after I'd left. I cursed myself for not being more patient.

But I no longer cared about being back for work on Monday. I had made that mistake before, two weeks earlier. I unfolded the note. Couldn't really read it. Didn't care. I would go.

"That's their address", he said.

London.

London.

In one small, provincial way I hated the idea of going, because I felt uncomfortable in the capital. I always had. But fuck that. Fuck it. Who cared? If the address had been in Scotland or on Mars I would have gone. I knew I wanted to see Alley. Desperately. And now it seemed that she wanted to see me too. And that was all that mattered.

I thanked John F. He had saved my life. I smoked a little more of the joint which had been lying, dying, in an ashtray, and passed him the rest. Then I almost ran out of the building to New Street Station. I would catch the first train I could. But by the time I reached the station it was already too late to travel that evening. There were works on the railway lines or something, and there were no more trains until the next day. So I went home and slept well instead. Very well, for the first time in a week or more.

Sunday. The last Sunday of August. Nervous, excited, happy. I couldn't eat anything. I caught a bus to the city centre, then a train to London. I just did it. Just went for it. I told my parents that I would be spending a few days at a friend's flat in Moseley, another suburb of Birmingham. The truth was that I would be clocked in at work by a friend and I could be away – and paid for it – for a few days. It was freedom of a sort. And a very real freedom. I was only 18. It felt wonderful.

It took me a few hours to get to the capital and even longer to find the address. Much longer than it should have done, because John F had written it down so hastily that most people couldn't decipher it. Eventually a very old man with an equally ancient white bulldog studied the scrawl and could tell me where it was.

Where it was, actually turned out to be only a few minutes' walk from where I had arrived on the Underground. At the end of a terrace was a large rambling townhouse that must have been pretty grand once. Now it looked rather broken-down and like it needed some love and care to bring it back to life. It reminded me a lot of a Glasgow tenement. The kind where my mother had been born. Only this building was London brick coloured rather than Glasgow soot black.

But what to do now? John F had said 'their address'. I was sure Alley wasn't seeing anyone else. I remembered her words that night in Handsworth. Held onto them. All the same, I would have hated to open the door and walk in to find her with someone else. So did I go in? Yes. She would have done. Regardless. And in any case hadn't she twice phoned John F – twice! – and asked him to find me? Yes. She had. And if there was something wrong, as John F seemed to think, then of course I had to go in. What the fuck was I waiting for?

All the same, as I walked up to the door and stood outside it, I just couldn't knock. I couldn't do anything. I was too nervous. Too excited. And I stood for a few minutes, wondering what to do. In fact, at the last moment, I was so wound up inside that even then I might have walked away, if a girl who I later discovered to be called Sarah – and who also came from Birmingham – hadn't come up to the big front door right at that very moment.

"Are you coming in?"

"Yeah, sure, I'm erm, looking for..."

"John? Alley? Viv?" she said, holding the door wide open for me.

"Yes." I was so relieved. Three names. Not just two. "Alley."

Inside that door the smell of damp was strong and not unexpected, but the smell of paint did surprise me. Clearly someone was trying to make the place a bit nicer. There were other smells too. Alcohol, and someone was cooking, and joss sticks and dope. The building itself was dilapidated and looked as if it could fall down. A faded glory or, worse, a shabby hand-me-down, broken and only defying gravity out of habit. Part of me winced, but another part immediately wanted to embrace it all, too. This was a building that screamed 'Growing up, moving out, moving on'.

And I wanted to do all of those things. Now more than ever.

"They should all be up there", said Sarah, waving at a broken-down staircase and then heading for a downstairs room. "They're always in and out of each other's rooms."

The walk up those narrow stairs seemed long and heavy. It was nerves, of course. And I wished I could stop feeling like that. But I couldn't. I knew by then just how much I liked Alley, and how much I wanted to see her again. So it was natural that I felt the way I did.

I reached a landing and a young boy with dark hair and wearing lots of heavy make-up peered out from a half-open door. "Hiya", I said.

The boy looked at me, but didn't say anything.

"Alley?", I asked him.

The boy smiled slowly.

"That little bitch?", he said, albeit with some genuine affection. "Find a room that smells of cheap perfume and you'll have found her." He said the words 'cheap perfume' quite loudly. They echoed.

"I heard that. It's not cheap, you're just jealous!" replied that strange voice, the one I already knew so well. "Actually it's the most expensive one they have."

And there, suddenly, framed by a doorway that, along with the rest of the building, looked terribly unsafe, was the gorgeous blonde hair, pout and smile, vibrancy, energy and sexiness that was Alley.

She stopped glaring at the other boy and turned to me with a broad smile. "Aww! What took you?"

It was evening, Alley wanted us to go out, and I loved the idea. The prospect of going out somewhere, anywhere, with Alley fully dressed and made-up filled me with delight. I so wanted, even needed, to see how others reacted to her. Not people she already knew, in venues with familiar faces, but strangers. I suppose that in a vicarious way – albeit for different reasons – I wanted to carry out the very same experiments that she, herself, must have carried out a few years beforehand. What would people say? Could they tell that she was a boy? Would most people be hostile, friendly or indifferent? There were all sorts of questions, and where she had once needed to discover the answers, I now needed to know too.

But first we, or rather she, had to get ready.

"It sounds so different from how it was for me", she said, holding a small bottle of nail varnish up and examining it closely, but not yet applying it. "What was it like?"

I was telling her about my own childhood.

I had four large older brothers. And one of them had more or less punched his way through the huge white-majority estate on which we lived. I wasn't boasting about it. It was just my reply to her telling me a little about her own background. She had been an only child and her father had died when she had been very young, so she had been brought up by her mother. Very much so.

"I remember watching my brother, and his best friend, the two of them", I said. "They stood in the middle of a patch of wasteland, back to back, and took on everyone that came. They knocked everyone down. Bare fisted. I was in awe."

"So no one ever dared touch you, then?"

I shook my head. "God, no. No one."

"I'm jealous." She sighed a little and then started applying the nail varnish. "I hated school. They try to fit you in and if you don't fit in... I left as soon as I could." She put varnish on a few nails. Then continued. "I was called everything. Puff, ponce, queer. Everything. I was picked on all the time because I was so much prettier than the rest." She stopped and looked up at me. "I looked like a girl. And then when I bleached my hair, it just went crazy."

"Yeah, I suppose... I suppose it must have done." I said. It was impossible for me to really understand. I felt quite angry, and had a strange hopeless sense of wanting to somehow equal things up. I should have been there for her. An older brother.

"I'd hit someone though, if I had to", she added quickly. "I'm not scared. Not of anything. I got over that years ago. I had to."

I believed her. She had a determination which could probably find release as aggression at times. I hadn't seen any of it myself, but I could tell it was in there. And so I could easily imagine her throwing a bottle at someone's head or going for them with a frying pan. And the thought made me smile. On top of everything else she *was* also a little bit crazy. And I liked that too.

"What was it like?" I asked her finally.

She was applying an extra thick layer of black mascara to her eyelashes as I asked. Curling and darkening them at the same time. Making herself look ever more stunning – as if that were possible.

"What was what like?" she replied, without stopping.

"You", I said. "Watching you, looking at you, the way you move, dress. When did you first do all that? I mean, outside? I guess lots of boys experiment, but they don't go out..."

She carried on applying the mascara and didn't answer me.

"I'm sorry", I said. "I shouldn't have asked."

She put the mascara down and turned around to look at me. Sort of blinking her eyes as she did so, to stop her eyelids sticking together. "Actually it was fun." I didn't expect any more of an answer. But to my surprise she elaborated on her words a little. "It was difficult. But it was fun too. I'm sure I must have felt uncertain, scared even, but I needed to do it. I wanted to show the world my real self. That's very important to me."

I didn't interrupt her, just listened.

"I knew I looked dazzling. Look at me." She pointed at her face with a small flourish of the hand. "And I'd practiced. Lots of times. I was gorgeous without make-up. And with it I knew I looked just fabulous. I so did. And if I hadn't done, if I hadn't looked so good, I wouldn't have gone out." All of that was said quickly. Then she turned back to her mirror and started applying a little more make-up to her eyelids.

I loved listening to her. That voice was beguiling. But I also found myself half-studying her when she spoke. The way she snapped out the words. It was often quick. And often accompanied by a flick of the hair or a lightning fast smile. Sometimes she would giggle to herself, just a little, after saying something quite funny, or even harsh. There was a very capable boy sitting in front of me. But also a rather shy girl.

I wanted to hear more about her life. To know it all. But it felt wrong to ask or push it at that moment, so I let it go at that.

"Shall I make us a coffee before we go out?" I said.

She nodded. "Mmm. There's a room on the landing which we all share. It's got a kettle and all that stuff."

While I waited for the kettle to boil, I tried to imagine what it must have really been like. Of course I couldn't know. But I was sure she was both very crazy and very brave. Dressing like that and going out. This was 1981. She told me that she had been dressing like that since about 1979. She was still a young boy at the time. Even now she was only 18. And although things were changing, this was still not an age where men and boys could easily wear women's clothes. From what I had seen in the Hostaria wine bar, it was moving that way – but mostly it was still not done. Nowhere close to being done.

The kettle boiled and I made some horrible coffee. The last of the milk in the shared kitchen was so old it could have stood up without a bottle, so it would have to be black. I picked up the two mugs to take them to her room, but as I did so, she came into the 'kitchen'.

I could have used countless flattering adjectives to describe her at that moment. But instead I said nothing. She knew that I thought them, though. She knew it and gave me one of her dazzling smiles. Sharp. Shy. Sexy. Crazy. Brave. Gentle. All of them.

"I'm ready", she said quietly, "let's sit here and drink them".

So for a while we just sat. And we talked a bit more. At first we talked about friends. Some people she had known. Someone I had known. I laughed at her stories. And she laughed at mine. I told her a story about something that I'd heard in the factory only last week and she was surprised that it was so easy to make so much money. But then, somehow, that led us to talk about feelings too. And we stopped laughing.

"Actually, people tell me I can be cruel", she said, looking straight at me to judge my response.

"I can imagine that", I replied with a slight laugh. I paused. More serious. "Sometimes you must feel almost totally alone."

Those narrow dark eyes fixed me again. "Often. Quite often."

"Well, I don't think you're cruel", I said.

She didn't reply straight away, just drank a small mouthful of her coffee. She opened a packet of cigarettes and took one out, but then put it back in again. "Why do you say that?" she finally asked.

"You're not cruel", I said again.

"Not with you."

I shook my head. I took a cigarette out of the packet, lit it and passed it to her. She took it from me and had a drag on it. I flicked the lighter on and off a few times.

"Why do you think I'm not"? she asked in a soft tone.

I thought of some of the faces I knew. From my estate in Birmingham. Of some of the things they did. They weren't friends of mine. "There are cruel people", I said at last. "But you're not one of them. Really. You're not."

She drew on the cigarette again and then slowly let out a long cloud of blue smoke. She smiled, but didn't say anything.

Suddenly, outside, there was the sound of a siren.

"What colour are my eyes?", she asked, shutting them both.

"Mascara black", I said with a laugh. "Not really. They're green pools with big brown ripples."

She opened them again. Her narrow almond eyes.

"And I haven't seen any cruelty in them", I added. "I think you're fun. And also very caring and gentle." I took another cigarette out of the packet and lit it.

A part of me had to stop myself. This was a boy I was talking to. What the fuck was I doing telling him that his eyes were green pools?

I had a few draws on my cigarette, and we sat for another minute or so in silence, listening to the siren fade away. It took forever. "You're very quick, too", I said at last, "and maybe sometimes that can be hurtful. You see a put down and you say it. Maybe that's what people mean".

She flicked cigarette ash into an overfull ashtray. "No. I think they just don't like me."

"Fuck them then", I said. "They're not worth worrying about. Keep looking gorgeous on the outside and, when it's time, open up and let someone into the other you. Inside is even more beautiful."

She raised her eyebrows at that. "I like that about you", she said. And she stubbed out her half-smoked cigarette. "That's something I like about you. Very much."

"What?"

"You almost tell me off!" she laughed.

I laughed too. "I just don't like you listening to others who don't know the first thing about you. Maybe they're jealous. Shallow. I don't know. It's too easy to judge. But if they say that about you, it's because they don't really know you."

I didn't know why, but inside me a voice told me that I was out of order, and I half-expected her to say something sharp or nasty to me, too. Instead, her hand reached across the table for mine, found it and held it. And for a few moments we sat there like that. A little like we were having a séance. Or maybe like an old couple who had known each other for 40 years. Or a million years. Odd. But I liked it anyway.

"Sometimes", she said, finally letting go of my hand, "I do hear myself doing it and tell myself off. By then it's too late. The quicker I speak, the more nervous I am. And the more nervous I am, the more I say something which others think is horrid".

I nodded. "So it's mostly nerves then. And defence sometimes. Let it go. Stop thinking about what others say. You're not cruel. Don't think that. Don't ever think that. You just have a very quick mind and that isn't a bad thing". I paused. "Maybe sometimes you just think too fast for your mouth!"

She smiled at that. "When we have a row here, and sometimes we do, I can be quite nasty, I think."

I shrugged. "When people argue, eight times out of ten everyone involved is as bad as each other", I said. "In any case, saying a few nasty things in an argument? Who doesn't do that at times?"

She licked her lips. Quickly. Almost imperceptibly. And flicked her hair off her face with her right hand; something I'd noticed she did often. "Shall we go out?" she asked suddenly.

"Yes."

"Where shall we go?" I asked.

She took my hand again, and just said "Come on".

And off we went.

A short while later we were out in the streets of the capital. Alley was dressed in a leopard print fur coat, black fishnets and black high heels. Her blonde hair was unmissable, even in the dark of the night. She lit the area up. And stood out a mile.

London streets appeared to fall into two types. Some were empty, and more or less dark, while others had crowds and bright lights, perhaps a few shops or pubs. But more than that I didn't really notice. I was far too fascinated watching the looks on the faces of people as we walked – almost strode – along, Alley holding my hand, head tossing from time to time. Heels clicking on the pavements. This really was her town.

Her town. Yes. But clearly some of the people she shared it with were not her friends. At one junction, waiting for the traffic lights to change, someone whistled at her and, when she half turned to look, they stuck two fingers up at her. Who they were, I had no idea.

To be fair, it was a big city and most people, as in any big city, didn't look twice at us. Not while we just walked along, hand in hand like any other couple going out for a night. But whenever we stopped or came face to face with someone, there was often a reaction of some kind. Sometimes a longer look than normal, or maybe a second glance. Sometimes a definite stare. Those made me smile. Especially when that extended look caused the viewer to stumble or even walk into a lamppost – as happened to one woman.

Alley appeared more or less oblivious to all of it. I guessed she was used to it by now.

At another crossing there was a group of young lads. They were talking as we walked up, but fell into a kind of silence as we stood next to them. I was sure that they were staring straight at Alley and trying to work out if she was really a gorgeous girl or something else. And as we finally crossed that road, I'm pretty sure that they still didn't know the answer.

Suddenly, I realised that I had got it wrong about Alley. She *was* noticing it. Most of it. More than that, she was deliberately aiming us at the busiest streets in the area now to maximise the responses she would get and I would see.

One man looked at her twice. And the woman he was with took offence at that and dug him sharply in the ribs. They were still arguing as they walked off. That made both of us laugh.

She had been right. It *was* fun. But there was something else too, for me, something that gradually nagged at me and I didn't like it. I realised, slowly, just how much she must be flirted with, chatted up, approached and god knows what else when she was on her own. I was jealous of that. And I let go of her hand at one point, feeling a bit sullen and yet also knowing how stupid that was of me. She didn't notice. And, fortunately, it happened just as we got to the pub, the change of pace and scene taking my mind away from those unfair thoughts.

The pub itself was rather plain. An ordinary corner pub in London. Not one specifically for gays or men with make-up or vertical hair. Just a pub. And I was surprised that she took us in there with such confidence.

"Actually I do come here quite often", she said in response to my query, as we sat in a small alcove with red-velour seating. "Well, not often. But sometimes. A few of us come here, because it's local and quiet. It gets us out of the house too, I suppose."

Inside was bright. Too bright. There were only a few middle-aged men smoking at the bar. And not much else to see. I was surprised that she came to somewhere so bare and almost run-down.

"Even I can't go to a club every night", she said with a small shrug.

We sat in that pub for an hour or so. A few of her friends came in. She spoke to them for a while. They left. It was all quite normal, really. Almost – almost, but definitely not – disappointing. Quiet too. And we just sat, talked, drank and smoked. Then half a dozen more middle-aged men came in. And they started talking louder and put the jukebox on.

"Do you want to go somewhere else?" she asked me.

I didn't care. So long as I was with her. Here. Another pub or club. At hers. I didn't mind. I was happy. Just being with her was fun. And it already felt right. Always.

Ten minutes later and the men were now sitting at the next table. And talking louder than ever. At the same time, I found it fascinating the way they kept glancing over at me and at Alley. Her, I could understand. But me? That struck me as odd.

A few more of their friends came in. They got noisier still. Alley pushed her glass away. "Go? Or another drink?"

"Another drink", I said.

"I'll go to the bar", she said. And she got up and walked to the bar. By now she was no longer wearing her eye-catching leopard print coat. Instead she was standing at the bar in a black dress which was partly off the shoulder, wearing bright red lipstick.

I watched the men. They watched her. And I almost laughed.

Two of them turned and stared straight at Alley's backside. Then turned back to the others and said a few things I couldn't hear.

I took out a cigarette and lit it. Then I looked at Alley, who was just collecting her change and picking up our drinks. So I took another cigarette out of the packet and lit one for her too. As I did that one of the men, one of the bigger and rougher looking ones among them, leaned across to me and said – in a voice that was quite deliberately audible to Alley – "Oi, mate. You do know that's a boy, don't you?"

Alley stopped, holding our two drinks.

I looked at her. Then I looked back at the group of men. Then I had a long drag on my cigarette, held it for a second, then blew it out and replied "Of course I know she's a fucking boy. I'm sleeping with her".

Alley widened her eyes just a little and sat down, placing my drink in front of me and picking up the cigarette I had lit for her. She didn't say a thing.

The man looked away. Neither he nor his friends said anything else. I took a sip of my drink and said, "Thanks" as Alley gave me my change. We talked for a while longer, finished our drinks and left.

By now it was completely dark outside, and back in the house with just one small pink lamp lit, Alley's room was pretty dark too. We stood, for a moment, awkward like two people who had never met before waiting for a bus at an isolated stop.

"How do you even see in here?" I said, thinking about her dressing and putting on make-up. And trying to make conversation.

She rubbed her lips back and forth as women do when they have freshly applied lipstick, then wrinkled her nose. "I just wait for daylight. Or I use some candles."

And then she did indeed light some candles, moving silently around the room and bringing it slowly into focus with their flickering firelight. There were three or four candles on a mantelpiece that had seen better days. There were another two on a chest of drawers, which leaned and had a drawer missing. There was a large one on the floor in a big heavy golden candlestick.

There was another small one in a long thin black candlestick standing right next to a bright green paper parasol.

She saw me looking at that as she lit the candle. "Hmm! I know. But it's Viv's." She meant the boy I had met on the landing earlier. "So if it burns, I don't care!"

She sat on the edge of her bed, which was nothing but a mattress on the floor. And I gazed around the room, with that same cold and nervous feeling I'd had a few weeks before in a large house in Handsworth. Trying to lose the sensation by focusing on other things.

The house was a random collection of rooms. Each person seemed to have their own space, while some rooms were communal, such as the kitchen. It was all pretty basic. There were small gaps in the floorboards – which meant you could sometimes see light coming from the room below. And yes, there were gaps in the walls too, around the windows. Needless to say it felt a cold and draughty place. The noise from passing cars came in easily. Dirt and wind probably blew through the cracks on some days.

Otherwise there was a rickety wooden chair and a very heavy velvet curtain over a cracked sash window. And clothes. Lots of clothes. Lots compared to the amount I owned, anyway. Some in a pile. Some in bags and boxes. Some in the chest of drawers. And coats. A fur coat. And a black coat of some kind. And a few pairs of shoes and even what I thought was a pair of slippers.

It was tough. A tough place made into an almost pretty home by a beautiful but determined person.

But it made me a little sad again. This was just a young boy after all. What the fuck was he doing living like this? Was it because he looked like a girl? Was life, was society, already driving him downwards, even at such an early age, because of the way he dressed? I didn't know.

But no. I tried to focus my mind elsewhere, but I couldn't. Not on any of it. Partly because we were now here, just the two of us, in Alley's bedroom. And it was late. And partly because the way I had replied to that man in the pub was still at the back of my mind. And I felt bad about saying it. A part of me was trying very hard not to make her feel pressured or too involved. She didn't want to let anyone in. Not yet. And we weren't a couple. Not going out together. We were just good friends.

"Alley", I began slowly, still standing. "About what I said. I only said it to shut those men up."

Her narrow eyes widened, and for one horrible moment I thought she was angry with me. But instead she laughed out loud. "No. Don't. I loved it", she said. "Actually it was just the kind of thing that I would have said. Really. They didn't know where to look after you said that!"

For me, it had just been a joke. A put down. But I still thought she might have been offended somehow.

"And did you see the face of that one guy?" she laughed. "He went purple. I thought you were going to be like your brother and fight them all at once!"

Relieved, I reached in my pocket for a cigarette. Took out the packet, but it was empty. I threw the packet at her, as a joke. Just gently. But without that prop, a cigarette, I wasn't sure what to do next. Or what to say. And for a minute or so we were both quiet. I stood and looked at some pictures on the wall.

Alley broke the silence. Quickly, quietly and suddenly she asked me "You are going to crash here tonight, aren't you?"

That she asked me, expected it, and had even asked me in her shy voice, immediately filled me with happiness. I wanted to scream. Shout. 'Yes. Yes please!' But instead I managed to be cool about it and just say "Yeah, sure". As if it was the most ordinary thing in the world.

Then I realised that I hadn't given sleeping over any thought at all. I had crashed on floors at parties before, quite a few times. And I suppose I would have expected to do so again. But I saw that I ought to have asked her first. "Sorry", I said. "I should have sorted something out."

Those narrow dark eyes narrowed still further. And, by way of reply, she picked up my empty cigarette packet.

"Do you want me to see if I can get you a few cigarettes off someone in the house?"

"No. No, it's fine", I replied, finally sitting down. On the rickety chair. Alley now sort of tucked up on the edge of her mattress. "I smoke too much anyway."

I looked at her. She glanced up at me. We were together in candlelight again. As we had been at the party in Handsworth. And I remembered her long pale legs pulling on fishnets the morning after that party. The thought flashed through my mind. Would I see those sexy legs again? Then a realisation. I wanted to. I wanted to see them. I wanted more. More of this boy.

A boy.

She was a boy.

For some time I hadn't felt that. Hadn't given it a thought. But here it was again. I wanted to see him, because he was such a gorgeous person to see. Because I loved watching the way he moved. He could stand like the statue of a goddess. Or stand awkwardly. I don't think he ever saw that. He was both. Both in every way. He walked like a woman. And sometimes he walked like a boy in heels. Everything about him, I wanted to see.

More than that. Much more. We laughed too. We always laughed. We had done so since we had first met on the train. And that was a huge attraction. We seemed to care and hurt in the same way. We talked – in fact we could talk and talk. I was attracted to him for those reasons too. And hear him. That too. To hear his voice. When he spoke quickly or when he was quiet, shy. A soft voice, effeminate. I laughed to myself. I even wanted to hear his heels click on the street. It was everything. All of him. All of her.

In a less guided or less strange life, I would almost certainly have done nothing about any of that for the single reason that Alley was male. I knew that, too. As I sat there, I knew it. And yet how fucking ridiculous was that? If two people like each other, what does anything else matter?

But this life did feel like it was being guided, somehow. Alley had seen that too, at the party in Birmingham. What was going on? I didn't know. When chances come, we must take them. And the way they arrive can be, is often, wholly unpredictable.

"I dreamed of you", I said at last. And with those few words I felt myself shiver.

Alley glanced up at me again, her dazzling blonde hair reflecting the flickering of the candles.

'Oh bollocks. No', I thought. I shouldn't have said that. About my dream. But out loud I just said "Now I'm not sure if I should tell you".

She tilted her head back, looking down her nose at me. And we watched one another in silence for a little while.

"Tell me", she said at last.

I got up off the chair.

But I didn't immediately sit down beside her on the mattress. I stood. Looked at a picture on the wall again. "Er... no. I shouldn't have said anything. It wasn't clear", I hesitated, "I mean, you know what dreams can be like".

I turned to face her. Still the head tilted. Still she watched me.

"Tell me", she said again.

Far too often I said things that I oughtn't to say. Big mouth? Maybe. Too honest? Maybe. But I knew Alley was the same. It was another thing we had in common.

She raised her eyebrows at me, she wasn't going to let it drop. Impatient to know.

I sighed. "You and I were asking someone to let us into a club. A really huge club. With golden doors. But they wouldn't let either of us in. You told them that you were always allowed in. To every club. But they didn't let us in."

As is often the case with dreams, sometimes the more you recall the more you remember. Detail came to me as I spoke, but I didn't want to tell her. "I can't really remember the rest", I lied.

"So... ?" she said. "What did we do instead? Did we go to a pub instead, like tonight?"

"Yes!" I lied again "Like the one tonight".

And I laughed. A nervous laugh. Uneasy. Standing in the centre of the room, not quite sure what to do with myself. Tense, and it must have showed pretty clearly.

Those eyes fixed me. Hardened. Narrowed. And I knew that she knew I hadn't told her the whole truth. She rolled her tongue around inside her mouth. I knew because I could see her mouth moving.

"Tell me the rest", she said at last.

Finally, heavily, as if reluctant, I sat on the mattress. Not right beside her, but not very far away either. I guess I hoped that she would let it go. I looked at the wall. At the ceiling. At a different wall. But no, she didn't let it go. She turned to look at me. Now only an arm's length away. Sitting at the head of the bed. Beside the pillows.

"Tell me", she insisted.

I pulled at a thread on my jeans.

"We... we. We had to think of something else to do. You were dressed up. Looking gorgeous. And so we had to think of something else to do." I said. Stopping. One last time hoping that she would leave it at that. And wishing, ever more, that I had never mentioned my dream.

"So what did we do?" she asked quietly.

By way of answer I just shook my head. Very slowly. And very slightly.

Then I turned back to her and half-smiled. And by way of reply to that, with those eyes searching right into me, understanding, she nodded. Also very slightly.

A curl of her blonde hair fell across her face and she flicked it away.

A few seconds of silence. I knew. And she knew.

I stared briefly at the floor in front of me. Was there anything there that I could talk about instead?

"Did we do something like this?" she said at last. And with those words she moved a little closer and reached a hand towards me. Entwining her fingers in my hair.

My back stiffened. She won't let anyone in. I told myself. She won't let anyone in. We don't know each other well enough. This is just us playing around. It's OK.

Well, all that may have been true, but her fingers still toyed with my dark hair. And I didn't know whether to move towards her, turn away, stand up, burst into tears or kiss her.

Suddenly she let her hand slip away from me. And I probably took a long deep breath. I'm not sure I had breathed once while she was touching me.

She lay back on the bed, her head now on the pillows.

"Hey", she spoke quietly. "It's OK. We don't have to be anything or do anything that we don't want to. I haven't forgotten what we both said."

Once again, I stared briefly straight ahead. There was a sketch pinned to the wall. I wondered if it was one of hers. Then I turned to face her. Those dark eyes were fixed unflinchingly on me.

"Come here", she said. "Next to me. It's OK. I promise."

I stood up. She moved over. And I lay down on the bed beside her. Then for a moment we didn't move, either of us.

Then we both turned, at the same time. So that we were face to face and very close.

"It takes months for me to trust anyone", she said.

Just those few words. Nothing else. I nodded. The smallest of movements again. Was I relieved to hear that? In part, maybe I was. In part no, I wasn't.

"But you're not just anyone", she continued, just there, right in front of me. "We both know that. We've both known it since we first met on that train."

With every instinct, every emotion, I wanted to reach for her. But still I didn't do so. I needed to respect her. How she felt. Not let anyone in. And, finally, I even managed to say what I was thinking, "We... We should probably stay as friends", I said.

She shook her head. Slowly. Three or four small movements. "Is that all you want?" she almost whispered.

That room. That mattress. Two boys. Face to face.

Open and honest. Learning to trust. Learning to love.

Soft-focused eyes searching for each other.

Searching. Learning. Trusting. Loving.

She had asked me. And I couldn't lie to her. Not about that.

"No", I replied, my voice almost hoarse. We looked directly into each others eyes. "No. I want you".

It had to be my decision. We both knew that. My decision. And I had just taken it.

Immediately and almost imperceptibly we moved closer. So that we were face to face with only a few centimetres separating us.

We hesitated. Or maybe I hesitated. She saw it. And lifted her head in the slightest of movements.

I guess, really, I had spent much of the evening feeling unsure. But that final, slight lift towards me changed everything. Suddenly I felt like me again. Much more like me, anyway.

I leant forward those last few centimetres, towards her lips.

Oh god.

But that moment lives with me still.

It will live with me forever.

The moment I first tasted her red lipstick.

It was quite a mild night in that big old house, and the shivers I had then, those ice cold shivers, were nothing to do with the weather or being hot or cold. I had never felt anything like this. Never. Not ever.

After a first tentative kiss, I moved away. Not very much.

Her dark narrowed eyes followed me.

They widened a little. Drew me in.

And I went back for her again.

And we kissed once more. But longer.

We stopped. Separated.

We both laughed. A quiet laughter. A shared smile rather than a laugh.

And then we leaned gently towards one another and kissed again.

And again.

And again.

For a while that was all we did. Kiss. Lying there in the candlelight in that shabby yet somehow magical room. We kissed and time seemed to stop. And we left a hole in it. In time itself. We kissed. And our actions became frozen forever. Always present. Always ours. Even as the years would pass. Once shared, always shared.

We kissed. We parted. We breathed.

Then we returned. Deeper. We kissed, and at one point I remember feeling our teeth hit, grind almost. We pulled apart. Laughed again, her eyes just dark slits, almost crossed. And I loved that. I loved it. I paused. Wanting to look at those half-crossed dark narrow eyes. To hold the moment. She frowned slightly at me and then arched her left eyebrow in a small suggestive way. And so we kissed again. Deeper, ever deeper and longer, ever longer.

I knew, of course. I felt it clearly then. She looked, spoke and moved like a girl. But she was a boy. I knew that right then. And inside, something screamed it at me. There are so many parts to us all. I knew I was with a boy, but I didn't care. Even if she was a boy, what did it matter if it felt like this? How could it matter? Yet some part of me did care. Somewhere. How many layers are there to each of us?

140

We kissed again. And again.

After some time, I didn't know how much, I rolled away. Needing to try and control the electricity racing through me.

I rolled onto my back.

Lying there, I reached out a hand. She took it. And for a moment we lay like that. Not speaking. Not moving.

A few quiet seconds passed. Our blood settled. Our nerves too. A little.

Then she pushed herself closer to me. Partly on top of me. She pressed herself so close that I could feel her heart beating. Even through all our clothes I could feel that. I could feel her every muscle. Those long pale legs. An image of them flashed through my mind.

I smiled at her, her face now just above mine. Blonde hair. Red lipstick.

"Hello", I said.

"Hello yourself", she replied.

We both giggled. Then we gazed into each other's eyes for a moment and then, and without saying another word, we slowly began kissing once more.

It was impossible not to put my hands on her somewhere.

Somehow. But where and how wasn't something I felt confident about. I didn't want to push too far. I wanted to respect all that she was and all that she had said. So somehow I managed not to touch her body by keeping my hands on or near her face. Then she rolled onto her back and I propped myself up above her again.

Alley seemed totally unworried about any of that. And at one point as we kissed, her hands ran up inside my white t-shirt and along my back. Along it. Up and down. Across it. Nails lightly digging into me. A feeling, a sensation, that made me weak.

Where were we going with this? Where were we going?

And then someone knocked on her door.

More than knocked.

They banged on it. And it shook in its rotten frame.

Alley and I instinctively separated. Moved apart. Like two naughty children who had nearly been caught doing something they shouldn't.

And we both lay quite still on the bed.

For my part, at first I thought it was the police. But then I realised that they wouldn't be outside and knocking on the door, they would have crashed straight in. So I knew it wasn't them.

Then the door was hammered again. "Alley", came an irate voice.

"I do know you're in there, Honey. I'm politely waiting out here, but not for very much longer."

After another short silence, Alley turned slightly and looked at me. I did the same. Then she put a finger to her lips. I nodded.

But it didn't work.

The door was banged for a third time and the increasingly irate voice shouted "Alley darling. Honey. I need that five pounds that I lent you. And I need it now, dear. Come out, come out, or I'll break in and pour a whole cup of cold water all over the pair of you."

Alley frowned. "Oh shit", she swore. "I promised him I'd give him that tonight."

I shrugged. "Do you have it?"

"Yes."

"I'll count to three", came the voice again.

Alley let out a long sigh. Then said loudly, "I'm coming, I'm coming. Give me a minute, can't you?"

To my surprise she leant towards me and kissed me once more, very quickly but still on the mouth, and then jumped up out of bed, fully dressed but looking quite dishevelled.

"I'll have to go", she said, and she quickly tidied herself up and went out of the room. Then she came back in, searched for and found her bag, took a five pound note out of it and left the room again.

What a bastard. That was my thought as I fell backwards onto the pillow. What imperfect timing. And for a while I just lay there, not feeling or thinking.

Slowly my mind did come back to earth from wherever it had been – from where Alley had lifted it to.

I could hear music coming from somewhere in the building or nearby, and it gradually rode over my world.

We've only kissed, I told myself. And I'd done that before.

But no, my little lie didn't fool me. I knew that this wasn't the same.

Not like anything I'd ever done before. Every time before it had been with a girl. That was one major difference. And there was something else too; with none of them had it felt as good, as right, as it had just felt with Alley.

What had happened felt wonderful. I admitted that. Knew it. I was fine with it. So why not just let it be? From here, anything could happen. Exactly as if I was seeing a girl. We seemed to laugh a lot. Get on. Enjoy being in the same space. And there was more than a little electricity between us. We had every chance.

Yes. I was positive. It was fine.

Though I did feel a bit guilty, too. Had I pushed Alley into doing something she didn't normally do? I didn't want to do that. I cared more for her than I cared for 'us'. I saw that too.

Those and similar thoughts, and totally unrelated thoughts, went through my head for a while longer. And then, slowly, and with no sign of Alley, I began to fall asleep.

In front of me was a long white concrete wall. Not quite white, but not concrete grey either. It stretched off into the distance. Up close, here, where I stood, someone had covered the wall with all kinds of patterns and shapes and colours. It was lively and vibrant. There was so much to look at. But the further away the wall was, the more it receded, the plainer it was. Here and there were patches of colour. Images. Some clear, some indecipherable. But ever less the further the wall was from where I was standing.

And to my mind that seemed a shame. Why couldn't the whole wall be painted like the bit up close? I asked the question aloud, of someone standing nearby, wearing a thick black coat.

You can't paint it all, they replied. *You aren't allowed.*

Fuck that for an answer. I picked up the pots of paint and the brushes that were lying all around on the ground in front of me and I walked away. Away to where some of the wall was bare. And I began painting it regardless. Vibrant swirling patterns. Pinks and whites. Then yellows and greens. And a splash of red.

145

Suddenly all sorts of voices were raised in anger. And I saw, to my horror, that a crowd of people were running at me and shouting. Telling me stop what I was doing. I stood back and admired my 'work'. It had improved the bare wall. My images were there for everyone to see. Not just me. Why was that wrong? But no, the crowd waved their fists and ran, and so I ran too. I ran away. Getting hotter and hotter. And hotter.

I woke up.

I had crept under the covers of Alley's bed, fully dressed, and I had got too hot. And, as often happened when I got too hot in bed, I had had a bad dream.

What the time was when I awoke, I didn't know. It was still dark outside, and pretty quiet in the house.

Was Alley here? No she wasn't. That pissed me off. Not hugely, but a little.

Then I realised that I was still very sleepy. So I took off my t-shirt, and pushed the cover down so that I could cool off. I couldn't take my jeans off because I wore nothing underneath them and that would have felt wrong.

I slept well. And at some point in the night, Alley must have crept quietly into the bed too, because she was there in the morning, lying almost, but not quite, beside me. Fast asleep.

5

It was Monday morning. One hundred miles away, I hoped, I was being clocked in to work at my factory. I lay there for a while, once more listening to the rhythm of her breathing. And at one point I decided that she wasn't really human. There was an extra breath. And I wondered if she was an alien. With a third lung or a second heart. That made me want to laugh out loud. Although I didn't, in case it woke her.

Instead I finally got up, still in my jeans, put a few more clothes on and went to make us both a cup of tea or coffee or something, depending on whatever bits and pieces there might be left in the 'kitchen'.

By the time I came back into her room, with two thin looking hot drinks, Alley was awake.

"I thought you'd gone", she said.

"No", I said, sitting down next to her and passing her one of the mugs. "You were fast asleep and I didn't want to wake you". Left? Just like that? I couldn't have imagined anything less likely.

We sat for a while, me on top of the covers and her still underneath. We said just a few words, then drank together in silence.

"I'm hungry", I said after finishing my drink.

"Mmm, me too", said Alley.

Through the not very clean window, partially hidden behind the curtain, we could see that the day was sunny, and it looked very inviting. "Let's go out and get a bite to eat", I said. "And get some fresh air too."

"Can we go to a cafe?"

I nodded. "Of course we can. Whatever you want. I'll buy us some toast or something."

Alley smiled and then yawned hugely. "I suppose I'd better get up then", she said.

I took her mug and got off the bed. First I decided that I was going to the 'kitchen' while she got up and got ready. Then I decided otherwise. I put the mugs on the dressing table and sat on the rickety chair.

I sat and I stared. Right at her.

Her hair was tousled and wonderfully all over the place. She looked edible. Exactly that. Edible.

"Come on then", I said. "Get up."

She blinked at me.

"Get up then."

I'm sure the look she then gave me would best be described as peevish. "I'm not shy!" she said. "I'm not even naked."

I shrugged. "I never said you were shy. Or naked."

Still she sat there. Half in and half out of bed.

"Come on then. Let's see you."

"Ooh, I hate you sometimes", she said, picking up a pillow as if to throw it at me.

"I'll look away", I promised. And I did so.

How odd. She could dance in public dressed as a girl or walk along a street wearing a tight black dress and stiletto heels. Men might hurl abuse, and she could shrug it off or blow them a kiss. She would tell anyone what she thought of them and only worry about it afterwards, and she had been acting that way since she was 16, if not younger.

Yet, at times, when she spoke, she spoke so fast that it could be hard to get exactly what was being said or, at best, to misinterpret it. And that was wholly down to being shy. And then there were moments like this. If I'd said nothing, she would've got up without another thought. Yet, because I had sat and watched and cajoled her to do so, she didn't even want to get out of bed in front of me.

I couldn't imagine that. Being so very bold and yet also so shy. But then I knew, had known since we met, that this was very much two different people. Both were her. Both were real. An outside and an inside. I understood that, because I shared it. But my inside and outside were less clearly defined. And if I could have been so bold... I think nothing would have held me back.

I turned back to watch her. And by now she was bent over a cardboard box full of clothes looking for something to wear. The long white t-shirt she'd slept in covered quite a bit. But not those sexy pale legs. And it clung quite closely to her slim figure and tight boyish backside.

And yes, I had been right. She looked edible.

A little while later, we were sitting in a cafe. I worked and so I had money. Not a lot, but enough to do things like that. The cafe was a nondescript place off the high street. The kind of place where plumbers or builders stopped and ate a bacon sandwich and read a newspaper and then returned to work.

One or two heads swung around to look at Alley as we entered. One man, I was sure, immediately realised that she was a boy, and an expression crossed his face which it took me a few seconds to fathom. It was shock, yes, but it was also fascination. But for most, at least most of those that noticed us, she was a gorgeous young girl in a loose fitting jumper sitting in a cafe with her boyfriend. They bought their egg sandwiches and read their papers and paid no attention to us.

"You're easily pretty enough", said Alley.

I put my coffee down and looked at her. "Thank you", I said. I had no idea what I was pretty enough for, but I was sure she meant it in a nice way.

"No", she said. "I mean you're easily pretty enough to change your style too. If you wanted to. Lose the t-shirt and jeans. Though not as dazzling as me, obviously!"

That was true.

"You could wear make-up, though. You have eyes like a deer."

I could feel myself blushing a little at that. "Thank you", I said again.

I glanced out of the window to try and cool myself down. Yet when I turned back to her those narrow dark eyes were still there, looking right at me. She had on a lot less mascara than the night before, but there was still some and it still weighed down her eyes; a look which I'd always loved.

"My features are too masculinc", I said at last.

"Noooo", she said. "No, they're not."

"I don't look like a girl", I said. "Not like you."

She shook her head and took a sip of her coffee and a bite from the toast I had bought her.

"No. You couldn't carry my look off. But I'd love to see you with the right make-up on. It would really accentuate your features."

"What would I wear?" I wondered out loud. An old lady sitting immediately behind Alley was now listening in to our conversation, and I wondered too what she was making of it.

"Skin tight jeans with heels. Not too high. A top knot for your hair."

"Skin tight jeans", I said. "With or without nylons underneath?"

"Your legs would look dead sexy in nylon."

A brief thought crossed my mind. She had never seen my legs. Except in jeans. But then I was equally sure she would be able to look at a man's legs in jeans, or anything else, and decide in an instant if he would look right in a skirt. And she had obviously been looking at mine to make that judgement. I liked that idea.

"My legs in nylon?" I took a sip of my coffee. It had been too hot to drink so far. And I noticed that the old lady was now, quite definitely, taking in our every word.

"Oh god. Of course you'd have to shave them first, though!" Alley gave that little giggle again.

I laughed. All the more so because, upon hearing Alley's advice, the old lady stood up and glowered at us.

Alley didn't see it, as she had her back to the woman and maybe that was just as well because, Alley being Alley, she would probably have made a point of deliberately saying something a lot more shocking.

As we left the cafe, Alley – seemingly instinctively – put her arm through mine. And for a short while, we walked along with our arms linked. I loved the feeling of her being that close to me. And I loved the fact we were walking through the streets of London like that. But then she moved away. Suddenly. And all the way back to the house we didn't even hold hands again.

"I was thinking", I said. "You know, last night when whoever it was wanted that money, the money you owed him?"

Alley was sitting on the floor, sorting through some clothes, and I was lying on her bed, half-trying to read but far too interested in her to be able to focus.

"How do you get by?" I continued. "I don't mean how do you get food or the basics, but how do you afford all your make-up and hairspray and stuff? And clothes?"

She stood up, dropped some material on the floor and then sat next to me on the mattress. "Well, I don't sell myself", she laughed. We both knew that. "But when I go clubbing, men are always buying drinks for me or offering cigarettes, and that saves me money. I never have to pay for anything like that. And although I don't have serious relationships with anyone...", she paused. "Not now. I mean before. Before. I'm happy to be taken out, I've nothing against going on a date. And who knows? I might even get bought a bottle of perfume or something."

I laughed. "That's a bit naughty."

She shrugged. "Mmmm. But I don't blame them! If people want to be seen with me for an hour, why not? Brighten up their lives."

"They aren't going to buy you clothes, though, surely?"

She got up and rummaged around in a cardboard box. And pulled out a very expensive looking black scarf.

"Pure silk", she said proudly. "He offered me a fur wrap but I didn't want real fur." She dropped it into the box and sat back down next to me.

"OK. But what about skirts? Or a dress?"

"Well... ", she began slowly, "sometimes you can find the most gorgeous things in charity shops like Oxfam. People don't really know what they're throwing away. I once found a jacket from the 1950s, cream brocade it was, and I wore that for ages. It was beautiful. Until someone spilt red wine all over it and then that was that".

I loved her voice. Effeminate, slightly accented. I could have listened to her talk forever.

"And this." She got up again and picked up a short black skirt off the top of a pile of clothes. "That came from there too. I wear it often. I love it."

I'd already noticed it, but she hadn't yet worn it with me. I tried to imagine her in it. She had a very slim waist and long legs and I was sure she must look stunning in it. "Wear that", I said. "Next time we go out."

"I will", she said, with a bright shine in her dark eyes. Then she dropped it casually back onto the pile and flicked a great loop of blonde hair away from her face. "And then there are all kinds of places you can buy materials and just make stuff up."

I nodded. "I know", I said. "We have the same shops in Birmingham. Indian shops. Asian anyway. Full of rolls of material..."

"Yes!" she said with huge enthusiasm. "Rolls of silk. In the most beautiful colours you've ever seen. Off cuts of leather or suede. All different lengths, textures and colours. And nylon. And cotton. All sorts of lace. If I find a pair of gloves in Oxfam, I can find the material to go with them in one of those shops. Make up a whole outfit. It's so easy to do." She paused. Pulled a bit of a sad face. "Of course I can never afford very much stuff. But by mixing and matching... anything's possible."

I nodded. "What about make-up?" I asked. "You must spend a fortune on that!"

She nodded. "I do. We all do."

"How do you manage?"

"I don't know. It isn't cheap or easy." She shrugged. "We're always fighting over the hairspray!"

"And perfume? Scent?"

She looked at me with a small scowl. One that I'd seen before, and which made me smile. "You know I sometimes just have to take it. You were there, you heard me tell Viv."

I laughed. "Yeah, I heard. Do you two get on?"

She nodded. "The best of friends. The biggest of enemies too. It depends."

"So how do you take it?" I asked her, meaning how did she steal things like make-up.

Both eyebrows flicked upwards for an instant. "Well, we go into the bigger chemists, like Boots, and, sometimes, a little bottle of perfume or a can of hairspray might fall into one of our pockets."

I frowned, remembering her magazines on the train. "Oh, you're a shoplifter!"

"A little bit of this. A little bit of that." She sang the words. We both laughed.

"You must look pretty obvious, though?" I said. "You and the others. Any of the others."

She nodded.

"We do have to be careful. We've been caught a few times but, so far, we've always been let off. Anyway... there are ways around it. So if Viv's with me, one of us might trip or hurt ourselves, and when everyone's focused on him, the other one pinches the perfume or whatever it is."

I wanted to laugh. I couldn't help myself. It was the idea that Alley or one of her friends could do that and think they were being inconspicuous or crafty. "You really are crazy!" I said. "And sweet. You really are sweet."

"It works", she said quietly, with just a hint of sulk in her voice.

"It might work once or twice", I agreed. "But you just said you've been caught a few times. It won't work forever. You stand out pretty clearly, apart from anything else. You'll get caught again."

"What else can we do?", she said. "We're not rich."

I shook my head. I had to help her. "Do you have any carrier bags?"

"Of course."

"Get me a couple."

"Why?"

"Just get me a couple", I said.

She reached underneath the chest of drawers, and pulled out a plastic bag with a few odds and ends in. She emptied it and passed it to me. Then she moved another pile of things. But there were no bags there. Then she opened and closed the drawers, one at a time, until she finally found another.

"Now give me that silk scarf... no. Something else like that. But be sure to make it an old thing that you don't mind losing."

"What like? Like another scarf?"

"Yeah, anything like that. Soft. But not too big."

She passed me a pink scarf which seemed to have fought and lost a battle with moths, and I put it in the bag.

"Now put some stuff you don't want in the other one. Like used nail varnish bottles." I picked one up and dropped it in the bag. "And another soft thing. A bit of material or something."

She looked around the room. And for a moment I expected her to complain and say that there was nothing there that she didn't want. But, clearly, that wasn't true. There were plenty of things that could be used, and so we half-filled the second bag.

"Come on", I said, standing up. "Let's go and visit Boots!"

She frowned. "Like this?" She was only wearing what could fairly be described as something comfortable. "I've hardly got any make-up on either."

I sighed. "Put a little bit on. So you feel OK. But for your clothes, dress down a bit. Just this once."

"OK."

A mere 45 minutes later, she was ready to go. High heels. Long, tight black skirt. Black jacket. Eyes quite heavy with black mascara. Lips a toned down red – but still red. Slicked back, ice blonde hair. "I've put nothing on my cheeks", she said by way of an apology for having taken so long.

"Don't you have any flats?" I asked her, looking at her shoes.

"Why?"

I shook my head. "You look gorgeous. But today, for me, put some flats on if you have them."

She frowned.

"Please?"

She took the heels off, dived into yet another large cardboard box and brought out a pair of flats. "These?"

She put them on and shrank about eight centimetres.

"Yes", I said. "That's much better".

As we walked down the stairs, Alley in front of me, I took a long long look at her. What a fantastic figure. Both in terms of shape and style. "Edible even in flats", I said, much more to myself than to her.

"Pardon me?" she stopped at the foot of the stairs.

"Nothing", I said. "Come on."

I'm sure it wasn't the lack of heels that made the difference, but a little while later, as we walked along Regent Street, fewer heads turned to look at Alley compared to the number that had turned during the walk to the pub the night before. I looked at some of the faces of the passers-by, and I figured that, during the daytime, people were mostly too pre-occupied with getting on with their own lives. Jobs to go to or do. Things to buy in a limited time. More people around. Less space to stand out.

Alley though, was a little bit annoyed by it, I could tell. And, eventually, as we neared Boots, the largest pharmacy in the high street, and suppliers of all types of make-up and perfumes and so on, she couldn't stop herself from expressing that annoyance.

"This is the last time I come out to the high street wearing flats", she said. "No one's looking at me!"

That was far from true. Plenty of men, and a few women, still turned their heads. But I laughed when she said it, all the same. One side of her was such an unbelievable show-off.

She would go far one day. One way or the other.

The shop was big. And it was situated on a corner. A corner busy with traffic and people, and controlled by traffic lights. Which made it ideal for a quick bit of shoplifting. The more stuff going on around, the better.

"OK", I said, giving Alley one of the bags. "Don't forget to bring it to me when you see me!"

I left her and went into another shop. And she carried on and went 'shopping' in Boots.

For a while all I had to do was wait. And so I just looked at stuff in the shop I'd happened to walk into. It was a clothes shop. And not really my sort of style. But it could keep me occupied long enough while Alley walked around Boots and put anything – and everything – that she wanted into the bag I'd given her.

There was, of course, a chance that she would be seen doing that. But she ran that risk, as they all did, every time they stole anything. At least my way she could make one huge haul all at once. And would not be caught doing so.

Eventually I went into Boots as well.

I saw Alley immediately. By a counter displaying some very expensive perfumes. And it was a bit of a shock to realise quite how much she stood out in there. But it was too late to change our plans now.

After a few minutes she spotted me, came over, swapped bags.

"Fuckin' hell", I whispered, "How much have you put in here? It weighs a ton!" I looked at her. And I could see that she was going to burst out laughing. "Don't! Don't you dare. Just go. Go on."

Barely holding in her laughter, she rushed out of the shop carrying the bag we'd half-filled with rubbish and empty bottles back in her bedroom.

Now it was my turn. And I had to wait. Wait until a woman, loaded down with bags and shopping, was paying at a till. Fortunately, with it being Regent Street, and consequently very busy, I didn't have to wait too long. A woman who I half-expected to have a chauffeur waiting for her with three dogs on one lead, all wearing diamond collars, was at the till, with a collection of bags.

I walked up to the till, put the bag full of Alley's 'goodies' down and then left the shop. The rest was really wholly up to chance. But if it failed and the woman left the shop without our bag, it would have cost us nothing. Just one old scarf.

Outside, pretending I didn't know her, I smiled at Alley as I walked past her. She then pivoted and went back into the shop.

The last bit was up to her. And I just knew she would play her role perfectly.

And so she did. A moment or two later the posh looking, overloaded woman came out of Boots carrying a clutch of bags, one of which was ours. No sooner had she done so than Alley came out of the store too.

"Oh, excuse me", she said, stopping the woman. "Excuse me. I'm terribly sorry, but you seem to have picked up my shopping by mistake." Alley smiled such a huge smile, and managed such an innocent look that the woman instinctively offered her the bag full of stolen things, glancing at it as she did so and clearly not recognising it.

"Thank you", said Alley, taking it off the woman. "And this one must be yours", she said in return offering the lady the bag we'd half-filled earlier.

"I'm sorry", said the woman.

"No", said Alley. "Really. Actually it's fine."

At that moment I thought to myself 'she's going to overplay this' – but she didn't. She did it perfectly. She turned very quickly on her flat heels and walked away. The woman didn't even look at the bag she had just been given.

As we crossed streets and changed directions once or twice we were both laughing so hard that tears were running down our faces. "Oh my god", she said at last. "That worked so well. It was so easy. Oh my god. Where did you learn that?"

"Like I said, I come from a big council estate", I replied. And then I stopped her. "Your mascara has run. I mean really run."

"Oh no", she said. "Let's get indoors again quick!"

That evening, for an hour or two, I lost sight of Alley. Somewhere in the building, and then even at another house a few doors away, which was also apparently divided up into lots of small dark bedsits. In one room or another, with one person or another, she was trading make-up for cash or clothes or shoes or who knows what. Like a child swapping Panini cards.

She did ask me to come with her, but instead I crashed on her bed and let her get on with it. I had brought a book with me – I always carried a book in those days – and I was happy lying there reading.

Happy? Who am I kidding? It was so much more than that. I was in the perfect place and, to some extent, seeing the perfect person. I couldn't have been happier or more content. I couldn't have been happier.

To some extent?

I turned a page or two of my book.

Then I noticed that I wasn't reading it. Not any more.

To some extent. That thought, those words kept coming back to me. Over and over. I closed my book and looked around the room. That broken-down room in that broken-down house.

To some extent.

I didn't care if someone I found attractive was a boy... I didn't. But I'd had the same thought a few weeks ago, when we first met. And it didn't seem to have progressed. I didn't seem to have progressed. She, my crazy, shy, sexy friend was actually a he. I didn't care. But where could it ever lead?

Always that. 'Always crashing the same car.' And always, so far, getting the same result.

Wait. Stop that. I told myself. I *was* in the perfect place and this *was* the perfect person. Full stop. Alley was the perfect person to every extent.

I opened my book again. Tried to read. But I couldn't. I put it down. Closed it. I wished Alley was there. If only she would come back. It would be alright.

But she wasn't there. And, instead, those awful thoughts came back. Kept coming back.

'You won't ever have children.'

Oh fuck off. Did that matter to me? In any case that was years away. I didn't care about that.

'There's no way you can ever tell anyone about him. Not without getting crucified.'

I told myself that that wasn't an issue either. Yet, I knew it must have been an issue. I was lying to myself. After all, who had I told so far? No one.

'He is a boy. Are you gay then?'

Gay? Was I? What stupid muddled thinking. Doubts and labels, naivety. What did any of that matter? And yet, yet... I had never told anyone, had I?

Where could this ever lead?

Robotically, I got up off the bed. I found my jacket. Searched briefly for a piece of paper and a pen. Found neither. So I tore a page out from the back of my book – which oddly, at that time, felt more wrong to me then than what I was doing to Alley – and, using one of her old eyebrow pencils, I wrote her a note.

I told her that I was sorry and that I'd had to go. But that it was nothing serious.

I walked out of the room. And, inside, I knew that I was walking away for good.

6

What madness was it that possessed me? I had no idea. I still have no idea. It isn't something I can understand. As I walked out of Alley's bedroom, I knew that I would never come back. Or rather, to be accurate, I knew that I would try to come back but that she would be cold and I would never see the inside of that room again. It would all be over.

As I reached the bottom of those narrow broken stairs, I stopped and listened. Behind a closed door I could hear Alley's voice teasing and taunting someone, not mean-mindedly but in the catty way that they did with each other. I even found myself smiling as I pictured her face.

Suddenly, I recalled Alley's own words. "Our meeting was more than an accident. Life has made things happen when we needed it to. And that isn't something either of us should just walk away from, is it?"

She was right.

I was wrong.

What was I doing?

I turned and ran back up the stairs, into her little room.

It was getting dark, there were no candles lit and the bulb had gone in the lamp. And there, where I had left it, on her pillow, was my note.

"Had to go. Sorry. Nothing serious."

What the fuck had I been thinking? I hadn't even signed it. I hadn't even put a kiss on it. Nothing. Six or seven cold and empty words. Words which were clearly and quite obviously covering some other reason or motive.

I picked it up and read it again.

"Can't do this. You're a boy." Those may not have been the words on the paper, but that was what the note really said. And that would have been exactly what it would have said to her, too.

I felt disgusted with myself. With my blind, stupid, selfish behaviour and my cold and callous words.

The last time we had spoken, just an hour or so before, she'd been happy and smiling, still talking about our 'sting' (as she had called it) at Boots the chemist. She had turned to me and asked if I was OK and sure that I didn't want to go out with her while she exchanged gifts. I'd said I was fine. She'd told me I looked "so handsome" sitting with a book in my hand and that she never expected to see me without one. Never. Then she had moved towards me as if to kiss me – which I would have loved – and only at the last moment decided against it. Too shy, despite all the public show.

That was where we were, together. At ease, laughing, talking. And now I was going to leave her a note which effectively said 'Goodbye'?

I screwed up the note. Then I took it back out of my pocket and tore it into tiny pieces. Pieces which I then burned in the ashtray.

Then I sat down on the old rickety chair.

There are moments in life that are given to us.

Moments where we can make a choice.

If only we make the right decision. We might change a whole story.

Suddenly I heard her. Running up the stairs. Calling me, and obviously very happy. And in the few moments before she entered the room, somehow, somewhere, I could understand clearly her sadness and disappointment had she done so at that moment and found only my note.

I had hit a crossroads.

And something had changed.

Changed yet again for the better.

"What is it?" I said as she came into the room, pretending to have just woken.

"I'm taking you out", she said. "You so won't believe how much money I've made!"

That night, having spent the last of my own money, and quite a bit of Alley's, we both crashed at hers, on her bed, in a crumpled heap. And we were still lying like that when the morning – very late morning – came harshly through the ill-fitting curtain.

As seemed already to be usual for us, for a little while we lay still and talked.

Not about anything in particular. Just about different friends who had done strange things. And some others who we felt would never do anything strange or even remotely interesting.

Somehow that led us onto talking about things we both enjoyed doing, apart from going out to clubs or bars or whatever.

"Walking", she said. "I love walking. I love fresh air."

"Me too", I said. And I told her about Sutton Park, back home in Birmingham. A huge unfenced green space I'd been visiting since childhood and still regularly went to, on my own or with friends.

"There's a park here", she said. "I don't think it will be as big as your Sutton Park, but it's big and I love going there."

"A park?" I said.

It didn't seem very likely. The area was heavily urbanised.

"Yes. And it's not far from here. It's really close."

I didn't say anything, because I wanted to see if she would say it.

She did.

"Ohh, let's go. Please. Let's go to the park and have a long walk? Away from people and crowds for a while."

There was that other side again. One side adored crowds and sought them out. The other side didn't like people at all and craved empty spaces and fresh air. For now, being so young, the former side won out. Mostly. As I suppose it did with me too – though to a much lesser extent.

I looked at her face. She had very little make-up on. Only the remnants of what she'd worn the evening before. "How long will it take for you to get ready?" I asked.

"Ohh... No. No. I shan't bother", she said. Adding, "Well. Maybe just a touch of lipstick. Five. Ten. Fifteen minutes maximum".

Almost an hour later – but wearing very little make-up compared to what I'd seen before and yet still looking quite beautiful – she was ready.

We went to the same cafe as the day before for a bite to eat and then, from there, we walked to the park.

I had never been to any London park before, as far as I could recall. And for some reason I expected to find just very short grass, flower beds and a few trees around a duck-busy lake. In fact although some of the park was like that, it was bigger than I had expected, and much prettier. There were different spaces. Some where the grass was long and wild. A few different areas of water. A few odd buildings. And as we walked, sometimes talking, sometimes not, we people-watched. We also looked out for squirrels. And, finally, we sat down on a bench.

In truth it was exactly the sort of day I might have had out in Birmingham if I'd just started dating a girl. A nice bright day. A walk in the park together after a long lie in. Idyllic.

Suddenly, as these things seemed to, from somewhere, a thought came into my head that brought clouds into our sunny afternoon.

Alley was talking about the club she was going to that evening – at the time, a very 'In' place to go. She loved it and was quite definite that I should come too. And I was about to say how much I'd love to do that when those dark thoughts arrived. I looked at her exquisite face. Those cheekbones. The eyes. The crazy blonde hair. And as I did so, I felt that our kissing seemed to have happened forever ago. And nothing like that had happened since.

Why? Why not?

At the time I knew, or at least thought I knew, that I'd pushed her too far and too fast. Nothing she had said or done gave me that impression. Not while we were kissing nor since. But from somewhere, somehow, that was the idea I had. If not last night in her room, I definitely had it now. If I was wrong, why was she sitting almost a metre away from me at the other end of the bench? Why were we not closer? Much closer?

Of course I was still young. Too young. It didn't occur to me that she might have felt exactly the same way.

"Are you going to come?" she cut into my thoughts. "Tonight."

"I don't know", I said. "I may have to go. Go back to Birmingham. I should go to work tomorrow."

I knew my words disappointed her. I could see it in her body language the instant I spoke. It was obvious. Really fucking obvious. And all I had to do was change my mind and say something else, like 'Nah, fuck work for one more day. Who cares about that? It'll be fine. There's nothing – nothing – I would love more than to go to the club with you tonight'.

But I didn't say that.

I stuck where I was.

"I guess if you have to leave...", she said, just that bit quieter than normal.

That small sadness ought to have been enough. But once I had started, too often I couldn't stop.

"Last night", I began, knowing even as I said it that I ought not to continue, "I wrote... I nearly wrote you a note and left. You know, while you were bartering the perfumes and stuff".

She turned and looked at me. Slowly. Too slowly. This would be trouble. And I knew it. I knew it. And I deserved it. But I had to be honest with her. Honest. Because *we* were all about trust.

"What note?" she asked at last.

Honest? Yes. But I white lied all the same. "Well, I was really supposed to go to work today for some meeting or other. And last night, well, I figured, I should have gone back then. To Birmingham...."

"What did the note say?"

"Oh", I continued to try to tell the truth but not be hurtful. "Nothing. I didn't write it."

She didn't stop fixing me with those dark eyes and I felt as if I was kicking a puppy.

"What did it say?"

"I didn't write it", I said, a little testily.

She stood up.

Bollocks. That was my thought right then. Me and my big mouth. All I wanted to do was hold her. And go to the club together that

174

night. But I felt as if she was keeping a distance from me and those thoughts were messing with my head. We should never have kissed, I thought. "We should never have kissed", I said out loud.

Oh shit.

That was enough.

Alley turned on her heel and began to walk away.

Do. Something. *Now!*

I jumped down off the bench. I had been clambering over it nervously for the last couple of minutes rather than sitting on it.

"Alley."

She was walking.

I hesitated. What had happened to those fucking crossroads? The last few times, I had got past them somehow or other without having to make decisions. Things had flowed. How and why that had been so, I had no idea. But I needed things to go on flowing. And I needed them to flow right now. I couldn't control this situation otherwise. I needed help.

She stopped and turned back to me.

"I'm sorry", I said. "That came out wrong. Totally wrong. I can be such an arse. I'm sorry."

I walked up to her. And she didn't turn away. That moment, where we had lost it... it seemed to have passed.

"I don't know how these things are happening", she said, fixing her eyes on mine. "But they are. And we have to go with them." She hesitated. "I want to go with them."

For a moment I was so relieved by those few words. But no. My relief was premature. I had messed up and she was letting me off the hook. But only in part.

"I want to go with them", she continued. "But I can see, I mean I know, I feel, that you have some doubts."

"Can we sit down?" I said. And we sat on another bench.

"We get on really well", she began. "You make me laugh. I make you laugh. I love listening to you, and we work so well together." She paused, then continued. "But, what it comes to, I think, is this; I am a boy."

Neither of us spoke.

"I am a boy who feels, every inch, to be a girl. I look like a girl. A gorgeous girl. And I feel like a girl... I mean, I feel things that way." She paused. "But I can tell you're not sure about all that or something."

That was hard to hear.

"Sunday night, when we were in bed, I thought any doubts had gone for you. When we kissed, it felt so right. It really did. But since then... "

I hadn't made any more of it.

"... you haven't made any more of it."

I wanted to laugh, but the feeling was too raw to laugh. She had felt exactly what I had felt. That the other person hadn't made any more of it since.

Oh, life.

"Listen", she said. "I care. I really do care. Already. And I wouldn't have let you in unless there was something very special and much more than the ordinary. You know that. But, for now... for now, I think it probably is best if you go home for a while. If that's what you need to do. Go back and see who you are and what you want before... Before I..."

She just let the sentence fade away.

From the house, Euston Station wasn't all that hard to reach. And it was the direct line to Birmingham New Street. So in terms of making the journey, from one city to another, it couldn't have been easier. But that journey, that night, all those years ago, was anything but easy.

Alley and I had walked back to the flat together. Neither talking nor arguing, neither holding hands nor laughing. Once there, the ice had thawed a little. And as Alley talked to some of the others about going out that evening, I sat and listened and once – just once – we smiled at each other.

But it was only once.

And when I heard Alley agree that it made sense to meet up at some pub or other before going on to the club itself, I had to go upstairs, out of the way, I didn't want to hear what I was missing, what I was making myself miss. A few minutes later and they were all beginning to get ready. I knew then that it was time for me to leave.

Alley and I said goodbye quickly, neither of us knowing what would happen next.

And I walked out of her home.

I had a long and miserable journey on the train, and I found myself back in Birmingham not much later than 9 pm. Every step of the way, every second, every minute, I wondered where she was right then. Tears pricked my eyes and I cursed myself for not being back there with her.

And once more on my own turf, that huge tough council estate, rather than go home, I went straight to my friend's house and invited him out for a drink. Then I realised I had no money left.

"I'll buy", he said. "I could do with a drink too." And we went out and drank far too much for a weekday night.

Getting up at 6 am the next morning for work would be hard. It often was. But this time, it would be much harder than usual.

*

The rubble of the factory, my factory, British Leyland, was a depressing sight. I walked all along the road where the buildings had once stood, with just ghosts for company.

How many years had it been there? Since the 1930s, perhaps? And how many lives had it shaped, affected, changed, broken? It was impossible to even guess at an answer.

I had worked with a man born during the Irish War of Independence, his father being killed in the fighting on the very day he was born. In the factory, I had run a book for him, collecting bets and handing out winnings. His profits being shared, in part, with me. Though nothing like half-shares.

I had worked with a man transferred from the HMS Hood a few days before it was blown up and sank with all but one of its crew. Long since resigned to that sudden loss of so many friends and colleagues, he told countless poignant, fascinating and often funny stories about the war. With a shock of white hair, and endlessly smoking cigars, he firmly encouraged me to leave the factory and find my own way in life. This is no place for a youngster with brains, he told me.

I had worked with a man who brought a whole new meaning to the word 'sour' – perfecting miserable and bad-tempered, he had wanted to work on after retirement at 65. Not out of love for the job, but out of dislike for his wife, children and home. And I had worked with another, who was as jolly and happy as it was possible to be, who everyone liked – and he'd died of a heart attack at the age of only 43.

In my own time, there had been a little cafe which still had a pinball machine from the 1950s, in working order and still in use every day. An old lady behind the counter poured acrid black tea from a Second World War tea-urn. And the owner, so it was said, even had a short affair with one of the senior bosses from British Leyland.

What had happened to all of them? Dead? Every single one? Or was the sour man still alive? If any of them were, it would surely be him. And where were their replacements? Men of my age, in their 50s? And the new apprentices, where were they? How would kids learn today from those older generations as we had learned? How could teens rebel if they had nothing concrete left to rebel against?

It wasn't that I over-romanticised the place. I didn't. It was dirty, polluting and noisy. But it also offered stability. Stability for men, women, youngsters who became apprentices, and for local families and businesses too.

It was worth keeping. An old way, yes. But worth keeping.

After that I walked for a while in the nearby park. At least that hadn't changed. And right then I needed that little green space and the water and the ducks. From there I went to some local shops, now mainly run by Europeans from countries like Romania and Poland. I sat for a while in one of their cafes and watched the cars and people go by. In a shop just there on the corner, I had long ago bought a Matchbox car. Now it only sold e-cigarettes. Did kids buy things like Matchbox cars now? I had no idea.

I finished my coffee. I felt a hundred years old inside. And for good reason. So much had been altered that I had to be a hundred years old to account for it all. Where I lived, in Ireland, overlooking sombre mountains and steel grey seas, nothing very much ever changed. No. That wasn't true. In some respects a lot had changed there too. But that was, somehow, more below the surface. Not as a result of poor civic and social planning.

People need stability. That was my clearest thought as I left the cafe. Ironically, they need it in order to be able to challenge things and change some of them for the better. Without stability there is nothing to push against. Everything exists in a state of flux.

That was enough. I caught the bus again. This time I was going back home. Or at least I was going back to where home had once been.

My hotel was a stately home. A stately home that I had known well as a child and once been very afraid of, as we all were back then. I had grown up living only a 10-minute walk from the place. It had stood empty, dark and terrifying for decades. And to our young eyes – those of my friends and I – it was unquestionably haunted. So scared of it were we that many was the time a gang of us had dared each other to walk through the disused gardens on a dark night or at Halloween. How we had ever found the courage to do so, I have no idea. But we did do it. More than once.

Then, one day, as a teenager and while some company briefly rented office space in the building, we had broken in and stolen enough paper clips and brown envelopes to keep us going for several lifetimes.

The place had a tennis court then. Totally disused, yet somehow it had remained playable. And over a threadbare net, but beneath a splendid clock tower, I had played – and beaten – most of the other boys from the estate at tennis.

Now here it was again, the whole place brought back to life. Back to a pretty glorious life. True, the tennis court was gone, but the ornamental gardens had been restored and were now even producing food for the kitchens. How wonderful. It was something of my city that was still there. Something that had even been improved. And that felt good. And after checking in – and being given what was named in the brochure as the haunted panelled room at the very top of the staircase – I took a short walk in the walled gardens.

The sun was shining strongly and it felt good to be here. At last, this was a positive connection to my past. There were herbs in the gardens. And fruit. Pears. Apples. And after the changes to New Street Station and the city centre, after Chinatown and the awful sight of rubble where so many men had once worked, this was re-invigorating. I wished Kate had been there to see it. Maybe one day in the future, I would return and bring her with me.

But it was also a strange sensation to be here like this. As if I had somehow travelled through time. Back to when the big house was lived in. Strange. But good.

There was a sadness too. Because my childhood home had been nearby. My mother and father. Brothers. Friends. All so close, once, and now mostly all gone.

When I first left the area, to take on my own run-down bedsit – very similar to the one Alley had lived in at such an early age – I had regularly returned home to see my parents and to take the opportunity to eat a decent meal and have my laundry done, sometimes going to the local pub with them for a drink too.

None of that was possible now.

Yet, as I sat there, in the sun, for a little while it all felt just like yesterday. So close I could still very nearly touch it.

That weekday night, all those years ago, after I'd left Alley in London, my friend and I drank too much alcohol at our local pub. He had been happy to do so. I had been everything but happy and had done so anyway.

That must have been the first time either of us had used that particular pub. It had only recently been built. But for quite a while afterwards it often played an important role – or, rather, various roles – in my life. I broke up with a long term partner there. Not with a dramatic scene, but with just one quiet drink and a sad goodbye. She and I had been together for maybe three years. A short while later I began seeing another girl there. We first met in that bar and first dated there too. Cheryl. She had been a wild sort of girl. Too many years younger than me, but for maybe six months or so we'd shared all kinds of crazy times together.

That was right. Yes. On another occasion there had been a party in one of the houses nearby. She and I had gone there. And I'm sure it was there that a boy had been stabbed. Or was it? No, someone tried to stab him but he hadn't been stabbed. For what reason? Some drunk had said that the boy 'looked gay'.

Looked gay? Fucking hell. If we were all to make such judgements about things we were uncomfortable with and take a knife to them... When will we grow up, as a race? Never?

In one of the other rooms, groups of older men had formed card schools and domino clubs. My father had joined both. And I would often sit with him for a while and watch him beat all comers at both games. He had learned how to play cards in the Navy during the Second World War. My mother insisted he cheated. I'm sure he was just very good.

When he died, his fellow domino and card players attended the funeral, all shaking my hand and saying how sorry they were. I didn't know any of them. But they struck me, to a man, as honest and decent and good. Real old fashioned men. Salt of the earth.

That was the pub I was going to, alone, this evening.

And as I walked through streets where I once used to run or play football or flirt with girls, I realised quite how much, and in how many ways, I had grown up and away from my own background. And quite how much, and in how many ways, I wished that I was young again and playing with a catapult or doing my homework for school tomorrow.

School. My old school was gone, that too levelled and now just rubble. I had heard that sad news before making the trip. So I didn't go near it. Didn't need to see it.

In a way it felt like I was being erased from history piece by piece. Erased while still alive. That didn't feel right.

Yeah. I needed a drink.

I wondered who would be in the pub. Would I recognise anyone after all this time? Would anyone recognise me? I wondered if they still sold the same cider. That was what my friend and I had drunk too much of all those years ago.

I needn't have wondered.

The pub was shut too. Boarded up.

Fucking hell.

*

That next day at work, after drinking too much with my mate, had been painful. Not because of a hangover from the night before, but because, just as with the journey back from London, every part of me, every moment, thought of Alley and nothing else. She had told me to go. Yes. That was true. But it was me who had caused that to happen. My fault. I knew that. And, at that moment, I couldn't see past it.

At work I just wanted to hide. Go and find a quiet bit of the factory, an old disused part, and speak to no one. See no one.

And I knew the very place.

There was an old disused canteen. One which, maybe in the 1950s, had been used for slightly more upmarket functions for the works. It had a sprung dance floor and a stage. An old wooden stage, like the ones I remembered from school. A few months earlier I'd discovered it with another apprentice. And for a while we'd gone there to sit and play cards. Sitting on the stage, in the wings. No one had known where we were. Then, one day, a handful of older men had come in and found us there and asked us if we wanted to join their card game. We had said yes and, to even our surprise, we followed them *underneath* the stage via a little wooden door.

Once underneath the stage, the door had been shut and bolted from the inside and some lights turned on.

"Here we are lads", they said.

To our amazement there were tables and chairs, dartboards, and, best of all, a whole keg of beer stolen – 'borrowed', as one of the men put it – from the management's own canteen and bar.

The Leyland factory really was that big, that rambling and that dysfunctional.

And so that was where I went again, the day after I walked away from Alley. To the old disused cafeteria. Hoping that there would be no card school, no friends, just no one at all.

To my relief it was, indeed, deserted. And I locked myself in, under the stage, and played a few games of patience. Then I put my head down on the table and slept. If anyone wanted me, they had a whole factory to search. I could have been out on a maintenance job almost anywhere. So I was fine.

The following day, the Thursday, I did the same.

I didn't want to think. Talk. See. Laugh. I didn't want to do anything. And hiding under the stage was the best place to be.

In the afternoon, however, the card school showed up. And for a while, I guess, I forgot my misery and played cards, losing virtually every game I played.

Friday. Although it was now September, the weather had turned very warm again. And on Friday afternoon, of all times, when I just wanted to hide, instead I had a particularly horrible job to do. It involved climbing up a long ladder and onto the top of a great iron furnace, which had only been switched off an hour or two beforehand. The work was a rush job. The furnace needed to be on again as soon as possible.

It was the last place on Earth that I wanted to be, in one of the oldest and darkest brick buildings in the factory, with a low ceiling, some of which was made of glass in order to let a smudge of daylight into the gloom.

Climbing up onto the furnace, to repair or remove the motor on top, was a hard enough job. The ladder was almost vertical and the tools I had to carry were heavy. Even worse, the air in the building was thick with oil droplets. I could see them, thick misty specks, suspended in the dim shafts of sunlight that reached down to where I was working. It was like something out of a Dickens novel. No wonder so many men at British Leyland had heart disease, breathing such air.

I was only young. But after no time at all working up there, I was far too hot. The sweat ran into my eyes, and I had to come down off the furnace and do a quick, partial strip. And by the time I came back out from behind the furnace – which provided great cover – I was wearing only overalls and boots, my other clothes in a neat pile on an old and rather oily chair.

I climbed back up the ladder with a huge length of heavy chain. The motor would have to be taken off and lowered to the ground. But in order to do that, I would have to unbolt the thing from the top of the furnace.

The bolts were at arm's length and hadn't been undone in my lifetime. The heat was fierce. The air was foul. As the sun came and went, intermittently I was plunged into dark and then dazzled with a blinding light.

I struggled with those bolts, in those conditions, with the top of my overalls now tied by the arms around my waist. I was only 18. And the job felt beyond me. I was strong enough, but not strong enough for those bolts. I climbed down the ladder and went to find help.

Back in those days, maintenance men were scattered around factories like bandits in the mountains, each with their own hiding place. Tucked in behind a large machine or squirreled away in an unused corner of a building, always with a little den furnished with old car seats, metal locker, table and kettle. I knew where most of them were because I was a maintenance apprentice and I'd already been passed around a number of those little dens to learn different skills.

That day I visited several of them but 'Old Harry' was the only other maintenance man I could find. The rest were either busy or had gone home early for the weekend.

I said hello to Harry and sat down with him for a few minutes. Then I told him what my job was, that I couldn't do it and that I needed help. By way of response he put down his cracked mug, filled with dark brown tea, and wiped his mouth. "What you want me to do about it?", he asked.

"Well", I replied, "I need help. The job's urgent".

"Well fuck that", he said. He was often quite blunt but he never meant it in a bad way. "You're a lot younger and fitter than me, son."

I nodded. "Sorry, Harry. But everyone else is busy."

"So?"

I told him again that it was one of the main furnaces, and urgent.

"So get back up on there", he said. "Stop sitting around in here pestering me. Get back up on there and try harder." And with that, he returned to his newspaper and tea.

He probably never knew it, but Old Harry, with those few words, helped me to grow up.

He was right. There was no one available to help. The job was mine. And I had to get it done. Me. No one else. I couldn't turn to anyone else. It was down to me no matter what. And during the next few hours, as I made my arms 50 centimetres longer than they actually were, and found that I had muscles which I had never previously used, I managed to get that motor off the furnace and down onto the ground. All by myself.

The impossible was possible.

It just took effort.

I felt so proud of myself when the other maintenance men saw that I had done the job. And even more so when the furnace was fired up again without too much loss of time after a new motor was raised into place and fitted with ease.

"That", I said to myself, "is the way I need to be. Do it. Just do it. Whatever it is. Don't rely on others. Just do it yourself".

Just do it.

Those three words rattled around in my head for the last hour at work and on the journey home; a journey that was often painfully slow due to the sheer volume of people who left factories in that area at more or less the same time.

The words rattled around. And once back on my big housing estate, I just needed Alley to have a phone. I knew what I had to do. Knew what I wanted to say to her. I just needed her to have a phone. I walked down the green hill towards my house, I walked past two phone boxes en route as I did so... If only she had a phone. I would have rung her then and there and put things as right as I could.

But she had no phone. So I couldn't ring her. And although the lesson was never lost for me, growing up doesn't happen overnight. By the time darkness fell, I was once again sitting in my bedroom wondering whether or not I should simply stay away. Courage is like that. Especially in young people. It comes and goes. It did that for Alley. It did it for me.

Bedrooms in council houses aren't big. Nor are they very private. The walls are often quite thin. The space is limited and, often, the room is shared with a brother or family member. I was part of a big family, but as my two oldest brothers had left home I did have a room to myself. And by then I needed it.

I had scraps of paper. All covered with words, thoughts, ideas. I have no idea how many times the thought 'He's a boy' went through my head and ended up on one of those pieces of paper. But it went through over and over and over. Each time it was offset by my cast-iron 'It doesn't matter. If you find someone attractive, what difference does it make if they're male or female?'. I really did think that.

But... But it wasn't only about me or how I felt. A relationship isn't just between two people. It's also between their friends, family, strangers.

I put some music on my stereo, turned on a small orange lamp and lay on my bed, hands behind my head. Lost in that sea of paper ideas and contradictory thoughts.

As the music played, I reassured myself some with very strong male thoughts: I had told those men in the pub in London that Alley and I were sleeping together. I did that because I wanted to defend her. I could and would do that for her. Anywhere. Anytime.

Yes. And that was true. I wasn't lying.

But nor was it the whole story, and I knew it.

I had also said that to those men without giving a damn what they thought. I'd said it because I'd felt it. I'd said it because I wanted it to be so. And that very same evening, it came true. Almost. A little. We had lain on her bed and kissed like I had never kissed before. More. I wanted to be back there with her. And I knew it.

But...

But I also knew that unless I could get my mind straightened out, the same issues would arise. For me, anyway. And I wasn't prepared to put either of us in that position again. I cared about causing upset. For her. I cared. And I didn't want to do that. And that was why, even though it was now the weekend, I hadn't made any effort to go out. Not to the Hostaria. Not up town. Not even to my local pub with one of my mates.

And then it was Saturday.

In the morning I just lay in bed, thinking back over the week. Each day registered with me. Clearly. Slowly. Starkly. Like time was crossing a thick heavy marsh rather than racing by on solid ground as it usually seemed to do. It was Tuesday that I had last seen Alley. I had left London and got home in the dark. Then on Wednesday and Thursday I had hidden at the factory. Then on Friday I had worked and learned, but I hadn't gone out in the evening. Now it was Saturday. Early September.

The same questions came. Would I ever see her again? What should I do?

The answer seemed to be in my own hands. It was up to me.

Downstairs, over breakfast, I watched Saturday morning television. A handful of pop stars were talking about their lives and how the decisions they had made a few years earlier had led them to meet and so led them to become a band and... now, here they were on the television. The presenters asked them how they had formed and then one of the pop stars said, "Well I don't think any of us wanted to get old without giving it a try. I know I didn't".

My hand stopped dead, holding the piece of toast I was eating. Just stopped, halfway to my mouth. The television was clearly talking to me. And I had to stop what I was doing and listen.

Don't get old without giving it a try.

I imagined the presenters turning to me and asking me that same question or a very similar one. "So, can you tell us, just why didn't you and Alley hit it off when you first met in 1981?"

And instead of the pop stars sitting there on the settee, being interviewed that morning, it was me. "Well", came my reply, "I decided to get old *without* giving it a try... "

What kind of an answer would that be? Regret something you *have* done. Don't regret things you haven't done.

They were right. I was wrong. And that was when I saw it. Finally and clearly. It wasn't that she was a boy. I really didn't care. It wasn't anything about that. It wasn't that I was unsure of myself. I wasn't. I thought Alley was gorgeous. The most sexy, the funniest, the most fun, the best dressed... oh, everything. It wasn't about any of that. None of it.

195

I had been right all along. None of that worried me.

My 'problem' was very much simpler than that. And it would have been the same problem if Alley had been a girl living a few doors away instead of a boy wearing red lipstick and living in a London bedsit. I had met someone who was stunning. Who I'd totally fallen for. But I just wasn't sure how they felt in return. And that was what all my doubts had really been about.

As simple as that.

Somehow, and perhaps quite naturally, I had been mistaken about what I was feeling all along. I had looked at myself, my world, my feelings and I'd come to the wrong conclusion; I'd assumed that I had those doubts because Alley was a boy.

But it wasn't that. It had never been that. Not really. Maybe for a moment, a few moments, at first, on the train, that first week and in the Hostaria when that Bowie track played. But since we first sat and laughed and talked in the wine bar, those particular worries were no longer there. I had assumed that they were. But no, they were gone. They were gone and had been replaced by a much more 'normal' doubt – did she feel the same?

Did she feel the same about me? That was my real issue.

Old Harry and the growing up.

How things clicked and finally fell into place.

I had spent almost the whole time I had known her wondering how I felt. Yet, had I looked past irrelevant gender-based nonsense, I could have answered my question two weeks earlier at the party in Handsworth. I wanted Alley to be my girl. My boy. My girl. Boy... I laughed at that. I no longer cared. Boy or girl, that was how I felt. And I knew it now. It was a revelation. A teenage revelation, but a revelation all the same.

I picked up my piece of toast. It had fallen on the floor while all those thoughts had whirled through my mind. I picked it up, and without thinking another thought, I ate it.

"Are you alright?" It was my mom.

"Yes", I said. "Yes. I'm fine."

"You looked like you were miles away."

Miles away. That was it. I was miles away. I was in London. "No", I said. "No, I'm fine. It's nothing. I was trying to sort something out."

"Well", she said. "Don't be too long over breakfast. We'll all be going out just before 1 o'clock, remember?"

I must have looked completely blank. "Are we?"

"The wedding?"

Shit. I had forgotten. It was today we were all going to a bloody wedding. I'd be there all afternoon. I didn't want to go. I wanted to race off to London. Right there and then. But I knew I couldn't get away. Not today.

"You'd better go and get ready", she said. "Or we'll all be late."

Oh fuck. It was going on into the evening as well. I wouldn't even be able to go to the Hostaria that night.

It wasn't that I expected Alley to be there. I didn't think that at all. It was just that, just in case, she had maybe phoned and spoken to John F... the Brummie telephone link for getting things sorted out. I had already missed Friday evening and now I would have to miss Saturday too.

But it would be OK. I would go down to the capital as soon as I could. Tomorrow. No. Fuck. I couldn't do that either. On Monday I was clocking my friend in at work. That was a promise, and I already owed him a few days.

Tuesday then. Yes. Tuesday. I could go then. I would go then. I would go back to London and to Alley. And that was my plan. As of Saturday lunchtime, that was my plan. My own mind was clear. Doubts all gone. I would go to the wedding and all the rest and then go back to my girl on Tuesday.

It was about 8 o'clock that evening that yet more doubts arose. Sitting talking to my cousin at the wedding reception, I suddenly looked at the clock and thought to myself 'What a shame I haven't been able to get to the wine bar and see if there's a message for me'.

See if there is a message for me.

Yeah.

And what if there wasn't one?

What if Alley hadn't called John F?

No. No. That could be fine. She had told me to go and clear my head. There was no need for her to try and call me.

I carried on talking to my cousin. And had a little bit more of my drink. He started to tell me about the things he was doing at work. And my mind went off elsewhere again. What if she *had* called John F and told him to tell me that it was all off?

Shit.

I needed to be there. I needed to go to the Hostaria and find out what was going on.

Suddenly my nerves started racing. What if she *had* done that? What if we were already over?

Oh god, no.

I had to get out of here and go to that wine bar.

"What time is it?" I interrupted my cousin.

"Ten to nine", he said. "Why?"

"Nothing."

Yes, sure, *my* doubts were gone. My own doubts. But what about Alley's? She didn't get into relationships easily. I knew that. She didn't let people in. Was I 'in'? Were we having a relationship? Or were we simply hanging out together and having fun? She had told me to go.

What was she really feeling?

I went to the bar and bought myself and my cousin another drink. But by now there was no stopping my mind. Oh how the thoughts, especially of the young and insecure, can race and torture.

We'd met by accident on the train. She didn't want to sit opposite me. She was in a rush. Then she hadn't flirted with me. Not really. I'd been wrong about that. And, thinking that she was flirting with me, I had kept looking at her. Gone red. She had seen that and thought I was trying to chat her up. She'd pretty much taken pity on me. I was good looking but going red, tongue-tied. That was how she'd seen it.

The invitation to the Hostaria had just been general. Maybe she hadn't expected me to go. And then when I had gone, I bought the wine. She had sat with me because of that.

Hold on, though. We got on well. And she'd invited me to that party.

No. Even that. She didn't necessarily mean for me to go. It was the way they all spoke to each other. I had definitely invited people to places before now, people who I didn't really care about. And sometimes they had shown up and sometimes not.

My inner dialogue was now getting quite heated.

'OK', my other side told me.' So why the fuck did she sleep next to you at the party?'

We didn't do anything, though.

'OK. So why did she invite you to fucking London, then?'

Just the way they all spoke to each other.

No. No that was wrong. I had myself there, at last. She had phoned John F and asked him to find me and invite me. And then, anyway, look at what happened in London. We had gone out a few times, to a pub, a cafe, a park. We had lain on the bed together. We had kissed.

That all seemed right. Yes. That was it. She *was* happy to see me.

So were we in a relationship?

Oh fuck. Fucking hell. I didn't know. I didn't know.

If only I could have got to the Hostaria.

Then one of my female cousins took me onto the dance floor for a dance. Then an aunt cornered me and told me what a good-looking young man I now was. Then an uncle shared a cigarette with me outside, neither of us being supposed to smoke.

And finally Saturday night was almost over.

If only I could have got to the Hostaria.

7

Tuesday morning. 6.30 am. It was an early start for a long day. The mild weather had gone. A cold drizzle fell. Real autumn weather already. And I hated it. It was early. But I wanted people to believe that I was going to work. The bus reached the factory at 7.30. And maybe in one life I changed my mind, got off the bus and did actually go to work. Who can say?

But this life was running a very different course. And I didn't get off the bus. Perhaps for one fleeting moment I considered it. But I didn't do it. And just 15 minutes later, I was in the city centre heading for the station. I crossed town, dodging the rain as much as I could, that furtive action fitting well with my whole adventure.

New Street Station was busy. And it felt a little odd to be there. I looked industrial. Almost Lowry-esque. Everyone else was wearing a suit or a smart skirt.

I had a bag with me – ostensibly for spending a few nights at my friend's house in Moseley – which contained a change of clothes. I went into the toilets in New Street and changed into tight pale jeans and a white t-shirt. I also had a black Harrington jacket. I needed something warmer but I also wanted to wear something that was stylish and suited me, and the Harrington was the only jacket I had to fit that description.

The wait for the London train was quite long. Not least because I deliberately missed at least one and then lingered over coffee in the station buffet. That wasn't because I was going to change my mind, I just didn't want to arrive too early.

Why? I asked myself. Was it just to avoid waking Alley, who had probably only gone to bed at 4 am? Or was there another reason? Did I want to avoid waking Alley and finding her with someone else? I was honest with myself. No. It wasn't that. Not at all. She had let me in. Me. No one else. I trusted her.

I had a book with me, as usual, and made myself read it for a while. Yet still some doubts crept in. She was unbelievably gorgeous. How had *I* found her? How had she found me? For all I was good looking, she was so very much better looking. How had all this happened?

Eventually I did catch a train. It left New Street at about 10 am and it got me to London a little before midday.

Even once there, although for a moment I almost went straight to hers, I decided instead that I would kill another hour or two in one of the museums. It was too cold and damp to sit in the park or keep walking around. And so that was what I did. I visited the British Museum.

A few hours passed there.

Then I took hold of myself and went to the house.

I walked along, trying to remember how I'd felt just a few days before, after Old Harry helped me grow up a little.

I could do this. I reassured myself. Of course I could.

I wanted to see her. I wanted that so very much.

It was just down to me.

I knew that the big old house was now only a block or so away.

Oh Lord. How I suddenly felt nervous. I honestly think that I could have been sick there and then. And might have been had there not been a handful of police chatting on the street corner.

Why do we feel like this? Any of us? Ever? What use does it serve? To be so nervous as to feel physically sick? Going for a heart operation, it might make sense. But going to see a person who you really cared for and were just longing to see again? Why did we have such an awful feeling?

I turned a corner.

There was their house.

There the front door.

I knocked on it.

It didn't take long before someone opened the door. It was a good looking boy about my age, but not a face I had seen before.

Fortunately any worries I had – and I did have them – disappeared immediately as Sarah, the girl I had met before, stepped out into the hall saying, "Who is it, Phil?"

He said he didn't know. And Sarah came up to him and held his hand.

"Who are you looking for?" she asked.

"Alley."

"Oh, of course, sorry", she said. "But I don't think she's in."

Erm.

"You can come in if you want to? But I don't think any of them are in", she continued. "A whole lot of them went out last night to a party or something..."

"No", said Phil. "It wasn't a party. It was a vernissage."

"On a Monday?" said Sarah.

"Yeah, I think so", said Phil, as I stepped into the house.

"Well anyway", said Sarah closing the door behind me. "They're none of them back yet, as far as I know. Listen?" And she put her hand to her ear in an exaggerated way. "Nope. Far too quiet. They must all be out."

"Oh, well... ", I began.

"Have you come a long way?" asked Phil.

"From Birmingham."

"Oh", said Phil.

"Well come in and have a cup of tea with us or something while you wait", said Sarah.

And so I did.

We sat in theirs, downstairs, and talked for a bit, then Phil said that I appeared tired. Which I was, having been up so early. And they both insisted I put my feet up on their old settee and crash for a while. "I'm sure they won't be long", said Sarah.

I was glad to switch off for a bit. In fact I even fell asleep. And I'm pretty sure that while I was asleep the two of them went out, did some shopping and came back, all the time just leaving me where I was. Which was very nice of them, and typical of the relaxed attitude in the house.

Eventually I woke with a start. A door had slammed, I think. In my dream it had been a gun or something. A bang. I didn't know what. Something had banged. Slammed. Was it a door? I blinked. Sarah and Phil were sitting at a table, eating chips out of a packet and drinking tea.

"That was the door", Sarah said, noticing that I was finally stirring.

A noise of people running up the bare wooden stairs. Heels? Definitely. Heels.

"I think that'll be them", she said.

I yawned and swung my legs off the settee.

"Oh, I'm sorry", I said. "I must have been here for hours. That was rude of me."

"No", said Sarah again. "It's fine. You poor thing. You must have been very tired."

"Yeah, I guess I was."

"Come and have a cup of tea", said Phil, pouring me one from a china teapot, of all things, before I had time to answer.

I wanted to just get up and go. Go and find Alley. For fuck's sake, I was in her house. She had just come in. Probably. And we were now separated by only one flight of partially broken stairs and a room or two.

But I felt I ought to have a cup of tea. I needed it. I was cold. And I had crashed on their settee for some time. It was the right thing to do.

I went over and picked up the tea, said thank you again. Then, with no more chairs to sit on at the table, I went back to the settee and sat down. Sort of perched on the edge of it.

"You know, last week", began Sarah, as if she were telling Phil and not me. "Last Tuesday it was, or was it Wednesday? No, definitely Tuesday. We all went out." She paused. Looked at me. Then turned back to Phil. "Well", she continued. "Now I'm not at all one to gossip, but some people, last Tuesday, were quite out of order at the club." She paused, smiled a small smile at Phil then turned to me. "From what I heard, somebody who lives in this very house, nearly took some man's eye out with one of their claws."

Phil laughed. I knew exactly who the 'somebody' was. At first I thought Sarah was being a bit catty. But then I realised that she wasn't actually getting at Alley, but just letting me know how things had been.

"Go on", I said.

"Weeell", said Sarah. "Some man offered this person a drink, and was trying to get friendly with them, you know? But she was in the most terrible of tempers about something or other."

"I heard that too", said Phil. "By all accounts she almost had to be dragged out of the club."

"Oh no", said Sarah. "It wasn't as bad as that. But she was spitting at everyone like a cornered alley cat all evening. That was definitely true."

Phil put his mug down. "Mm", he said, joining in the game. "And why was that, then?"

"Well", said Sarah, pretending to lower her voice. "I heard that she'd had a big row with her boyfriend."

I had heard all I needed to hear. My heart was racing. Last Tuesday. Alley had been upset. Really upset. That was down to me. That was about us. She cared. She must have really cared.

Wait. Care. Cared. Which tense was I using? I just wanted to run upstairs and see her. But hang on a minute. Was it care or cared?

"Did you see her at the weekend?" I asked. "I mean, did she go out at the weekend?"

Sarah nodded knowingly at Phil. They were only about my age. Maybe a year or so older.

"Let's just say, there was not a single sign of her for several days after Tuesday's performance."

"Not even on Friday", added Phil.

"Ooh, no", said Sarah. "Friday there was that slanging match with Viv. We all heard that."

Phil nodded. "She must have been very upset about something."

"Did she go out on Saturday night?" I asked, thinking back to the wedding and my thoughts racing all over the place, a few short days ago.

Sarah shrugged.

"I don't know, we were out ourselves on Saturday. But I know the same man came around. The one she had nearly blinded."

My heart sank. No. Not sank. It plummeted. Nearly stopped.

Sarah looked straight at me. "Though, personally, I shouldn't worry about that. I don't think he or anyone else has got a chance. I'm pretty sure our alley cat is already in love with the boy she was pining for last Tuesday."

I got up and put my cup on the table, which turned out to actually be some sort of packing crate with a tablecloth made out of red and white gingham tea towels sewn neatly together.

Then I walked across to the door.

"Thank you", I stopped and said. "For the sleep. The tea. And the news. All of it. Thank you."

I left their room and hesitated. Still I wanted to run up the stairs at top speed and burst into Alley's space to see her right now.

But no. That was no good. What if she was in there with someone else? No. This wasn't the time for those horrid thoughts again. Of course she wouldn't be. But it would still be wrong to just walk in. So I started to walk up the stairs instead.

Pretty slowly.

Then I stopped.

It felt impossible.

Where were those fates that had been chasing our story around? I needed them to do something right now.

What was I going to do? I couldn't go up to her room. Could I stay there on the staircase and wait for something to happen? No. Obviously not. But what else could I do? It felt just as impossible to go back downstairs, out of the house and knock on the fucking door. That would have been like some sort of sketch from a TV show.

Awkward instant.

Then up above me a door opened. Footsteps. Not heels. And they were coming this way. Coming down the stairs.

I made as if I had been walking upstairs all the time and bumped straight into Viv.

Half way up. Half way down.

He stopped and frowned at me.

"Oh, it's you", he said, and with that he carried on past, down the stairs. I turned and looked at him. He stopped. Looked up at me and said, "Thank god you're here. She's been completely impossible". And then, with a quick wave to shoo me on my way, he added, "Go on, go on. It's fine. All clear".

I continued up the stairs. Feeling ever happier. But once on the landing I stopped again. Only quite deliberately this time. To slow myself down. To be cool. To find myself. Just for one last moment. And as I stood there I listened, but could hear no noises coming from Alley's room.

Then I walked to her door.

Still there were no sounds. Nothing.

I took a deep breath. I could feel my nerve going.

Did I knock? Did I walk straight in? What should I do?

"Who is it?" A voice from inside. Sleepy. Her voice.

I pushed the door open gently and went into her room and there, sure enough, on the bed, but covered in a thick quilt, was a soft-focus blonde dream. Sitting up a little. Hair tousled. Eyes almost stuck together.

The pouting lips.

The angular face.

And finally, that smile.

Not the quick smile she used so often, but her long, slow and wide smile. Happy not nervous.

"What took you?" she said. Those same words again.

Her room felt cold and maybe also damp. That wasn't a surprise given the condition of the house and the fact that it had been drizzling all day. I hated the place for being broken down and I hated her being alone in there. Yet, at the same time, I loved the room and I loved her being there – as long as I was with her.

"Aren't you ever going to say hello to me in a nice way?" I said, half joking, as I walked over to her bed – mattress – and sat on the floor next to it.

She blinked at me. Smiled and said, "Hello". And then sat up a little more. "Ever?" she asked.

She was so perceptive. Missed nothing.

I nodded.

"Tell me then", she said. The same words I had heard before in that very room.

I sighed. Then I gave her the outline of my week. What I had done and, most of all, what I had thought and felt. "I so wanted to come down on Saturday. As soon as my head was clear. But I couldn't. I hated that. Because I didn't want to leave things any longer."

Alley nodded. "I know. I was the same." She sat up fully. I could see her thinking about whether or not to tell me and deciding to do so. "I did phone John F. I told him that if you came into the Hostaria, he was to get hold of you and make you come back here. Whatever it took. Even if it was just to tell me that we wouldn't see each other any more. Even that. I just had to know if things were on or off."

I understood.

"Just to know", she said again.

I smiled at her. What a tough week we'd both had. I felt guilty about it.

"I didn't want to hear that it was off, though", she added.

And, to my surprise, I still needed to hear even that. To have that extra reassurance.

"So you didn't go out at all at the weekend?" she asked.

"Only to that wedding."

Then I smiled to myself. Thinking about the gossip I'd heard downstairs. I couldn't resist it. "And what about you?" I asked. "Have you been going out at all?"

"I went to a club last Tuesday."

"You didn't feel like it tonight, though?"

She knew. She could tell. "What have you heard?"

I laughed. "Oh, just something about somebody being short tempered, hissy fits. That kind of thing. An alley cat. Nearly taking someone's eye out."

She sniffed. "He deserved it. But I can't stop him from trying to go out with me."

I let that go. But it registered and I felt it immediately start to nag away at me. Bloody hell. Why did she have to say that?

"So did you go out at the weekend?" I said, trying to escape my own jealousy before it showed itself in how I behaved or what I said.

"I did. We all did. On Saturday", she replied, and then she added, "but it was pretty dull. Last night too."

"So you weren't all that miserable then?" I said. "You went out when you had the chance."

"I was. I was *that* miserable," she said sulkily.

For a moment we said nothing more.

"Go and make me some coffee or tea or something", she said at last, "But bring it back in here, OK?"

"OK." I said. I guessed she wanted to sort herself out, her clothes and her hair and so I went and made a coffee for each of us and took my time about doing so.

By the time I got back to her room she had already made it look much cosier. All of the candles had been lit again. The lamp too. The curtain was drawn, mostly hiding the gloomy grey twilight outside and the condensation-covered window. And Alley was up, sitting on the floor and sorting through a pile of clothes.

I put one mug down beside her. Wondered if she was sorting out all her clothes, looking for a change of style. They seemed to be all over the floor. I didn't know.

There was something else I didn't know too. 'Someone who keeps trying to go out with me'. I was sure the answer was no. But me being me, I had to say it there and then to get it off my chest and out of my head. I could be like that, sometimes too much. I knew it. But if it was there I had to know. The truth mattered.

"Are you seeing anyone elsc?" I asked. Still standing up with a mug of coffee in my hand. Feeling uneasy.

She sighed. "No." That was all she said. But she knew who I was referring to.

She got up off the floor with her drink and sat on the edge of the mattress.

"I have men and even some women, boys, girls, all sorts, who hit on me all the time. I'm always, always being chatted up. People are always trying to go out with me. Hit on me. Drinks are bought for me. And that happens whenever I go out. Every time.

Sometimes it gets uncomfortable. But mostly I can handle it. I love the effect. That's why I do it." She paused and looked up at me. "But I don't let anyone in. Remember? I told you that."

That was a longer and better answer for me than a simple 'no'.

I glanced down at the floor. Then back at her and smiled. A sad sort of smile. "I'm sorry. It's just. I don't know. I'm tired, I guess. And it's been a while..."

"I'm seeing *you*", she said. Cutting me off, and for the first time almost raising her voice at me.

And how that cut me off.

If a pin had been dropped three streets away we might have heard it. Such was the magnitude of the silence which followed her words.

'I'm seeing you.'

Nothing could ever have prepared me for those words.

More. I know it sounds daft but she melted my heart with them. The way she said them.

At that moment, with those words, in that candlelit semi-derelict room, I wanted time to stop.

A feeling I would have several times in my life. But rarely as intensely as then.

More. I had never forgotten that she and I, both of us, were still quite young. But there was something about her that, mostly, made her seem ageless. Any age. She had a way of moving. A confidence. Such that she rarely seemed to be just a teenager. But at that moment, with those words, she seemed so small and young that I wanted to hold her, and hold her forever. It didn't matter how tough the exterior was, the inside was raw, gentle and almost innocent.

And me. How those few words changed so very much for me. She looked like this. She went out whenever she could. She lived in London. She knew the people she knew. People were always buying her drinks or chatting her up. And yet she had just said, thought, felt, without any hesitation that *we* were going out with each other. Us.

'I'm seeing you.'

Wow.

Suddenly I felt rotten. Small. Small minded for doubting her. I knew why I had done so. But I had been wrong to do so. She didn't let anyone in. And if she did, then she meant it. Of course she did.

Despite those thoughts, or maybe because of them, for another minute or so – which must have felt like an age to her – I still stood there. Stood there and looked around at that room, taking it all in again. It had been a week. It felt like a year. That damp stain on the ceiling and on one of the walls. The neon light, from the street, shining through the gap where the curtain didn't quite fit. The odd things everywhere, junk almost, and a lot of pictures. Pretty things too. Very pretty. A few silk scarves. Something made of lace. And even a few flowers in a vase. I had missed it. Missed all of it.

"I don't know what to say", I finally said. "It all feels odd somehow. Odd to be back. Like I never left. Odd to have been away...." I stopped. I didn't want to talk about being away. Not again.

Alley glanced up at me. "I know", she said at last. "I feel like that too, a bit."

She got up and went across to the one shelf, cluttered as it was with things. She picked something up. A dusty object. Wooden, I think. She examined it. Then apparently without thinking threw it down on the mattress. And then she sat back down, sort of tucked up, as she had done once before.

"Do you have any music?" I asked, trying to find a way forward for us.

"I can borrow some tapes", she said. And without my having time to say 'no, it's OK', she got up again and left the room.

What the fuck was I doing? I just wanted to get closer to her. To hold her. To be nice. I was angry with myself for not doing those things. But, then, I also knew that I was being hard on myself. We had been together once, wonderfully, a week ago. Since then, nothing. So it wasn't easy. And it wasn't as if this was anyone remotely ordinary. She looked, he looked, just fucking gorgeous.

I sat down on the mattress.

Alley returned, with a tape player and a collection of tapes. They all appeared, like the furniture, like the whole house, as if they were on their last legs too. Had they found them and the chair and the chest of drawers in a skip or something? Probably.

She crouched on the floor. She was wearing a long white top, reaching almost to her knees. And almost invisible underneath it, a short pale skirt. And something I hadn't expected to see – a pair of long, thick socks.

She put a tape in the tape deck. Pressed Play. Nothing happened. She took the tape out.

Again and again she seemed very small to me then. No. Not small. Young and slight. And despite her style, despite her obvious strength of character, she looked vulnerable too. And once more I wanted to just hold her. But I couldn't make myself move. Not yet.

I smiled. It was all so... What? Too good? Unbelievable perhaps. Yes. But real all the same.

"I'm pretty shy really", I finally managed to say.

She put the tape back into the player. Pressed Play again. And finally, music started.

"I am too", she said, she looked at me as she said that. To see if I doubted it. "I know I might not se-eem it", there was an extra e in the word when she said it. "And I can be a bit, a little bit sort of... But that's only a part of the real me. Just one part."

She hesitated and shrugged.

I knew all that. I had known it since we first met.

"What's that?" I meant the music.

"Oh that", she said, still sitting, crouched by the tape player, chin on her knees now. Another brief look up at me. "Something I was given. I believe it's supposed to be a...", her voice faded out. "Oh. You mean the music?" She had thought I meant the wooden thing which she'd dropped onto the mattress.

I smiled.

The music. She told me who it was. What it was.

Of course. Yes. As soon as she told me, I knew what it was.

I was just trying to reach for her. For us. So I didn't reply and carried on sitting on the edge of the mattress, her bed, on the floor.

"Well, I like it anyway", she said. Wanting to reassure herself.

"I do too", I said.

For a minute or so the music played. And neither of us spoke. Then I swore about housing and landlords. And she laughed. Maybe out of politeness. Then we talked a little more about the music. Seemingly neither of us wanting to say what we were really feeling.

But time was passing. The whole relationship too, perhaps. Unless we could close this gap between us. I could feel it slipping. The two of us sitting there *'trying to play it so cool'*.

No. I told myself. Stop this. Don't just let it all go. No. The moment. It's now. I felt it. It was almost a tangible physical thing. A moment. It was there. In that room.

And Alley must have felt it too as, almost imperceptibly, she moved a little closer to me. *'Not knowing quite what to do.'*

"Sit here", I said, at last. "Sit by me."

With those few words – I knew it – I was changing my whole life.

It was her room. Her bed. But I had asked.

And after the events of the last week, we had needed me to do that.

Alley got up. That blonde, carefully tousled hair. She got up and sat next to me.

"I brought this", I said, taking a small bottle of brandy out of my jacket pocket. "I don't know. I figured somehow we'd not go out and... I'm sorry, I don't have a glass." I opened it. Passed it to her. She took the bottle and sipped it. Sipped again. Then passed it back to me.

I took some too. A fiery warm taste. Making me realise that I was cold.

"So much for September", I said offering her the bottle once more. She just shook her head and I tucked it back into my jacket.

"Fucking hell", I said suddenly, putting my face in my hands, then looking up and directly into her beautiful, narrow, dark eyes.

Without speaking, with no obvious change of expression, she suddenly seemed quite lost. Thoughts crossed her face. Had she been too quiet? What was wrong? He was here. He had come back. But was he now going to say 'no'?

Act. Speak. Open up.

Before it's lost.

Instead she just said, "What?" She, too, was unsure, but longed to go forward. Was she being rejected? Had I come down to say goodbye? "You have to take chances sometimes. I mean..." Her words were indirect. Hopeful. "You can't say what the future might hold."

I looked at her.

She was such a strange mixture. Confident, intelligent, determined. But then somehow nervous, unsure and closed. Maybe even as nervous as I was. As sensitive too, perhaps more so. But she was also irresistible, in any case. And simply the most gorgeous person I had ever seen.

I stood. I wasn't playing games. I was just trying to find my own courage.

She made no movement. Sat quite still on the mattress.

But I wasn't leaving. I walked over to the door of the bedroom, which was still ajar from when she'd came back into the room. I pushed it shut. Walked to the bed. I kicked off my old suede boots and lay down on the bed. Inside I was shaking. And it wasn't due to the cold.

"Alley", I said, and I reached my right hand for her.

She turned towards me. Reached her hand to mine. It was the first physical contact that evening.

"Come here", I said. "Lie beside me."

And she did. And for a minute or so the two of us just lay there. Side by side.

The music kept playing. Now strange stuff, unfamiliar to me, but somehow it felt so right. There was the candlelight. It was cold. I lay back and stared at the damp patch on the ceiling directly above the bed and I smiled. Things mixed up. Patterns. Light. Smells. Tastes.

She was very close, but still unsure. "What are you smiling at?" she asked.

"Nothing", I said. I was lying. "No. Everything. Everything. I'm smiling at all of it."

The damp patch overhead formed a strange shape. Two dark circular patterns with a black ring in the centre.

I turned to her. And we were lying face to face.

Face to fucking face on her bed.

"God", I almost laughed. "I so want to be here with you." I looked away, trying to stop myself from laughing. But I was so happy, so moved, that I did laugh. It just burst out of me. I glanced up at the damp again. Focused. Controlled myself. I looked back and into her eyes. "I want you. And I'm absolutely sure of it."

Release. Both of us.

Fears all gone. Both of us.

Smiles. In that flickering light. Both of us.

"I want you too", was all she said. And without hesitating she put her arm across me. For a moment more we didn't move. Then she reached up gently towards my face. She paused. So I took her hand and brought her fingers up to my lips. I kissed her fingertips.

Two boys. Both 18 years old. Not really knowing the world at all. One quite beautiful. Learning the hard way. With an amazing public persona. The other less sure. But, at this moment, on this evening, leading the way. Two boys, lying side by side. In a world where that was still considered to be so wrong.

She touched my lips. My forehead. My cheeks. Carefully, gently.

And then in return I finally touched Alley's face. Also carefully. Also gently.

She didn't move as I did that. She didn't flinch. We were together, and getting closer all the time.

I did it again. I stroked the contours of her cheekbones. Touched her hair and her hairline. Then my fingertips came to rest on her lips. Those sexy red lips. She pouted. And lightly kissed one of my fingers. Then she smiled. As she did so very often.

We moved closer. Pressed together. She looked up at me. And then her lips met mine. They met mine over and over and over.

And over.

And over.

Inside I was truly shaking. Maybe even breaking. I wondered if she felt the same. I knew that if we had both died right then, that would have been fine for me. What future could be as wonderful as this present?

Her tongue touched mine. I responded. And we kissed harder. Deeper.

Her hands went to my hair. My hands went to hers. We pulled into each other and started to almost bite. Rougher.

I stopped. Drew breath. I had to. I held her and looked at her. She was so gorgeous. Just. Totally. Unbelievably. Beautiful. And I knew that was true on the inside at least as much as on the outside.

She came back to me. For more.

"Oh god." One of us said that. I'm not sure which.

I felt a numbness in parts of my face. A real numbness. What was my body doing? Was I dying? Falling apart? No. I was being taken apart.

Alley bit me. Gently. But a bite all the same. On the lip. I thought I could taste blood. But it wasn't. It was lipstick. Our minds perceive more than reality. Reality is greater than we perceive.

She bit. And I pushed her away a little.

I moved her hair. Exposed her neck. Bit her neck. Kissed it. Ran my tongue along it. I wanted to drink her fucking blood. I bit her harder. She arched her back slightly as I did that. So I did it again. Longer. Slower. And I used my tongue again. Along her neck.

She moaned. Then breathed sharply through her nose. Short of breath, just like me. We were both going through this together.

I smiled.

The music continued playing. Keeping time. Like it was all meant to be.

Time passed. And we kept kissing. Half biting.

The first song came back on again. Re-recorded. And some of the words from it had been written just for us:

'And then we touch. Much too much.'

At that very moment Alley sat up. Half sat up. A little over me.

We both took another deep breath, I think.

We both knew where we were going.

Then she tugged at my white t-shirt. And then slid a hand, with painted nails, beneath it.

She touched me. Scratched. And my body shook.

She pulled her hand out. Tugged at my shirt again.

I pulled at it too, and took it off.

She looked down at me. Her eyes seemed to be hazy. Metallic, almost. She curled her lips. Looked away. Looked down at me again. And then I lost sight of her. Just that blonde hair. That was all I could see. And I knew I was lost to this boy forever. At least in part this would be forever.

"I will love you endlessly", I half whispered half spoke. I had no idea where the words came from. And I'm not sure she heard me. They belonged to a song not yet written. But I needed to say them right then.

As I lay there and she ran her tongue down me, to my stomach, I was no longer me. I was no longer anyone. Nothing I had been, nothing I would ever be, none of it counted. Not then. Maybe never again.

I half laughed to myself. She paused, glanced up and said, "What?" in a quiet and gentle sort of way. "Nothing", I replied. And then once more all I could see was her blonde hair.

That laugh. I knew it all then. At that moment. I knew everything. And that was why I laughed.

I knew that gay or straight didn't exist.

I knew that money didn't matter.

I knew that there was so much more to the world than we would ever realise.

I laughed because I was not me.

I laughed because I knew I was part of this other boy. And that he was now part of me. And that the same was true, the same carried across to all of us. We were all a part of each other.

So I laughed.

Not loudly. Not too much. But I laughed.

Then her fingers touched me more. Much more. As I felt her unbutton my jeans.

Then her wet tongue. Her soft lips. And I laughed again as I clutched at the bedding. Trying hard to stay with it. And failing.

I laughed as I arched my back too.

And Alley? She just took me to pieces.

For a while, afterwards, I lay there, unable to move. I had never been touched like that before. It was as if everything beforehand had been a poor rehearsal. Something so much less than it needed to be or could be. And now this. On this night, in this place, I had been introduced to the best that there was or could ever be.

I lay and I didn't want to shiver. Yet I could do nothing else.

I lay and begged the moment to last forever. Yet I knew it would not.

I knew I had experienced something that people would wait a lifetime for. And most would never meet its like. Or even get close.

From nowhere I heard – or was it being played in another room? I wasn't sure – and I understood Bowie's words; *'We can be heroes, just for one day'*. And I understood more the line *'Forever and ever'*. Even if it was *'just for one day'*.

It all made sense then.

I turned. Not focusing properly. Alley was quite still. Saying nothing and not moving. Sort of crouched, sort of lying, near to my stomach. She still had the white top on. The skirt too. But I think the long knee socks had gone. Then a hand, and I realised it was my own hand, reached slowly towards her. And touched her blonde hair. Very lightly.

Slowly, very slowly, my senses came back to earth. But when I tried to speak, "Jesus", was all I could manage to say. With that word though, Alley finally moved. Lifting herself up, onto her knees, still on the mattress.

She ran both of her hands through her hair. Ruffling it up ever more.

"It's still early", she said, in a very husky voice.

And she was right. I had got to London early, but the day had now turned into evening. But only a few hours had passed together. And we still had a long night ahead of us if we wanted it.

She looked at me, her eyes first narrow and dark, then suddenly widening. "You don't want to go out, do you?"

It was a genuine question, but every part of me knew that she wanted the answer to be 'No'. On the one hand it was Tuesday night. One of the main club nights at that point in time. But that didn't seem to matter. Not then. Importantly, much more importantly, I couldn't really move and I just didn't want to.

"No." I croaked it rather than said it.

She lifted her shoulders in a slow shrug. Held them there. "Nor do I." And with those words she came up to me again on the mattress and leaned down to my face, her own disappearing in a soft-focus blonde mass.

And I felt her lips once again. And somehow, my own managed to respond too, and we kissed once more. Long and longer and yet longer still. So that I had no will left, nor any sense of myself. She had taken me over.

Somehow I turned my head away, just a little. For air. For reality. For my own sanity. And I saw our shadows merging together with the flickering candlelight on the walls all around us. They entwined. They entwined more than we were doing. How was that possible? What was making this all happen? I didn't know. But I remember seeing our shadows and thinking that.

I remember, too, that I wanted to speak right then. To say something. But there were no words. Nothing would have ever sufficed. Not then. And just as my mouth opened, her tongue stopped me from making any coherent sound.

I responded with my tongue. Our teeth clashed together again. We were almost trying to eat each other.

As we kissed, I felt her hand again. All over my chest. Her hand. Yet again.

I felt more besides. Those nails. Yet again.

Sliding slowly down. Yet again.

And then, once more, her face slipped away from me and all I could see was that blonde hair.

For a while, I don't know how long, I lay there and her mouth moved all over me. Just as it had before. How could she do that? How could she make me feel like this? How could I respond again already?

Her lips were wet. And I smiled as I pictured her red lipstick. Instinctively I licked my own lips and tasted it there too, and more besides. I wondered which of us had the redder lips.

Low. She almost bit me. And I almost let her. She wrapped her tongue around me but this time, somehow, somehow, I found some strength, from somewhere, to push back. I would have her now. It was my turn.

My fucking turn.

I moved, lifted myself a little, and managed to get half way down the bed as her face came back up towards mine.

Our eyes met. Her lips curled again and I took her full bottom lip in my mouth and bit it. Not hard but not gently either.

She pulled away and tossed her hair, and almost scowled at me.

I didn't care. And I loved that scowl.

We were no longer human. We weren't even animals. We were something altogether different, not part of the world, and we took from each other and we belonged to each other. We might die tomorrow. This was the time to live. Now.

I reached for her and gently pushed her head back. Hesitated. Waiting. Making the moment last. Then I found her neck again. Ran my tongue down it and she practically purred. She had a necklace on. I bit that too.

My mouth stopped. I was there, at that necklace.

But I wanted to go further.

She wanted me to go further too.

Life wanted it.

It just had to happen.

That white top of hers. A sort of long, mid-sleeved, t-shirt. I moved away from her again. Studied it. The image of a band. In black on white. A screen print. I looked at her face. Breathed. "Take that off", I said.

And she did.

In one silky movement up and over her head. Suddenly topless. Right there. In front of me.

Oh my god.

For me, I suppose, that was *the* strangest moment of my life. Even since I can recall nothing that comes close to it. Nothing.

Why so strange?

Because ever since we had first met, first kissed, she had been a girl to me. A very young woman. Red lipstick. High black heels. Painted nails. All of it.

She had been all of those things until that moment. That very moment. The moment she took off that t-shirt.

And now?

My eyes must have widened then. I must have frozen or had a strange expression, I think. I must have done something like that. I know I must have. Because for one short, horrible second, she looked at me, eyes into my eyes and appeared scared.

'King... Queen.' The words from Bowie's 'Heroes' echoed. In my head? Or from outside? I didn't know where they came from. But I heard them. *'King. Queen.'* And I finally saw that it made no difference.

I looked at that young and unbelievably girlish face, and I shook my head very slightly and smiled. She was clearly reassured. And I moved back to her again.

Inside, as I did so, there was a voice, not mine, which repeated the same two words over and over. Fucking hell. Fucking hell. Fucking hell. Once more not the most poetic of thoughts, but it was where I was. I was in heaven. Beyond my own limits and desires. Somewhere new and unbelievably wonderful. I didn't know. I didn't know anything. Just "Fucking hell". That was all I could hear.

The instant my lips touched her naked chest, I knew – and, strangely, for the first time – that we were lovers. I was now the lover of another boy. And he was my lover. And I had no idea how it had happened, nor any idea why anyone would ever think anything wrong of it. This boy, my girl, was beautiful. I'd have killed a hundred men, perhaps many more, to defend her. Then and forever after.

Then I kissed the chest of my lover. It was firm. And slim. A boy, not a girl.

Without asking them to do so, my fingers moved across her chest. Circling. Just gently. I paused. I licked the tip of a finger and touched her there again. She tensed as I did that. And so did I.

I leant forward and kissed her, the same place, the same way, gently. And time suddenly began to slow again. And things began to blur once more.

I recall that skirt. What was it? Short. Pleated. I had no idea. But I know that as I ran my tongue down to and over her flat naked stomach she wriggled and somehow pulled that skirt off. I can see it still, that wriggle.

Lying on the bed as we were, at that moment I lifted my head slightly, turned to look at her. To look along her. To see that her legs were now bare. Feet too. Top. All gone. She was almost completely naked.

Almost but not quite.

She still wore a necklace and, I think, what were probably cream coloured silk panties. But I didn't know. Silk. Cream. I didn't know. And I didn't care what they were.

What happened then was the most natural thing in the world.

Everything about it felt right.

Why would anyone ever think otherwise? If you like someone, find them attractive, get on, laugh, love the touch of their skin... what else should matter?

I remember licking her. Down across her stomach again. I remember pulling back that soft material too. And pulling it down just far enough. Then I continued to move my tongue across her tight young body.

And as I took her in my mouth, him in my mouth, in just a very few seconds I had swallowed her. Wholly.

And she arched hugely as that happened. And then fell back onto the mattress afterwards. Seemingly exhausted and limp like a puppet whose strings had been cut. Still and not moving. Except for a finger or two which seemed to claw slightly at the bedding.

I sat up. Licked my lips. Tasted the last of her and swallowed again.

This. This was life. This was it.

Nothing else mattered or would ever matter.

All the fighting in the world, all the pressures and stress, all the hate or running, the commuting or struggling. At the end of it all, what mattered was connecting. Loving. Like this. This was all that ought to matter.

I glanced at her pale, young body. Now wearing only a necklace.

Even the red lipstick was all gone.

And immediately I looked at her, all other thoughts were gone too. I just wanted to protect her now. Minutes beforehand all we had felt was passion, desire, excitement. Now I wanted to look after her. Whenever. Whatever. For as long as I could.

I watched. And she turned half onto her side. She bent her legs. Folded up to sleep.

How vulnerable people were. Could be.

Still with the music playing, I reached across the bed and grabbed the thick cover lying there, and I dragged it up and over us both. And we lay still.

Exhausted.

Elated.

One.

Under the covers, after a few quiet moments, she suddenly re-awakened. Turned onto her back. I kissed her lightly. Those sculpted cheeks. And, after a moment more, like two children, we giggled. Then we got too warm and pushed the covers down a bit.

What she said then amazed me. "Well?", she whispered and wrinkled her nose a little as she said it. "Boy or girl?"

I think I took that the way she meant it and I laughed.

And then she laughed too. And I held her. And kissed her.

After a few minutes, she reached out of the covers, found and grabbed her white t-shirt and crawled out from under the bedclothes.

Somehow she also found my brandy. And she threw the bottle to me in bed. Then she walked slowly and gracefully around the room blowing out the candles and counting them out loud as she did so.

As the last candle went out, and we were plunged into a mixture of neon orange and darkness, she took her top off again and climbed back under the covers with me. There was a clunk as her necklace hit the floor too and she was finally, finally, completely naked and next to me in bed. I still had my jeans on. Open and unbuttoned. But on. Strangely I then did them up. I don't know why. And then I put my arm around her. She laid her head on my chest and we were quiet.

At first I expected us to fall asleep. But we didn't.

In a quiet voice, a sultry, muted, husky whisper, she talked to me. Those words were private. I was surprised by them. A short tale about something she had had to do once. I was glad she told me. Trusted me. But I was sad to hear them too. And I held her a little tighter.

"I will love you without any end", I said again. And I meant it.

She soon fell asleep. And I lay there hating the world for the harshness it could show. This person was to be held, not hurt. Never that. Never hurt. And then I fell asleep too.

8

We should have slept well. It had been a long day for both of us. An emotional end to an emotional week. Mentally, physically, sexually, stretching out into the universe itself, we had somehow connected. Both had given and both taken. Eventually, with just two people in a lifetime, I would know that difference – the difference between making love and sex. Sex could be fun, energetic, gentle, all kinds of things. But Alley was the first person with whom I experienced the other type – making love. It is deeper. It is rarer. It touches every part of our being. Time stops. Space ceases to exist. Making love with someone is being anywhere and nowhere, all at once. It is two becoming one.

So yes, we should have slept well.

But despite the day seeming to have lasted forever, we had, in truth, crashed into bed quite early. And throughout the rest of that never-really-quiet building, others were rushing around and making noises. Getting ready to go out. Letting people into the house. Shouting. Slamming doors. Playing music. All kinds of noise. Every kind of noise.

So any sleep was disturbed, over and over, and eventually broken.

At one point, with one last slam of the front door, maybe around 11 pm or so, finally the house fell silent.

By then, both of us, Alley and I, were half awake and half asleep. In a sort of twilight of consciousness, eyes only able to see in grayscale.

I lay there and was sure that I could smell fireworks. Fireworks. Bonfire night. A distinctive smell. And Alley told me she was sure it must have snowed outside, because there was again something distinctive about roads and road noise when the snow has fallen. Yet it was neither the time of year for fireworks, nor for snowfalls. We talked about it. Sleepily. And agreed that perhaps it was true, after all. Both of those things. Perhaps we had connected so intimately that time and space had really changed. Perhaps it was snowing, in London, in mid-September, and fireworks were being let off to celebrate that fact.

Despite talking about that, and other strange sensory events, all the same, sleep did come and go. And at one point I awoke to find myself lying with my arm over Alley, both of us on our sides.

Was she asleep now? I lay and listened. Yes, she was. On her right hand side, with both hands somewhere underneath her pillow. With the covers pushed half way down, in true dark now – but for the gap left by the curtain – I carefully moved my hand to her side and then gently stroked her, my hand running smoothly across her soft, naked skin. Her waist was so narrow that there was even a pronounced curve above her hips. I too had that curve. Less so, but it was there all the same. Men don't normally have that.

Just like a girl, I said to myself.

Earlier, some part of me had been stunned – very briefly – when Alley had taken her top off. Because that part of me somehow expected to find a real girl underneath the clothes, and the sight of a boy's naked chest had made me freeze for a moment.

I wondered what might have happened, or rather, what I might have felt, if I hadn't had that week to sort my head out. Alley was a boy. Like me. Yet she was a girl too. Very much so, and in so many ways. It wasn't just the clothes, the outer appearance, although that was a very real manifestation of a part of her. The lipstick, blonde hair, high heels. All of that. Nor was it just the effeminate voice or mannerisms, her name or the careful way she might sometimes eat and drink. No. It was everything. That curve. The silken skin. The narrow waist. Those things, too, made her female.

And as I lay there watching her, it struck me again. What a stupid mess people make of issues like gender. In truth, we were all, all of us, just somewhere on a sliding scale. A shade of grey. Not black and white.

I stroked her back a little more and soon fell asleep again.

It must have been maybe 3 am when Alley woke me up.

"Are you awake?" she whispered, barely loud enough to cut into my sleep.

I awoke anyway, but only slowly. And I could see the dream I was having slipping away as I did so. Someone had been touching me. Stroking my back. For real? Maybe? I wasn't sure, and now the dream faded away.

"Are you awake?" Again quietly.

"What is it?" Equally quietly.

"Take your jeans off."

I was just about awake enough to hesitate and say, "No".

She lay still. Then, inevitably, asked, "Why? Why not?" She would never let things go. And I loved that about her.

Of all the strange answers I could have given her, I told her the truth. The real reason I had fallen asleep with my jeans on. Even buttoning them back up. "I can't", I said slowly. I knew that answer wouldn't do. So I added, "I'm not wearing anything underneath".

For a moment we were both quiet.

"I know you're not", she giggled.

And, in my turn, I knew that right then, in that dark room, her face was lit up with one of those fast cheeky smiles.

"You're a bastard", I said, reaching for the buttons on my jeans.

"Just take them off", she replied.

I did so. And as soon as I had done I realised how strange it had been to continue to wear them in bed. "Sorry", I said, turning towards her so that we were face to face. She shook her head a little by way of reply. And I knew that she understood me. She had understood that as she understood so many other things.

Morning arrived. Our third or fourth or fifth together? I ought to have known and probably did. But I was too sleepy, too tired and just too fucking happy to care. It was morning. I awoke. And we were both tangled around each other. What more could I ever want?

In my imagination I reached for a button. A big red button. I pressed it and blew us to kingdom come. Right there. Right then. With Alley none the wiser, because she was asleep as I reached for and pressed it. Reality was out there. Outside the bed. Outside the room. Outside the window. And I didn't want to see it. Not then. Not ever again. I just wanted to stay here, hold her and have her hold me.

That was, I suppose, in part, because I knew that nothing ever lasted. No matter how wonderful it was. I knew that. I knew it even though I was only 18. That million-year-old man. Sitting inside and giving it to me. Sometimes good news. Sometimes bad. This morning his message was stark and it was bad.

Well, maybe that was so, but it was also for the future, I told myself. For now, and for another hour or so, I would lie there with my girl, my boy, and everything else could just fuck off.

And so we did stay like that for a while. Entwined. Soft moments. Shared. Just ours. Then thirst, and hunger and other necessities came calling, and we reluctantly got up.

People quickly form patterns of behaviour. Habits, almost. And Alley and I were no different in that respect. Once we had got up – somewhat shy of each other – and dressed, I took her out to 'our cafe' again. The same one. Maybe even the same table. The one where we had offended an old lady with our talk about shaving legs and wearing stockings.

We sat there for an hour or more. People-watched. Ate. Drank. From there, that Wednesday morning, we then walked to the park. And I expect we walked virtually the same route we'd taken just over a week before.

But, today... Alley was in flats again, which had made me laugh when she put them on. But then she'd told me to stop it or else she would find her highest heels and wear them instead. She also wore a heavy looking leopard print coat. And we walked along holding hands. From the back or from a distance – I know, because I visualised it several times – we looked like exactly a gorgeous girl and a very good looking boy. Which, really, is just what we were.

We sat down for a few minutes on a bench and it was only then that we realised we had no cigarettes. We'd smoked the last one the previous evening and had none since. And, until we sat down on that bench, neither of us had even noticed. How strange.

Later on and back in her room, we even planned another shoplifting raid on a different chain store.

Habits. Patterns.

At first, Alley wanted to swap roles for the shoplift. But we soon realised that was no good – I wouldn't have known which lipsticks or perfumes or whatever to steal. Then she disappeared for a while. Quite a long while. And by the time she came back, she was clutching a list.

"What's that?" I asked.

"A shopping list!" she beamed. "Orders from some of the others."

"Bloody hell."

By the time we finally went back out, the shops weren't far off closing time. So we had to move quickly. Would we have enough time to find a woman waiting by the till with enough bags? I wasn't sure.

To my surprise it all went really well. At first.

Alley filled a carrier bag with all kinds of goodies.

We swapped them over and she left the shop with the bag of rubbish.

I waited barely five minutes before I spotted an ideal target and put 'our' plastic bag full of things down next to her. I left the shop. And, as before, Alley walked into the shop just as the woman was leaving. It was going well. Too well.

"Now", I said to myself.

Where was Alley? She ought to have swung around and followed the woman out.

The woman flagged a taxi and one stopped.

"Where is she?" I spoke my thoughts out loud.

At the very last moment, Alley dashed out of the shop. She went straight over to the woman, who was half way into the taxi, and then switched bags.

"That was close", I said, as we hurried away. "What took *you*? We nearly lost her."

"Oh", Alley replied, "there was a gorgeous new shade of lipstick. Right by the door. On a display. I had to try it".

I shook my head.

By now we were a few streets away.

"Let's have a look then", I said. "What did you get?"

Alley opened the bag. Reached in. And pulled out a heavy white package.

Waxed paper.

"What's that?" I asked her.

"Ugh I think it's someone's Sunday roast", she replied.

I looked at the package. And then at the bag. "You must have swapped the wrong bag! She's driven off in that taxi with all your perfume and stuff, and you've got her dinner!" I laughed.

The look of horror on Alley's face made me laugh even more. Although for a minute I actually thought she was going to be sick.

"She's got it all!" said Alley, finally adding in a quiet voice. "What am I going to tell the others?"

Then it was Wednesday evening, with almost everyone in the house having had some of the roast beef. No one was going to a club, so a few of us decided to go to a pub for a drink, just to get out for a while. To escape the escape that was, in turn, that old rundown house. To show off a little. To be shown off a little.

And, once again, those habits surfaced and we went to the same pub as before.

To begin with, the walk there was almost a farce.

There were a half dozen of us and I was the only one not dressed as if I were in a circus parade. At every crossing, the traffic stopped before the lights turned red. And waving and laughing, the circus carried on. Performing to its night time London audience. I expected to see seals. Or a lion tamer. Acrobats or a fire eater.

More than once car horns were honked. A police car slowed down to look. Another car sped up to get away.

More than once a southern voice shouted words like, "Hello darling! Goin' anywhere nice?"

More than once a southern voice shouted, "You bunch of fucking weirdos. Go and get a job!"

"Isn't it wonderful?", someone said. "Isn't it awful?", said another.

Outside the pub itself, a few men – possibly the same ones that Alley and I had encountered before – were standing around smoking and talking. "Uh oh, the posers are here", said one of them, making sure he said it audibly enough for everyone to hear.

None of 'the posers' seemed to care. Some of them laughed. Alley took my hand and led me into the pub. I wondered if she'd done that to stop me saying something to one of the men? I decided that was exactly why she had done it, and I thought it was rather sweet of her.

Was I one of the posers too?

No. I was in jeans and a t-shirt and wearing a black Harrington, and my dark hair was just starting to get long again.

But then again yes. Because I was sleeping with one of them. The Queen of them. So on balance? Yes, I was, at least an honorary poser.

Once inside the pub, the razzamatazz dropped off quite a bit. There wasn't a very substantial public to perform to. It was cold. Damp. Mid-September. Midweek. What else had we expected?

For a while I thought it was going to be one of those dreadful nights where, for entertainment, we would buy two packets of peanuts and count the contents of each to see who had the most, with the loser having to buy the next drink. And I remembered the time, in another pub, with other people, that two halves of peanut, found in separate bags, had definitely, unequivocally, undeniably matched. Fitting together like pieces of a jigsaw. Not just the shape, but their colour and texture too. What were the chances of that? Or were peanuts always so totally similar to one another? I didn't know the answer, but I recalled that we examined a lot of the others and none of them matched so perfectly. Not from different bags, anyway.

Looked at from another angle, a boring night was also quite reassuring. If these people, wearing these clothes, in London, at this age, could have such seemingly dull nights, there was hope for all of us. Even those that lived on remote Scottish islands and could only look forward to a game of darts on a Saturday night and a visit from a mobile chip shop with a bright interior light. Dull could crop up anywhere, everywhere, at any time. Or so it seemed for a while.

But no. Fortunately not. This was not going to be a night quite as bad as that. A few jugs of sangria helped liven the mood, as did the arrival of some other friends, one of whom had a Spanish guitar with him and could play it pretty well.

"Oh, we should dim the lights and get some candles on the tables", said Sarah, the girl from downstairs. "It's like a Spanish tavern."

"An Andalucian tavern in 1750", said Phil, her partner. "And we're all hiding inside from the wild storm raging outdoors."

"Oh how romantic", said Viv. "And who will be my Don Juan?"

"Mmm, I've got mine", said Alley, hooking her arm through mine and squeezing.

"Oh please", said Viv. "I think I'm going to be sick."

Sadly, just as I was beginning to visualise it, the whole 'Spanish tavern lost in a storm in the Pyrenees' idea then went out of the window. Not only did the landlord refuse to switch out the lights or find some candles, but the juke box suddenly burst into life with a track by Ian Dury; 'I want to be straight'. I suspected that the men, those same men, who were now laughing, had probably picked it out on purpose.

It didn't faze any of the posers though. And the boy who had the guitar immediately picked up the riff and sang along to it. As did they all to the chorus – posers and men both – 'I want to be straight, I want to be straight. I'm sick and tired of taking drugs and staying up late... '.

It created a good and positive atmosphere. And as more tracks were selected on the jukebox, both 'sides' even talked and joked together.

It was nice to see.

More drinks were bought and what I had thought was going to be dull became a fun evening. Much better than any visit of a mobile chip shop in the Hebrides.

At one point Alley danced with the guitar player, to a track called 'Give me the night'. Inside I was green as she did that. But I tried not to show it. Of course she noticed, she noticed everything, and before she went to the bar, she stopped by me and whispered something in my ear that meant I immediately forgave her and even went a little red.

We all left the pub in a much better mood.

Glad of the night out.

The walk back to the house was almost as outlandish as the walk there, but not quite. That was largely due to the fact that it was now raining and there were a lot less people about and a lot less reason to perform.

Back at the house, Alley and I sat for a while in one of the other rooms and shared coffee and a joint. Then we, or rather Alley, made tired noises and after assembling a thick joint for ourselves, we went upstairs to her space. It wasn't just us being rude – though it was partly that, because Alley didn't particularly like something someone had said about her 'new' lipstick – but it was also because we were still quite damp from walking back in the rain.

Once back in her room, I think both of us felt that we could relax again. I mean relax more. Be our real selves, our real inner selves.

The public faces could be left at the door. Not that I had one down there in London. Not really.

"Wet things", said Alley. "Put them on the back of the door or the back of the chair. If we put them away, they'll smell."

I hung up my Harrington. She hung her coat next to it.

I sat down on the mattress as Alley rummaged for some clothes in a box.

I noticed a biker's leather jacket on the floor, in the far corner of the room. I hadn't seen it before. "Is that yours?", I asked her.

"That leather?" she said. "Yeah, I've had it a few years. I really ought to get rid of it now. It isn't me anymore." She picked up a saucer which was in use as an ashtray. "When I first came down to London I was sort of a punk with make-up, I suppose. Actually I keep the jacket because it reminds me."

She sat next to me on the mattress and lit the joint. She took a long draw on it.

"Let's get into bed", she said.

That was fine by me. I think it was exactly what I wanted to hear. So I took off my t-shirt and then climbed under the covers. Only then did I take off my jeans. I think I might still have kept them on if they hadn't also been damp.

"Alley?", I said, sitting up in bed. "We're not such a different size. Pass me something to wear in bed, I'm a bit cold."

She was still sitting on the end of the mattress. Still smoking the joint. But at that she stopped smoking and laughed. "No! You can sleep like that. I want you just like that, with nothing on."

Alley picked up the saucer ashtray and passed it to me. She still held the joint, though. I sighed. Theatrically, heavily. "OK. You too, then. Strip off and get in here with me."

She lifted her head high, walked over to one of the piles of clothes and dug out a large woollen cardigan. Shapeless. Like a sail without any wind. She put it on. And under cover of that, she stripped the rest off.

I saw very little of her. But there were those long pale legs again. My eyes took them in. And I knew, felt, inside, that they represented more than what we had so far done together. But that, somehow, was for another time.

A few moments later, we were both naked and both in bed, her cardigan being slipped off at the last second. In bed. Sitting up. Me holding the saucer full of ash for her and Alley still hanging onto that bloody joint.

"Let's tell each other something. Anything. A secret", she said, as she blew out the smoke again.

I laughed. "A secret? I'm not sure I have any."

Alley flicked ash into the saucer. "Oh, you must have. Of course you do."

I really didn't think I had any but I wanted to play, so I said, "OK, I'll tell you something if you tell me something first". And with that I tweezed the joint from her fingers, as she seemed reluctant to let me have any of it.

"Ha!"

"No", I said, taking a long draw on the joint, and holding the smoke in for a moment. "No. It's your game. Never mind 'ha'. You go first or I just won't play."

Alley lay back, her head now on the pillow. I glanced at her pale, lightly freckled shoulders but continued to sit up.

She lay there and, for a little while, her hand ran up and down my naked back as she said "Ummm" to herself a few times. Then she stopped stroking me. I turned to face her. She half hid under her hair. "Oh no. It's not fair. Actually, I can't think of anything. Why do I have to go first anyway?"

"OK, you don't", I said. "But if I tell you one, you have to tell me one afterwards." And with that I stubbed out the last two or three centimetres of the joint and lay back on the pillows beside her. "Promise me?"

"OK", she said. "I promise."

"OK then", I said. "Well... when I was small, I always used to hunt around in the house and find my Christmas presents."

Silence.

Somewhere in another room someone coughed very loudly.

"Was that it?" she said at last.

"No", I said, in truth still trying to find a secret to tell her. "And every year, without fail, I would find them. Sooner or later. And every year I regretted it. It always spoiled some of the surprise on Christmas day. But I couldn't stop myself from doing it anyway."

Alley laughed.

"But the one year", I continued, "It was almost Christmas day and I still hadn't found them. And then, I realised, that there was only one place where they could be..."

"Where?"

"Well, there was a big old suitcase in the airing cupboard in the bathroom. It was always there. It had been there for years. But this year, suspiciously, it was locked."

"They must have been in there then", said Alley, her eyes lighting up conspiratorially.

"Sure they were. But it was locked."

"So what did you do?"

"Well on December 23rd, very close to the day now, my mom popped out without her handbag. Only a few doors away to see one of our neighbours. I knew she wouldn't be long because she said so. So I rummaged around inside her bag and found the key."

"That was a bit risky", said Alley. "She could've come back at any moment."

I shook my head. "No, no. I didn't go upstairs with the key. I just pressed it quickly into some plasticine to make an impression of it. So that I could make a copy."

Alley laughed out loud. "Oh my god!", she said. "That is sooo devious. How old were you?"

I wasn't sure. "About 8 or 9, I think."

"So what happened then?" Alley asked. "Did you make a copy."

I nodded.

"Later on I melted some plastic from an old Airfix kit into the plasticine. And once it had cooled down I had a plastic copy of the key."

"Did it work?"

I shook my head. "No. It snapped off in the lock. First time of use."

Alley laughed out loud again.

"It was a very good Christmas though", I added, trying to salvage some pride from the tale. "I had no idea what my presents were going to be."

We looked at each other. Leaned towards one another, and kissed lightly on the lips.

"OK", I said. "Now it's your turn."

"No. I don't want to", she almost squeaked.

"You promised", I insisted. "Don't break a promise to me."

She smiled. That shy smile.

"Go on", I said, reaching under the covers and pinching her on the thigh. She yelped. "Tell me. Tell me something."

She sighed. "OK", she finally began. "I will tell you." And suddenly, to my surprise, her hand reached for mine and took it. Holding tight as she spoke. "When I was about 14... I don't know why I did it, there was no clear reason and I've often thought about it, but there wasn't one, I first tried on some women's clothes."

She stopped.

I didn't say anything. But right then I wished that we had another joint to light up and share.

Alley sighed a little again and then continued. "It was in my bedroom. And it, well it just felt right. I can't explain how it felt right, but it did. And then, soon, I don't know how long, I realised that I somehow felt safer when I dressed like that. Maybe older. More mature. Does that make sense?"

She looked at me. Those dark narrow eyes. But it was hard to see what she was thinking in the dim light of the small room.

"Yes", I said. "Older. Somehow safer. Because?"

Alley, still holding onto my hand, glanced up at the ceiling. Then back at me. "Because, at school, I was always being picked on. Because I was so pretty. Some boys called me a girl. But in the evening, if I put those clothes on, I felt older. Not a school boy any more, not even a girl. I felt like a woman. I felt above the kids at school who were just children, no matter how nasty they were to me."

I hadn't expected Alley to tell me any of this and, in a way, I felt stupid for telling her what I had told her about my Christmas presents. But, at the same time, I was very glad that she felt she could open up to me about such an important but delicate subject. "How did you move from there to going out dressed like that?" I asked quietly. "That must have taken a huge amount of courage."

Alley nodded. "I suppose it did", she said. "But I looked so good, so absolutely gorgeous, that I knew I could carry it off." She paused. "It began with those clothes, but then I practiced with make-up too. For hours. And I was so beautiful."

Which was true.

"Where did you go?" I asked.

"Clubs", she answered. "Night clubs. Bars. Wherever felt grown up. And while those boys at school were at home watching TV or out playing football or whatever and then being sent to bed, I was out going to clubs until the early hours of the morning."

I laughed. A little. It was impossible not to.

"Oh, I know", she said. "My school had no idea. I fell asleep in class a few times and got detention. But I didn't care. There's other stuff in life apart from school and exams."

"So in the day", I said. "You were pretty, but picked on. A boy. Picked on by people who, in the evening, in make-up, you totally outgrew. You just blew them away. Left them behind. They were children compared to you. And the more you did that, the more the gap grew?"

"Yes", she said. "Exactly like that." And she squeezed my hand a bit harder. Then let go of it.

"Wow", I said shaking my head a little. I looked at her. In the dim light of her bedroom, with just a few candles still flickering. She was a boy. I wasn't remotely interested in boys. She was a boy but she was really a girl in so many ways. It all seemed so fucking muddled. "You're so strong inside. I mean, you did that. That was so, I don't know, so... Just so brave."

Then, for reasons I couldn't really fathom, my eyes suddenly filled with tears.

Alley saw them immediately.

"Oh no", she said moving closer to me. "Don't". She raised herself up on one elbow, her blonde hair hanging down on her bare shoulders. She leant towards my face and kissed me on the lips. Then she lay back down on the pillow next to me again, but closer than before. "How do we all turn out the way we are, so

264

different from each other, when really in so many ways, we are all so very similar?"

"We are all so similar", I agreed. I had been thinking about that a lot. "All people. And all of us need a chance."

For a short while we lay in silence. Then it came to me. "At school, my background made me so secure", I said. "Poor, but secure. So eventually I could hide my inner self behind an outer self. Inside, I was so sensitive, too sensitive. And that's still how I am. But that outer self, it's just as real." I paused.

I suppose I expected Alley to say something, but she didn't.

So I continued. "That outer me. Fuck. I'd play up. Act out a part. But it was a real part too. And girls, in my case, loved me for it. I was good looking anyway and I get that all the time. But boys, most of them, males, they hate me. They call me... well, guess what they call me?"

"Arrogant", Alley said the word without hesitation.

"Yeah." I laughed.

"Arrogant, too sure of yourself, a show-off..." She laughed.

I laughed again. "That's it. All of that."

"I don't see any of that." She looked closely at me, an almost stern look crossing her face.

"Thank you", I replied and then added, quite sincerely, "I don't see that in you either. I can see why some people might say it, but I can also see beyond that so easily. I don't know why others can't."

"And you get the same?"

"Yeah."

"No", she said. "No, I don't see that either. I really don't."

I shrugged. "That's because this is your world. Your friends, clubs, all that. Back in my own world... well, I'm like you. Not the clothes. Nothing like that. But even recently, two people I know quite well, one of them said 'Oh him, he's got such a mouth on him sometimes'. That was the boy. And the girl, she said 'No. He's alright. He's just like the conductor of the orchestra. Always driving things on. I wish more of you were like that'."

Alley sniggered.

"Thanks for that", I said quietly.

"Sorry", she said, again touching my face gently. "But that's so similar to me. It really is. We were separated at birth. You and I. Actually some people hate me too. Quite a few. While others love me and defend me. To some, I'm irritating and a bitch. To others I'm wonderful and the only person to know."

"We're just the same really," I agreed.

I watched her face. She wanted to add something else and so I waited. And eventually she did. "But", she said at last. "I'm, well, like I am. You know." She paused. "And you're so similar, I mean, what I've seen these past weeks, how gentle you are, how caring. How we get on. The things we've done. I see a lot of myself in you and I know you feel the same too. And now what you've told me. But... look at me. Then look at you. You're straight."

I raised my eyebrows, but Alley cut me off.

"No", she continued. "No. You know what I mean. This is where we're different. We are different too." She paused. "Just look at me. I need some new heels. But you probably need new work boots with steel toe caps or whatever they're called!" She did that quick little giggle that I'd heard so often and loved so much.

The truth was that she was right. And we both knew it. We were somehow so similar. Too sensitive. Hiding inside an almost arrogant exterior. Also real. But somehow we were very different too. And Alley had gone far, far beyond what I'd done or ever could do. My own outer world was safe, easy. I was self-assured and that seemed to be a problem for some people, but it was nothing like what Alley had done. My own alter ego, for want of a better description, could live comfortably within 'normal' society. Whereas Alley had to redefine what was 'normal' in order to have an authentic life.

Those thoughts made me want to hold her.

But instead, for a little while, we just lay and talked about other things. Nothing serious, nothing very much. And eventually we crashed and went to sleep. Just sleep. Nothing else. No more than that. And maybe, at times, that was all both of us needed. After all, we were still only young. In some ways we were still kids. At times we were wild. At times lost in each other. But sometimes, I felt, we both just needed someone we could trust to be there. To be close. At such moments – and this was one – she was almost like a sister. The one I'd never had. And I was almost like her brother. The one she'd never had.

*

I don't sleep well any more. I haven't slept well for years. Something is missing. I know what it is but can't get it back. But those nights with Alley were very different. Lying in her room, in her bed, with her beside me, I could have slept forever. My sleep was childlike. There was something so totally reassuring about being there with her that nothing else mattered.

And as I woke up, after a bad night's sleep, in yet another hotel room, I just wished that whatever it was she had given me all those years ago had since been bottled and could now be bought in a pharmacy.

It wasn't the fault of the hotel. This hotel. This room. No.

The room was comfortable and so was the bed. It was me. A young Polish doctor once told me that I was not 'happy in my skin', by which she meant that I was not living the life I wanted to live. And she had been right.

But I had a lot less to complain about than very many others. So I didn't let myself dwell on it.

Instead, with a shrug, I got up, showered and went downstairs for breakfast. I had a lot more freedom than most. And I knew I ought to just be glad of that. And, often, I suppose I was.

After breakfast I planned to go for a walk. Not around the streets I'd once known so well, but instead along the river valley. But at first there was a pretty heavy drizzle. The receptionist assured me it was forecast to pass. All I had to do was wait.

So I waited.

I took my laptop and went into the bar, which was also, in part, a library.

How wonderful it must be, must have been, to have lived in such a grand house. To have owned a library stocked with leather books on all kinds of subjects. The leisure and money to study and learn. And as I cast an envious glance at the crowded shelves, I wished I had lived there two hundred years before.

But what was *that* book? Right there. Lime green. Thin. Hardback. Why did it stand out so much?

269

I looked at it more closely and tried to figure it out. On either side of it, other books leaned away. Each neighbour was a shade of red. So that was it. The reds contrasted with the green, the leaning away formed a sort of passageway. That was all it was. A clash of colours that caught the eye. No. It wasn't just that. There is more to life than we know. It stood out with some purpose, its cover almost waving to me. Hello. Look at me. Here I am.

I reached for it and took it off the shelf. What was it?

Andre Gide, 'Strait is the Gate'.

If I'd been the kind of person to have felt dizzy, I might have felt it then. I had a room upstairs which was supposed to be haunted. Was the library haunted too?

Wasn't this one of the very books that I had been reading in autumn 1981? Not the first time we met, not that time on the train, but afterwards, when I was making those trips back and forth to London, never really able to focus on it. Always putting it down and staring out of the window instead, my thoughts drifting forwards or backwards, to what Alley and I would do, or to what we had done.

Yes. I was sure of it. This was the same book. More than that, it was even the same edition. The same cover. The same cream coloured pages. Printed in the early 1930s.

I flicked through those pages. What had it been about? Did I remember it? Had I ever finished it? Maybe not.

I turned to my laptop. What was the book about?

Wikipedia would tell me. Or remind me.

And there it was: *'(Gide's work) probes the complexities and terrors of adolescence and growing up... and the misunderstandings that can arise between two people'*.

I pushed the laptop away. Just to hold that book again. Not open, but closed. I held it in my hand. A small volume. A gentle but clear weight.

No wonder I hadn't been able to read it. I was living those complexities and terrors myself back then. Afraid of the misunderstandings.

How strange. The very same book. Here in this library. Today.

And what would we say about that now? A coincidence. Ha ha. No. I'd given up believing in that empty notion years ago. The world was a much stranger place than we gave it credit for. Not being able to understand it was no excuse to file everything away under the blanket term of 'coincidence'.

I opened the book again and turned a few more pages, read a couple of lines. And then, as had happened so long ago, my mind wandered.

Away from the text and out into times past.

What had happened back then? The following morning? After she had told me her 'secret' and we had fallen asleep together.

If I remembered rightly, it had been a Thursday, and I'd had to go. Away from Alley. Home to another city. This one. Back to a world I didn't really feel in touch with. Not then, not any longer. Work. Even family and friends. By then, Alley already meant much more than any of that to me.

Then? Over the next few weeks, we'd met as often as I could manage it. Each weekend spent in London with Alley. My friends in Birmingham wondered where I was going, why I wasn't going out with them on Fridays or Saturdays. I'd just told them that I was seeing someone who lived out of town.

I'd also stolen days from work at random during the week. But money had gradually become a problem too, as it soon dwindled on train fares.

Hadn't I taken to fare dodging? Yes, I had. As frequently as possible.

We were sleeping together, too. Sharing a bed, anyway. As Alley had said one night – and I had pinched her pretty hard for it – we were 'almost lovers'.

Almost lovers...

I came to myself again, back to today, the present, and flicked through the book a little more.

Was it in here? Somewhere? In these dry pages? A memory of our time together?

No. Of course not. Everything that we were. How we laughed. Listened. How we touched. Kissed. Held. It had gone. Only memories remained. The words of the book hadn't changed. Yet where were we? Where was all that we had been? Life was brutal.

I put the book back on the shelf, careful to close up the gap between the two red books. Whatever the little green hardback had been trying to say, it had said it. There was no need for it to reach out to anyone else.

I sat down.

That Polish doctor. Yes. She had been right. I'd never been happy, in myself, of myself, not since I made such a bad mistake back then. The book knew that. And so did I.

But the past could somehow be changed. Changed to make our present better. Wasn't that what it had said in that philosophy text? The passage I'd read aloud to Alley on the train the day we first met?

I glanced out of the library window. The drizzle had finally stopped, as forecast, and the sun was even coming out. Walking beside my river today might be damp, but I would still be able to do it. All the same, I decided to leave it for another hour to give it a chance to dry off a bit. I ordered a coffee. It arrived and I watched a very thin haze of steam rising from the patio.

I turned my attention once more to my laptop. I had several business related emails to answer. Then a check of social media. A few 'what you up to?' sort of messages. A gig I could have gone to, in Birmingham itself, if only it had been a week earlier, but no, by the date given I would be back home in Ireland.

And there, finally, one other message. From an old friend. Alan Birch, now a professor at Aston University. It was a message I had been waiting for, checking almost hourly for, another reason for this visit to my home city. And I was relieved to see it.

I hadn't spoken to Alan for quite a while, but before making this sudden trip to Birmingham, I'd fired off a quick 'Can we meet up ASAP?' type mail. I hadn't said it was urgent, but I'd implied as much.

I felt a little guilty about that, all the more so as – during a short working stay in Ireland – he'd contacted me on a few occasions to suggest meeting up, and I hadn't taken him up on any of those invites, somehow not even finding the time to reply to him.

Yet here was a message from Alan full of friendship and quite insistent that he would make time, at short notice, so that we could at least meet up for a coffee.

When? I could do tomorrow morning. And so I wrote back suggesting as much and also took the opportunity to apologise for this and that, as friends sometimes have to do.

I was still working on the laptop when I received his reply.

Yes. We were on for a coffee tomorrow, around 11 am. I looked forward to it. Just like Megan, Alan was one of the people who I still knew and cared about – even though we hadn't seen each other for some time – from the 1980s. We'd once been very close. We knew a good deal about each other, but not everything.

But first, with the sun now out in a seemingly cloudless sky, an afternoon walking along by the river.

My river. A water I had once known like the back of my hand.

Built in the 1950s, during the post-war need for better housing, mine had been – and still was – a large suburban estate which lacked character. But it did have one huge advantage over other similar housing pile-ups; it was situated on the very edge of the city. The countryside still reached in for us all, and long fingers of grassland concealed a river valley full of kingfishers and Himalayan balsam. Overlooked by many, it had been adored by us as children.

Sadly, much of that precious humanising green space had been built over when I was in my late teens. But the valley itself remained. And thanks to successive councils and the hard work of local volunteers, not only was it intact, it had been replanted carefully and allowed to grow wild again in a much healthier way than before.

At the start of my walk, the old grey metal pontoon bridge was gone, and I missed it. It had been built as a temporary structure after a storm washed the concrete one away and, as children, we climbed all over the iron girders and often got into trouble for doing so. Yet it had still been there as recently as the year 2000.

From the new and rather characterless bridge, I climbed down onto the path that now ran along the river bank. Again, as children, that hadn't been there for us. We'd hacked our own paths through nettles and brambles. We'd waded knee-deep in mud and, quite often, waste. Waste made up of old bottles, boxes, saucepans, dumped newspapers, bits of carpet, even stolen car parts. Pretty much everything. And we found a use for all of it in one game or another. But it wasn't like that now. It was pretty. Easy going underfoot. A proper path, and probably better for it. Where once we had been told there was typhoid and tetanus, there were now willows, streamer weeds, butterflies and dragonflies. It was still my river but it could have been anywhere. It was calm, quiet, and almost tranquil. Rural despite being in the city.

How many times had we sailed sticks on this river, often remaining out until after dark to finish a race? How many times had we built mud dams here, only to cross the water and then throw stones at the dam until it broke?

As I walked along, it struck me that we were, slowly, mostly, improving our handling of the natural environment. At least on a local level. And that felt good. Places like this were better respected now than they had been in the 1970s. Conversely, especially here in the UK, there seemed to be less and less respect for the human environment, rushing to knock things down and cram the spaces left behind with ever smaller houses and ever bigger cars. And increasingly, or so it seemed to me, people sat in those oversized cars to avoid sitting in those undersized homes.

I rounded a corner, a bend in the river, and found myself by our 'Victoria Falls'. And the sight made me smile. I had quite forgotten these.

We had all called it the 'Victoria Falls'. We gave each part of the river its own name. How else could you arrange to meet a friend at a certain point? But really it was no more than a shallow weir, formed during the collapse of another concrete structure, a narrow walkway. In practice the rubble caused not much more than a crease in the water. But shallow or not, this had been one of the places where we'd spent most of our hours. Sometimes wading into the deeper water at this point, sometimes trying to bridge it, impossibly and always failing, with planks or logs, whatever we could find.

I began to feel a little drowsy and the remnants of an old brick pier above the weir provided an ideal spot to sit. As I did so, I noticed that a heavy grey cloud had appeared, seemingly from nowhere. The sky had become much darker. The air still.

I threw a handful of small stones into the water. Realising, as I gathered them that the ground was no longer moist. That surprised me, I hadn't expected it to dry out so quickly or so thoroughly.

Wasn't this the very spot where I'd once stopped, with the best-looking girl from my year, and we'd fooled around in the long grass, kissing each other as though there were no tomorrow? Her blouse undone. My shirt too. Was I remembering the right place? Yes. I was. An old man walking his dog almost literally stumbled across us and that had scared us both to death. From then on we'd stuck to kissing safely in bus stops, phone boxes or on the doorstep of her house, with her being told repeatedly to 'come in now'.

Fifty metres away from me, upstream, a man was walking a dog.

I watched him for a while, only able to see his silhouette, really, none of the details.

He bent for a stick. Threw it into the river.

I couldn't see his dog, as it fetched the thing, but as it came back out of the river, wet and jumping up with excitement, I could see it quite clearly.

The sight made me smile.

The build of the man, and even that of his dog, reminded me of my eldest brother, Joe.

Dead these last 10 years.

The thought, the impression, whatever it was, made me feel uncomfortable.

I was sitting just a short distance away from what we used to call the witches' tree.

Had there been something in that name?

Was that really my brother and his dog?

No. Of course not.

I sighed. Glanced up at the sky.

Overhead the thick grey cloud continued to shroud the afternoon sun, refusing to move.

I turned back to the water, not wanting to look at the man any longer. It felt for a moment as if the water had stilled, the weir fallen silent. Neither were the case but the sensation was unpleasant.

Why was I feeling like this?

That man. The dog. My brother Joe.

Joe had been my oldest brother. We hadn't met, nor spoken, for over 20 years. And for half of that time, he'd been dead. A heavy drinker and an even heavier smoker, his hard living had taken its toll quite early. He had died aged just 60. I was in the USA at the time and knew nothing about it. No one had been able to find me or contact me until the day before his funeral. I'd then done everything I could to be there, but hadn't been able to make it.

My other brothers, and their wives or partners, and children and relatives, put my absence down to our family feud. Joe, the oldest, and me, the youngest, having fallen out many years beforehand, our views, political and social, being simply irreconcilable.

I had never told anyone about Alley.

But I had wanted to tell him.

I had wanted to do that so very much.

At the time, and unaware of his faults, he was the person I most looked up to.

My big brother.

Still that cloud lingered above me.

I took my phone out of my pocket. Brought up Kate's number. I wanted to hear her voice. To have her make me laugh or smile. I dialled. There was no answer. So I texted her. Just something, anything, to bring me back into contact with the man I was today.

I waited. But there was no immediate response.

And so my mind drifted back to Joe.

If he had been here, now, today, if that man with the dog had been him? What would we have said to each other? What would I have wanted to say?

"Joe. I once dated a boy who dressed as a girl. More than that. I fell in love with that boy."

And so I made myself say those words, out loud, even saying them in the direction of the man and the dog, who were still playing with the stick.

And Joe? What would his response have been?

I had no idea.

And back then? If I had told him back then?

He might have killed me.

Or he might have shrugged his huge shoulders and told me that it was fine, it was alright to love someone. That he would look after me.

I shook my head.

If Alley had been a girl, I mean born a girl, unquestionably a girl, Joe and everyone else would have adored her.

But because she was a boy, a boy who was also a girl, the world would have been cruel. To her. And to me.

Or would it have been?

Would Joe have been cruel? As he could be.

Or would he have made everything alright?

I had no idea.

Should I have told him?

I had no idea about that either.

The man and the dog had gone, walked further upstream. I was now completely alone. Just me, the river, and the witches' tree.

"Joe!" I shouted. "Joe! Wherever you are! Alley was a boy and I loved her. Can you hear that?"

The cloud overhead finally moved away from the sun. And as it did so, the river seemed to start flowing again, the rippling noises of the 'Victoria Falls' once more audible.

The sun returned too, weakly at first, then with a harsh intensity.

I sighed. Then felt myself smiling. Unable to prevent it.

A huge smile. I had told him.

Now, today, here, beside my river, I had told Joe about Alley.

I rubbed my eyes. Imagined myself to have been asleep. And for a few long minutes, unable to think, walk or even move, I simply sat. The sunshine now warming me and bringing me back to life.

Suddenly my phone bleeped.

A text message from Kate. "Sorry missed U. Ring me ASAP if u need to. Love K xxx."

I called her straight back.

And for a few wonderful minutes, as we chatted, I felt wholly at peace with the world. My daughter's voice and her laugh connecting me with my present. The river and the words I had just said out loud connecting me with my past.

I promised to call again later that night.

Kate insisted there was no need.

But I told her I would do so anyway.

It was time to go.

A few minutes later, I reached the other bridge. The end of the section of the valley that I knew so well. That valley where, for so very many hours, I had played as a youngster. I stood on that bridge and thought about the years. How we think we make the best of them but, mostly, we don't. And then, before we know it, our time is all gone.

And yet, and yet... all those years ago, and for lots of reasons, I had told no one about Alley. I had believed myself alone. But now? Today? I'd told Megan, and somehow, just now, I knew it, I'd even told Joe.

Another sudden flash in the water made me smile. Fish! In my dirty old river. How wonderful. What an improvement that was. People used to say that there would never be fish in it. That it was impossible. But no, Nature – with a little help – was incredibly resilient.

I loved that little river. I could believe that it, and not blood, ran through my veins. I had a river flowing through me. Yes. I liked that idea.

9

Late September 1981. A Wednesday. I planned to go down to London again on Friday, and to be there for the weekend. In the meantime I expected to go to work. I meant to do the right thing.

But that morning? That Wednesday? No. My good intentions had no chance. It was such a perfect autumnal morning. Still. Quiet. Cool. Damp. Just birds singing. Almost no other sound. And as soon as I set foot outside the house, I could feel myself being pulled off course.

Then as I walked up the low wooded hill for my bus to work, I suddenly found myself entering a long mist, a white veil which wove itself back and forth through that old avenue of trees. Trees that were now turning rusted colours with their acorns and chestnuts covering the ground. Food for the grey squirrels that needed to eat well for the winter and who were already up and foraging for their breakfast.

From somewhere, deep inside, a voice arose. What the fuck was I doing going to work on a day like this?

And as if to emphasise that point, just as I reached the top of the hill, my bus rolled slowly past from right to left. I had missed it. I was two minutes late.

Two minutes meant a fifteen minute wait for the next one.

And five minutes late for work meant losing a whole hour's pay.

I hated that. It always seemed far too harsh.

Nevertheless I did still try. I stood at that bus stop and waited. I was going to go to work today, tomorrow too, and on Friday I would get my own back. I would be clocked in at work and go to London for the weekend. I had found my own way of getting past their system. That was what I told myself as I stood there. Waiting.

Waiting.

I noticed that the air was fresh too, fresh but not quite crisp. It was moist and beginning to smell of leaves and wet ground, earth and mud the sun wouldn't dry out for another six months or so. A smell I loved. Yet, somehow, a smell that also told me life was short. 'Do what you want to do, and do it now'. I didn't think I ought to be feeling like that at my age.

But still I waited.

I could see the road for quite a way. And there was no sign of the next bus. I could also see that the bus stop, down there, the one before mine, was already quite busy. I looked around. There was no one else up here at the top of the hill. Just me.

I watched a squirrel run up a tree as a big black dog appeared from nowhere. I was late. Late. Despite my best efforts.

Finally the bus appeared at the bottom of the hill. It stopped. Down there. In the distance. And that long queue of people boarded it. Then, slowly, it crawled up the road towards me.

But it didn't stop.

Instead the driver flashed his headlights, and as the bus drove by, I could see that it was already full to, and beyond, capacity. He couldn't stop. The bus was full.

That would mean another fifteen minutes to wait.

I sighed. Took out and lit a cigarette. And as I watched the blue grey smoke drift slowly up into that still cool morning, yeah, I could feel myself being pulled off course.

Fuck it. Work could wait. I would do something else.

And I knew what.

I wouldn't wait until Friday, I would go to London today.

I finished my cigarette and walked back down the hill, the mist gone already, its job done. It had enticed me. It had won. I knew that what I was doing was wrong. It was foolish. I was making a mistake. No one was expecting to clock me that morning. I would show up as absent. Not paid. Just absent. And I would need to explain that away at some point.

I knew all that.

More than that, as I walked back home, although there would be no one in just now, I knew I would have to explain myself there too. Write a note. Explain why I hadn't gone to work on time and had, instead, come home to grab some clothes so that I could spend another four or more days away, ostensibly at 'my friend's in Moseley'.

Half way down the hill, those thoughts became a little too much and I hesitated. Considered turning around and going once more for my bus.

But no. Something else was drawing me on by now. Something much more powerful than any job or any awkward explanations or anything rational. It was almost October. And the life that was calling felt real. Heavily and intensely real. Full of joy and madness. A place I wanted and needed to be. And nothing else came close.

Back home once more, I changed my clothes and wrote a note. I screwed the first one up and put it in the bin. The same with the second. The third one would just have to do.

Mom, I'm going to be away for a couple of days. Staying in Moseley again. Love. xx

It was only a partial story. But I figured that I had a few days to come up with a more complete one. Then, as the place was all mine, I stopped and sat around in the house, not wanting to have to move too soon. Taking it easy and eating and just watching the time tick by. About 10 am I went up to my bedroom. I set my alarm for 1 pm, lay down and fell asleep.

The alarm went off. Still the world was silent. Still the house was all mine. Still there was no one else in.

But I knew that they'd soon be back.

It was time to get moving.

Wash.

Dress.

Skinny black jeans. Bought last weekend. Tight fitting to show off my legs. I had good legs and a good arse. I'd been told that quite a few times. Once, on a sponsored walk for the school, we'd all been allowed to wear our own clothes instead of school uniform. I wore jeans. And a bunch of girls, from the year below mine, made sure they walked right behind me and my friends for the whole eight mile walk. Commenting, as often as they could, about 'that arse', 'those legs'. On another occasion, or so my brother's girlfriend told me, she and some other girls had sat in school watching us boys walk past. And it had been my arse that they'd all picked out as the best. Even their teacher had done so.

White t-shirt. Black Harrington. Old suede boots that really did need to be repaired. I rummaged around and found an extra bit of money. Not much. And that, too, was a mistake. And I knew it. After all, if I'd waited until Friday, as planned, I would've had a whole pay cheque. (A cheque? In truth we were paid in cash. Little brown envelopes stuffed with pound notes and coins.)

But it would have to do. It was too late now. I had been pulled off course. I had enough cash to get to London. Enough for some drinks. Some food. And more than that, who cared? I just wanted to be back there, with my girl once more.

I left the house and set off in a different direction. A short walk across my river valley, and beyond that past other factories. Buildings and chimneys which smelt of aluminium and seemed to stain all the privet hedges in the area with a fine coating of silver dust. Then homes. Plain red brick boxes very much like my own. And then, finally, a small and run-down local railway station built of grey concrete.

From here, direct, a train could take me to the capital. It would be slow. This was no express. It would stop at almost every station. Virtually no one chose to travel this way between cities. But I didn't mind any of that. Not at all. I didn't want to be in London too soon. Timing mattered hugely. And if the thing was empty, that meant I could relax more. Find my other self again at my own pace. I could just be me.

Me. Me, as the rattly old train took me slowly back to where that me really wanted to be.

London.

London.

At last.

And I walked along feeling apart from it all.

I might have crossed one road. I might have crossed ten. I didn't know. The driver of a black cab might have pulled over and wound his window down and sworn blind at me for walking straight in front of him. Or he may not have done that. I couldn't be sure.

It had been chaotic, the last few weeks, visiting at random. A day here. A day there. But this time it was different, and that felt wonderful. It was different because this time it was only Wednesday. Late afternoon. And I was going to stay until either Sunday night or Monday morning or beyond.

This would be the longest time Alley and I had spent together. And it had happened because an autumn mist lifted my spirits and made me do what I wanted to do – instead of what I was supposed to do. And that was what so much of this was really all about. Doing what we wanted to do. We were young. Hurting nobody. So why not? And that lesson should have been drummed into us at school, instead of Geography or History.

And that bus too. I ought not to forget that either. I'd missed the first one and the second one had been full. I felt that I ought to say thank you to each and every person who had filled up that bus. Or to the people who made buses that little bit too small. Or to something. Or someone. To whatever it was, whoever had caused this, I wanted to say thank you.

I was nearly there.

Suddenly I was also hungry and thirsty. And remembering the lack of food and drink or, worse, the condition of any food and drink, in the house, I decided to stop and get a bite to eat.

In the first shop their sandwiches looked awful. I didn't want crisps or chocolate or rubbish like that. I needed something good. Something that felt healthy. Something to suit my mood. But what? No. There was nothing in here.

Two doors further on, a small shop run by Asians offered a much better selection. There was fruit, there were spices, drinks, savoury foods... all kinds of things. I bought a mango, a couple of bananas, a small pot of something that I thought was a yoghurt but actually turned out to be cream, a half bottle of brandy, a packet of rolling tobacco... and then that was it. I had already used up most of my money.

Money. That annoyed me. It was great to be back here. But if only I'd waited a bit longer in Birmingham and collected my pay packet so that I had more to spend. I was cross with myself. How could I stay for so many days with Alley without any money? She had a lot less than I did.

I left the shop eating one of the bananas. Opened the brandy and took a mouthful of that.

Had I messed up the weekend by not waiting to be paid? Oh fuck. I looked at the odd collection of things I'd just bought and decided that Alley and I would share them. It was the least I could do.

As I neared the house, I could see that the front door was open and that a few people were sitting or standing around outside. One of them with bleached blonde hair. It was Alley, of course, and as soon as she saw me she stood up, threw her cigarette away, and almost ran to greet me.

"Wednesday?" she laughed, throwing her arms around me. Meeting in the middle of the road, hugging, we nearly got run over. "What day. When's day. It's only Wednesday. And you're here! How? Why? Tell me! Oh, but I'm so happy!"

We walked back across the road, arms around each other, my hands full, my pockets full. I said hello to some of the others and then told Alley about the mist and the bus and the note and how I'd wanted to be there for longer this time, longer than we'd ever managed before. And then I told her that I had already used up most of my money. And how that made me feel. And how I wondered if I'd messed things up by doing that.

"No", she laughed. "Oh god, no. Guess who did a 'shop' on Monday and sold enough lipstick and mascara for us to go out for a whole week? I've never had so much cash. If you hadn't shown me how to get it... what a difference!."

From nowhere, really, and for no great reason, a whole coil of tension had settled onto me; money, feeling that I ought to have waited, that note... and suddenly, with those words, it was lifted. Gone. She could do that. So often. Just one reason why being there mattered so much.

We hugged again.

By now the others had gone in. But Alley and I continued to sit for a while on the step. I took out the tobacco and rolled us both a cigarette. We smoked them in silence. There was something about the air that cool autumn day. A moment to share. But a moment to share without speaking.

A short while later. Indoors. In her bedroom. Strangely it wasn't cold. It had felt colder in there a month before. Why was that? Is it that the shock of September is greater than the gradual arrival of winter? It must be something like that. We acclimatise. Adapt to anything.

So no, it wasn't cold. But between us we drank most of my half bottle of brandy anyway.

We smoked too many cigarettes, too. We smoked them as we sat on her mattress. Sat and talked and listened, listened because that matters too, listened as we told each other about what we had been doing for the last week or so. And in between our words we also spoke with our smiles and our agreements, our odd slight touches of fingers and we heard how, somewhere, somehow, in the events, we had each been missed by the other.

Then Alley unfolded herself from the mattress, got up and sat almost cross-legged on the floor, fiddling with clothes as she often did. Examining, talking, sorting. Holding them up and laughing with me. Chucking one item aside. Carefully refolding another and putting it away.

We did that for a while.

Time passed. It was now dark outside.

We didn't care.

Then, slowly, she began to get changed. I didn't even notice at first. Talking, sharing, just took over any visual imagery. But at one point I realised that she was now wearing a long black skirt with fishnets underneath, and trying to find her black leather heels. Shoes which had disappeared half under the chest of drawers. She reached for them with her stockinged feet and pulled them towards her and then put them on.

"What top shall I wear?" she asked herself out loud.

I looked at her. She had on a thin grey cardigan. "Wear mine!" I said. My white t-shirt, the one I was wearing. We were almost exactly the same size. I was a little bit bigger around the shoulders and chest. But not much. Not back then.

She raised her eyebrows. And then laughed. "Why not!"

"Give me your long one, the one with the screen print," I said.

It was on the floor, near the foot of the mattress. She found it and threw it to me. In turn I took off my t-shirt and threw it to her. I pulled on her shirt. Really it was too small. Clearly I was bigger than I had thought. Or she was smaller. So I took it off again. Searched around and found a baggy black cardigan and put that on instead.

"What else did you bring with you?", she asked suddenly. She got up, picked up my jacket and emptied out the pockets. All that was left was the cream and the mango. She had eaten the other banana sitting on the step.

"Nosey", I said.

She threw both things onto the bed, then seemed to lose interest and turned back to her mirror and started applying some make-up, getting ready to go out.

I watched her for a few minutes and then thought about making a coffee. Then I saw the mango and the cream on the bed. And instead of coffee, I went to get something we could eat those with.

I came back with two small plates, one of which was chipped, and a couple of teaspoons.

"Are we going out"? I asked as I sat down on the bed.

She finished applying some mascara. Widened her eyes, then turned back to me. "Well, yes. But not if you don't want to?"

I didn't want to.

Alley had borrowed the tape player again, but we were listening to Radio 1, the evening show, which was playing stuff that I liked even though I didn't know who it was by.

"So what shall we do instead?" I asked. And even as I asked it, I felt the answer. Felt it. Since the brandy I hadn't been cold. Yet my own words had just given me a shiver. I knew what I wanted to do. I wanted to get closer to my girl. I missed the touch of her soft skin and the feel of her lips. What shall we do instead? *That* was what we should do.

Alley rose. Blinked her eyes again a few more times to stop the mascara from sticking and sat down next to me on the mattress. She was wearing my white t-shirt now and while it didn't exactly swamp her, it did look bigger on her than on me, and she looked cuter than ever.

I passed her a plate and one of the spoons. "Let's eat these before they go off", I said.

"Oh, mmm, I love mangoes", she said. She took the small pot of cream with her and sat back on the rickety chair.

Life?

Life can take unexpected turns.

Strange events can change expected events into something quite different.

The unusual can then happen.

And sometimes, it's almost as if it were fated to do so.

As Alley opened that little pot, she suddenly squealed and jumped up, taking the pot with her but allowing the cream its liberty to travel in another direction.

Out of the container. And downwards.

"Oh my god!"

"What is it?"

"A spider, oh my god, it's big enough to put a saddle on", she gasped. "It ran right across my leg..."

I laughed. I looked. I couldn't see anything.

"I'm alright, it was just the shock of it, really. That's all."

"Well it's gone", I said at last. "It's alright, it's gone. It's already gone. It was more scared of you, I think."

Alley frowned. And turned the little pot over in her hand. "The cream has all gone too", she said.

She was right.

It had.

But where?

We both looked down.

"Oh no. Uck." Her right ankle, foot and shoe were all covered with fresh cream. "Oh no."

I laughed again. None of the stuff had landed on the floor. She had somehow managed, inadvertently, to catch the whole lot.

"Oh no. Help me... " she began.

"Aww," I said, still smiling. "What can I do? At least it didn't go all over the place."

She paused. Looked at me. Looked at the cream. Then she looked back at me again. Her eyes flashed and a naughty smile passed quickly across that gorgeous face. "I need it cleaning off."

"What with?" I said. "Just take off your shoe, and the stockings too."

She sat back down in the chair, and I thought she was going to do just that. I threw the mango up in the air and caught it once or twice.

"Help me!" The words were the same but her tone had changed.

I tilted my head on one side and looked at her.

"Clean me off."

"I can't do anything", I said, in all innocence. Meaning what I said.

She nodded. That smile returned. One that I only vaguely recognised.

"Clean it all off for me." That was almost an order. Not a request.

I opened my mouth to say something.

But she stopped me. And just pointed. At the cream.

"Here!"

What a strange world I'd suddenly entered. Where had that big spider suddenly come from? What was life doing? What games was it playing?

"Get down." She licked her lips and then laughed.

I glanced back at those dark eyes, trying to see into them. But the heavy mascara kept them shielded. "You bastard", seemed to be the only words that were suitable.

She didn't say anything.

Just pointed her shoe towards me.

Since we'd first met, from somewhere, I didn't know where or why, I'd had a kind of fascination with her legs, and with those leather heels of hers. With the black nylon encasing her legs too. What was that? I didn't know. So how did she know? She always took everything in. That was the truth.

She lifted her ankle a little higher. Off the floor. "Hurry up, it's running into my shoe."

I wanted to slap her arse. I really did. But I also wanted to do what she told me. And she won. So I leant forward, my face level with her black nylon clad ankle.

"Clean it", was all she said.

And for a few minutes – I wasn't sure how long – I did exactly what she had told me to do. My tongue ran all over her. Around her ankle. Onto her foot. Tasting nylon and Alley and cream in equal measure.

Then I sat back. Looked up at her and licked my lips.

She examined her shoe. Her ankle. Turned them around.

"That's not bad", she said. Then she looked at me. "But take that cardigan off, too. I want you topless."

"You're loving this", I said. But did as she asked anyway.

She shrugged. "Got to clean them somehow."

She looked down at her shoe again.

"And my shoe?" she said.

Suddenly I noticed something. Her voice had changed. Subtly. And I knew why. She had tried to be in control here but wasn't really in control any more than I was. I could win this game too. That was what I thought. So I took her shoe off.

She lifted the little pot and poured the last of the contents into her leather shoe. Then she tilted it up and pointed it at me.

"Open your mouth."

I did as she asked. But now I did it because I knew I wanted to. In one way I didn't want to stop. The feeling was strong. Sexy. But now a part of me was also thinking 'You bastard. I've got you too'.

She tipped the cream from her shoe directly into my mouth. And then, dropping it onto the floor, she gave me one of her 'I've won' smiles.

I licked my lips. Swallowed the cream. And shook my head.

Yeah. This was working both ways. I liked that. And if I'd had one of her wicked smiles, I would have given it to her right then.

I picked up the shoe. Showed her the inside. She looked at it. Took it off me. "Clean enough", she said, with a naughty smile.

"You taste very nice", I said turning towards her. Licking the last of the cream off my lips and still kneeling on the floor in front of her.

"Oh thank you", Alley laughed, but it was a nervous laugh, an aroused laugh. "And did you prefer the taste of me or the taste of the leather, I wonder?"

I half stood. Kissed her, closed mouth. But full on the lips.

"Mmm. Not sure", I said.

She giggled. I smiled.

I kissed her again. And she pushed back, her teeth biting at my lower lip. It was a long kiss. The longest since I had arrived. I loved the feel of her soft lips, of her tongue, the sensation of her desire. Mine too.

We came apart for breath.

"I thought we were going to have the cream with the mango", she said.

"There's still some left", I replied, and I reached for the nearly empty pot. Ran my finger around it and then sat back on the floor. Licking the cream off my fingers.

"Give me your knife", said Alley, finally moving from the chair to sit on the mattress just to my side.

I was shocked. "My knife?"

She nodded. "Yes. Don't think I don't know you have one. You always have one with you."

She was right. I always carried one. A lock knife. It looked like a flick knife but it wasn't one. Sometimes I carried it in the pocket of my jeans. At other times in my coat. And that was where it was right now.

I wiped my finger around the inside of the pot of cream again. Reached for Alley and smudged the last of it onto her mouth. She licked it off. Then I found my coat, and with sticky fingers, I took the knife out of my pocket, gave it to her and knelt on the floor just in front of her.

Alley took the knife and very quickly cut some chunks from the mango. "We used to have these when I was little." She smiled. "I've always loved them." Even though she had cut the thing quickly and easily, in just those few movements she'd covered her fingers with both fruit and juice. "But they're very messy", she added.

She tossed my knife onto the floor and held out a piece for me to eat.

I shook my head.

She held it still.

"No", I said.

"No what?"

By way of answer I ran my hand slowly across my bare chest. "You too, first", I said. "Take your top off as well."

She sighed. But stripped her top – my t-shirt – off anyway. Then she picked up the mango again and held it out for me once more.

I wanted to eat her. But for now the fruit would have to do. So I took the piece she offered me and ate it.

She shook her head. "No, not like that. We have to share it." She put a second, larger piece in between her teeth. Gripping it there. And maybe inadvertently squeezing it as she did so.

"You're gonna get covered in that juice", I laughed. And she was. She already was. But by way of reply she just sort of grinned at me.

I knew what she meant. We each knew what the other meant so often. So I leant towards her and bit the mango, the big piece that she was holding in her mouth. I took a chunk of it. Directly from her teeth. Bit into it. Tore it away.

And as I did so the juice and the fruit went everywhere.

Every. Where.

I leant back. Gulped it down.

There was yet more of the mango in her mouth.

"Don't you dare swallow it", I said. "That's mine as well."

Again I leant towards her, Alley still sitting on the edge of the mattress, me more or less kneeling on the floor in front of her. Still wearing my skin tight jeans but nothing else. We half kissed as I ate the mango from between her teeth.

As I swallowed the last of the fruit, we didn't move apart. Juice running into her mouth, into my mouth, down onto our bodies, down onto the mattress, we just carried on kissing. Tongues twisting. licking juice and teeth clashing as we did so.

Then we did pull apart. "It's going everywhere", Alley laughed.

And it was. It really was.

I leant back on my knees. Stretching. Leant back and looked at her. I picked up what was left of the fruit and cut myself a slice of it as I did so.

There she was. Mine. Right in front of me. A topless teenage boy in a skirt and black fishnets. Shoes lying on the floor somewhere behind me, cleaner than they had been before.

I looked at the angles of her body. Those lines along the neck which we all have. I didn't know their names. But they added to her gorgeousness. Her slim shoulders. Arms on the right side of thin.

I bit into the piece of mango I had just cut, watching a fine long line of juice running down her neck as I did so. It would keep on going. "Mmmm", I said. I was still eating and couldn't make any real words come out.

"Oh no!", she shrieked suddenly. "Stop it. It's going down my back!"

I took hold of her by the top of her left arm, and turned her towards me. I stared at her thin boyish frame. Transfixed by her. For a moment more I hesitated. Watching the juice pool on top of her lightly freckled shoulders and then, slowly, but surely, begin to run down her long slender back.

"Stop it!" Alley reached a hand to try and stop the flow. But I wouldn't let her do that. I was stronger than her and held her hand captive.

"Say please", I said, finally able to speak.

"Pleaaaase", she begged, giggling as she did so.

One more longing look at her pale shoulder and then I licked the pool of mango juice clear away. My tongue didn't stop. It continued down, along her back. As far as the liquid had already run. Tasting both her skin and the sweet fruit as I did so. Unsure which flavour I enjoyed the most.

"Oh fuck", she moaned. And that wasn't any kind of complaint about the juice running down her back.

"Oh fuck", she said again, turning towards me and putting her arms around my neck and pulling me to her.

Face to face we rolled onto the bed.

I don't think, I can't see, I don't understand how either of us could have been able to breathe. How was it possible? We were buried so deeply into each other at that moment, that it must have been impossible. Yet we did breathe, somehow. We must have done.

A few minutes. Then we pulled apart again. "Jesus Christ", I said. "I feel so weak when I'm with you. This is just not possible. How are you doing this to me?"

She looked back into me. Those dark, narrow, beautiful, black outlined eyes. Melting into me. "God, I fucking adore you", she said.

Yet either of us could have said either thing. I knew that. And she knew that too.

I leant into her again. Like two parts of one machine, meshing together.

And we stayed that way for a long long time, her 'oh fuck' still sounding clearly in my head. She could have read the most beautiful poem ever written, and, right then, it wouldn't have sounded as good as those two words and the way she had said them. 'Oh fuck' meant 'I'm losing it'. It meant 'I want you'. It meant 'Nothing else matters'. It meant 'Now'. Oh fuck. Oh fuck. And I felt it too. The very same. As we kissed and burrowed into each other.

Somehow, though, I did manage to pull away again. I sat up. I hadn't quite finished with this girl or that mango yet. And I watched as she wriggled out of her nylons.

Still the skirt. Wearing something underneath. But now no more than that.

I sliced the remainder of the mango into segments, without peeling the skin off. Thin, orange-like segments.

"Lie back. Lie still", I said. "Tilt your head up a bit."

She did so.

I lay next to her.

The first segment of the fruit I squeezed into her mouth. The pout parted. The mouth opened. Her tongue licked and swallowed.

We kissed. I wanted to taste that same piece too.

The second segment I took myself. And with my mouth directly over hers, I bit into it. Not so hard that the fruit exploded and went everywhere, but hard enough so that the juice ran from my mouth and straight into hers.

Again that tongue. Again licking it. Swallowing.

Again we kissed. This time licking each other's lips dry.

"Where else?", I almost whispered.

"Fuck off", she replied, in less than a whisper, her hands pulling me down to her mouth again. "Never mind the mango. Just fucking eat *me*."

God knows we were messy at that moment. And God alone knew how we would ever get clean again. But none of that mattered. What mattered was doing as she had asked. I bit her lips. Bit at her teeth. I moved my mouth to her neck. Bit at that too. Hard. Then harder.

She squirmed around underneath me. And I felt her hips rise towards my body. Rise towards me. Then fall away. Rise towards me. Fall away.

Her shoulders were still glistening. With mango juice? Was it where I had licked her? I couldn't tell. Either way I ran my tongue all over them again, drying her skin with my breath and my mouth.

A half turn of my head, and her naked chest was right in front of my face. She pushed my head down onto it. There was no taste of fruit juice there. Just naked boy. I knew to be gentle. Mainly. Mostly. It was more erotic that way. Lick carefully. Lightly. Kiss the same. Then, every now and then, that bit firmer. But only briefly. Then gently. And on, and on, and on.

"Oh fuck." Those two words again. Her hips rose and fell.

This was a boy who needed to find some relief, and quickly. I knew it. I felt it too. But I wasn't quite at that same point.

Still teasing her chest. I moved across. Softly biting her. And as I did so I let my hand slide slowly down her body. Just stroking her hard flat stomach.

I lifted myself away from her a little.

Her narrow dark eyes had become almost metallic. Blurred. Soft-focused. Full of passion. Full of life. Burning into me in a way that sex itself could never achieve. This was so much more than that. This was some kind of universal connection. And we both knew it.

My eyes and hers were the same just then. She nodded. Not able to speak, that was my impression. My hand still circled her stomach, but a fraction lower now. At the waistband of her skirt.

I paused. Stopped completely. For all I could make her feel like this, as she could do to me, I didn't know whether or how to ease that skirt away from her body. I tugged gently at the waistband. She understood. Wanted me to. Her shoulders lifting off the bed a little, she found the energy to undo it and push it down.

That was all I needed. I pressed her shoulders back onto the bed. And her eyes closed as she fell. They closed as my hand stroked her stomach one long last time and then went slowly down and down until my fingers wrapped around her.

And then? A different kind of stroking. Slow. And deliberately erratic at first.

Alley's eyes widened. Not something they did often. And I saw it. And I laughed. I leant forward to her and whispered in her ear, "Being a boy too", I said. "I know just how to do this, you bastard."

Those eyes widened a little more. "Bastard yourself", she said back to me. Hoarse. She wriggled a bit too. A small, but not very determined effort to move me away from her.

I shook my head. Pinned her down more firmly. "No", I whispered. Also hoarse. "You're mine. Right now. And forever. And I'm going to make you pay for that cream earlier."

I scratched her with the sharpest of my finger nails, and pressed it into her. Just there. Just where it needed to be.

She pulled my face back up to her own and took my lower lip in her mouth and bit me. And then I touched her more. In ways that a woman might take a lifetime to understand.

I moved away. A little. Tasted blood in my mouth. "Bitch", I said, smiling.

Moaning, teeth gritting, I watched her every expression with an almost sadistic pleasure. A wicked smile.

312

My hand could do whatever it wanted to do. I didn't even need to look.

My eyes were enjoying her face too much to move.

Again she tried to lift off the bed. Again I stopped her. She was strong. But I was stronger.

Her "No", became "Nooo", became "Nooooooo", the words groaned rather than spoken.

Then I felt it. There is a moment where you know. And I knew. I knew that just one more quick hard stroke, that bit firmer, would have her and me both glistening again. But this time it wouldn't be with fruit juice.

I hesitated. Then gave her exactly that. And she came. And she screamed as she did so.

It wasn't an ordinary scream.

It was brought up from deep inside. And that, I knew, wasn't down to me. I knew that. That, that much, that scream, that was wholly down to her. However good I was, had been, even I couldn't have brought so much out of that boy just then. No. This was more than even making love. This was more than even connecting at some deep and unknown level. This was a fusion of life and death. Of all pains gone and all pleasures to come. From everywhere. All at once.

God. The whole house must have heard. Maybe even the whole street.

Moments passed.

Silence.

"Jesussssss", finally one of us hissed. I think it was me. But it may have been Alley. Perhaps it was both of us.

Those seductive dark eyes flashed. Quite literally, they flashed. A light shone from them. I'm sure of it. They flashed at me. And burned the memory of it all into the very back of my own eyes. An image I could never forget.

"You", she shook.

I leant towards her. Caressed her forehead. "No", I said, and I shook my head as I said that. "No. That was you."

"Us." She said. Barely getting the word out.

She was right.

It had to be us.

Both of us.

It was what we were together.

I looked at her. Felt one with her.

Her body was limp. Her voice, by now, was barely audible.

I lay down beside her, trailed a finger across her wet stomach.

She turned to me, the mascara running, her eyes overflowing. And that made mine do the same. But when she did finally speak, it almost scared me. "You. Don't forget", she spoke slowly, very slowly. "I'm a boy too. I know how to do all that as well."

It was the sexiest threat anyone had ever made. Ever.

I awoke in the morning to find a boy named Alley tucked in next to me wearing a long cotton nightshirt. She must have got cold in the night and climbed out of bed and found something to wear. I wished she hadn't done that. I had woken and wished she was still naked. But I didn't mind too much. She was warm, fast asleep and looked as pretty as a girl could ever be. And to my eyes – not for my own deceit, quite the opposite, out of respect for her – she was just that, a girl.

Over the next few days we found and lived our habits once more.

We walked in the park. A squirrel ate a piece of apple from my hand. Alley called me Dr Doolittle. She said that animals all seemed to love me. I agreed. I felt that most people did not.

We sat in the cafe. I ate little and drank less, because it was her money and not mine. She spotted that and told me off. And as I sat back down at our table after a visit to the loo, I found a huge toasted sandwich waiting for me. I leant across the table and kissed her on the cheek. Then I ate it. I was ravenous.

We visited the pub. But it was shut. For good? We weren't sure. So we went to another, which was softer, cleaner, low lights, muzak, superficially so much more the kind of place I expected Alley to want to sit in – and we both hated it. We drank a strange cocktail and left most of it, keeping the plastic mermaids from off the top as a memento.

Friday night. Saturday night. These nights were more serious.

I nearly died of old age waiting for Alley and the others to sort out their make-up and finish squabbling over the hairspray.

As for the number of costume changes? They must have been on a par with those being carried out in the nearby theatres that very night. Alley appeared in a jacket with a velvet collar. I pulled a face. That went into the pile on the floor. The leather biker jacket was worn for a couple of minutes, before that, too, went into the pile because Viv said that someone else was going to be wearing one they'd bought in Camden Market earlier that very day.

In truth I could almost have gone up to Birmingham, on a train, collected my pay packet, and caught a train back to London in the time it took them all to sort out what they were going to wear and ensure they didn't clash too much with one another.

And it was like that on both nights at the weekend.

The second evening, the Saturday, about 7.30 pm, I stripped off a little and got under the quilt with my book.

"Aren't we going out?" Alley asked me.

"Sure", I said. "In the meantime, while you all get ready, I thought I'd finish my book."

She took it out of my hand. Looked at it. "You're only about half way through it!"

I laughed. And she threw it back at me.

I loved the clubs. I loved the madness of it all. And I was envious that Alley had this, and had already been living this way for a long time. She was so much more grown up than I was in some respects. More grown up? Yes. Although in some ways she was less so and could be a bit of a brat too. So when someone spilled her drink, which, to be fair, she had been wafting around, so it wasn't really the spiller's fault, she let go a pretty hostile few sentences. "Don't be so horrible to people", I told her. And by way of reply she rubbed her nose against my cheek. It was sweet. It was also childlike.

In one way, I hated it when a night out finished, the buzz over for another week or whatever. I loved being there with her, watching her performance and laughter. Watching her fire off quick sarcasms. Watching her check my face to see if I was going to tell her to stop it. All of it. And to have it end? It felt a little like Christmas morning after the presents have been unwrapped

But then again... I didn't hate it. Not really. Because once the night was over I knew it meant that Alley and I would soon be back in our own space. Just the two of us. And that was so very much better.

The following weekend I went down to London again. I'd tried to steal a day from work midweek, but our 'clocking-in' racket had almost been foiled. So we'd all agreed to leave it alone for a while. I hadn't wanted to agree, because that meant I would only be able to see Alley at weekends. But I'd had no choice and in the end, reluctantly, I had said yes, it made sense to stop doing it for a few weeks. Temporarily. Then I could go back to seeing my girl as often as possible.

"It'll only be for a little while", I told Alley. She was sitting putting her make-up on again.

"How long?" she asked.

"A few weeks?"

She pulled a face. I hated it too. But there it was. I had no choice.

I had no choice? Time together. Not enough of it. It was the biggest issue we had, really. What was going to happen unless I moved to London? How long could we go on seeing each other on odd days and weekends? I guess we both knew that was a problem. A huge problem. But neither of us wanted to address it there and then. I told myself that lie – 'I have no choice' – and Alley knew the truth but didn't want to press it either. So instead I just told her that I was sorry, and gave her a small kiss on her neck and then sat down on the mattress to read my book while she went and squabbled with some of the others about hairspray again.

Maybe the vaguest of voices spoke to me. Inside. 'No, it *is* up to you to do something about this. You *do* have a choice.' But it wasn't loud enough. My million-year-old man had gone on holiday and I was all alone. Aged 18 and not smart enough. If only I had been.

In the end it was just as if nothing had been said and half an hour later we were play-fighting on the bed and she pinched me so hard that I bit her hand. It hurt her. I apologised. And we started to kiss, only to stop as the door was pushed open and Viv came in to scold Alley for using up the last of the hairspray again.

After Viv left the room, Alley sat up. Her hair was all over the place from our fooling around. "I'm going to go out with it like this", she said. It looked as if she had been making love for hours. And we both laughed. It looked great. Better than ever.

It was a good night out. And she was very full of herself afterwards once back in her room. Which I loved to see and hear. Shy and sensitive, yes. Feeling and loving, yes. But such a show-off too, and when she did that she shone, quite literally, her confidence radiating throughout her whole being.

On Saturday afternoon we walked in the park in the rain. Just the two of us, or so it seemed, everyone else hiding indoors or in cars or ducking from one shop to another.

And then on Saturday evening, we went out to a club. But money was short for everyone and the night lacked the buzz of the evening before. It felt flat. So Alley and I left the club a little earlier than everyone else and went back to hers.

And then it was already Sunday. Already Sunday and we both knew that I would be leaving that evening. And that it would be a full week before we could meet again. Neither of us mentioned it. Not directly. But it was there. And we both felt it. And I guess that was why we were both already thinking ahead. Alley much more so than me.

"I've been thinking", Alley was lying with her head on my shoulder. "Y'know what I'd love to do?"

I stroked a lock of her blonde hair away from her eyes where it had fallen across them and hidden her from me. "What?"

"When you come here, really, this is my world. Always. You come here to my world."

That was true.

"I want to come and see yours", she continued, lifting her head off my chest and looking at me with those beautiful, heavy, dark eyes. "I want to see who you are. Back there, I mean."

I didn't reply. But I'm sure I smiled. In fact I nearly laughed because she sounded almost like a child asking to be bought a bicycle or something.

A finger touched my cheek. "Yes", I said. Then added more enthusiastically, "Yes. Definitely. I'd love that".

Alley was happy. "Me too. I'd love it too. Let's do that next week? This next Friday? You can take me to your places. Show me around. Show me off. Just look at me!" She tossed her head.

This time I did laugh. "You vain cow", I said.

She laughed too.

"OK", I agreed, "Yes. I love the idea. I'll sort us out places to go. Things to do!"

"Yes!" she said. "Oh yes! Oh it will be lovely."

For a while we talked about it, Alley trying to get me to say where I would take her. Me not sure and not telling her that.

Then she wondered if there was anywhere to get another pair of stylish high heels. I told her that there was.

"How will we do it?" she asked.

"What do you mean?"

"Where will we meet?"

Where did everyone meet in Birmingham? "At the bottom... no, at the top of the ramp. By the railway station."

She frowned at that. "The top of the ramp? What ramp? How will I find it?"

"Ask someone."

"OK. What time?"

"7.30. Friday evening."

We lay down, her head back on my chest. It was still Sunday. I would still have to leave in a few hours time. But at least we had a plan for the next time.

We were both happy about that. And I started to fall asleep.

"Where will we stay?" she asked at last.

I had no idea. "I'll sort something", I said.

10

Work. Bloody work. I had no right to complain. Not really. No right at all. I had been paid for so many hours of work when I hadn't actually been there. But why was it on Friday – and this Friday of all Fridays – that there had to be a special meeting for all the apprentices? And why did it have to be held after work?

4 pm came. The time we usually finished. But instead of going home, we were all to wait around.

4.15 pm came. And I was already clock watching. Even if I'd had no plans for the evening, I would have been annoyed. But this evening? With the plans I had? I couldn't believe it.

4.30 pm. And finally Mr Wood arrived. He was the kind of man who loved the sound of his own voice. How long would this go on for? What was it about?

Oddly, the meeting turned out to be just good news. Very good news, really. It was all about bonuses. The scheme was changing and we were all going to get a new bonus. Higher. Which meant more money. So it was great news. And all we had to do was sign a form that said we agreed to the new terms for the bonus.

I already had a pen in my hand. But then everyone else started talking about the new scheme. And some of them even asked questions. I looked up at the clock again. 'OK', I thought. 'It's great news. Now please let's all stop talking about it and sign the papers and go home. I need to eat, wash, get changed and then make my way to town. I have a very special date at 7.30!' It was already creeping towards 5 pm. Fucking hell.

Eventually I was in front of the piece of paper.

"Good news isn't it?" said Mr Wood.

"Yes. Yes", I said. "It's great."

"Oh, you don't look all that happy."

Inside I thought 'Shout. Shout. "I'm meeting a gorgeous boy in two hours. I don't give a fuck about anything else"'. But instead I merely said, "Yes. Of course I am. It's very good news". Good. Good news. Very good. Great. The same few words kept being bandied around as if we had all just, collectively, discovered them and were now trying them for size.

I signed the form and turned to go. Was briefly stopped by one of the other apprentices, then made my excuses and left. "See you all on Monday!"

Finally outside, and with the time quite comfortably after 5 pm, I didn't even wait for a bus to take me home. I knew that if I walked, it would take 30 minutes exactly. Whereas if I waited for the buses, running late on a Friday, I might still be at the bus stop in an hour or more.

So I walked.

Home.

"You're late?", my mom said.

"Yup."

"Any problems?"

"No."

"I heard someone in the shop talking about you getting a new bonus at the factory. That's good isn't it?"

"Great."

"Do you want some dinner?"

"Yea... no thanks." Suddenly I realised I was so nervous and so excited that I had no appetite at all. I couldn't have eaten a thing.

I ran upstairs, stripped as fast as I could and threw my work clothes somewhere. Had they landed on the cat? No. She was fine. But she gave me a stare Alley would have been proud of.

The bathroom was empty, thankfully. And I had a quick wash. But where was my aftershave? I sighed. There was none left. And then I wondered where Alley was right now. Was she on the train already? She was going to be there, wasn't she? Wasn't she?

Such thoughts saw my nervous tension go up another level. I pushed them away. Get changed anyway, I told myself. Just do it.

I did.

And then I found a little bit of cedarwood oil. The last little drop. I had no aftershave but cedarwood was nicer anyway. I'd smell great. Perhaps not everything was against me?

Downstairs and the clock had already raced on to 6.30 pm. I had only one hour left.

I almost ran out of the door. Almost. But not quite.

Then up the hill in the dark. Past the trees. A monster hidden behind every one. Or so my Dad had once told me.

A fucking bus going past. How long would I have to wait for the next one?

I stopped.

Wait, I told myself firmly. Wait. This isn't a bad thing. None of this is. I'd had the wrong attitude so far. I was getting wound up. Tense. This was all wonderful. So bloody wonderful. Here I was, on a cold October night, looking good, going out to meet the most beautiful person I had ever known. And she, he, she was mine.

That thought lifted my spirits.

It was like a rush of pure adrenalin.

How *good* was all this? How much was this *really* like being alive?

Oh my beautiful trees. The lessons you teach me! Thank you for slowing me down again and letting me see. This was all something to savour not stress about or wish away.

So I stood and waited, searching for the pale yellow lights of the next bus, but no longer feeling rushed. No longer impatient. Just loving it. Loving every fucking moment of it.

Finally a bus did appear. It crawled up the hill. I got on. And it crawled slowly away.

I didn't care. The light was now within me.

Then town.

Friday night.

A city of one million. A catchment of three million.

Busy. Alive. Vibrant.

I walked through the city centre streets, past the big shops with their brightly lit window displays, savouring every step.

Right there was a cafe I had sat in, aged maybe 10, and eating a cake the bottom of which had been strangely wet. It had been the end of a school trip, a day out up town, and I had complained about the cake to my teacher. She had eaten it instead.

And there was the record shop where I'd bought my first LP. I couldn't recall the name of the album or the band, but I could still remember the smell of ink and cardboard from the album sleeve; a smell I had always loved ever since.

There was the department store where my parents took me for my first school uniform, and where we'd met Father Christmas every year. We stopped going the year they started to charge extra for the 'Lucky Dip'.

I was 18. And all this was mine. All of it. My city.

Above a jeweller's shop, there was a large black and white clock with an ornate face. It had always been there. For as long as I could remember. And it had always been difficult to see the proper time. The Roman numerals and ornate ironwork made it tricky to read. But not this night. This night it was clear. It shone for me. For us. It said 7.20 pm.

And there, ahead of me, was 'The Ramp'.

I had made it.

With 10 minutes to spare.

I walked slowly up the ramp to the top. To the entrance to the shopping centre. I stood. Looked. There was no one there except an old woman. And with her, partially hidden and in the dark, another figure, who was bending down, retrieving something from a large straw shopping bag.

No one else.

The entrance to the railway station was just inside the shopping centre. So rather than wait, I decided to walk down and take a look at the arrival times. Maybe I would bump into Alley on the way.

Oh no.

No.

This can't be happening.

At the foot of the escalators, which led to the station, a large paper sign warned travellers that the London line would be shut, unexpectedly, from 8 pm that night.

I dashed over to the timetable.

The last train had arrived from London a short while ago. But if Alley had been on that, she would have been at the top of the ramp by the time I got there.

The next train? No. It had already been cancelled.

I ran over to the ticket office and asked them about it. What was going on? They were polite and friendly. But there was nothing they could do. There would not be another train that night. There hadn't been an accident, but there was a fault in the overhead power lines.

All trains were off.

For a few minutes I stood in dumb shock. Just stood there in the station concourse, totally deflated. Of all the weekends, why did it have to happen on this one? All around me there were people greeting friends or lovers. Other trains had made it, from places like Manchester and Newcastle. Their weekends were starting. Why wasn't mine?

A woman walked past talking to her friend. "We were lucky, that was the last train from London tonight, apparently."

Why wasn't I lucky? That bloody meeting about the bonuses. I'd known it then. This wasn't going to happen. I wanted to kick something, to shout, scream, to punch someone, but finally, meekly, I settled for lighting a cigarette instead. And then I turned and walked away, heavily, sadly, back the way I had just come.

What a disaster. What misery. I felt desolate.

Slowly I left the bright glow of the shopping centre. And at the top of the ramp I threw my cigarette end onto the floor. Maybe I could catch a train down to London the next day? Yes. And in the meantime? Drink. I would go and drink too much.

"Hello! Where have you been?"

A familiar voice from my left.

In the shadows.

I turned. Was I imagining it? How was it possible? Alley was there. She was already there. "I've been looking at cheap summer holidays", she smiled, "In the travel agent's window."

"Alley!", I laughed. Almost cried. Wanted to cry.

"Hon-ey!" she laughed back, mimicking a voice we heard so often at hers. Then added, "What is it?", because she could see I was shocked, upset, or something.

I was so happy.

She was so happy.

We threw our arms around each other.

"I was beginning to think I'd missed you", she said. "I thought this was the wrong place."

I shook my head. "No. Oh god. No." I was breathless. Just so surprised and relieved. "No. When did you get here? The London trains have all stopped running."

"Oh, I know", she shrugged, "But I've been here for ages already. My train got in early. And you'll never believe it. I spent the whole journey talking to an old lady. Y'know, she didn't know. She had no idea".

"An old lady?" I said. Sudden realisation. "Did she have a big straw shopping bag?" I asked.

331

"Mmm, yes", said Alley. "Yes she did. How did you know? And then she lost her glasses, poor old dear and she couldn't see a thing."

"Did she have a spare pair in her bag? And you found them for her?"

Alley's eyes widened. "Yes. She did. I did. But how... ?"

I laughed. "Never mind. It doesn't matter." I took her hands. Stood back. Looked at her. "Fucking hell, you're here. You're here. That's all that matters!" I put my arms around her and pulled her close. Hugged her. And we kissed.

"Mmm, you smell gorgeous", she said. "What is that?"

"Cedarwood oil", I said.

With my arm around her, we slowly walked back across my city. And as we did that together, I made a point of noticing the expressions on every face we passed. On every male face, anyway. And, I'm sure, that without exception, every single one of them looked at least twice at Alley. Not because any of them thought 'Is that a boy?', but because every single one of them just thought 'Wow! Look at her'.

And no wonder.

That evening, carrying a largeish shapeless designer bag, Alley was wearing a short, white fur jacket. ("Fake fur", she quickly explained.) Skin tight black jeans, with a shimmering finish, and black leather heels. Her ice blonde hair was slightly, but quite deliberately tousled. Her lips were a dangerous red. Her eyes narrow, and heavily blackened with mascara. And she had highlighted her cheekbones to create an almost sculptural effect.

She looked stunning.

Provocative and enticing.

And as we walked and talked and laughed, she smiled and scowled in equal measure at the world which unfolded in front of us.

"So where are we going first?" She asked as we passed under the jeweller's clock, the time of which I could once again no longer decipher.

"To a hotel", I replied. "The Grand Hotel."

She laughed. "Ooo. That sounds *so* me."

Outside one of the big department stores we walked past a line of faces waiting to meet their own dates. Most of them, male and female both, turned to look... turned to stare, at Alley.

Suddenly Alley stopped and spoke to someone. It was an old lady. The old lady with the straw basket.

"Oh", said the old lady as I waited and watched. "And is that your young gentleman?"

"Yes", Alley replied, taking me by the arm. "Isn't he gorgeous?"

The old lady smiled. "She's come all the way up from London to see you. I hope you're going to take good care of her."

I promised that I would.

"Aren't old people nice." said Alley as we walked away.

We checked into the hotel and, briefly, there was a problem. The receptionist, who had probably seen everything in her time, and whose job it was, in part, to look twice at guests, was quite happy for us to have a key, have the room, all of that. But when I asked about bringing breakfast to the room, and she took our order, she hesitated over which words to use to refer to Alley.

"Yes, I'll have orange juice", I said answering her question.

The receptionist looked up. "And... and for...." She didn't know what to say. The lady? Your friend?

"For me?" Alley said helpfully.

"For you, Madam?" This time she managed to find the word.

All three of us smiled.

"I'll have some orange juice too."

Upstairs, the room was large. Warm yet also fresh. It had the biggest double bed I'd ever seen. There were two large windows, each draped with metres of expensive, thick curtains. Old cast-iron radiators. A desk and chair. And a newly done en suite bathroom with an old fashioned, long and very deep enamelled bathtub.

Alley took one look at that, her eyes lit up and she started to undress. "Oh, look at that. Wow. Run it for me, please?"

I began running it, emptying complimentary shampoo bottles into the bathtub as I did so. "Aren't we going out, then?" I asked her.

"Mmm, yes, of course. But I'm going in that first", she said, already out of her coat and heels and unzipping her jeans. "And you can scrub my back!"

I grabbed a voluminous white towel off the towel rail and draped it around her. "Cover yourself up first, you tart!"

She laughed as she wrapped the towel around herself, and with just a few slight wiggles dropped her jeans and underwear to the floor without exposing anything at all to me.

A few minutes later, she was in the bath, sitting in a sea of soap bubbles.

A few minutes more and I was rubbing soap into her back and her pale, lightly freckled, slender shoulders.

A few minutes after that and I was sitting in the warm water with her.

We splashed around and got water everywhere. Soap too. Slipping and sliding all over the place. Then I got out, hid myself in another massive white towel, and lay on the bed. Then she got out, wrapped herself up too, and came and lay beside me.

"How have you afforded all this?", asked Alley, turning to face me.

"A big bonus", I lied. The truth was that I had saved up a few hundred pounds over a year or more at work, probably expecting to go on a summer holiday abroad with friends. But any such plans all seemed so distant that I was happy to spend that money now on the two of us.

"Have you been shoplifting and selling stuff as well?"

"Maybe that was it", I said, moving closer and kissing her gently on the lips. She kissed me back. And I traced my fingers around her incredibly fine cheekbones.

And then for a while we lay there and talked about nothing very much.

Then she put her head on my chest.

And for a while we lay completely still and quiet.

I'm sure we could have lain in bed together like that for the whole weekend. Longer. Much longer. We could have stayed there and either grown old or died. I don't think either of us would have minded. It was wonderful.

The windows were wide open, and from outside the noise of the street flowed in, coming and going, taxis, cars, the odd laugh or shout. People having a Friday night out. It didn't matter to us. None of it. If anything, we enjoyed it.

I felt as if I was floating, lying on that mattress, adrift with this blonde boy beside me. A shallow warm sea beneath us. A warm sun overhead. A gentle breeze blowing from the south.

"Shall we just stay here and drift forever?" Alley asked, cutting into my thoughts.

Had she had the very same impression? I didn't know. Life was strange. But when it played with you, rather than against you, it dealt you things that were beyond any rational explanation.

A short while later, we were in one of my favourite bars. A small and intimate wine bar with pale blue walls, cream linen tablecloths and candles. Big windows that allowed us to look out but which, somehow, prevented others from seeing in.

"What shall we have?" I asked Alley.

"White, please", she replied. "Something sweet. I need to drink something sweet."

I went to the bar. The staff more or less knew me. And I asked for a good bottle of Sauternes.

The wine bar was situated next to the Birmingham College of Food and Domestic Science, and crowds of students used it. The food was good. The wine was better. But, often, by about ten at night – and it was after that already – the place emptied out a little and took on a much more sedate feel.

"I like it in here", said Alley as I brought the wine back. She was wearing a contemporary dress, in white, with a deeply slashed neckline which she had dug out of her huge designer bag just before we'd left the hotel. In addition to that, high heels and chunky, sparkling necklaces. In the candlelight, once more, with bare shoulders, she looked edible. "It's got a Parisian feel... Like something in one of the backstreets that's only used by artists. But actually the whole world is walking past and there's plenty to watch."

I was glad she liked it. It was exactly that – somehow both busy yet a little out of the way. That was one of the reasons I liked it too and used it quite often. On one hand, people were still coming in and out of the wine bar itself, and there were crowds walking to and from the Repertory Theatre and the college and the pub on the corner – another popular place for the students. On the other hand, as we sat and watched the world and drank the wine, it felt like we were still on a floating raft, as in the hotel earlier, and that no one could even see us. That was how it felt. Yet we could see everyone else... Just the two of us.

And I think that was how we both felt, too. We only cared about each other. Nothing else mattered.

"How often do you come here?" Alley asked, touching my hand across the table. "And who do you come with?"

"I've been using it for a while", I replied. "I usually come with a couple of friends, a mate, Tom, and his girlfriend, Annie. Sometimes there's a few more of us. But we don't usually stay here all night, we usually go on somewhere else."

"Like where?"

"Oh..." I sipped my wine, trying to think. I hadn't been there for a while, since I'd met Alley, and my life before her was feeling increasingly distant, as though it had never been real. "Just a nightclub or something. Maybe a restaurant, an Indian, you know. Or maybe someone's house to drink and talk and crash. Or sometimes to a party. It all depends."

"Mmm. And now you're here with me", said Alley with a slightly smug tone.

We smiled at each other.

Then laughed.

And then, for a while longer, we sat and drank and watched people, inside the wine bar and passing outside. And I loved that we could do that together. Talk or not talk. Laugh. Or be serious. Whatever we needed to be, we could be for each other. It was just right. Easy. Natural. And it had been that way since our first encounter.

I lit Alley a cigarette and passed it to her, refilled her glass.

The music in the wine bar wasn't loud but there was a small dance floor, old wooden floorboards with a few subtle orange and white lights.

It wasn't the kind of space you could hide in, though. It wasn't empty. But it wasn't crowded either.

So if you did dance, you were very visible.

Alley watched a couple dancing. She said nothing but I could see her opinion of the girl's outfit quite clearly. She leaned across the table a little, fixing me with her dark eyes, and said huskily, "And your arse is much sexier than his, too". Then leaning back, she added brightly, "Let's dance? Us! The next slow track they play. It's just for us!"

"Yes. Definitely", I said, emptying my glass. Although really I was thinking, 'Oh fuck'. I was fine on a bigger dance floor. In a nightclub. Somewhere darker. But this was a bit too intimate for me.

Suddenly there were shrieks and shouts from outside and we turned to see a half-hearted fight in progress between a couple of students – lots of swinging arms and random kicking. And as we watched in fascination, I heard a slow track start. So I started talking about what was happening outside, hoping that Alley wouldn't notice the music.

But of course she'd already noticed.

She always noticed everything. And as soon as I'd finished talking, trying to keep her ideas away from the dance floor, she stood up. "Come on", she said, holding her hand out to me. "Dance with me. Don't be so shy." Shy. She had seen that, too. I wanted to pinch her for that.

I stood up and took her hand. And as I did so, I had a quick fleeting image of the party, a few weeks beforehand, where she had reached for me to dance and someone else had cut in between us and prevented us from dancing together.

Incredibly, that was about to happen again.

Well, almost. But not quite.

The wine bar always played chart music. And as we got to the edge of the dance floor, the slow track ended. It had been too short for us. We had missed it.

"Awww", I said, looking at her.

Those eyes narrowed at me.

But I braved them and took one small step away from the dance floor in any case, heading back to our table.

And then a song by Barbra Streisand came on.

Barbra Streisand. 'Woman in Love'.

I stopped. Turned to Alley. And I knew. I just knew.

Alley's face had lit up.

I couldn't believe it. Not Barbra Streisand. This was fate having a joke. Surely? The song couldn't have been more... more... more gay. Not really.

But once more the hand was there, and held out for me.

So I took it again.

Alley laughed. And, finally, we began to dance.

Life is a moment in space

When the dream is gone

It's a lonelier place...

At first we both laughed as we danced. It was fun. That was all it was. We were just dancing together to Barbra Streisand. Just dancing together, with Alley's smile lighting up the room.

But as the music played on we stopped laughing. We began to hold each other closer.

And closer.

We looked into each other's eyes. And we began to dance better. Moving more tightly in time with each other and the music.

Around us, candles flickered. People came and went. Drinks were bought and consumed. Cigarettes were smoked. But some tables sat, now seemingly transfixed, I was sure, by Alley's every move. Mine too, perhaps, as we moved ever more smoothly, ever more seamlessly.

When eyes meet eyes

And the feeling is strong...

Increasingly we began to fix each other's gaze. She mine and I hers. And slowly, subtly, it became much more than that. More intense.

It may have been said elsewhere.

It may have been said about others.

But with her and me, just then, it *was* true. Her eyes were reaching into me and had found my very soul. We began to merge. To unite. To become one.

I stumble and fall

But I give you it all

I am a woman in love...

Alley sang those words at me. Straight at me. Her lips moved barely centimetres in front of mine. Mesmerising me as she danced smoothly. Effortlessly. Perfectly.

I, too, found it so easy. And that shocked me. I was a good dancer anyway. But this? No. This was beginning to feel like something else. Like I was possessed, almost. It was as if the moment was now dancing. Not me. Not us. The moment itself.

And perhaps that was it? Time and space were dancing with each other. And we were there to allow them to finally meet and face one another in physical bodies. On a dance floor. Possessed by them. Part of them.

With you eternally mine

In love there is no measure of time...

She pressed herself closer to me. Not just close to me. But into me. Into. We moved as one. Breathed as one.

As one. I pushed one hip forward. Just a little. Her hip moved back the very same distance. I tilted my head one degree to the right. She moved her head one degree to her left. It was hypnotic. And it wasn't coming from us. I knew that now. This really was coming from somewhere else altogether. A deeper, stronger place that touched every life – if only we allowed it to.

We may be an ocean away

You'll feel my love

I'll hear what you say...

Something else was happening, too. At first I sensed it rather than knew it. It was all around us. I couldn't hear any drinks, footsteps, conversation. Nothing. Except for the music, the room seemed to have fallen silent. No one else was dancing.

A part of my conscious mind returned. Not very much of it. A small piece. Just enough to look past Alley, once and briefly, to see that now, it really was no longer only the people at a few tables who were transfixed, but every table. Everyone standing. Everyone. The bar staff too.

In the doorway, even. Half a dozen were standing there. Watching. Watching time and space embrace on the dance floor. Embrace. Interlock. Captivate. What must have been going out from us into the universe? How was this happening?

I tried to get hold of myself. Was I going crazy? Maybe I was.

I looked back at those eyes. Leaned to her, she leaned to me, and our lips pressed briefly together.

I am a woman in love

And I'd do anything

To get you into my world...

Finally the music began to fade out, and then stop. We stopped too. I couldn't breathe. Alley looked shocked, almost scared.

Would we be able to separate? Yes. Though moving apart did feel strange. There was a charge. Like static electricity, but stronger.

I half expected a round of applause. But of course there wasn't one. There was a stunned silence. People still stared. Some seemingly frozen. Slowly, others gradually thawed out and went back to their own worlds. Two girls, students maybe, shook their heads and talked about us, openly and, clearly, in a positive way.

As we sat down, our senses coming back to us, smiles huge on both of our faces, we began laughing again.

Then the manager came over with two large glasses. "My god", he said, shaking his head as he spoke. "I've been running clubs and bars for 40 years, and I've never seen anything like that. Never. Whatever it is you two have, you should get together and bottle it and sell it. Please. Please take these. They're on the house!"

Mine was a huge single malt whiskey. And, strangely, I was half Irish.

Alley's was a large shot of Cointreau. And she, really, was half French.

In a way, we had almost been given our own national drinks. How did life do that? What had it whispered in the manager's ear?

As for the dance, I wasn't sure what we had done. Or how it had been done. Three or four minutes had become a permanent moment. Captured forever. Somehow. Somewhere. I didn't know if that was actually true or a kind of madness. Real. Fake. An idea. I didn't know what it was. But I did know that I would only ever be able to do it with this unique blonde boy in bright red lipstick.

*

Buses and trains. Buses and trains. Everyone who lives in Birmingham, and probably most people who live in most cities in the West, are so used to them. Public transport. It takes us everywhere. When we're children. When we're teenagers. When we grow up. When we revisit. The cities would stop without them. Just grind to a halt.

The last bus journey of my visit took me from Castle Bromwich in the suburbs back to the city centre. I had a few hours before my London train. And before that I had a meeting with my old friend, Alan Birch.

Alan and I had known each other since the mid-1980s. I think we first met drinking in a pub and playing a few games of pool. Something like that. Back then I was about to start at university and he - a road sweeper at the time, of all things - was also thinking of giving up work and returning to study. I had been a bit of a hot head. Studying philosophy. And for all it may be one of the most personally useful subjects in the world, in terms of a career it was pretty much right down at the bottom. No one wanted clear thinkers. Few employers wanted thinkers at all.

348

Alan, by contrast, was much more career minded than me. Despite a few false starts in his early years, and despite the fact that it may well have been my words, my books, my quotes, my actions and all round intellectual attitude that persuaded him to finally become a student – at the advanced age of 25 or so – it was his own pragmatic approach that had led him carefully, step by step, into psychology and then clinical psychology.

And that was where he was now. Still. In some specialised part of the field that I couldn't quite grasp. Established, writing, with a PhD to his name. High earnings. Respected. All of that. He was solid, reliable and occasionally brilliant. He had done well and I was glad of it. But to me? He was rather like an older brother. Someone I could turn to if and when I needed advice or help. And, back in the late 1980s, that had been exactly what I'd done. Into the early 1990s, even. He had often been there for me.

Those years were now long past. And today we only stayed in contact at a distance. This would be the first time we had seen each other for several years. All the same, I was glad that we were meeting up. I knew his work crossed into other areas and guessed that he knew more about certain subjects than I did. I'd pick his brains. See what he thought and what he had to say.

We had arranged to meet in Digbeth, at the Friends of the Earth cafe, an organic and wholefood place off one of the main roads into Birmingham city centre. An area once full of factories and dodgy second hand car dealers, resprays for stolen cars, done dirt cheap and for cash up front. Now it, too, was being given a new identity. Given it. This was, apparently, now the Irish quarter, and many of the old industrial buildings were being converted into venues for music or places for students to meet up. I supposed that was a good thing, overall. But I still preferred and missed the dodgy car dealers.

Alan hadn't changed, not really. And he looked pleased when I told him that. The hair was greyer, of course, but then he'd had grey hair even in his 20s. And, just like me, he now had his fair share of wrinkles. He also wore glasses all the time. I managed to still avoid them most of the time. But my turn will come. That's how life is.

We went into the cafe, which was all wooden tables and green paint, signs and posters about the environment and chances to get involved in saving things or helping other people. All good and honest stuff. We bought some organic food. A slice of carrot cake and a cup of fair trade coffee each. And we sat down at a table in one of the windows.

At first we talked about how long it had been. At least five years. More like seven.

We laughed when I reminded him of a badly behaved evening in the green room of a club, in the 1990s, when I was putting on music events in Great Malvern and Cheltenham. He had shown up, drunk too much and possibly sniffed a little of something and

– despite being happily married for many years – flirted terribly, and hopelessly, with various female band members.

Then we moved on, quite naturally, to talk about work. He asked me where I was now. I told him and he was surprised and pleased in equal measure.

"I always knew", he said. "That you'd either do well or end up in a cell."

That line sounded vaguely familiar to me. "It isn't too late to do the cell yet", I laughed.

Then we talked about his work. About specific psychological conditions that affected various criminals. And how these could or might be handled or even treated.

A lot of it was above me. I had stopped reading psychology years ago. But I listened, and I think I made one or two positive comments.

After that, we moved onto life in general. Or, rather, I moved us onto life in general. I was pleased for Alan that he was, clearly, so involved with his work. But the subject matter was depressing. Humans who had completely lost their way. Prospects for any progress, with any of his clients, appeared so bleak, so few, so limited. For me, it would have been very hard to pursue such work year in, year out.

I knew that his wife had worked for many years in the field of gender and gender studies, and I knew that he, too, had done some work in that area. And a part of me wanted to talk about that. In truth, it was more than something I wanted to do, it was something that I needed to do.

A big part of the reason I had visited my home city again, and why Kate had been so adamant that I did so, was to talk about Alley. To clear things up a little for myself. To talk about Alley with people who had known me back then, all those years ago.

So yes, I wanted the conversation to move around to the subject of gender. Because I wanted to tell Alan all about Alley.

But even now, after so many years, and with views and opinions, generally speaking, so much more enlightened than they had been back in the 1980s, even here, talking to someone who had been my best friend, I still couldn't just make myself say it outright.

'Hey, did I ever tell you about the boy I went out with? The one who was a girl?'

In a way, it was the very same block I'd had all those years before. And as Alan told me about his wife, Jill, and her work, and how well she was doing, I heard very little of it. Heard very little because I was angry with myself.

This was my friend. I hadn't told him all those years ago. But now? Today? We were two grown men, with a lot of experience, not afraid of being honest. Why the hell couldn't I just come out and say it?

In truth I knew the answer. I felt that I had betrayed our friendship by not telling him about Alley all those years ago. More than felt. It was a fact. I had failed him as a friend. Myself too. And Alley.

I had to say something.

"I went out with a transgender", I suddenly blurted out.

I didn't even know for sure if we were still talking about gender.

Alan said nothing, presumably waiting for a little more explanation.

"A long time ago", I inhaled and tried to look out of the window. It was rather steamed up and not easy to see through. I had never told anyone. But this trip was about changing that. Slightly. Subtly. Slowly. I finally needed to talk about myself.

"It was 1981." I continued. "You remember. Back when we used to go to Bogarts club and the like. I met, I mean I had a short lived affair with a boy. Only..."

I wasn't quite sure about continuing, or even quite sure how to continue. This was an old friend. We ought to have discussed this years ago. Or never. But it was too late now. I had begun.

Alan sipped his coffee. "Only?"

"Only he wasn't", I said. "Well. He was. He was a boy. But he wasn't. God, I must sound so out of date. I mean, he'd been born a boy. But really, I think he was a girl in most respects."

It was probably just my imagination. But for me, at that moment, the clock appeared to slow right down. Down, down, down. Each second taking a full minute to pass, my mind having the time to consider several possible responses.

What would Alan say? Would he be hurt? Would he be angry?

No.

Instead he just nodded. Smiled. Sipped his coffee and even, finally, laughed a small laugh.

I laughed too.

I suppose it was a release of tension.

"What?" I said, "What's funny?"

Alan shook his head. Just a little.

"I'm not surprised", he said. As if what I had just told him was the most natural thing in the world. "You were always the sort of person who would, and did, do just about anything and everything."

And that was it.

As simple as that.

We continued talking and even reminiscing again for another 15 or 20 minutes. Alan asked me nothing about Alley.

And as he told me one of his dreadfully long-winded jokes – something he had always been guilty of – I realised once more why it was that he and I had been such good friends all those years ago. He, like me, and maybe even more so, was a genuine man. A man who accepted others for who and what they were. No questions asked. It just wasn't important for him if a person was gay, straight, black, white or anything else. If you were a decent person, you were a decent person.

A short while after that, it was time for us both to go.

Outside, the sun was shining. Pale and weak today, but at least it was there.

We stood for a few more minutes on the pavement. I told him that he really had to come to visit, soon, maybe in the late autumn to see the colours and storms. And he promised me that he would. And I realised, as we said those words, and made those promises, that we meant them too. And that felt good.

Then we said our goodbyes and I turned and walked slowly up to New Street Station. I still had plenty of time before my train. I was in no rush.

Even back in 1981, it had soon stopped mattering to me who I was, who Alley was. We loved each other. Passionately.

Intensely. We shared. We connected. And that was all that mattered.

But if labels *had* to be applied? What was I? Who was Alley?

I understood now. Better than I had before.

In the last few days, sitting in hotel rooms with my mind wandering away from work, I had studied all kinds of articles on gender and transsexuality.

My own reading, combined with the impressions I had got from Alan and Megan and just from the modern world in general, was that I was straight. Plain old straight. I had once met a boy who was probably a girl, in most ways. And I had found her incredibly attractive and we had fallen in love. But physically and sexually, males did nothing for me.

True, there were straight men who would not – could not – have fallen in love with Alley. There were others too, very many it seemed, who would use transsexuals for sex, but not even consider having an authentic relationship with them.

Degrees of straightness, then?

Probably so.

And degrees of transgender too. Any gender. All gender.

We use 'male' and 'female' because that makes things nice and simple. On the surface, anyway.

And Alley?

I'd read descriptions. And I had decided she was transfeminine. Someone who doesn't identify wholly as a woman, but identifies more as a female than a male.

And I had decided that Alley fitted that description.

But how inadequate it felt. And with a shrug, I recalled my usual anathema to labels, and happily retreated back to my label-less world. The truth was that I had simply fallen in love with Alley. Labels shouldn't matter. It's love that counts.

I laughed to myself as I walked along. How ironic – that I had confirmed all that by finally telling others about our affair.

Life is strange. It really is.

And now?

I had a train ticket to buy.

A trip to London, for a flight back home.

So why, then, did I still feel unhappy?

No sooner had I asked myself the question than I knew the answer.

I'd always felt I'd betrayed Alley.

And I had.

I had betrayed her.

I ought to have been open back then with others and told them
that I was dating a boy. More than that – that I was in love with a
boy. But I had run away from doing so. Told no one. With that
sense of betrayal being a part of my world ever since.

Yes, for sure, I now felt different. Different to when I had arrived
in Birmingham. In one way, the visit had lifted a weight from me.
But, as I got closer to the station, I realised that the sense of
betrayal still remained. I might feel different. Somehow better.
But that other, much heavier weight was still there. It was
something which, seemingly, nothing could ever shift.

Oh, I could try and justify my actions to myself by saying that
things were less clear, at that time. People were gay or straight
and there was no room for manoeuvre. We had no other ideas.
Not back then. But I knew that – for me, anyway – these were
almost excuses. I ought not to have sat on the fence in 1981. I was
tougher than that. I should have stood up for what I was doing. I
should have stood alongside Alley and people like her. No matter
what the case, the risks or anything else, I should have told people
we were dating.

Well, there at least, something had changed for the better today.
Hugely so. Now, we did know the difference. Or, at least, we

were beginning to know the difference. Gay, straight. There were countless shades in between. It was about identity. Not genitals. And it was about degrees of identity. And whilst it was all far from being accepted, it was much more acceptable today than it had been in the early 1980s.

Yet there was something else too.

What was it?

I entered the station and bought my ticket for London. And as I did so, two police officers wrestled a man to the ground, a few metres behind me. Someone who might or might not have been some kind of threat to those around them.

I did nothing. Others did nothing. It wasn't our place to intervene or even ask questions.

Yet that was it. Exactly that.

The times Alley and I had shared. How much easier had it been for me than for her? Oh sure, back then, it was OK for her, too. Mostly. Living in that almost communal house. Despite their bickering, they had all cared for each other. Up to a point. But beforehand, before she found that space in London, when she was at school in Guildford, and the evenings as an adolescent, how hard must that have been for her? Who had stood up for her? Who had stepped forward to intervene?

No.

No. I had that wrong.

Even in London, those men in the pub had said, "She's a boy".
How had that felt for Alley given that she considered herself to be
female? I was so glad I had stood by her that night. Very glad.
But how many times must she have heard that kind of thing?

In so many ways – ways that really mattered – she wasn't a boy,
she was a girl. Imagine being told, over and over and over, that it
was the other way around. At school too. Only there the others
had said the opposite. There they had said that Alley was a girl
and not a boy!

Fucking hell.

We understand so little. And can hurt one another so much.

11

Saturday. The 10th of October.

We were woken at 10.00 am.

Someone was knocking at the door. "Room service, you ordered breakfast?"

Whose dumb idea was that? We both laughed. I hadn't been up so early on a Saturday for two or three years. Not since I'd played rugby for the school. Turning to look at Alley, I got the clear impression that she'd never been up this early on a Saturday. Not ever. Not unless she'd had a paper round when she was about 10 years old. And I couldn't imagine her having ever done that.

I got out of bed, dragging some of the sheet with me for cover, and started to look for my jeans.

"Just open it like that", said Alley, who was leaning out of the bed watching me. "You look very sexy. Give the girl a treat!"

I snatched more of the sheet, wound it around myself and opened the door.

Now sheetless herself and totally tousled, Alley squealed and hid under the quilt.

"Thank you", I said. I closed the door, took the breakfast tray and put it down on the desk.

"The last time I had breakfast in a hotel was...", I tried to remember. I laughed. "Oh my god. It was this summer. July. In Devon with my parents!"

What a difference.

A few months ago, I was their youngest son, on what was probably going to be my last holiday with them. And although I did chat up some girls who were foreign language students, I was more or less behaving myself. A summer holiday. Not quite bucket, spade and sandcastles, but not so far off that either. And yet now? Here I was in a hotel in Birmingham city centre with a *boy*; and not just any boy, but a boy with bleached blonde hair and bright red lipstick!

I found my jeans and pulled them on. Then I yanked most of the quilt off Alley, to encourage her to get out of bed.

"Your long legs are exactly the same shape as mine", I said. "Just as thin. Or slim. Depending on how you want to put it."

We each got a bit more dressed and sat and ate breakfast with the windows wide open. Then Alley stood in the window and smoked a cigarette. I always tried to avoid lighting up for as long as possible on a new day, and this morning that allowed me to watch her for a while. Her inquisitive expressions as she looked out onto the street below, combined with the hollows beneath her cheekbones as she drew on the cigarette. Then a pout as she let the blue smoke out. She looked, for all the world, like a black and white art print, despite being in full – if somewhat pale – colour.

"You are so good looking, it's ridiculous", I told her at last. "We have the same legs almost, the same arms, though mine are more muscular than yours...", she held one of hers up and examined it with some pride. "...the same narrow waist. Angular faces. And in some ways we're like two brothers."

"Brother and sister", she interrupted. The eyes narrowed, but the mouth smiled.

"Like brother and sister", I agreed. Laughing.

"We're both naturally dark haired, too", Alley added.

I laughed again. "I know that now", I said. And I was sure she blushed a little as I said it.

"Both spoiled by our mothers."

"That too", I agreed. I finished my coffee and drank the last of my fruit juice. "And we're both too sensitive. Inside. And we both try hard to hide that from others."

She nodded. Flicked the last of her cigarette out of the window with a deliberately insensitive gesture, laughed and came back over to me.

"But you", I said, shaking my head. "You are so beautiful. It's as if a sculptor had spent decades carving out the most perfect face and then given it to you", I paused. "Sorry. Am I embarrassing you?"

I was. A little. And I knew it.

"No", she said, going into the bathroom. "But I can get ready while you tell me some more. I can hear compliments just as well from in here!"

Again I laughed. "You little tart!" So, where was I? "Those cheekbones. Your eyes. Your lips. You have the most beautiful features I've ever seen. You're just perfect. You really are."

I stopped. Was that all? No. One more thing. I got up and walked into the bathroom, where she was standing in front of the sink starting to sort out her hair. She had a towel on. On her bottom half. Nothing else. I put my arms around her. "I'm so pleased you're mine."

She smiled. I let go.

She turned to face me, put her arms around me, and we kissed. Long and slow. The first time that weekend.

Despite having slept in the same bed the previous night, despite our bewitched dance, despite lots of things, this was our first real kiss of the weekend.

"So where are you going to take me today?" Alley asked, a little while later.

Fully made-up and wearing the same white fake fur and sharp heels, but once more in her shimmering black jeans. She was finally ready to go out.

I had been ready for a while and was lying down and listening to the world outside the window. "Shopping", I said, swinging my legs off the bed. "In the Rag Market."

"The Rag Market?" she echoed. "Ohhh. Yes please. I've been there before I think. I'm sure I must have been. Are there all sorts of second hand clothes and stuff?"

I nodded. "Clothes. And jewellery. Hats. Glasses. Materials. Boots and shoes..."

"Shoes!"

"Shoes." I held the bedroom door open for her.

"Mmmm, I really need some more heels. I really do. These ones won't last much longer. One of the heels is going to break soon, if I don't get some more."

Outside it was grey, cool. Drizzling too. Not a lovely day in terms of weather. But I couldn't have cared less. Here I was. In broad daylight, in the very centre of Birmingham, my own city, with the most stunning girl in the world on my arm.

And the heads turned, just as they had last night.

And, just as last night, I knew that few if any of those turning heads were doing so because they thought that Alley was a boy. It wasn't about that. Not at all. It was all about her. Alley's hair, her attitude, her style, they all worked. And she lit up that grey day. She shone. And *that* was why people turned to look at her.

Then a wonderful thing happened. Wonderful for me. For me personally. As we turned into a narrow lane, one with a well-known rock venue in it, I saw faces up ahead that I recognised. All boys. One of whom was even a fellow apprentice from my factory.

At first, I suppose, somewhere inside me, a part of me – a small part by now – must have started in fright. After all, I was walking straight towards them with Alley. And they were already staring at us. All four of them.

"Alright, mate", said David, the apprentice, as Alley and I approached.

I liked these lads. David in particular was a good kid and a lot of fun at work – but I could taste the envy as he looked at my girl. I could have rounded it up, folded it and put it in my pocket. Where it would have weighed pretty heavily.

"Alright, Tat", I replied. That being his nickname.

"Are you going into the beer keller?"

"No", I said, "I don't think so, mate". I couldn't resist adding, "My girl's not really dressed for it, is she?"

I wanted to laugh out loud as I said that, but somehow I managed to stop myself.

I turned to look at Alley. Her red lips were smiling broadly like the Cheshire Cat's. She exaggeratedly brushed a few invisible particles of dirt off the sleeve of her fur coat.

"This is Alley", I said, introducing her. Alley just nodded very slightly at them.

As we walked away, I knew, I just knew, that the four of them were watching us, watching that dazzlingly blonde hair or maybe even Alley's arse in that tight denim-like material. Watching her walk away and thinking something along the lines of 'Jesus. Where and how did he pull *her*?'

Alley must have been having similar thoughts because at that very moment she chose to put her hand on my backside and squeeze it.

"You're as bad as I am", she laughed.

And then we walked around the corner and disappeared into New Street.

New Street itself, one of the main streets in the city, was packed. And on any given Saturday, on that street, it was pretty hard to turn heads. But some turned all the same. And we both enjoyed watching the reactions. But then the drizzle started to fall more heavily, so we left New Street and cut through the Bull Ring shopping centre.

I suspect that the sound of Alley's heels alone, echoing in the corridors of the shopping centre, might have drawn some attention. But when those heels were connected to that body and that hair, the effect was magnified many times over. Everyone, and I do mean everyone, paused to look.

"Isn't it just like walking along with a dream?" said Alley.

"Show-off", I said, squeezing her side.

Alley skipped a step to escape me and that was all it took.

Snap. A heel of her shoe was gone.

Just as she had predicted.

She stumbled but somehow managed to stay upright and even look pretty cool.

"Told you I needed some new ones", she said, casually taking off the other shoe. "Is it far to the market?"

"Nope", I said.

I shall never forget the rest of that walk through the shopping centre. With shoes in her hand, barefoot, Alley looked as if she had just left the Casino in Monte Carlo at 3 am on a Sunday morning. I half-expected people to come up to us, to her, and ask for an autograph. One group of lads stopped and watched her without even trying to hide their fascination. Mouths open. Eyes on stalks.

The last part of the walk wasn't easy though. It was now raining quite heavily and there was a short open section, exposed to the elements, between the shopping centre and the old market hall where the Rag Market was situated.

We stood there for a while and watched the rain.

"You've no shoes. The wrong coat for rain. Everything", I said.

Alley looked at me.

I looked at her.

And she smiled.

I sighed. Sometimes we spoke like that. Without words. I took off my suede boots and gave them to her.

She put them on. "Well you did say we were almost the same size." She started crossing the road. "Come on! Let's go!"

I wanted to slap her arse or something... but that could come later.

Suddenly the skies opened up fully. I ran. She ran. And in just a few wet seconds, we were in the market.

When it was closed, the Rag Market was a large, grey, industrial-looking warehouse, open to the elements in places. It didn't have the appearance of anything very exciting.

When it was open, however, with all the traders in place, it resembled Aladdin's cave. Aisle after aisle of crowded stalls, selling everything from carpets to buttons, records to period clothes and military insignia to lipstick. Aladdin's cave it was. But there was a touch of Ali Baba and the Forty Thieves too as, unless you had your wits about you, you might end up paying five times as much for something as it was actually worth or having your pockets picked.

It was sharp. Exciting. Busy. A bargain hunter's paradise. A thieves' paradise too. It had everything.

Walking through it wearing wet socks wasn't much fun, though. So it was with a huge sense of relief that, having been there for only about ten minutes, Alley found and bought a stylish pair of leather high heels dating back to the 1950s or early 1960s.

She bought them, put them on and gave me back my boots.

And that felt like a gift from heaven, wet socks or not.

I said 'Thank you' to Alley and was about to suggest we went to look at another stall when a familiar voice suddenly cut me short.

"Hello, I thought it was you."

I turned and found myself face to face with an old school friend, a girl called Debbie, who I had known since the age of five. We had spent 11 years at school together, always in the same class. But where she had left with lots of qualifications, I had left school with none.

She smiled at me, and we gave one another a quick hug.

"Why were you walking around with no boots on?"

"Well", I began, laughing. "Actually it's a long story..."

"It was my fault", said Alley, before I had a chance to finish my reply. "I lost a heel. And like a gentleman, he loaned me his boots while I went on a hunt for some new shoes." And she pointed at her 'new' pair of old shoes for Debbie to see.

"Oh they're lovely", said Debbie looking at the shoes. "Wow. I'm so jealous!"

Debbie looked at me. Something, a twinkle in her eye, just the slightest change of expression, maybe a very little smile, crossed her face. But she said nothing.

"Alley", I said, "this is Debbie. A friend of mine. Debbie, this is Alley. She's up here from London."

"Hello", said Debbie, giving Alley a quick kiss on the cheek.

"Hello", said Alley.

"I think I've seen you up here in the market once or twice, haven't I?"

Alley nodded. "Probably", she said. "I've been out here a couple of times. But I don't come up to Birmingham very often."

"So what are you up to, Deb?" I asked. "Are you still working in Oasis? I keep meaning to drop by and have a chat."

"Noooo", she replied. "No. Didn't you know? When did we see each other last? I got married. We've moved now. It's all about mortgages, painting and decorating, the garden..."

"Oh that's brilliant news!" I said. "No. I didn't know that. Congratulations!"

We chatted for a while longer and then Debbie had to go. She was meeting her husband and they were off to buy a three piece suite.

"Hopefully see you around sometime?"

"Maybe", I replied. But after so many years of knowing each other and growing up together, her world and mine suddenly seemed to be very different.

Alley and I continued to walk around the Rag Market for a while, Oohing and Aahing at various things that we found. At one stall, I came across a tough-looking 1950s leather box jacket. I just had to have it. So I bought it, and wore it straight away.

"Oh you look gorgeous in that", said Alley, putting her arm through mine as we looked at a few more stalls. Then she let go. Because in front of her was a stall selling just about every colour of lipstick and blusher that you could imagine.

There were old period shirts on the stall opposite. So I left her to search through the make-up whilst I browsed through the shirts. Now and then looking up at Alley. She was lost in a crowd of people, and all I could see was her startlingly blonde hair.

A little while later, carrying a brown paper bag full of lipsticks, we moved onto another stall. Jewellery. Then another. Dresses, period dresses. Alley held up a long pink frock in front of herself and posed with it. It was ghastly, really. And very expensive. But somehow she managed to make it look sexy and I half wished that we had the money to buy it.

We bumped into other faces I vaguely knew. Said hello. Moved on. Felt them watching us, or, rather, Alley. Probably asking the same question as before: 'Where the fuck did he find her?'

It was fun.

And we could have wandered around there for hours more.

But it was getting colder and we were hungry.

"Come on", I said. "Let's go into the indoor market and have a coffee and something to eat."

The indoor market, or the food hall, was different to the Rag Market. It was partially heated and the stalls were permanent. For me, it also had a firm, and happy, association with my childhood. Because I had often been taken to the market by my father and we had sat and eaten cockles or whelks at one of the many fresh fish stalls.

Virtually everything sold in there was food of one kind or another. And in each corner of the food hall there were also small steamy-windowed cafes, similar to the one Alley and I had taken to using in London.

We went into one of those and sat in a window that faced out onto the street.

To begin with we both had coffee so strong it could practically hold up the teaspoon by itself. Then we bought a few sandwiches and ate them. And then I bought us both an orange juice. None of it was very exciting in terms of food and drink, but it was all they had and we were so hungry that we didn't care.

We finished eating and I lit her a cigarette. I took a draw on it and then passed it to her, then I lit one for myself.

Alley drew a heart on the steamed-up glass. And I watched, wondering if she would put our initials in it. But before she had a chance to do that, a man walked past outside with what appeared to be a three-legged dog, and we both wiped the window frantically so that we could see out.

It was indeed a three-legged dog. We watched them for a minute.

"They look happy", I said. "Both of them." Which was true.

"Aww", said Alley. "Isn't that sweet?"

Now that we had cleared the glass, for a short while we just sat and people-watched; something we both loved doing.

"You fucking queers", said a voice from inside the cafe, suddenly.

I stubbed out my cigarette and turned to look. Alley must have heard it too, but she just kept looking out of the window. I guess she had heard it so often before that she knew to ignore it.

There were three lads, our age, or a bit older, sitting at a table adjacent to us. They were each a good bit bigger than me. And they had faces suggesting that Darwin might have been wrong about evolution.

"Swwwweeeet", said one of the lads, trying to mimic Alley's effeminate voice and missing it entirely.

Alley turned to look at them. And I saw the gleam in her eyes, and I knew what she was going to do next. She was going to goad them further.

"Don't", I said quietly and shook my head. "Just let it go."

Thankfully Alley didn't say anything and turned away again.

Outside it was still daylight. Getting towards evening but not yet dark, despite the rain. And there were lots of people coming and going. But inside it felt pretty uncomfortable, and I was beginning to wonder what we should do, whether we should leave or sit it out. I wasn't sure.

"That's a fucking boy under all that muck?" came one of the voices.

"Fucking disgusting", came another. "Shouldn't be allowed."

I half smiled to myself at that moment as I had the sudden clear impression that listening to them or, rather, having to listen to them, felt like hearing a person vomit. These were not really words being used. There was no sense to what they said.

I glanced at Alley. She was still looking out of the window. Neither of us were full of anger or hostility. Neither of us were insecure, at least not in that sense, and neither of us felt the need to spew words or threats at harmless strangers. We were not at fault here.

"What are you fucking smiling at?" said one of them, aiming that at me.

Three of them. One of me. I felt myself tensing up. I knew I'd do something about it. Outnumbered or not. That was my background. It was what we did where I came from.

But the fact that I would also have to protect Alley. That worried me.

Suddenly the cafe door opened. And a squat burly figure came in wearing a crash helmet and a long heavy coat. He took off his crash helmet and stood dripping at the counter. He looked up at the price list, glanced at the sandwiches and mumbled an order. Then he turned and saw me.

"Alright, mate?" I knew him. It was a lad called Micky Gould. He and I had worked together for a few months in the factory. Then he had disappeared. Apparently sacked for stealing parts – which lots of people in the factory did, but Micky had been caught trying to walk out of the main gate with a new bonnet for a Sherpa van.

"Hello, Micky", I said. "I didn't recognise you with that big overcoat on. Have you got a motorbike now, then?"

He nodded and looked at Alley.

"My girl", I said.

"Hello", said Micky, holding out a heavily tattooed hand.

"Hello", said Alley, gently shaking his hand.

Back when we had worked together, Micky had stolen a metal sign off one of the machines that said 'Made in England'. He'd been going to sew it onto his coat. He was British and white and often vocally proud of both things. Yet, on another day, playing cards with some Pakistani lads, he threatened to punch someone for racially insulting one of them. I always felt his heart was in the right place. It just didn't always mesh with his actions.

"What you doing up here, then?" Micky asked.

"Oh, you know, having a coffee. Been shopping in the Rag Market." I replied. "Alley bought a pair of shoes."

I didn't at all like the three lads who had been taunting Alley and me. But their timing was awful. Because they chose that very moment to have another dig at us. "Queers", they said again.

"You don't want to get too close to them, mate", said one of them, "they're a couple of queers".

Micky looked at me. Then at Alley. Hesitating a little longer than he might otherwise have done. I guess he saw it then. He must have done.

Then he turned slowly to them.

Now it was three of them. One of him. But he was bigger than me. And crazier too.

"What did you just fucking say?" he said, looking the biggest of the lads straight in the eyes.

No reply.

Micky took a step or two closer to their table and leant down towards them. And in a voice that was only a bit louder than a whisper – a very aggressive whisper – he "Why don't you three cunts leave? While you can all still fucking walk."

They hesitated.

But only for a fraction of a second.

Then they began to get up.

"Go on", said Micky again. "Fuck off."

They got up.

They left.

Micky then sat down with us without mentioning the lads or anything else. He had a cup of tea and four huge sausage sandwiches. We talked for a while, mainly about the factory and what he was doing now. He offered each of us a cigarette and then he got up to leave.

"Micky", I said, as he pulled on his overcoat. "Thanks for that, mate".

He shrugged. "No way to talk to a girl, was it". And with that he picked up his crash helmet and, with a quick smile at Alley, left.

Alley smiled too, then wildly ruffled her bleached blonde hair, quite deliberately making some of it stand up. As if she wasn't already both startling and stunning enough.

I laughed and shook my head.

It felt as if Alley had no idea how close we had just been, the two of us, to a difficult situation. Of course that wasn't true. Far from it. Alley had been experiencing situations like that for some time now, on and off.

"You *are* crazy", I said. "But beautiful and fun too."

She wrinkled her nose. Shrugged. "I can't help it if people feel they have to talk to me, but the only things they can find to say are nasty."

I didn't want to push the issue. But I did still feel tense. And understandably so.

"My Alley cat", I said. "You are rapidly using up your nine lives, I think."

Alley's response was to meow, scratch at the air and light a cigarette. The same gesture she'd made in the Hostaria when she first told me her name.

"I..." She took a long draw on the cigarette before continuing, "I am going to do very well, thank you very much. With the right man, of course. With my luck, and my looks. I will be a star. In one way or another."

I took the cigarette out of her hand and took a long drag on it.

"What will you do then, Miss Wonderful?"

"Fashion", she said. "I adore material. Jewellery. Make-up. Glitz. It's all so me. Fashion, or something very like it."

A short while later, we left too.

There was no sign of the three lads outside. And for a moment I wondered what might have happened if Micky had not shown up when he did. For myself, I wasn't too worried. But for Alley, I actually felt both upset and afraid.

"Mick was very nice", said Alley, interrupting my thoughts. "Oh look, it's stopped raining!" Evidently she had taken the whole experience in her stride.

Saturday evening. I had thought of taking Alley to visit my council estate. But that thought had survived less than one full second in my head. She and me, both, would have been fed to the dogs within ten minutes of getting there.

Then I thought of doing what so many people in Birmingham did, and for which it has since become renowned; go out to a restaurant for an Indian curry. But no. I didn't want to do that.

A wine bar? No. We'd done that yesterday.

The Hostaria again, or somewhere like the Rum Runner? No. She almost certainly knew more people in those places than I did.

In the end I realised that I didn't actually care where we went. I didn't care so long as I was with her. And she didn't care so long as she was with me. So without having made any decision, I just washed and changed and then lay on the bed while she got ready.

I had asked her to tell me how she did that. How she got ready. Make up. Hair. What did she put on first, second, why and how. And so as I lay there, from the bathroom came a very descriptive and entertaining recital of how she applied what, where and in which order. Between each stage, she came out of the bathroom and showed me how she looked.

Of course all that took quite a while. And the clock, wherever the nearest one was – because neither of us had a watch – moved around pretty fast.

Then she decided that I had to try some eye make-up. And that stole a little bit more of our evening out. But, finally, we did get away from the hotel.

At first, all we did was walk. Through the city streets at night, people watching again and showing ourselves off. I loved it. Alley loved it more. She was such a natural poser and show-off.

And it struck me that that was a good thing, too. How might her life have been if she had not been able to pose like that? Much harder, that's for sure.

Eventually we ended up near to a pub I knew well but which wasn't really somewhere I was going to take Alley; the Golden Eagle. It was a dark, loud and sometimes slightly rough place which often had live punk or rock bands. In truth I knew it very well and I was almost tempted to go in. But no, I wanted to go somewhere where she would be visible. The Eagle was just too dark for that.

Still unsure where to take her, from there we walked down towards New Street Station and then, at last, I remembered the old theatre bar; The Victoria.

The Victoria was a very old fashioned pub, almost music hall-like. Brightly lit, with brass and wood fittings, slightly dilapidated velour upholstered furniture, the walls were covered in old theatre posters and signed photographs of actors who had played in the theatre next door and occasionally slept in one of the rooms upstairs. It was a place that still attracted a few actors from time to time. As well as those who liked actors. And those who liked the whole acting scene.

We went in.

"I love it", said Alley squeezing my arm as soon as we entered the door.

It was already quite late and so there weren't many tables or chairs free. But we found one small table and stole a couple of chairs from another. We were almost in the centre of the room.

Alley sat and took her coat off, and heads turned from every direction, wondering whether she was from the theatre. And I went to the bar, leaving her to sit and shine.

We had only been in there for long enough to have one drink when two elderly gentlemen, one in a cream old-colonial suit and the other one in shirt sleeves and a lilac waistcoat, insisted on sitting with us and buying us both more drinks. And they wouldn't take no for an answer.

It could be that kind of place.

They were quite genial. Telling us all kinds of stories about the theatre and certain actors they had known personally.

"Oh, mind you", said the lilac waistcoat, nudging his friend a little as he spoke. "Back then, eh? Well, things were a lot more under the counter than they are today, shall we say. Things have changed a lot since our youth."

"Oo yes", the other agreed. "You youngsters have it much easier than we did. It's good to see that some things have changed for the better."

Another drink or two and they were both adamant that Alley was "clearly a boy, but a very dear boy" and also "absolutely the most gorgeous creature" they had ever seen. They were equally adamant that she would "most certainly end up on the stage". Or "in very deep trouble", the lilac waistcoat laughed.

It was a totally unplanned evening which was, as they said as we left some time later, "delightful, just delightful". Alley gave each of them a huge kiss. And I think that they probably went to bed very happy. Together.

By the time we returned to the hotel, we'd shared a bottle of wine and had quite a few extra drinks bought for us too. It may not have been a huge amount of alcohol for some people, but for us it was more than enough. We were both quite slightly built and neither of us was able to drink a great deal before feeling the effects. And as we lay in bed, I think that for both of us, our heads were turning more than we would have wanted them to.

And then, to make sleep just about impossible, Alley got a fit of the giggles. I pinched her and tried to get her to stop. And she did try. But it didn't work. And soon I started laughing too.

When you laugh about something, it usually stops pretty soon. But when you start laughing about nothing, it can go on until your face aches. And even beyond that.

"Stop it!" I said. "Stop it. I mean it!"

Alley more or less bit her lip and managed to stop. But as soon as she looked at me, she burst out laughing again.

"Don't", I said. "Stop it! Let's try and take our minds off it." We were getting louder and louder all the time.

She put her hand over her mouth and, eyes shining, nodded her head. And we lay still for a moment.

"Let's talk about religion or politics", she said at last. "Anything. Something boring to take our minds off it."

"Oh no", I said. "Let's not. Not that. Anything else."

"Oh go on, it'll only take a minute."

"OK, go on then", I agreed. Anything to stop the giggles.

"What politics are you?"

I gave it just a few seconds' thought. "Where I come from, you're communist, fascist or you have no idea."

"Ooh, so which are you?"

I turned and looked at her. "I'm too opinionated to have no idea", I said.

She agreed. "Fascist, then?"

"Would I be here with you if I was?"

"Mmm. Some of the gayest men have been fascists." she laughed. "It makes a great cover."

"Well I'm not."

"Oh... So I'm sleeping with a red, then? Oo, I like that thought."

I shrugged. I didn't know about that. But it was better than the other two alternatives. "I'm not going to ask you", I said. "I'm bored of it already."

"So am I", she replied.

I laughed. I reached for her and lifted some of her blonde hair away from her eyes. Then I turned onto my back. "Well, you were right. That did only take a minute."

"And it stopped us giggling", Alley added.

Then for a little while we lay calm and motionless again, the cool breeze from the open windows helping to slowly clear our heads, the noises outside not really intruding.

"Lie here, on me", I said at last, putting my left arm out so that she could lay her head on my chest. But she had already moved over to me before I'd even finished asking her.

That position. That position. I loved to have her there. Just there. Her head on my chest. Sharing and shared. We might lie quiet and still like that, neither needing to move or do anything at all. We might lie and talk, either one of us, the other listening in the dark or replying just now and then. And hours could pass that way. And for all I cared, my whole life could pass that way.

Ever since the party at Handsworth, where Alley had been cold in that huge bed and I had held her, we had often lain like that. Very often. Sometimes maybe only for a few minutes, but sometimes we would lie like that until one or the other of us fell asleep and beyond. For both of us it felt relaxing, comforting, close and intimate. It made me feel protective, and I'm sure it made her feel protected. And neither of us had any issue at all with taking such clear and almost stereotypical roles. Out there, our public face, we might pinch one another or laugh, we might smoke or drink or even steal, we might dance or talk, hold hands or kiss, but once together, in our own space, our inner selves, we were totally comfortable with being who and what we were.

She was a girl, who wanted to love me and be loved by me. And I was a boy, who wanted to love her and be loved by her.

"I wonder..." she began.

My hand had been stroking her hair. But it had stopped. It had stopped because I was half asleep, though still holding her.

"I wonder, would you put me in your autobiography if you ever became famous?"

The question woke me up a bit. My hand began to stroke her blonde mane again. Would I what? Had I misheard her? "I think if either of us becomes famous, it'll be you. Not me," I said, at last.

She didn't reply, not at first.

We moved apart a little. She lay back on her pillow and I raised myself up on one elbow to look at her.

She turned and looked at me, those dark almond eyes. Searching. Fathoming. As they always did. "Do you really think so? Why?"

I shook my head. "Just look at you", I said. Quiet. Almost a whisper. "You have the most beautiful face in the whole country."

She smiled. Quickly. "I have", she said. We both knew she believed that. She really did feel it. And with good reason, too. "But it takes more than looks. Anyway, you're gorgeous too."

I shook my head again. "No. No. I'm good looking. I know that. But you're totally different. People don't have looks like yours. They just don't." It came out a bit clumsily, but that was how I saw it. "And anyway, you can dance, sing, the way you dress, you've got crazy friends, you live in London. Cars stop when they drive past you. Something'll come along. For sure. And you, your personality. You're very strong. It's really only a case of deciding what you want to do and when."

She didn't reply, just moved her lips over each other, as if rubbing in fresh lipstick. It was one of so many of her facial gestures that I adored. Then she stopped, and simply lay still for a moment. Thoughtful. Pouting without meaning to.

"Will you put me in yours?" I asked her. My own words had made me see it. I ought to have known it before. She was obviously destined to do something. Just as those two men had said in the pub. She would get in real deep trouble or have some sort of rocketing career in the public eye. Or maybe both.

Probably it would be both. So she might well write such a book one day. And I liked that idea.

Alley shook her head slowly. "No", she said. "No. I don't think so. I don't think I will. I mean, I won't put you in it."

Her answer surprised me. I was disappointed, too, a little. Not angry. Nothing like that. But yes, surprised and a bit taken aback. "Why not?"

"No. I'll tell everyone all about everyone. All about everything", she pressed her lips together again, then turned and gave me an achingly sad smile. "But I won't tell them about you, about us."

My turn to not reply.

"You don't belong here," she continued. "This isn't your world. And what we have together, what we've done and shared, I shan't tell others about it. They'd never understand. They'd never feel it or get it. Not even close. They'll just bring it all down to their level. And for you, that would be so wrong. They'd tear you to pieces."

At those kind and considerate words, expressing what I, too, knew would be true, I could feel tears rising in my eyes. Prickling. And I didn't want them, not right now. So instead I just leaned towards her and kissed her forehead. Trying to reassure her that I did understand. Which I did. "You really are so thoughtful. You really are." I meant that, too.

Lying face to face as we were, I noticed that her eyes were sparkling too. A single tear even escaped and rolled down the angle of her cheek.

"How others can't see that in you", I added, touching her moist cheek gently. "That's scary. How blinkered people must be not to see it in you."

She wiped the eye that had revealed her sadness. "What about you?" she asked.

"What do you mean?"

"If you do ever become famous. Would you put me in your autobiography?"

Was it the same? I wasn't sure. "I guess... on balance... yeah, I think I probably would."

"You would. Why?"

"Well..." I wasn't sure, but I could see a difference and it made some sense to me. "The opposite of you I guess. I want people, say 'normal' people, to read about how loving someone is possible. Exactly that. Just possible. Even when the person you love is the same sex as you. That it isn't about being gay or straight. It's just about caring for someone, connecting to them. Being close. All of what we have. All of what we've done together. That's what really counts."

She laughed. A small laugh. "Are you saying I'm not normal?"

I leant towards her and kissed her on the mouth. Just lightly. And as I began to move away she put her arms around my neck and pulled me back to her, kissing me in return. Then we moved apart again.

"You know what I mean", I said, lying back on my pillow.

In the half-light of that hotel room, for a few minutes I listened to the sounds of the world outside. Muffled and faint but somehow fascinating all the same.

I liked it. It was as if the vagueness of those noises emphasised our being alone, together, in this bed.

Mistakenly, I thought I heard the distant sound of a train. A train in the night. A sound I had grown up listening to and, as a child, had found reassuring. It was soporific.

I guess I just expected to go to sleep then, too.

But was that all I wanted?

To sleep?

In part, I suppose it was. There was always that side to us, after all. We were young and in so many ways insecure. An important part of the attraction was that, with each other, we found a place where we could hide. The other could be trusted. We had known that from the beginning. Alone together, we might just hold each other and lie still. As we often did.

But there were other times, fewer of them, but they were very much there; times when we wanted to be more than safe. More than secure. When we wanted to push our own boundaries, and those we shared as well. Moments when we could form an even closer bond. An ever deeper trust.

So was that all I wanted? To sleep?

No.

Still lying flat on my back, I turned my face once more towards Alley.

I knew she would be doing the very same thing. Thinking the same. Feeling the same. I knew it before I moved.

And I was right.

I turned and those narrow almond eyes were there. Wanting. Those eyes, weighted down heavily with dark black mascara. She also needed a closer bond. Was also searching for that ever deeper trust. Her mind, her body, feeling just like mine. I knew it. We continually did the same things. Felt the same things. We had done that since we first met.

For a moment her eyes searched mine.

I was now used to the way she did that. Not in any way bored with it, but used to it in the sense that I understood it. She examined, she looked for the right signals, she read people, she worked on feelings and instinct and her eyes fed her the information she needed. So I lay still. Knowing her and enjoying it. Letting her do it.

Then a slight head movement, a small order, to pull the bedding down a bit. Down and off myself. Not far. She wanted to see a bit more. Just my chest and my stomach. Then stop. Another small head movement. Those eyes still searching. Looking at me and into me. But I loved the game. Loved it just like she did. So now I searched back. And that made her turn her face away from me, a fraction, as if momentarily unable to focus.

That felt like a little victory. Not in any way a competition, just a little victory. Something to make me smile. Something to make her push back against.

And she did push back. She took me wholly by surprise by leaning right across to me and suddenly running her tongue along my cheek. Like a cat licking up cream. Then she pulled away. Smiling.

I laughed. A quiet laugh. She laughed too.

Then we moved closer. Once more.

Closer, face to face, until our lips met and our bodies almost touched.

But this was no polite kiss. No thought of goodnight. We pressed our lips together harder, opening our mouths instinctively as we did so. I put my hands either side of her face, that unbelievably beautiful face, and held her still and kissed her. Softly. Then hard. Deep. Deeper with passion and almost with force.

She responded in kind.

I loved her tongue. I loved her mouth. But how insufficient are those words. Her kisses were like life itself to me. Better.

Then she surprised me again.

She pulled away, wholly, and just lay on her back. Face towards the ceiling. She didn't move. Didn't speak.

"You're beating me", I whispered. "You bastard." And I had no choice except to move so that I lay almost across her. At least in part. Which was, I knew, exactly why she had lain like that.

Now she was partly underneath me. My face above hers. Her blonde hair on the pillow.

Propped on my elbows I stroked that hair so it was totally away from her face. I wanted to see every angle, every line. To miss nothing.

"Who's the best?" she asked. A quick smile.

"You", I answered, leaning down to her.

And we kissed again.

"You. Every time."

And again.

And as we kissed, we pressed more into each other, her hands reaching around my back, touching my bare skin. Sending shivers down my spine.

I wriggled the cover down further, so that it was below my arse but still covering my legs. I had done that because I wanted to see her more clearly.

To look at her, to look and want and need.

And to take.

My head went down her body. My tongue, my lips running around her stomach. Flat. Sexy. Male. I bit her, gently. She made no effort to stop me. And I moved down further. So that her narrow hips, even narrower than mine, were in front of my face. I ran my tongue across them. Enjoying her squirming. Enjoying it because she was squirming. I bit her hip. Moved my head a little to the left and took her into my mouth.

But only for a moment. I came back up the bed, back up her body, back so that we were once more face to face.

She gave one of those small almost imperceptible nods. And

slipped down underneath me. Doing to me, from beneath, what I had just done to her.

We knew, each time, every time, what to do and how much to do it. We connected that much.

Then her mouth let go of me and, in turn, her long pale body reappeared from underneath.

Our faces met, her head on the pillow, and we kissed ever longer.

I changed position, more on top of her, lifting myself up, moved so that my arms were now either side of her slim young body.

Raised up onto my hands. Press up position. Totally naked, face to face, the length of our bare bodies touching as we lay there.

I looked down at her. At her chest. Her neck. Her shoulders. Taking it all in slowly and carefully.

I looked at her face. That bewitching face. And those glistening lips.

And in return Alley glowered back at me. That was exactly what she did. She glowered. I almost flinched away from that look. It was hard. But it was beautiful too. Like fire. And I knew why she was doing it and who she was doing it for. For me. For herself. For both of us. I knew, too, what both of us were feeling at that moment. Both of us. We wanted. We wanted each other. We needed each other too. And nothing else mattered. Not this time.

I tried to glower back. But she was better than me. Faster. More in touch, even. I fixed her eyes but in response she flared her nostrils. She flared them with passion and flared them to breathe and flared them because she was burning with life. Yes. I had been right. We were beyond any language now.

I pressed my pelvis into hers.

Nothing deliberate.

Just one thrust.

I hadn't meant to do that. It just happened. Instinctive.

Her response? She exhaled sharply from between her teeth. Almost a hiss. I felt the air pass across my naked chest. She breathed while searing into me with those eyes. Captivating. Capturing. Taking me. And winning.

Then, instinctively, with both of us adjusting slightly to allow her to move in such a way, her legs, those long lean legs, simply parted. Parted so that I was no longer lying half on and half off her body, but lying on the mattress and completely in between her slim, soft thighs.

We held still.

So much of our love was in these moments. The pauses. The glares. The eyes. We held still.

We held as if something invisible, thick and clear and strong, fused our gazes together.

We held still, and I felt that every sight she had ever seen, I now understood. Every colour or image in my head, she had seen too.

Watching.

Breathing together.

My flat stomach felt hers move. Hers felt mine move.

Then slowly, very slowly, I leaned down and towards her mouth, and slightly, she raised her lips to mine. We kissed again, so gently that it barely registered. Her eyes closed. Ecstatic closure. I studied her features. The very ideal of beauty.

Lightly I ran my tongue across her lips. Just moistening them.

The eyes opened again. Suddenly. Sharply.

"Please." She said it in what was no more than a faint, husky whisper.

Leaning down, I kissed her lips. Her cheeks.

Her legs moved more. Not apart. But around. Around me. Not fully. But enough to pull me in, to tell me what we were doing, to let me know how she ached. As I did too.

In response I changed my own position. Just enough. And with that movement of mine her legs, those long lean legs, finally wound completely around me. And brought me right up to her. For the first time ever.

Still our faces watched each other. For every sign. Every passion. Every breath.

My hips moved down towards her.

Her nostrils flared again. My teeth were almost gritted.

Then her eyes narrowed. Narrowed as much as it was possible to do so without actually closing.

Her mouth opened a little.

She paused, then whispered just two words.

"Fuck me."

Deep and magic moment. Timeless.

I held still for one last look at my girl. My boy. The words, her two words, now a part of my life forever. Tattooed onto my soul.

Then she said it again. With even more passion.

"Fuck me."

She didn't speak the words. She breathed them. And this time she breathed them almost viciously. Almost a plea. Almost desperate.

But it was also so much more than that.

The words said connect.

Connect to me. You *are* my lover.

Connect to me.

Connect to me forever.

That night, for two full hours, Alley cried. We sat in bed and she sobbed. Over and over.

It scared me. She cried so hard I thought she would make herself ill. I really did. I didn't know what the pain was. I found out later, but by then everything had changed.

At first I tried to calm her. But no words worked. Nothing could get through. These were tears beyond words. She begged me to do so, so I promised to just hold her and let her cry. I promised not to let her go. She held onto me. And I held onto her. And she cried.

During those hours, I tried to move twice. Just a little. But each time she sobbed even more. "Don't go", was all she could whisper, through a voice that was unbelievably thick with emotion and tears. So I held her closer still. And slowly, the worst of it gradually subsided.

Eventually she fell asleep in my arms. Twitching once or twice, like a kitten having a bad dream.

And finally I fell asleep too.

12

The journey from Birmingham back to London on the inter-city train was uneventful. It was more than that, it was unpleasant. There was no proper air conditioning, no windows seemed to open and – outside of First Class, which I was fortunate enough to be able to use these days – it was hugely overcrowded, with people sitting in the aisles and standing up between the carriages.

When I was young, trains always had ten or twelve coaches. And now there were only five or six. No wonder they were so full. We could open windows back then, too. Like that carriage when I first met Alley all those years ago.

I used to love travelling by train. Not any more.

Fortunately, it was no longer my country. It wasn't my business. And the rest of the journey passed quickly enough for me, anyway, as I had my laptop to work on and lots of emails to answer.

And then we reached London.

London, Euston.

Crossing the main station concourse and heading for the Underground, I stopped abruptly as a girl with brilliant blonde hair walked past in front of me.

All those years ago. I wondered. That house, that dilapidated terraced house, full of condensation and potential, filled with love, music and laughter it had been only a short walk from here. Should I take the Underground direct to the airport or should I go and take a look at the old place? I had time for the detour. But should I do it?

Yes. Yes, I'd go and look. I had a few hours to spare.

So I went.

And I soon wished I hadn't.

Firstly, once away from the station, the walk itself felt rather sad. Time flies. My parents had told me that – often – but I'd never believed them. When we're young, we think we have forever. But where had forever all gone? How was it already so long ago?

What would I have given for it to be 1981 again? Making this same journey, but to be just 18 and going to meet Alley. Going to meet Alley by walking these very same streets. I hadn't done it since then. Not this very same route. And I somehow felt the ghost of my younger self, within me, as distantly familiar sites went by.

But it was more than lost youth which made me sad, much more. It was about change. And not just my own change. But an all pervasive, uprooting, overly fast-paced change that appeared to be affecting everything and everyone. Only rarely for the better.

The shop where I had bought the mango and cream, for instance. It was gone. Actually I wasn't certain which one it had been. But as the whole row had been demolished it was definitely no longer there.

The cafe, too. Our cafe. Gone.

I wondered if the pub was still open? That, surely, should have stood the test of time. Or would it now be a Starbucks or a Chinese restaurant? Perhaps fortunately, it was too much out of my way to go and check.

And then, suddenly, there it was – the house.

Or, rather, it wasn't.

Because that fine old building, which had been so run-down in 1981, had also gone. As with so much back in my home city.

I hadn't expected it to still be a squat, but it should have been smart flats by now. It had been a large, stylish Victorian house, maybe even Georgian, and it would have made wonderful flats once converted. But to be gone? Totally knocked down and replaced by some nondescript modern thing? No. I hadn't expected that. I thought the capital would have had more sense. More style.

Like so many other things from my past, it was just as if it had never existed.

From London, feeling a little low, I took the tube and train to Luton Airport.

And after only a short wait I caught my plane to Knock, the windswept airport that served western Ireland. And home.

Kate was at the airport to meet me, and I was very pleased to see her. She would be going in another day or so and I knew I would miss her terribly, but she had extended her own visit to cover for me and even pick me up from the airport on my return.

Unusually it took quite a long while to get home from Knock as the Irish roads which – away from Dublin, anyway – were normally so quiet and often empty were partially gridlocked due to an accident.

Ordinarily I would probably have found that traffic to be annoying. At the end of a long day, it's the last thing you need. But on this occasion it actually gave Kate and me the chance to talk a little. As if the traffic had been put there quite deliberately to give us the opportunity.

That thought made me smile, and I felt the approaching presence of the 'holy' mountain as we drove along, and of the countless magical tales associated with it. Perhaps the mountain had put all these cars in our way.

"So", said Kate, looking a little bit older than her years for once. "How are you? How was the trip? Did it work? Help? You know."

In all honesty, at that moment in time, I felt pretty flat. As if the trip had made things worse by bringing so much back into focus. But I also knew that, in many respects, the trip had been very positive for me. A good thing to do. A visit to try and understand myself and my own past.

And with just one quick glance at Kate's frown – a frown caused by driving in the dark, the wet and the traffic, but also a frown of concern – I knew that I had to forget the negativity for now, and be as upbeat as I could manage.

After all, in no small part, the whole thing had been done at Kate's insistence. And now, I could tell, she was worried about how I had found the experience.

"Good", I said at last. Firmly. "Very good. And don't think I've forgotten that it was thanks to you that I finally went. You were right. I should have done it years ago."

That worked.

Her frown disappeared. And the dazzling smile she had inherited from her mother appeared once more on her face where, so very often, it usually was.

"I met a few old friends. And made promises to see them again. Cleared up a few things, too."

Kate nodded.

From there I told her more of the detail. The places I had revisited. Some of the old familiar sights. And how, one day, very soon, we would both have to go, together, to see my river valley.

Finally, the traffic ahead was thinning out, as we left Westport and approached Mulranny Bay itself.

"Well, I'm glad you had a nice time", she said, navigating a tight bend in the road which had half-filled with a large puddle. "I was worried about you, Dad. It seemed like something you had to do. But once you left, I felt bad, as if I'd made you do something that might not help, if you see what I mean."

I smiled at her, tired, but glad to be home and even more glad that Kate was there.

"And then, when I found that photo of yours", she continued. "Oh my God. I was so shocked. There were so many similarities with Mom., I mean, you know in photos of Mom when she was younger."

I thought about that for a moment. I could see what she meant. "Yeah. There are," I agreed. "I suppose that's just my type."

Kate didn't reply, and I knew I needed to explain a bit more about us, about Lisa, about her Mom.

"Your Mom", I said, "and I've always felt this, was the woman I loved most of all. We met at school and I had a crush on her there. And that never faded. Not really. And through all the years we had together, we had some fantastic times. Don't ever think otherwise."

As we pulled into the drive, needless to say, it was raining again, and pretty heavily too. County Mayo truly seemed to enjoy being wet. But I was glad to be back, anyway. Very much so. The air was fresh, and the sky was dark. Quite different to how it had been in Birmingham and London.

And, as I took a deep breath of that clear night air, I knew that out there, across the bay, the great mountain stood impassively waiting for a new day.

And I promised myself I would say hello to it again just as soon as I had the opportunity.

A little later, I was sitting at my computer, when Kate, now ready for bed and wrapped in a blanket, suddenly came back into the living room.

"You haven't told me how it ended", she said.

We had been in for an hour or so, and I thought she had already gone up to bed. We had said goodnight. And maybe she had gone too, but I guess the question had been nagging at her for a while and she wanted to know the answer. She would be leaving in the morning and it would be a while before we could meet again. And it wasn't really the kind of thing we could talk about via email or whatever.

"How did it end, between you and Alley? What happened?" she continued. "You haven't said."

For the first time in my life, and long overdue, I had told some of my closest friends about Alley. But I had never told anyone the ending.

Now, surely, it was finally the time to do so.

And there was no one else as important to me as Kate, my daughter.

Who else could I tell?

Who else would matter?

Kate had felt the need to ask me, and I felt the need to tell her.

So I pushed my chair back from the computer, where I was half-heartedly quoting for a job, and took a deep breath as Kate sat down on the settee.

I knew it well. How it ended.

I had been over it countless times in my own head.

"It was late in October", I began. "We hadn't seen each other for about ten days but I was going to go down the next weekend. It was a Tuesday. I even remember the day. Outside was cold with a strangely dark sky. It was that kind of late autumn, you know, that looked like the end of the world."

I paused.

I was surprised by how raw this felt and how much it still hurt, after all these years.

Maybe that was just because I was telling someone else. For the first time ever.

Kate nodded. "Shall I get you a drink, Dad?" she asked.

"Yeah", I said. "That would be nice. A whiskey please. Thanks."

I had a small bottle of whiskey in the kitchen. Kate, with her blanket trailing around behind her, found a glass and poured me a large shot of it. "Here you are", she said, putting glass and bottle down in front of me.

I took a big swig of the drink.

"Go on", she said, sitting down again. "Late autumn?"

"Well, I came back from work on that dark, dreary day. I'd almost certainly spent most of it at work thinking about Alley. Daydreaming. That was how I got through my time at the factory. Planning to go back down to see her and so looking forward to it..."

*

"There's a letter for you".

A letter? For me? I didn't recognise the writing. No one wrote to me. Not ever. I might get a card or something from an aunt on my birthday, but otherwise nothing.

"Who's it from?" my mom asked, as she passed it to me. "Is it from a girl? It looks like a girl's writing."

I had no idea. I couldn't think of anyone who would be writing to me. Well, that wasn't quite true. There was a girl. A Swedish girl. We had met in Devon the previous summer and begun writing to each other. Only one letter a month. But this wasn't from her.

Even so, my stomach turned. And I suddenly felt quite uneasy. Why was that? I couldn't say.

It was as if the envelope itself was emitting some kind of signal. A hugely negative one. Something like that. Or maybe it was the weight? Did such a little letter normally weigh very much? No. Of course not. Yet this one did. Or at least it seemed to. I felt a weight, both in my hand and in my chest.

I turned it over and noticed the postmark: London.

Then my brother came in.

"He's got a letter", my mom said. "From a strange girl, we think."

Those two words.

That did it.

'Strange girl'.

As my mother said those two words, I immediately knew who the letter was from.

Alley had written to me. But why?

The nausea returned. But stronger, this time.

What was the last thing we had said to each other? I tried to think. What was it? Where? The station. A week or so ago. That was it. I'd seen her off on the train back to the capital. We'd been in Birmingham all weekend and it had been wonderful. We had made love for the first time.

What had I said to her? Nothing. Nothing. We were fine.

No. Wait. There had been something. I told her that I couldn't come down to London last weekend. I mean, the weekend after Birmingham. I'd said that it would have to be two weeks before we saw each other again.

I hadn't wanted that. But I'd had no choice. It had made me sad. It had made Alley sad too. And she asked me if I could come down during the week instead. "Two weeks is too long", she'd said. "I need you with me. We should be together now."

But no, I hadn't been able to come down during the week. The whole clocking-in scam at work was still on hold. It was too risky.

"Are you trying to get rid of me?" she had asked. And she had meant it too.

"God no", I had replied. "That's the last thing I want. I'd do anything for you. Anything."

The look on her face when she'd asked me that broke my heart. But with my answer, that look passed as quickly as it had come. And by the time she got on her train, we were smiling. We kissed goodbye. Classic railway station departure.

And that was it.

So why was she writing to me now? I felt sick. I just knew it had to be something bad.

I tried to stop the sensation. I told myself. 'No. Don't be stupid. Why would it be bad news? We love each other. Life has brought us together. This isn't something to walk away from. Alley herself had said that. And she had been right'.

"Aren't you gonna open it?" said my brother, trying to take it out of my hand.

I didn't want to. I put it down the side of my chair, between the arm and the cushion. And for a moment I tried to ignore it. I had been drinking a coffee. Eating a biscuit. It would be fine. I would go up and have a shower in a minute. I could read it then. Maybe it wasn't even from her?

No. Of course it was from her.

I tried to stay calm. But it was no good. I just had to know. I put down my coffee and wolfed down the last of the biscuit. And I took the letter upstairs.

By the time I reached the top of the stairs I was shaking. I went into my bedroom. Tore open the envelope and skipped straight to the last line or two.

Jesus Christ. No. Please. No. Not that.

I shut my bedroom door. Found a record. Anything. The first thing I could find. It was an album by Tom Rush. A sort of country rock. I put it on. Someone had loaned it me. I hated it. But there was one track on the album that I did love. And it was that one which the needle found. Life being strange once more.

And when the track reached the end, it would play again as records did in those days. And then again. Just that one track, a sad one about losing love called 'Driving Wheel'.

The music began. And inside, I knew – knew, because the music told me – that this was the worst moment of my young life. Then, despite knowing that, and still just about able to stand up, I made myself read the letter.

It *was* from Alley. And what follows are the very words she wrote. I know that these are the exact words because I still have that letter. Though no one, except for me, has ever read it. Five small pieces of pale blue, tear-stained paper that broke my heart and ended something quite beautiful.

So very many times over the last few days I have started this letter, but I don't think I will ever get it right. How do you tell someone you love that now is the best time to say goodbye? Is there a right way to do that? I don't think there is and if there is, I can't find it, I'm sorry.

The last time we met we danced and kissed, you took me out in your town and showed me off. I loved it all. So very very much. I needed to see who you were back there, to see if there was any difference, and to see if the real you was any different to the you that I already knew so well and loved so much. Well, there was a difference – because the real you is even lovelier!

I felt more connected to you, not less, and I fell more in love with you than ever, if that were possible.

That night when we made love, I cried and I cried and you couldn't stop me. Though you held onto me and held on and held on and for that I loved you even more. I cried because it all hurt too much. It hurt, not to make love, but to be so loved and to be so in love. I knew then with every part of me that we belonged

416

together for all time and not just at weekends, not just on odd days now and then, but for all time. And we do belong together. We connect outside all the limits of this world. We really do.

But then when I came back to London and looked around at my world, and thought about you in yours, so far away, I saw that we just can't do it. We just can't be together as we should be, not in this life, not in this world. My life is here and it is and will be so different from yours. The glitz. I live here and I live like I do because it is who I am... I mean who I really am. For good and bad, and there is plenty of bad. But I really don't have any other choice.

I don't have any other choice – but you do! This is so not your world. You have uncountable future options, all of them away from my sort of disorder and troubles. You will go to university. I know you will. And you will write or paint or whatever it is that you need to do. You belong with me, but you don't belong here. And the same is true in reverse, I belong with you but I don't belong there.

I know as you read this you will hate me. You will hate me and that makes me feel horrible and so unbelievably sad. But I know you will hate me because I would hate you forever and ever if you wrote this same letter to me. But please please believe me, none of this is about wanting to go, none of this is about having any doubts about us or not loving you enough. It is all the opposite, the very opposite. It is about loving you so much that it hurts and hurts and then hurts some more. I am part of you and I know you

417

feel the same about me. But how can we ever be together? And knowing that we can't be together properly hurts even more. So it has to be better to stop it all now, doesn't it?

You told me once that if we lose someone special, someone really special, we owe it to ourselves and to life itself to get back out there and search for someone else. Because there is someone else out there, you said, they are out there and we have to try and find them. Please go and do that, and please forget me, forget me as soon as you can and just go out there and find that someone special. Please.

You have changed so much about me and about who I am. All for the better. My past is changed, my future too. I don't listen any more to people who only see my outside. My shield, as you once called it. I have shared my inside now, at last, with you, and you have given me a strength I never had before. You are my someone special. And I know I will be able to handle losing someone else special when they finally come along, because they will not be you.

I have to stop now. My heart is breaking as I write this. I can't see the paper properly, my eyes are so full of tears. The paper is getting wet. I am so sorry. Please go. Please don't come and find me.

Love always, always true and forever

Alley xxxxxx

I read it. Then I read it again. The first real response I had was sickness. A nausea. I felt very close to retching. Because of that, and because I didn't know what else to do, I simply sat down on my bed. Sat down, with that track still playing.

Just called to tell you, that I love you.

And then, clutching the paper, I began to read the letter for a third time.

But I couldn't read it. Not again. Not yet.

It wasn't that my eyes were full of tears. Though that was coming. And fast. I couldn't read it because I was in shock. I couldn't understand any of the words any more. I tried, but they blurred. All I could see for sure was the pale blue of the paper. The black of the ink. And those strange small spots where both had discoloured as tears had fallen onto them. Like tiny Rorschach ink spots. That was my thought. Those marks looked like little ink spot tests.

There was a sudden tap at my bedroom door. It opened. My mom. She could hear, could tell, that something was very wrong.

"Are you alright?" she asked me.

"No. Not really", I replied.

She came over to me and noticed the letter. "What is it? A girl?"

I nodded. "We're over." That was all I could manage to say. Now I could feel the express arrival of those tears. They were close, getting closer and about to break.

My mom hugged me. That was gentle and kind of her. She said a few words. I don't know what. The kind of thing that mothers know how to say. But right then I just needed some space. "I'll be OK in a bit", I lied.

She left me, telling me that if I needed anything she was there.

Now it was finally time to cry. And I did. I read the letter again and sat on the bed once more. And as I read it for that third time I began to cry. Really cry. Uncontrollably. I cried and I cried and I cried.

It hurt so much and I cried so much that I thought I would die. An echo of Alley's tears ten days or so beforehand in our hotel.

I felt like I was drowning. Asphyxiating. Yet still the pain came.

I read it again and again. Always, now, searching for a word, for something, some phrase, some let out, some get out, a way back, a way around the utter emptiness and bleak sadness that had suddenly enveloped my whole being.

In truth, within those words there was probably everything I needed.

But I saw none of it.

Not then.

I held the paper close to me. Pressed it against my heart. And burst into tears again, slipping off the bed and onto the floor. Where only days before I'd had a very real body to touch, a hand to hold, hair to stroke, laughter to hear and lips to kiss, I now had just tear stains on a few pieces of paper. And that realisation made me sob even more.

How could that happen? How could life allow a lover, a real warm living caring being, to be replaced by words written in ink on a scrap of paper?

I hated, then. At that moment. I hated Alley. Yes I did. I hated her because I loved her so and missed her so. Already.

Why had she done this? Time after time, events, fate, whatever it was, had tried so hard to bring us together and keep us together, and now she had written a letter to tear us apart? That felt wrong. Wrong, as if Alley was challenging Life itself. She was going too far. This was something we wouldn't be able to overcome.

My thoughts raced on.

She must mean it, then. She must mean it. Even Alley would not have made such a challenge unless she really meant it.

Somehow, finally, I managed to get up off the floor.

I walked downstairs like a dead man. Took a coat and shouted

"Going out", and went out, quickly, before anyone could say anything. I walked down to my river. Not to hurt myself. I was hurt enough. But to have some space, the space that I needed, the space to cry and sob and howl the hurt. And that was what I did. Sobbing and aching until I had no tears left.

I stopped. And poured myself another glass of whiskey. I couldn't say any more. Not straight away. Finally telling someone else how it had ended, even my own daughter, made it almost as raw as the day it happened. And I was crying a little as I told Kate.

I drank that second glass and sighed. Hugely.

"What did you do?" asked Kate at last.

I shrugged. "For maybe, I don't know, ten weeks, without ever giving it a conscious thought, I went to bed knowing that I had the most wonderful thing in the world waiting for me in the morning. Whether we were together or apart, I was loved. Loved by the most special person I could hope to find. And I knew even back then that if I lived to be a hundred years old, I wouldn't find her like again. Nor come close."

Kate nodded. "So what did you do?" she said again. "You didn't just let her go like that, surely?"

I had been waking every morning feeling that the world was mine, and now that sensation was gone. Now there was no reason to get up. My world was empty. Grey and desolate. And that was my morning the very next day. Despite the fact that the sun shone brightly on a bitterly cold and crisp morning, or maybe because of that sunshine, I woke and felt exactly like a man going to the guillotine. My world was at an end. I felt dead. I was dead.

Dead, yes. Yet still I moved. Somehow.

Somehow.

But what could I do? What should I do?

Why get up? Should I just give up? Accept her letter? Was there someone else? Is that what was really happening here? Would we ever meet again? What should I do?

Questions. So many questions, all rolling around, coming and going. Contradicting one another. Upsetting me. Then giving me hope, then taking it away again just as quickly.

Yes, questions. Lots. But finally one answer roared back at me.

It didn't begin as a roar. It arose quietly from some deep part, a part that actually belonged to my distant future and whose voice I didn't then recognise, but as it climbed and found strength, it grew louder and louder until I could hear only it and nothing else.

Go and get her.

That was it. Go and get her.

Questions didn't matter. Action mattered.

Go and get her.

Yes. Of course. That was what I should do!

Go and get her.

And with that single, striking, clear idea in my mind I managed to stay with it. Calmed down a little. Enough to get up. Out of bed. To have a wash. Enough to say "Hello" to my parents, who were already downstairs eating breakfast.

Yes. I could see it now. It was the right thing to do. I knew it. I would go and see her. Get her back. Do whatever it took.

I managed to eat a little. The death sentence had been lifted. The sunshine, that day, was there to cheer me, not condemn me. It all made sense. A better sense. A positive sense. And soon there was no doubt left in my mind. I made myself a coffee. Told my parents that I would be going to work and I would just have to be late that day.

That, of course, was a lie. I wouldn't go to work. I would go to London. I took my coffee upstairs. Sat down on my bed, still positive, and read the letter again. Yes. I was right. Of course I was right. I picked out some of the more encouraging phrases:

'I felt more connected to you, not less and I fell more in love with you than ever.'

How could I have missed all that last night? I thought myself intelligent. I wasn't. I had been stupid. I had panicked:

'It hurt, not to make love but to be so loved and to be so in love. I knew then with every part of me that we belonged together for all time.'

There was so much there that was positive. This was not over.

I knew what to do. Of course I did. I really would go to London. I wouldn't let it end now. Not like this. Not with just words on paper. We were bound together by more than that.

That dance. In the wine bar. The owner told us that he had never seen anything like it. People stood and watched us. We weren't two people, we were one. Two halves of one person.

I would go to her. I would put it all right.

And that wasn't all.

I would move down there too. Do whatever it took. There was so much that Alley and I had right. We couldn't let such 'normal' things as housing or distance tear us apart.

I would go and get my girl back.

That was settled

It was only about 30 minutes' walk to the nearest station. And from there the trains went all the way up to London. There was no way I could take a bus or taxi to the station. I was too upset to do that. So I walked. Besides, despite the pinching cold, the day was bright and fresh and it was something to savour. A walk would be good.

But no.

I left the house feeling positive. Determined to find a way forward. But that walk haunted me. Or something haunted me.

Something? Maybe not even that. Maybe it was just me. Maybe I was too young, or not as perceptive as I thought.

It began as I crossed the metal pontoon bridge above my river valley, I paused, looked, and remembered the night that the old concrete bridge there had collapsed. I must have only been seven or eight years old at the time. Yet I could still visualise it. Something solid like that, collapsing. Washed away. I could see it clearly. But the metal bridge had replaced it. Life had gone on.

And as I went on further, ever closer to the station. I remembered that only a few years previously, on Saturday mornings, I often walked these very roads to go and play rugby for the school. And now I felt that I already missed those days. Wanted them back. School days. That simplicity. That ease.

Odd memories. Flashbacks. Creeping in for no real reason as I walked along. Talking to me. Voices I didn't want to hear.

426

That afternoon when we first met, Alley and I. It, too, returned to my mind as a crystal clear image. The girl with blonde hair and red lipstick. Sitting on the train. She had nearly missed it.

What if she had missed it?

What if she had chosen a different seat?

And then her shoes. Rubbing against mine.

A train journey. A misunderstanding. Those were the things that brought us together.

Accidents. Innocence. Chance. All playing a role.

Finally I reached the station, where I checked the time of the next train. I had about 40 minutes to wait. 40 more minutes in the cold, with the sunlight now fading into a thin but impenetrable grey cloud. A cloud like a sheet. An opaque sheet.

But that was OK, I told myself. I'd wait. I'd do it. I'd go and get my girl. So I bought a ticket, my mind made up. I'd do whatever it took. I owed it to myself. To us. And most of all to Alley.

I walked heavily down the steps to the platform. There was no one else there and I was glad of that.

I sat on a bench, trying to be calm. Trying to hold onto the positive mood I'd had for the last few hours. But I could feel it slipping.

Then I had another flashback. Image. Impression.

The girl on the train was a boy. We *had* talked. And for some reason we'd even made plans to meet. At the Hostaria wine bar. That was the image. The wine bar. Only we had nearly lost each other again, hadn't we? I was leaving because I couldn't find her and she'd caught me at the very last minute, as I was right by the exit.

I shook my head.

That memory disappeared too.

Other people gradually arrived on the platform. One of them, a woman, came and sat near me. She had far too much perfume on, so I got up and moved further away.

The party. Again. The same thing. At the party we got on fine. We had begun to learn to trust each other. And that mattered hugely to both of us. But the following day, Alley almost left me and dashed off to London. If she had done so, would we ever have met again? But Life stopped her.

Life pushed us together, over and over. We were meant to be.

But, right now, we were no longer together. Why was that?

How much longer before the train?

I looked up at the station clock.

Still 15 minutes.

I took out and lit a cigarette. My hands were shaking.

There were now quite a lot of people waiting.

I hadn't expected that. I had expected to be alone, or almost alone. One of them, a man, came up to me and asked for a light. I didn't want to be polite. I wanted to just tell him to fuck off. But I gave him a light all the same, and then took a few more steps away. I wanted to be alone. I needed to be alone.

Another memory. This one of London. We had met again and we had got on so well. But that weekend... wasn't that the weekend I wrote her that lousy note and almost walked out? Yes. Yeah. I was sure it had been then. How close, so often, we were, we had been, to losing it. Yet we had hung on. Gotten closer and closer. Until now.

Until now.

I looked up. There was a train coming into the station.

But it was on the other platform. From the capital *to* Birmingham.

Those early days. Yes, how close, how often, to losing one another. Yet Life had kept finding a way. We kept finding a way. We had done it. Even when I had lost the ability to go and see her during the week, and money had got tight, we had still fought through.

We had made it.

Yet now I had that letter. This one, here in my pocket, telling me
it was all over. She had written to tell me it was over. She had
challenged Life itself. That was wrong. Why had she done that?

I wanted to shout, to scream. I looked up at the sky. A fine rain
began to fall from that grey sheet overhead.

What had been her words? "This isn't something either of us
should just walk away from."

Yet now she had written me this letter. The one that now weighed
so heavily on my soul.

Another train approached the station.

Finally, it was the London train.

My train. Our train.

It stopped. And the doors opened.

I finished my third shot of whiskey, stood up and put the empty
glass down on my desk.

I looked at Kate with tears pricking at my eyes, her face as wide-
eyed and as innocent as that of a small child.

"A minute or so later, the doors all closed. The train pulled away from the station. And I was still there. Still standing there. I hadn't got on it. And as I walked out of that station, back home, back to a world I knew so well, I told myself over and over that Alley was right. Right to end us. It couldn't work. It just couldn't. We were too different. Or, at least, our worlds were too different. We... we had to move on and find the next someone special. Because they *are* out there. Just as I had once told her they were."

I stopped. There were no more words.

And the two of us sat without speaking for a few minutes.

I wanted another drink, but I didn't pour myself one.

"Why?" said Kate, finally breaking the silence.

By way of an answer, I just shrugged. A hopeless, long-gone, sad sort of a shrug.

"I was scared, I guess. That walk. That wait. The tension. I was so scared of losing her. I thought that if we met, face to face, she might have told me to go. For real. And I couldn't have handled that. By walking away, instead of going down to London, I probably felt I was leaving myself with some sort of hope..."

Kate shook her head slightly.

And once more we sat in silence.

Of course I knew, and I had known for years, that I had got that decision – that last decision for us, for Alley and I – totally wrong.

Almost the final words I ever said to her were, "I'd do anything for you".

That was why she wrote me that letter.

She had to know that I'd meant those words.

She had been right, we couldn't go on as we were. I needed to move down there. To be with her. To commit to her as she had done to me.

That was why Alley had written me that letter.

To make me do just that.

Do it for her. Do it for us. So that we would be together.

But I didn't do it. I didn't catch that train.

I failed her. I failed us.

There are moments in life that are given to us.

Moments where we can make a choice.

I had made the wrong one.

*

Kate left the following morning.

I was sad to see her go, but she promised me a return visit very soon and we agreed that, together, we would make a trip back to my home city.

But those were not the last words she said to me. Instead, car engine running and window down, she hesitated.

"Go and find her, Dad."

I made some excuses about that being too difficult. Where would I start. But Kate knew me too well.

"At least try", she said. "Start with social media. Or talk to one of your old friends, someone like Megan. Why not?"

I promised I'd think about it.

In the afternoon, alone in my big house once more, I had another huge scaffolding job arrive by email. This was going to be used on a towering office block. And I would have to visit London again, in all likelihood, to see the project on site. But not for a while yet. Not for a couple of months.

I started working on the job straight away, but after only a few minutes I realised my heart wasn't in it.

And taking the photograph with me, the one that Kate had found, I made myself a cup of coffee and sat on the old rough wooden bench overlooking Mulranny Bay, watching as shafts of sunlight illuminated the peak of Croagh Patrick; the 'holy' mountain.

I had climbed that mountain a few times. It wasn't difficult. There was a path to the summit. The hardest thing was finding a suitable day.

Today, it struck me, would have been one of those. Not warm, not cold. Clouds, yes, but it was dry and bright.

The view from the top would have been worth the effort.

I drank a little more of the coffee and took a deep breath of the good, clean air.

I put my cup down and looked at the photo, being held so carefully in the palm of my hand.

That smile. Those almond eyes. Her bleached blonde hair.

It felt like forever. Yet she still took my breath away.

Of course the truth was that I had looked for Alley.

Once.

A long time ago.

I *had* tried.

But it wasn't easy. Not then.

All we had, any of us, were hand-written letters and phones.

I smiled, sadly, as I remembered the hours spent searching through a phone directory. To no avail.

But now, with social media? The world really was much more connected. So yes, perhaps Kate had been right, maybe I should go and look for her again, for Alley.

But... was that something I really wanted to do? Would it be right to just crash into someone's life after all these years? And what might I find out if I went looking for her? Good news? Bad?

I shook my head a little.

No. No. I would not let myself believe that.

Not Alley. She would have made it. She would have found her glitz. And much more besides.

I could feel that she was still out there. Somewhere.

She must be. She had to be.

Dear Reader,

If you've got this far.... please consider giving the book a review on Amazon.

It doesn't have to be a written review - though they are always nice to see - just take a moment to click 5 stars... or 4 stars... or 3... or... whatever YOU feel is right! Thankyou.

For more information, more books or to contact the author, or just to say "Hello", please feel free to send an email to geofff@geoffbunn.com

Other books by the same author

FIVE lives... only ONE ending
DYING in BRIGHTON
The story of five people, who find themselves moving to Brighton. And the story of what happens to them when they get there.
Available NOW on Amazon:
https://www.amazon.co.uk/dp/B081854HBJ

Printed in Great Britain
by Amazon

64487152R00251